Oddjobs 2:
This Time it's Personnel

by Heide Goody and Iain Grant

Pigeon Park Press

Published by Pigeon Park Press

www.pigeonparkpress.com

Cover artwork and design by Mike Watts – www.bigbeano.co.uk

Monday

Nina Seth watched her feet on the uneven ground as she made her way across the demolition site. Work had stopped and much of the workforce were gathered around a single spot. As she approached the edge of the circle, a construction worker looked back and saw her.

"Oi. You can't come in here. This is a hard hat area."

Nina looked up. Two massive cranes were angled elsewhere and there was nothing above her but blue sky.

"Why?" she said. "What's going to hit me?"

"You're not allowed on the site without a hard hat."

"Then you'd best get me one," she said.

Nina was barely into her twenties and had a figure that she liked to think of as petite but was probably better described as tiny. Being a tiny young woman conferred fewer benefits than people suspected. The ability to get children's tickets on the bus and buy VAT-free children's shoes hardly made up for being patronised and ignored by others, particularly by large, older men who thought they knew better. But, even as the builder began to protest, she slipped through the circle of men and to the centre of their attention. Two of the men wore ties and carried tablets. Site management.

Nina flashed them her ID.

"Nina Seth. Consular mission to the Venislarn."

"What's that?" said one. "We called the police."

"Uh-huh," she said. "Ricky and his lads will be here soon enough. But I was on my way to work and I heard you found something."

The man simply pointed at the block of stone in front of them.

"It's Portland stone. A single piece. It was being broken up."

"It's from the Jurassic," put in the other manager to labour the point.

Nina looked at the stone: a white-grey cube, two feet to each side. It had been cracked open but the object within was still firmly embedded in the rock.

"And did they have weird, freaky-ass Rubik's Cubes in the Jurassic?" she asked.

The site managers looked at her.

Birmingham was undergoing a transformation. It always had been, and it always would be. Buildings came down. Buildings went up. Traffic was diverted this way and then that... The city was a constantly shifting maze and its million or so inhabitants negotiated each new surprise with the tolerance of philosophical rats.

The three squares at the city's civic heart, Victoria Square, Chamberlain Square and Centenary Square were virtually adjacent. However, in years gone by, pedestrians could only go from Chamberlain Square to Centenary Square through a shopping arcade that ran beneath the inverted concrete ziggurat of Birmingham Central Library. Now the huge, shiny and rarely open Library of Birmingham dominated Centenary Square. The original Central Library was a pile of rubble in Chamberlain Square, the three squares were reduced to two and anyone wishing to walk from Victoria to Centenary would need a thorough grasp of local geography, some of it subterranean.

Behind the screens that separated the library demolition site from the public, Nina and a bemused workforce considered a lacquered wooden puzzle cube encased in prehistoric stone.

"Yup," she said, "I'm going to need to take that."

"Is this some kind of hoax?" asked one of the site managers.

Nina crouched down and waved her fingertip over the iridescent symbols painted on the cube's individual panels – curved, complex squiggles like octopuses at a disco. "This is third-variant *aklo*, the welcoming wards for the entourage of *Prein*."

"It's a Rubik's Cube."

"It's a tunnelling device for passing between worlds. And, I guess, if you twisted it into the right configuration we'd see some next level stuff – leather, spikes, flagellation – like a Tory MP's ideal weekend but without safe words."

"It's a hoax."

"It's an OOPArt," said Nina, straightening up. She brushed her hands.

"Pardon?" said the site manager.

"OOPArt," she said and looked up. "I've always wanted to drive a crane." Light clouds scudded across the sky. "Does it get windy up there?"

"Is it dangerous?"

"Is it terrorists?" voices called from the wider circle.

Nina looked round to try to locate the individual.

"Terrorists? Terrorists planted a magical toy in a block of stone so you could knock off early for lunch?"

"Are we knocking off early for lunch?" called someone else.

"It's nine a. m.," replied a site manager tersely, without even looking up.

"It's an Out of Place Artefact," said Nina. "We're getting a lot of them lately. Some weird vase underneath an Iron Age fort. Spooky dolls. An alien typewriter – we think it's a typewriter – in the roots of an oak tree. Dig it up. I'll take it away."

"And that's it?" said the site manager.

"What more do you want?" she said.

"But it's impossible!"

"Yes, it is."

"It must mean something."

"Mean something?"

He spluttered as his brain struggled.

"You know," he said. "The end of the world or something."

"Sure," she said and gave him a comforting pat on the upper arm. "It's the end of the world. Happy?"

"It's not the end of the world," said Rod.

"I can redo it," said Annie.

Rod Campbell took the offered cup of tea. "A spoonful of sugar won't kill me. You've got a smashing view." He gestured with the cup at the morning cityscape visible from her balcony, sloshing an inch of accidentally-sweetened tea into the canal five storeys below.

"Thanks," she said, as though it were her own handiwork. "It's the main reason I took the place."

Oh, yeah, thought Rod. Fabulous views of Birmingham all year round with the bonus of pond scum stink from the canal in high summer.

"So, tell me about your encounter, Annie," he said.

"Encounter," she said with a nervous smile. "You make it sound so official."

"It is official," said Rod. "You called the authorities. It's my job to listen."

"It's not an actual ghost," she said.

"I understand."

"I mean it's not something I've even seen."

"Go on."

"Well, there's the noise." She stepped back into the flat and crossed through a living room furnished only with an armchair and a dozen packing boxes. "Sorry. I've not yet moved in properly. Only sorted out the broadband this morning. The noise, it comes from sort of here. It's like a clanking and a thumping."

"A clanking and a thumping," said Rod.

"And then there's the smell."

"What kind of smell?"

"An awful smell. Like something dead. Dead and diseased."

Rod sniffed. There was something and it wasn't the canal.

"There can often be funny smells in a place, can't there?" he said. "So, the old tenant moved out a month ago?"

Annie whirled round, her fluffy dressing gown flying out.

"That's exactly it," she said, wide eyes aglitter. "Did she?"

"Did she what?" said Rod.

"Move out."

"I'd have thought so. Wouldn't you have noticed if she was still here?"

"Thing is, Detective Campbell…"

"I'm not police, Annie."

"She never looked all that happy when I came round to view the property. I don't think she liked the landlord very much. And, I got to thinking, there's been all those suicides in the local area recently."

"Has there?"

"There certainly has. And here's the shiznit, detective. The previous woman, she worked over at the Mailbox and I remember her telling me she always got home bang on six o'clock."

"I see," said Rod, who didn't. He sipped his tea and winced at the sweetness.

"The noises and the smell, they always sort of begin at six o'clock. It's like... It's like she's come home. You get me?"

Rod processed the idea. He gave it time.

"Did the old tenant smell particularly?"

"Well she would now she's dead, wouldn't she?"

"Suicide?"

"Or..." Annie's eyes widened further. "Is she bricked up in the walls, eh? Eh?"

Rod looked at the plasterboard walls.

"Aye. Do you mind if I have a poke about?" he said.

"Be my guest."

Rod walked into the kitchenette and poured his tea down the sink. The boiler was mounted on the wall beside the sink. He pressed a couple of buttons and looked at the boiler clock and timer settings.

He walked back through to the living room and went directly to the radiator. He ran his hands behind it.

"Okay, Annie," he said. "Good news and bad news time."

Shortly afterwards, Rod jogged down the stairs to ground level and exited onto the canal towpath. He sniffed his fingers experimentally. They smelled faintly of apple-scented soap and strongly of month-old prawns.

"Tell me, are you happy with your current provider?"

Rod looked at the man with a clipboard full of papers who had materialised in front of him. The top of the young man's left ear was missing and a roadmap of minor scars criss-crossed his entire face. He was either a really bad cage fighter or had lost a war of attrition with a feral cat.

"I'm not religious, mate," said Rod.

"Good one," laughed the man. His head bobbed and twitched constantly, perhaps reliving his most recent tussle with man or cat. "I'm talking about your phone, broadband."

"Not interested," Rod said and, with the weakest of smiles, pushed past.

"The most competitive rates," the man called after him but Rod paid no attention.

To his left was the junction of the Birmingham and Fazeley Canal and the Birmingham Main Line. The concrete roundabout island at its centre had been aggressively colonised by a family of nesting ducks. To his right, the Birmingham and Fazeley stretched out towards the BT Tower and the tunnels under Snow Hill. Ahead of him, his colleague Morag Murray waited at the apex of a humpback bridge across the canal.

Morag was only three weeks into her job with the Birmingham consular mission to the Venislarn and Rod had already decided that he liked her. She was Scottish, ginger, enjoyed a drink, didn't back down from a fight and generally acted like tomorrow was always going to be worse than today. It was like she had bought all her personality traits at Caledonian-Clichés-R-Us. Perhaps that wasn't fair. Morag, like the rest of the consular mission, lived in the inviolable knowledge that humanity's tomorrows were well and truly numbered, so Rod could forgive her a certain pessimism. Also, he had seen her eat both fruit and vegetables so she wasn't totally Scottish.

"Does this city of yours breed nutcases?" she said, strolling down to meet him.

"Not my city. Don't pin it on me," he said. "I take it that rumours of a man-eating shark roaming the canals of Birmingham were unfounded?"

"You take it right. Just some mad local who thinks that three halves of bikes he's fished out the canal are evidence of a giant predator. I take it there wasn't a ghost haunting that fifth-floor flat?"

"No. Just a disgruntled former tenant doing the old prawns-stuffed-behind-the-radiator-revenge prank."

"Prawns?"

He sniffed his fingers again, hoping the smell had miraculously gone in the past minute. Nope. Still there. Rotten shellfish and apple soap.

"Smell that," he said and held out his hands.

"No, thanks."

"I'll be washing that off all day."

"And you said you liked Crackpot Mondays."

Rod shrugged. "Beats processing mad occultists or babysitting a thousand baby godlings that spit acid."

"Those wee godlings liked you," said Morag.

"Too much," said Rod. "Right. Who's next on the list?"

There were gods. Small g. The Venislarn. Vastly intelligent or dribblingly insane; it was hard to tell. Hideous and angelic. Strange and formless. As familiar as childhood terrors. Hungry. It was impossible to say where or when they had come from. They were recent arrivals from a place beyond the reach of human understanding and they had simultaneously been here forever. They lived below, within and throughout the world we knew and were biding their time until the day when they enveloped the earth and everyone in it in an endless technicolour hell: the Soulgate. In the meantime, they were a state secret because, hey, there's no mileage to be gained from telling the kiddywinks that monsters are real. The consular mission to the Venislarn were the god appeasers, the end-of-life carers for an oblivious planet. They were the secret keepers.

But, sometimes, the secrets crept out.

Morag was in another canalside apartment block, a hundred yards down from poor Annie who had been haunted by prawns. This time it was the devil, not ghosts. Apart from that and what Rod suspected was a great slice of Catholic guilt, the pieces were the same. A naïve lone tenant with an over-active imagination, a dollop of urban dislocation from the real world and an inability to make a decent cup of tea. Rod let Morag do the talking and tuned out completely until Catholic-guilted Rhona said something that brought his attention right back.

"Sorry. What was that? What you said before, Rhona," said Rod.

Morag looked at her notepad, as though she had been making proper notes in there and not just composing a shopping list.

"He told me I was going to hell," said Rhona.

"His eyes, Rhona. Pink and silver."

She nodded vigorously. "Pink, with a sort of silver pattern running through them."

"Can you show me where you saw him?"

Rhona crossed to the window. Morag tapped Rod's knee and gave him a questioning look.

"Right there," said Rhona.

Rod joined her.

"Outside the window? What, floating in the air?"

"I think he was holding onto something."

Rod opened the window as far as it would go, then he released the safety catches and pushed it out fully. Below, there was a narrow back street and the canal beside that. Rod spotted dusty pitted marks in the brickwork to either side of Rhona's window.

Rod climbed up onto the window sill and, holding onto the upright with his right hand, swung himself out onto the exterior wall so he could reach one of the marks.

"Oh my God!" exclaimed Rhona to Morag. "Isn't he going to hurt himself?"

"He does this kind of thing," Rod heard Morag say.

"Dangerous things?"

Rod touched a hole in the brickwork. It felt like someone had driven a piton into it. He looked down and saw more holes running up from the ground floor – two sets, eight feet apart – as though a team of climbers had raced each other up.

"Is that how he lost his finger?" Rhona asked. "Doing dangerous things?"

"Half a finger," said Morag. "He gets touchy about that."

Rod didn't get touchy about much, reflected Morag as they made their way downstairs. As long as no one accused him of having lost a whole finger in a tussle with the murderous servants of a subterranean god, or mocked his unnecessarily large collection of wearable survival gadgets (which included a belt that could be turned into a hunting bow, an hourglass key fob filled with explosives, and a shirt that turned into a magnesium-infused red-smoke-spewing emergency flare when burned). Apart from those unlikely triggers he was unflappable. Morag wasn't sure if his easy-going nature was because of, or despite, the fact that he was built like a brick wall and had spent much of his adult life in the army. If there was such a thing as Small Man Syndrome, Rod had the opposite. He was big and beefy and the gentlest man that Morag had known in a long time.

If he had a flaw – at least in the workplace – it was that his Venislarn knowledge wasn't up to scratch.

"So, what is it?" asked Morag.

Rod kicked among the weeds alongside the canal, as though he might find some clue there, and then looked up at the wall of the apartment block.

"I can't remember what it's called. *Nurgle* or *Numf-numf.* Definitely summat beginning with N. Ingrid would know." He stopped. Ingrid, tech support in the mission Vault, was dead, eaten by a god she'd been foolish enough to summon. They'd cremated an empty coffin as there had been nothing to put in it. "Nina will know."

Morag looked up too. Rhona was watching them from her apartment window.

"So, she didn't make it up. She saw the devil."

Rod shook his head. He crossed to the wall and stretched out his arms: six feet from fingertip to fingertip plus another foot to the mark on either side. Eight feet.

"They're claw marks," said Morag.

"Feet. Like a spider."

"That's a bloody mahoosive spider," said Morag. "I'll call Nina and find out if we should wash it down the plughole or try to trap it under a glass."

Nina was in the Vault, the consular mission's storage facility. The Vault occupied a vast basement level of what was notionally Birmingham's flagship public library. The consular mission's office occupied most of the library's upper floors. The Library of Birmingham had been built with great fanfare at the taxpayers' expense and then all but closed due to said expense.

It was a good excuse and it did a good job of keeping the public away.

The Vault was supposed to be organised and run by the mission's tech support officer. However, the most recent tech support officer, Ingrid Spence, was dead. Nina's last encounter with Ingrid had ended when Nina threw Ingrid off the upper balcony of a shopping centre. (It wasn't the fall that had killed Ingrid...) Without a tech support officer, the mission staff had muddled through as best they could. New Venislarn artefacts, which were cropping up at an increasing rate, were being stored wherever they could find room.

Nina was clearing space on a shelf when her phone rang.

"Nina Seth, professional sex kitten and twenty-four-hour party girl."

"Nina. Morag."

"Hey, Braveheart. How was the weekend?"

"Not bad. Richard and I took a trip out to Stratford. You know, to do all the Shakespeare stuff. We found this lovely tea room where –"

"Wow," said Nina. "That sounds so unbelievably dull. But, hey, whatever makes you old folks happy."

"Are you in the office yet?"

"Yup."

Nina plonked the Rubik's Cube of *Prein* down next to the vase of multiplication they'd found at the Berry Mound Iron Age fort. Along with the alien typewriter, the keys of *Trek-lehn*, the *pabash kaj* effigy doll, a wand of uncertain origin and a purse containing coins from a period of history that never happened, that made seven OOPArts this month alone.

"Rod and I are down by the canal near Fleet Street, checking out a crackpot story. Rod's found some claw marks and – oh, he's now found some slime. He's very excited – he thinks it might be some sort of giant spider thing with pink and silver eyes."

"*Dinh'r*," said Nina.

"*Dinh'r*," said Morag.

"I was close," she heard Rod say.

"You said they were called *Nurgles*," said Morag.

"It has an N in it," said Rod.

"They're psychic parasites," said Nina. "We used to have thousands but there shouldn't be any left in Birmingham."

"No?"

"They live and feed on *Yoth Mammon*. They're her personal fleas. And since she left for *Kal Frexo leng*-space, whenever that was, they should either have gone with their goddess or died."

There was a creak of metal. Morag made a noise that might have been an ah of wonder or an ugh of disgust.

"Yeah, I don't think they've gone anywhere," she said. "Are you busy at the moment?"

"That's a trick question."

"I think we might need you and Vivian down here and possibly some police to guard the entrance."

"Entrances. Plural," said Rod.

"Entrances?" said Nina.

"Yeah," said Morag distantly.

Nina arrived ten minutes after the police and a good hour before the two British Telecom engineers Rod had summoned.

Nina craned her neck to look up at the tower.

"Hundred and fifty meters," said Rod, consulting his phone. "Birmingham's tallest landmark."

"The hundred and fifty meter high club," mused Nina. "It could work."

While Chief Inspector Ricky Lee, the local police-Venislarn liaison, consulted a sheet map and sent pairs of coppers off to guard certain unmarked doorways and service hatches within in a mile radius, the BT engineers sauntered over to inspect Rod's discovery.

Attached to the brick façade of the apartment block was a grey, windowless structure as tall as the building itself but no wider than a parking spot. It had a small, steel door at ground level. The lock was broken, and slight buckling around the latches suggested it had been forced open from the inside.

"Did you do this?" said the older BT engineer.

"Ripped open a two-inch steel door with our bare hands?" said Morag.

"Did you?"

The engineer had a round, lined face, was bald on top and had thick stubble on his chin. He looked like one of those optical illusion faces that change expression when you turn them. Morag wondered if his upside-down face looked as surly as this one.

"This is the Anchor Telephone Exchange, isn't it?" said Rod.

"Maybe," said the engineer. "Let's see some ID, mate."

Rod presented his photo card. The engineer looked at it closely.

"And this is mine," he said, holding up a card.

Rod was polite enough to bother to look at it while the engineer looked at his.

"This must be what Grindr was like before they invented the internet," Nina whispered to Morag.

"It all appears to be in order," said the engineer, in the tones of one who thought things were only *just* in order.

"Thank you, Colin," said Rod.

"Now," said Rod, reaching to open the door.

"Excuse me," said Colin primly. "That's BT property. It can only be opened by authorised agents of BT Group PLC."

Rod gestured to the door and Colin pulled it open. The narrow space contained nothing but an uncovered manhole in the floor. A ladder led upward, toward a metal grille in the high ceiling. Leaning forward, they saw that it also led downward, into the darkness below.

"So, we're going down here," said Rod, "and we need to know if there's owt we should be aware of."

"Only authorised agents of BT Group PLC are allowed down there, mate. There's some complex and expensive telecommunications equipment down there."

"We're not interested in the telecoms stuff," said Rod.

Morag pointed to a grape-like cluster of spheroids seemingly glued to the inside wall of the shaft. Each of them was the size of a cricket ball, had a silver sheen to its leathery outer layer and, more importantly, was split open and empty. Nina crouched to get a better look.

"*Dinh'r* egg cases." She sniffed. "They stink of bad fish."

"No, that's Rod's hands," said Morag.

"You've got fishy hands, Rod," said Nina.

"He's been touching prawns," said Morag.

"That's a euphemism," said Nina.

Rod counted fifty-five rungs to the bottom.

In the end, they'd decided that seven of them would go down: Chief Inspector Ricky and his pet sergeant; the two engineers plus Morag; Rod and Nina.

"You didn't bring Vivian with you?" Rod said to Nina.

"She's sifting through job applications for Ingrid's replacement," Nina replied.

"How come she gets to do that?"

"Because no one told her she couldn't. God, she loves it though. Wasn't even interested in the OOPArt I'd brought in."

"Another?"

"*Adn-bhul* Rubik's Cube of doom."

"I had a boyfriend who wrote his master's thesis on them," said Morag.

"Rubik's Cubes?" said Rod.

"OOPArts."

Rod stepped aside at the bottom to make room for Ricky and waited in the foetid black until Colin found the light switches. Strip lights clicked and tinged into life.

"*Muda,*" Morag swore softly in Venislarn.

They were in a square concrete tunnel, ten feet to a side, like the world's deepest pedestrian subway. The tunnel, like the strings of telecoms cabling on one wall, stretched off in both directions as far as the eye could see. No sign of *Dinh'r* though.

Rod realised he was smiling.

"The Anchor Telephone Exchange," he said. "Never been down here. Always wanted to."

"And this was built as a nuclear bunker?" said Morag.

"BT Group PLC can neither confirm nor deny," said Colin superciliously.

"Excavated in the fifties," said Rod. "They told the public it was going to be an underground railway."

"It's one of three target-hardened telecoms centres in the country," said Colin.

"And how far does it stretch?" said Ricky.

"Jewellery Quarter," said Colin. His pointing hand swung from one direction to the other. "Southside. Mile and a half. There's sleeping quarters, a canteen and offices down that way. Even a meeting room for the mayor and those councillors who might be lucky enough to get down here after the three-minute warning."

Colin unclipped a bunch of torches from a charging rack on the wall.

"You'll need these. The lights can go at any time."

Rod produced the pencil torch that hung from his hourglass key fob.

"I'm all right. Got my own."

"It's not BT Group PLC authorised kit," said Colin.

"Not been tested," said Colin's mate.

"Two hundred lumens," said Rod. "If it's good enough for the Israeli Defense Forces…"

"But Colin's is bigger," Nina pointed out helpfully.

"It's not about the size," said Rod before he had time to filter-check what he was saying.

"Says the boy with the smaller torch."

"Can we get on with this?" said Ricky. "Some of us have proper work to do."

16

"But which way?" said Morag.

Rod looked back and forth.

"You haven't even said what you're looking for yet," said Colin.

"Spiders," said Rod.

"Spiders?" said Colin. His mate sniggered.

"Sort of a sea urchin-mushroom-spider thing," said Nina.

"Foreign spiders, are they?" said Colin.

"Sure. Whatever."

Rod had already drifted towards the southward tunnel. He wasn't one to be taken by hunches or "feelings" – growing up in South Yorkshire, folk didn't take kindly to people with "feelings" – but there was something in that direction that gave off dark and weird vibes. The stark light on concrete, the movement of the air, the almost inaudible murmurs of a bustling city hundreds of feet above. Weird vibes.

"You know," Rod said to no one in particular as he led the way, "this reminds me of another tunnel. I mean, this isn't Iraq and the tunnels I found mesen in there were far smaller but –"

"So where are they from?" said Colin. "These spiders. They from Mexico?"

"They're not from Mexico," said Morag.

"There was that bloke who got bitten by a spider that had come over in some bananas. Gave him rabies or something."

"What's the plan when we find them, if we find them?" asked Ricky.

Rod smiled grimly. "Nina, these *Dinh'r*. They're fair game, right?"

"Totally," his young colleague replied. "They're parasites. Not gods. Not offspring, allies or vassals. Go crazy."

Rod drew his Glock 21 pistol from the shoulder holster under his jacket.

"Big spiders then," said Colin.

Rod clipped his pencil torch into the slot under the barrel and continued.

Nina was first to smell it. Or at least the first to think it worth mentioning.

"Something stinks," she said. "And I don't mean Rod's fishy fingers."

"It's kind of close in here," said Rod.

"Bad plumbing?" suggested Ricky's pet sergeant.

"This facility was built to house up to a hundred workers for an indefinite period," said Colin defensively. "Flawless in design and execution."

"Oh aye?" said Rod. "Wasn't this place accidentally built below the water table?"

"Not true," said Colin. "The local water table rose following the decline of heavy industry in the seventies and now a system of pumps, controlled by operations panels such as that one there, continually pump out the lower levels."

"Shush, the pair of you," said Nina. "You can all smell that, can't you?"

"God, yes," said Morag.

At that moment, the strip lights flickered and went out.

There were sighs, mutters, fidgets and the illumination of seven torches.

"Rod's *is* brighter," said Nina. "Small but mighty."

Colin's mate was already at the operations panel, torch gripped in his teeth, flicking switches.

"I'rr 'ave uh gno 'ack an' rrset uh 'uses," he said.

"Eh?" said Morag.

Nina looked ahead. Her torchlight had picked out a pile of something in the tunnel. A neat and gently sloping pile against one wall.

"He'll have to go back to where we came down and reset the fuses," Colin translated.

Nina approached the pile. It was reddish brown and nearly as tall as her.

"I think we should all stick together for now," Ricky was saying. "We can rely on torches for the time being."

"If you're worried about him bumping into one of your spiders, he's got his big stomping boots on," said Colin.

Nina saw dark red smears on the concrete floor around the pile. Straight lines and curved lines. Someone had used a brush or a shovel to gather it together. It. Nina suddenly had a very good idea what it was.

"This is wrong," she said. "Guys!"

Morag and Rod were almost instantly at her side. Both put their hands to their noses. Rod made a disgusted noise and switched hands.

"That's a big pile of rotting flesh," said Morag.

"Yes, it is," said Nina. "Neatly piled, like someone clearing snow from their drive."

"Human flesh," said Morag.

"How can you tell? Got a lot of experience with rotting human flesh?"

"Well," said Morag reflectively, "that's a scrap of denim. That's a shoe. That's a phone."

"Aw, crap," said Ricky. "And now we have a crime scene."

Somewhere behind them, Colin's mate was throwing up noisily. No one paid it any attention.

"Have you had a lot of people go missing in the local area?" asked Rod.

"Nope," said Ricky. "There's always some. The homeless. People who fall between the cracks."

"Those are high heels," said Morag.

"You can be homeless and classy," said Nina.

"We've had to do clean-up on more than the usual amount of suicides recently though," said Ricky.

"Someone mentioned that to me earlier," said Rod.

"That'll be the *Dinh'r*," said Nina. "They're psychic parasites. They induce bad thoughts, hallucinations even. They feed off them."

"Like telling people they're going to go to hell."

"That'd be enough to tip some people over the edge," said Nina.

"So, they fed off *Yoth Mammon*'s bad thoughts?" said Morag.

"Like those birds that clean crocodiles' teeth."

19

"But these aren't suicides," said Morag, waggling her torchlight over the terrible pile.

"And that's what's wrong here."

"Ah," said Rod, understanding. "The *Dinh'r* don't actually eat people."

"Nope," said Nina, the loud plosive 'p' echoing down the tunnel. "Or chew them up and spit them out."

Nina produced a pair of latex gloves from her pocket, crouched beside the pile and teased the phone from the clotted goo with her fingertips.

"We need SOCOs down here," said Ricky.

"Let's not bring any more potential victims down here until we have to," argued Rod.

The phone came away with a grim sucking sound. Nina tapped the screen but it was dead.

"If we could ID some of these people..." she said.

"We've still not found sign of the *Dinh'r*," said Rod.

Nina recognised the tone in his voice.

"Let's Scooby Doo this one. You and Morag go bug hunting. Ricky and I will get all wet and sticky here."

"This doesn't gross you out?" said Ricky.

"This girl isn't scared of nothing," said Nina.

"This girl's got no sense of smell," said Morag and turned to the BT engineers. "You guys can stay here."

"I think I'll be coming with you," said Colin, holding his nose. "Matt, you can stay here."

Colin's mate did not look happy about that. He didn't look happy about much, at the moment.

Once the explorers had headed off, Ricky and his pet sergeant put on rubber gloves and, while the pet sergeant took photos of the pile of human offal on her phone, Ricky joined Nina in the world's grimmest Lucky Dip game.

"First one to find actual cash buys the cocktails tonight," said Nina.

"We're cops," Ricky reminded her.

"All right. Buys the lagers. Whatever you lot drink. Hang on," she said. "What's this?"

The pet sergeant angled her phone camera round.

"Booyah! Mama's about to strike it rich," said Nina.

The object was heavy and flat and slapped wetly onto the floor once Nina had pulled it from the pile. It was an old-fashioned leather school satchel. The buckles were already undone. She flipped it open. There was barely anything inside it. A few pens, a highlighter, a bottle of Tipp-Ex. Ricky bagged each as it came out.

Nina pulled out a sheet of lined paper in a poly pocket.

"What I Did On My Holiday by Croesus Smith-Mammonson," she read. "Aw, crap."

"These things have been dismembering kids," said Ricky.

"Worse than that, Inspector," said Nina. "These things have been dismembering Venislarn kids."

Ricky Lee, goofy-looking but cute Ricky Lee, frowned at her.

She stood, stripped off her gloves, took out her phone and vainly hoped for a signal.

"See, the *Dinh'r* are vermin. Nothing more. And people," she said, waving at the pile, "are expendable. No one actually gives a shit about people." Nina ignored the confusion on the BT engineer's face. "But the Venislarn," she said. "Yeah, they get kind of tetchy if their loved ones get turned into kebab meat. Tetchy as in city-squashing tantrums tetchy."

Ricky stood too.

"You're telling me that the Venislarn, these transdimensional god-things, send their children to schools. Our schools."

"Well, probably a grandkid or great grandkid. And only one transdimensional god-thing does it." There was no signal on the phone. "I need to call Vivian."

She clicked her fingers at the BT engineer.

"Hey, Broadband. Where's the nearest ladder to the surface?"

The engineer looked backward and forward and then pointed.

"Let's go," said Nina.

Ten minutes and half a kilometre down the tunnel, the lights flickered and came back on. Morag turned her torch off. The lights went out. She turned her torch on again. The lights came back on once more. She kept her torch on.

The tunnel stretched away toward a distant corner. Ahead, Morag saw doors and recesses in the wall.

"What's that?"

She looked at Colin. He was pale. A slag heap of people bits would probably shake most people.

"Colin," she said. "What are these doors here?"

He looked, as though for the first time.

"Refuge areas. Sleeping quarters," he said. He rapped his knuckles on a submarine-style bulkhead door as they passed through it. "Blast doors, little lady, in case part of the tunnel was compromised in a nuclear strike."

Little lady, thought Morag. The colour had returned to Colin's face along with the casual sexism. It hadn't taken him long to bounce back. Maybe guys like Colin didn't have the intelligence to stay shocked for long.

"So, what? You reckon immigrants did this or something?" he said.

"Immigrant spiders?" said Rod.

"I meant the…" He waved his hand toward the distant and invisible flesh pile. "You know, they let anyone in the country these days. And give them benefits."

"And a free house?" said Morag.

"And a Rolls Royce as soon as they jump off the back of the lorry?" said Rod.

"I'm serious," said Colin.

"Aye," said Rod. "I can see that."

Nina, two cops and a BT engineer who looked like he might never venture below ground level ever again had come up through a manhole near the law courts, giving the two uniformed cops guarding it a scare. While Ricky got on the radio and briefed his officers, and the BT engineer took deep cleansing breaths and eulogised to no one in particular about sunshine and fluffy clouds and loving each day like it was the last, Nina called Vivian.

Nina didn't ask Vivian to come to the scene. Nina didn't want Vivian to come to the scene. But Vivian came anyway because Vivian wanted to and because Nina, who wasn't afraid of anything, was mildly terrified of Mrs Vivian Grey.

Vivian Grey was, in Nina's estimation, approximately two hundred years old, had probably fought the Nazis in World War One and knew more about the individual Venislarn entities living in the city than anyone else. She wore her grey hair in a tight and functional ponytail, had a fine figure for an ancient, and with those cheekbones and that attitude could probably earn top dollar as a dominatrix. Nina was mildly terrified of Vivian and a little bit in love. Nina planned on dying young and leaving a ravaged corpse but, failing that, she hoped she grew up to be just a smidgeon like Vivian.

Vivian drew up beside the pavement in her modest and eminently sensible car. She didn't get out. She just waited silently for Nina to get in.

"You didn't have to come down," Nina said to Vivian once she had gotten in.

"Seatbelt," said Vivian.

Nina obliged. Vivian pulled away.

"We going to Dickens Heath?" said Nina.

"To speak to Mammonites," said Vivian.

"I thought you were busy helping Vaughn with the job applications."

"I was and then you interrupted me with your phone call."

"I just wanted some advice on how to approach the Mammonites."

Vivian indicated to get onto the slip road for the Aston Expressway. "And what did I say?"

"You said they'd eat me alive."

"Indeed."

"I've dealt with them before."

"You've allocated them housing. You've not dealt with them."

The morning rush hour was going in the other direction. Vivian pootled along at a fuel-efficient fifty-something miles per hour and briefed Nina on the Mammonites of Dickens Heath. Nina already knew ninety percent of it but wasn't going to tell Vivian that.

Trying to understand the Venislarn was like trying to understand the earth. Most people dug down and found some rock and soil and considered that to be the earth. Others drilled boreholes and based their understanding on what they found there. But there were always deeper layers. Of the tiny fraction of humanity who knew anything of the Venislarn, the vast majority believed the coracle-paddling *samakha* or spindle-limbed *presz'lings* or unholy congregation of *fyek-yah* to be the Venislarn. They weren't. Others, who thought they knew better, looked to their parent-gods – *Daganau-Pysh, Khazpapalanaka, Zildrohar-Cqulu* – and thought they were the Venislarn. They weren't. Apparently paraphrasing some science dude Nina had never heard of, Vivian had told her, "If you think you understand the Venislarn, you don't understand the Venislarn." The true Venislarn were beyond all understanding and any attempt to do so would probably end with your brains leaking out of your nose.

Yoth Mammon, the corruptor, the defiler of souls, the dredger in the lake of desires, was about as deep a Venislarn as a human could have any chance of comprehending. She was universally regarded as a *she,* even though no one could ascribe any physical characteristics, sexuality or partners to her. She was the embodiment of greed and venality, had annexed a corner of the West Midlands for her unholy offspring and then, some years ago, had slipped sideways into the *Kal Frexo leng*-space and beyond human comprehension.

The Mammonites themselves were dangerous, for two principal reasons. Firstly, their mother-goddess loved them and had made them powerful. Secondly, they were quick learners and had decided that certain key elements of human behaviour were worth emulating. (Vivian was quite vocal in her opinion regarding the value of humans as role models.)

"Remember," she told Nina, as they drove back in along the Stratford Road, having taken a great loop round the city from north to south on the motorway. "The Mammonites always remember.

24

Anything you say, they will use against you. Any promises you make, they will hold you to."

"Sounds fair," said Nina.

"And exact an entirely justifiable punishment if you are not true to your word."

"Less so," said Nina.

Dickens Heath was notionally a village. It might once have been the site of a genuine village, nestled between the city and the Warwickshire countryside. If so, every remnant of indigenous architecture, and even the original street plan, had been replaced by what might better be described as a housing estate: street after curving street of narrow shoebox houses, all in the same rosy brick, no door distinguishable from any of its neighbours except by its brass numbers. In a picket-fenced green, four toddlers played solemnly on the swings and slides. At the village's designated centre, at the entrance to the small delicatessen-cum-grocers and from the windows of the Italian brasserie next door, women silently watched Vivian's car go by.

Vivian took a left.

"I always get lost in this place," said Nina.

"Of course, you do," said Vivian, taking a second left. "It's based on Zhuge Liang's stone sentinel maze and is designed to deflect the innocent traveller back out as soon as possible."

"Huge Wang what?" said Nina.

"Zhuge Liang. He built a maze with just eight standing rocks. Some say eleven. And despite its simplicity, once inside it, the unwary could never find their way out. An inversion of the same was used in the planning of Dickens Heath to create –"

"Yeah, yeah. Mystic Chinese bullshit. I get it."

Vivian took a third and fourth left and then a turning that Nina wasn't sure was either left or right.

"Seventy-six Alderway Lane," said Vivian. "The registered home of one Croesus Smith-Mammonson. I shall come to the door with you but will allow you to tell the Smith-Mammonsons that their little boy has been eaten, however improbably, by a *Dinh'r.*"

"Thanks," said Nina tartly and got out.

She pressed the doorbell and then rapped the knocker.

"Is it necessary to do both?" said Vivian.

"They've got both," said Nina.

A woman opened the door. Except, of course, it wasn't a woman, not really. It was a Mammonite and, once you knew what you were looking for, the signs were impossible to miss. Greg Robinson, Nina's first boss at the consular mission, had described Mammonites as being "like one of them Picasso paintings," but that was an exaggeration. They didn't have eyes on the sides of their heads or ears in the wrong places. The Mammonite look was subtler than that. Rod's opinion was they looked like Hollywood types who'd had too much plastic surgery and resorted to further plastic surgery to fix it. Nina could see what he meant but that still didn't convey the very wrongness of the Mammonite's physical appearance. It took her a while to develop her own perspective on it and, when she did, she realised that the thing they most resembled were the Disney characters painted on the sides of children's fairground rides.

Lots of fairground rides had Disney characters painted on them (and DreamWorks characters and Pixar characters). They weren't authorised or licensed images. The magic of the fairground ride Disney character was threefold: firstly, no individual piece of the character was wrong (those were Pinocchio's eyes, that was Simba's jawline); secondly, there was never any doubting which Disney character each of them was meant to be; thirdly, but most confusingly, the renditions were nonetheless subtly but quite undeniably and even nightmare-inducingly wrong.

The Smith-Mammonson woman was tall and beautiful, part supermodel, part Californian babe, part reality TV media whore. Bleached teeth, sharp cheekbones, big hair and an uncannily effective skincare regime made her age utterly unguessable. And yet, her beauty was ever-so-slightly skewed. The eyes, well, they weren't too far apart but it was just that they… they… Or maybe it was the mouth? Too wide? A bit wonky? No, not either of those but… It was as though the woman's skin was a fancy dress costume and… No. Not that either.

"Good morning. How are you doing today? I hope you haven't been waiting long. My name is Melanie. Can I take your names?"

The Mammonite spoke quickly, like a radio voice giving the terms and conditions for a high interest loan.

"Um. I'm Nina Seth. This is Vivian Grey."

"Hello, Nina. Hello, Vivian. Can I call you Nina and Vivian?"

"Yes," said Nina.

"No," said Vivian.

"Are you lost?" smiled the Mammonite, flashing two rows of perfect (and perfectly sharp) incisors. "Do you want directions? You must come in. I've been baking and there are muffins fresh out of the oven. I haven't eaten yet." She glanced up and down the street to check it was empty and then returned her hungry gaze to the women. "It is just the two of you, isn't it? I'm sure I can fit you in."

Nina liked muffins and never knowingly turned one down. But this creature had 'stranger danger' stamped through her like a stick of rock.

"No, thank you," said Vivian and showed the woman her consular mission identification. The smile shifted.

"Thank you, Mrs Grey," she said. "Now, was that a 'no' to the coming in or a 'no' to the muffins? If you don't like muffins, I can make you something else. Gluten-free options are available. You can eat in the back garden. We've got a *lu'crik oyh* in the pond that is simply the envy of the whole neighbourhood."

Nina looked past the Mammonite, down an obscenely clean and bright hallway that was surely far too long for this suburban semi. At the far end, she glimpsed dark stone and an open fire. Chains clanked distantly.

"We've come about Croesus," said Vivian, giving Nina a nudge in the ribs.

The Mammonite gripped the doorframe. Her fingernails were long and glossy.

"Is this a legal matter?" she said suspiciously.

"Are you his mom?" said Nina.

"I might need to refer you to someone else to answer that."

"We just want to speak to his family."

Fingernails beat a pattern on the doorframe.

"I am authorised to tell you that I am his mother."

"And when did you see him last?"

"A few hours ago. When he went to school."

"This morning?" said Nina, surprised.

"I could check my records, if you'd care to wait."

Nina thought about the satchel and the rotting pile of meat it had been buried in and the time it had been found. She thought about the distance from here to the city centre. None of it really added up.

"We found your son's bag, a brown leather satchel."

The woman's face became pinched, momentarily disgusted.

"Satchel? He has a Nike rucksack. Are you sure you have the correct information?"

"And he is definitely at school?" said Nina.

The Mammonite drew back a little, like a crocodile sliding back under its rock or wherever it was crocodiles lived. Nina wasn't up to date on the habits of crocodiles.

"Is there anything else I can help you with today?" said the Mammonite.

"No," said Vivian.

"But we've not had a muffin yet," said Nina.

Chains clinked. The Mammonite's eyes glittered like a carnivorous Kardashian and she stepped aside for Nina to enter.

"We are leaving," said Vivian.

The Mammonite looked disappointed.

"Thank you for coming. I hope I've been able to answer your queries. On a scale of one to ten, with one being very dissatisfied and ten being very satisfied, how would you rate my helpfulness?"

"Oh, definitely a ten," said Nina.

Vivian took hold of Nina's elbow and steered her away, not turning her back on the woman-thing until there was respectable distance between them.

The door closed slowly.

"Muffin-denier," Nina muttered.

"She would have eaten you," said Vivian.

"YOLO," said Nina. "To school then?"

"To the school," said Vivian.

"And next the canteen."

Morag followed Colin as he pushed the door open. The lights inside were already on.

It was, indeed, a canteen. Four rows of metal tables, chairs neatly tucked underneath. Stainless steel cabinets off against one wall, perhaps full of government issue plates and cups and crockery. Hooks on the wall on the other side. Three sets of plastic overalls. A clipboard on a hook, the sheet on it mouldered to an unreadable yellow.

"Cool," said Rod, crossing to the hanging overalls. "These are actually fallout suits."

"That's what I got told," said Colin.

"Amazing."

"I'll get you one for Christmas," said Morag.

Rod scoffed. "You can try but, when you do, MI5 will 'take an interest.' Trust me."

Morag didn't touch anything. The place was like a museum piece and she'd been raised not to touch things in museums. It was affecting to think that there was a time, not so very long ago, that such a place had been necessary, that people had planned to hide down here and keep civilisation ticking over while the world burned above their heads.

She looked up.

"Ah," she said.

The ceiling lights were suspended on chains and now Morag saw that the dark space above them was occupied. The *Dinh'r* didn't look much like a spider. It looked like something growing on the base of a tree in a damp woodland, a huge fungoid sac, veiny and bloated. True, woodland fungi didn't tend to have four-piece mandibles, segmented legs and purple-silver eyes waving around like deely-boppers; but it sure didn't look much like a spider.

"Rod," she said. And then it dropped on her.

Thatcher Academy in Dickens Heath, two glass-fronted storeys of thrusting and shiny corporate-sponsored educational newness, was surrounded by sports fields, light woodland and high security fences to keep out humans. While Vivian and Nina waited in reception, a wall screen rotated through photographs of children going about the business of learning, which apparently consisted of exciting science experiments, looking thoughtfully at pieces of paper, and belittling others in sporting events.

The headteacher was a Mammonite woman whose movements were both expressive and efficient, like an uncannily human-like (but not quite human enough) robot that had taken up acting lessons.

"Mrs Grey," she said, "So very nice to see you again."

"Thank you for taking the time to see us, Miss Cook-Mammonson."

The headteacher held up the tablet in her hand. "This is not a scheduled visit. How can we help you today?"

"We are conducting a missing persons inquiry."

The headteacher nodded in acknowledgement. "And who is this?"

"My colleague, Nina Seth."

The headteacher looked down at her. If she had worn glasses, she would have peered over the top of them.

"You're very short, Nina," she said.

"Petite," said Nina.

"Which means much the same thing, Nina. I assume it's due to poor diet or subpar genetic heritage."

"I was raised on chip butties by a tribe of kick-ass pygmies," said Nina.

"I assume that's a joke," said the headteacher.

"You assume a lot. Croesus Smith-Mammonson."

"Yes?"

"Is he one of your students?"

"Is that a formal request for information, Nina?"

Nina looked at Vivian and then the headteacher. "Yes," she said.

The headteacher gave her a small, economical smile.

"He is one of our students. Year seven."

"Is he here?"

"Yes."

"Are you sure?"

"Why would I not be sure?" said the headteacher. "Do you have evidence to suggest otherwise, Nina?"

"No, she does not," said Vivian swiftly.

"But you would like me to check nonetheless?"

"That would be lovely," said Nina.

"Then we shall do the tour." A bell rang out. "The end of lunch. Everyone has fed and is back in lessons. This way."

Pink and silver mandalas of light battered at Rod's vision.

He blinked, tried to turn, and found himself in a tunnel. Not a concrete blast-proof tunnel beneath Birmingham but a far older tunnel, far away in time and distance. To be precise, 4th May 2005, somewhere on one side or the other of the Iraq-Syria border, one week and twenty miles away from the bloody battle of Al-Qa'im.

Rod crouched on the tunnel floor, his fingertips inch-deep in cold white sand.

(It's not real, shouted a tiny voice deep inside Rod but he ignored it.)

He took a personal inventory. Weapon-wise, he had the MP5 submachine gun, the Browning pistol, two flash-bang grenades, a mini-claymore mine and a knife. He'd lost the 60mm anti-tank mortar. God, he wished he still had that.

He had two clips for the Browning but only one for the MP5. He'd used up most of his rounds on those men, those creatures. He sniffed as he recalled the recent firefight. They hadn't been men. Their heads were like toads' heads and their knees were in the wrong places. They hadn't been men.

The LION thermal imaging scope hadn't even picked them up in the dark.

"Cold-blooded," he said.

Equipment-wise, he had a water bottle, rations, a survival pack, a torch, the thermal imager, PVS-7 night vision goggles, the

UHF radio, the GPS receiver and the map which had lied to him and said there shouldn't have been anything within ten miles of this place except sand and rocks and dead insurgents.

One of the toad-men's rags had had the red triangle of the Iraqi Republican Guard on its shoulder.

"Messed up," said Rod.

The tunnel sloped downwards away from the echoing pool chamber in which he'd fought the toad-men and left eight of them dead. Moving down wasn't necessarily a good thing but moving away was.

Rod readied the MP5 and crept onward. The walls of the tunnel were a mixture of rough and smooth, as though sections had been replaced, piecemeal, over the ages. Chunks of sandstone, occasional pieces of black granite (carved with silver sigils that seemed to writhe when Rod wasn't looking directly at them), even lumps of modern cinderblock, hacked down to fit into place.

Twenty yards further on, the narrow corridor opened out into a much larger space. Its walls, rising up into darkness, were all of the ancient black stone. It was a perfectly round room with at least four corners. Rod tried not to think about that.

At the centre of the room was a pedestal and on it sat a shallow bronze bowl, a double-headed serpent forming both its lip and the handles at each side. In the centre of the bowl sat a red jewel, the size of a plum, the colour of blood (or cranberry juice, thought Rod. You could've said cranberry juice) and expertly but irregularly carved into the shape of some stylised beast, crouched, poised.

Three thoughts immediately occurred to Rod.

The first thought was that the red jewel would be the answer to all his problems, a genie's lamp, a wish machine, a limitless credit card. He knew this as a simple and irrefutable truth that required no explanation.

The second thought was this whole situation was as dodgy as a seven quid note. From the business with the toad-men to the mad architecture of this temple-like sanctum, it was a rum to-do and no mistake. Fubar.

The third thought was the clincher. Rod had seen that bit at the beginning of *Raiders of The Lost Ark* and he knew what happened when you took ancient gubbins off the big pedestal. He'd also seen that bit at the end and didn't want his face melted by something from beyond the dawn of time.

"No thanks, mate," he told the blood-coloured (no, *cranberry*-coloured) jewel.

And then, as in a dream, he instantly knew that something bad was about to happen to him. A creature was going to appear behind him. Its name was *Azhur-Banipal*. It would reach out to him with black, cloth-bound arms and compel him to take the stone, to make the world his own for a time...

Rod whirled with the MP5 but the creature wasn't there.

Of course, it wasn't. It would appear behind him. Whichever way he turned, it would be behind him, reaching out for him.

Rod was suddenly terrified. He had faced fear before. Army training and the SAS training that had come later had taken that fear and channelled it into something else. But he had never destroyed his fears. They were still there. And Rod was terrified.

(This isn't real, screamed the tiny voice inside him. It's a memory. A dream.)

He turned again, torch light swinging, his breath quickening.

Something brushed his cheek. He whirled, his hand going to his face in surprise.

The stink of rotten prawns filled his nostrils. Prawns? They were hundreds of miles from the coast.

Azhur-Banipal reached out to take hold of him.

Prawns? Seriously? In the Syrian Desert?

(Wake up!)

Rod blinked. He was on his back, staring up at the strip lights hanging from the canteen ceiling and at the hypnotic pink-silver eyes of a *Dinh'r*. He felt the grip of his Glock 21 in the palm of his hand.

"Cheeky bugger," he said and shot the creature three times. One shot for each eye and one for where any sensible entity would keep its brain.

"Thatcher Academy was, until 2010, the Tythe Barn Lane secondary school, a failing local authority school which turned non-work-ready and non-aspirational eleven-year-old humans into non-work-ready and non-aspirational sixteen-year-old humans," said Cook-Mammonson, the headteacher, as they walked across the empty playground. "And then, thanks to your government and the sponsorship of Mammon-Mammonson Investments, the Thatcher Academy was born, a self-governing non-profit charitable trust that uses private-sector best practice to further Mammonite integration with and supplanting of human society."

"Supplanting?" said Nina.

"Yes, Nina," said the headteacher. "It is a word that means to supersede and replace. Tell me, Nina, did you make best use of your school years?"

Vivian, who knew full well that Nina's school qualifications amounted to GCSEs in English and PE and a failed A-level in Digital Media (Photography), watched a little bit of class-envy and social discomfort play across her young colleague's face. Vivian took no pleasure in it but felt that a little humility would do Nina some good.

"I was the lead in the school production of *Grease*," said Nina. "And I sold cigarettes to all the sixth formers. My cousin Hari had a supply from his dad's shop."

"Yes. But what I meant was – Sorry, excuse me a moment. You! You! Stop there!"

This last was bellowed at surprising volume at a uniformed Mammonite lad emerging from a set of double doors across the way.

"You! Why are you out of lesson?" said the headteacher, drawing a smooth round pebble from her jacket pocket.

"Toilet, miss," said the boy.

The headteacher nodded and then hurled her pebble with impressive accuracy. It clouted the lad on the side of the head and tumbled him over into a flower bed.

"Attend to your toilet on your own time!" she shouted and then turned back to Nina, clearly indifferent to the lifeless lad in the borders.

"Is he dead?" said Nina.

"If he has a weak bladder and a thin skull then it was a kindness." She seemed to taste this last word as she spoke it, as though it was an entirely alien concept. She continued on, leading them round the building and alongside the rear playing fields where a school army cadet unit was undergoing weapons training. "Your qualifications, Nina. Straight A stars? Perhaps one or two As?"

"No," said Nina.

"That's disappointing, particularly from someone of your ethnic background. Such things might be expected from our Afro-Caribbean friends –"

"Woah," said Nina. "Time out on the rampant racism."

"It's not racism if it's true, Nina," said the headteacher. "I would not be so rash as to suggest that the academic weakness of black children is hardwired in their genes or specific cultural modalities but the statistics nonetheless bear out certain truths."

"You do not have any human pupils here at present, do you?" said Vivian.

"Does that have any bearing on your investigation, Mrs Grey?"

"Professional curiosity only."

"We have some human employees," said the headteacher, waving a hand towards a bent-backed cleaner who was collecting litter by a wall and would soon need to decide whether to tidy up or work round the pebble-struck boy. "But, no, we had a couple of children start with us last year. We tried to discourage them but the parents, enamoured by our results, were insistent."

"And where are they now?"

"They couldn't keep up with our rigorous standards. Excellence in everything, all of the time. That's our motto."

"I thought it was Equal opportunities for all," said Vivian.

"Yes, but we had to change that after some people, including the aforementioned humans, thought that meant we should treat everyone equally rather than allow everyone an equal amount of opportunity in which to succeed." She looked at Nina. "It's about giving everyone an equal start in life's race, not giving a medal to everyone who crosses the finishing line."

The headteacher stopped to admire the army cadets as they took up firing positions before a row of mannequin targets.

"Live ammunition," noted Vivian.

"We don't pretend here," said the headteacher proudly. "We asked to be part of the latest army cadet initiative in schools but have expanded in creative ways. We have a fully stocked armoury in the sports hall. The true purpose of education is to show progress, to put a numerical figure to a person and say, 'This person is better than that one.' How can we instil British values such as fortitude and personal endeavour if we do not have the failures of the rabble to learn from?"

The mannequins twitched and danced under semi-automatic rifle fire. Recoiling, one raised an arm as though to protest before it was riddled with further bullets.

"How can there be social mobility, if there are no bodies to climb over?" said the headteacher.

Rod wriggled out from under the dead *Dinh'r*. It was bulky but not heavy. Its body was as soft and light as marshmallow. Its skin tingled unpleasantly to the touch like glass wool. Rod got up and checked on Morag and BT engineer Colin, who were laid out on the floor nearby.

Colin grunted and spasmed like a dreaming dog. Morag blinked slowly and stared at nothing.

"You okay?" said Rod.

She looked at him and said dreamily, "I put the shotgun in her mouth and – boom – killed the bitch."

"Of course, you did, lass," said Rod, taking her hand in his and tapping it. "And now it's time to wake up."

Morag took a sudden deep breath, blinked once more and then said, in a far more normal voice, "Where's the *Dinh'r*?"

"Killed it."

"Good. Damned thing gorging itself on our *adn-bhul* nightmares."

She sat up. Colin whimpered.

"They can't cancel *Downton Abbey*," he sobbed in his trance. "What'll we watch on Sunday nights?"

"Obviously, some nightmares are more nutritionally filling than others," said Morag.

"You don't know that," said Rod. "Maybe he really loved that show."

Nina looked on as the headteacher's mobile rang and, with a gesture of apology, she took the call.

She spoke very little and listened intently and, as she did, her expression hardened increment by increment. She ended the call.

"You lied to me, Mrs Grey," she said and there was a world of subtext in her voice.

"I do not lie," said Vivian.

"She doesn't," Nina chipped in. "I once asked her what she thought of my new haircut."

"You told me you were conducting a missing persons enquiry. You did not say you had found a body."

"We haven't," said Nina. "We found body parts. Who knows if that's half a person or six?"

"Nor did you tell me where you had found these... parts."

"Is that significant?" asked Vivian.

Vivian had a wonderful poker face, one of the perks of being a 24/7 resting-bitch-face old moo.

"I'm afraid I need to speak to our chair of governors," said the headteacher.

"Is that who that was?" said Vivian. "Perhaps I ought to join you."

"To explain yourself," said the headteacher.

"To further our mutual understanding."

Cook-Mammonson inclined her head slightly. "And Nina here can go and check that Croesus Smith-Mammonson is alive and well."

Out on the field, the army cadets were cutting the heavy mannequins down from their posts.

"It's room G4 in that building there, Nina," said the headteacher. "But do feel free to wander as much as you like. Explore."

The way she said it, it sounded like some ancient Chinese curse.

Nina went to the indicated building while Vivian and the headteacher headed back to the admin offices. The corridors were pristine, empty and silent. There was none of the shouting, lesson skiving or casual graffiti that Nina recalled from her own school. She peered through the window of the nearest classroom door, half expecting to see children strapped to chairs, wire speculums holding their eyes open as they were forcibly indoctrinated. But, no, the young people in this room, a chemistry lab, seemed to be fully enjoying their practical lesson, playing with strange earths and white metals over Bunsen burners. Apart from the lack of safety goggles and the sooty blast patterns on some of the walls, it could have been any school classroom.

Nina moved on to room G4 and peered in. Thirty children, not more than twelve years old, sat in a neat grid of desks before an electronic whiteboard. Nina knocked and entered, flashing her ID at the Mammonite teacher.

"Don't mind me," she said. "I'm just having a look round."

The teacher returned to her class. Each student had a thick book on their desk, some of them open, some closed, and beside that a tablet, all open to the same app.

"So, how should an individual respond to a social problem such as homelessness?" she asked. "Mansa?"

"They shouldn't," said the boy. "The homeless should be ignored."

On the board, next to a lesson title of 'Individualism v Collectivism in The Fountainhead' there was a list of names, all with decimal scores between one and ten next to them. Mansa Mason-Mammonson's crept up a fraction. Croesus Smith-Mammonson, wherever he was in the room, had a healthy six point eight.

"Ignored entirely?" said the teacher. "Cassius?"

"Our charity should be limited to good wishes, miss."

"Good wishes?" said the teacher distastefully.

"We do not know if that hobo might one day turn their life around and become a success, someone of note."

"They're already a failure," said a pig-tailed girl snidely.

"Yang, do not call out."

The girl fixed her teacher with a stare straight out of psycho street.

"Are you sure you want to tell me what to do, miss? Your approval rating is dangerously low as it is."

The teacher glanced nervously at the board and then at Nina. Nina noticed that above the students' names was 'Miss Carter-Mammonson' and a score of one point nine. The girl, Yang, tapped on her tablet as did several students around her and the score dipped to one point eight.

"I might only be a supply teacher but this is my classroom," began the teacher.

"Do you own it?" said the girl. "Is your name on it?"

"There are rules."

"Do you want to show me these rules?"

"You... You shouldn't speak out of turn."

"But it was my turn," said the girl. "Can you prove otherwise? Do you have evidence? You don't. But do you know what I have?" She pulled out a mobile. "I've got the chair of governors on speed dial. Would you like me to call him?"

The teacher, in her distress looking even less like a human than most Mammonites, murmured something to herself and then bowed her head.

"My apologies, Yang. It was your turn to speak."

Yang and her cronies tapped at their tablets. The teacher's score went down a further notch.

"Weak," said Yang.

The teacher looked at her, broken.

"The homeless, by the act of becoming homeless, have already shown themselves to be weak," said Yang. "They have failed."

"What about second chances?" said Nina.

Yang gave her a furious glare.

"Everyone gets one chance," said the girl. "And this is it."

"I'll remember that," said Nina.

"Miss," said Yang, not taking her eyes off Nina, "who is this person?"

"I'm from the consular mission," said Nina. "Just come to check that everything is okay. Which one of you is Croesus?"

A dark-haired youth looked sharply at her. "What do you want with me?" There was a note of worry in his voice, not of actual concern but of social embarrassment.

"Nothing," said Nina. "I just wanted to check that you were here. You don't happen to own a brown leather satchel?"

There were some laughs in the classroom and, among the general giggles were some very knowing laughs.

"Does perhaps someone else own a brown leather satchel?" she suggested.

"We don't have to answer your questions," said a boy with tiny ears.

The supply teacher looked like she wanted to say something but she didn't. Nina didn't miss the relevance of the Yang girl's finger hovering over her tablet. It didn't matter; Nina already had a solid idea whose satchel it was.

Morag smiled at Colin's tone.

"*Downton Abbey*?" he said, pressing manfully ahead.

"Yes."

"No," said the engineer. "You must have misheard me."

"Back me up here, Rod," said Morag.

Rod kept his eyes on the tunnel ahead.

"If the feller's not willing to admit his love for a bit of gentle period drama, I'm not going to argue with him."

"It's not that I'm not willing, mate," said Colin. "I don't like it. My good lady watches it. And the *Strictly* and the *Bake Off* too – well not since it went to Channel 4 – and I might be in the room but I don't enjoy it."

The canteen and the dead *Dinh'r* were some distance behind them now. They had shoved the Venislarn critter into a corner before waking Colin.

That solitary *Dinh'r* had, probably, been the only resident of the defunct bunker but there were still unanswered questions regarding the empty egg sacs (which that creature had either laid or, conceivably, emerged from) and the unfeasibly neat pile of sliced 'n' diced flesh. And so, along cable-lined tunnels, from one blast door to the next, the three of them had progressed.

And now, as Rod was on the cusp of delivering his own verdict on dancing and baking shows, they came across something that, whilst not providing any answers, cast the questions in a new light.

"This shouldn't be here," said Colin.

And yet it was, and looked like it had been there for a good long time. The tunnel descended by a series of wide steps into a round and vaguely conical cavern, at least fifty yards across. The sound of dripping water echoed from low-arched tunnels cut into the bottommost steps.

"It's like an amphitheatre," said Morag.

"Like the Colosseum," said Rod. "Ah."

And several pieces of the visual jigsaw fell into place. The dark patches in the earth at the centre of amphitheatre. The shadowed cages on the far side of the chamber. Even the out-of-place stained wheelbarrow down in the centre of the pit.

"Like throwing Christians to the lions," said Morag.

"Because the *Dinh'r* don't eat people but they might –"

"Rip them apart for the entertainment of their masters," said Morag.

"But this shouldn't be here," said Colin. "It's impossible. Look, all that cabling's been rerouted. Neatly too. Like one of our lads did it. And the water pipes. Look."

"Someone's been mucking about with local space-time," said Morag.

She made her away around the huge chamber, walking along one of the circling step-seats. Instinctively, Morag did not want to cross the arena floor. To do so felt like an invitation to cause trouble.

When they were halfway round, the lights went off again. Colin and Rod were reduced to points of torchlight. There was a scrape of movement ahead, from the cages. Caged *Dinh'r*, kept cooped up until they were needed to fight? Morag played her torch over the cages as they neared. At the furthest edge, just outside the cage, a bell hung from the ceiling, a battered open-ended tin box like a cowbell for the world's biggest cow. Below that, something shifted in a cage, ragged and bloody.

"That's a person," said Rod.

As he said it, a hand grasped the bar of the cage. Morag ran forward.

It was a young woman, filthy, and wide-eyed with shock. In her other hand, the woman held something. At first, Morag thought it was a walking stick or a staff and then she saw the wide, blood-caked end. It was a broom.

"Are you okay?" said Morag.

"I clean. I clean," said the woman.

"She's foreign," said Colin. "Told you. Immigrants."

"Shut up," said Rod.

"I clean," the woman repeated, like a broken robot.

"Of course, you do," said Morag gently.

The woman stared. She didn't blink.

"They don't even pay me minimum wage."

Morag gestured to the bars. "Possibly not the worst thing about your current situation," she said and began looking for a way to open the cage.

Vivian had mixed opinions regarding the Mammonites.

It was true that they were utterly alien, their superficial resemblance to humans thoroughly deceptive. It was also true that they were ruthless, rapacious and relentlessly acquisitive. They killed without remorse, assassinating rivals in business, removing parents who had aged beyond their usefulness and even despatching their own children if they failed to live up to expectations. They worshipped wealth and status, not for what it would bring but for its own sake. They were the questing mouths of their mother goddess and would devour the entire world if the stars would allow it.

On the other hand, they were honest. Honest of purpose at least. They were what they were and wore their personalities on their sleeves. Their near-human appearance wasn't a deliberate deception. Humanity was a mould. They had no more chosen their form in our world than a puddle chooses its shape. They spoke plainly. Within the confines of their incomprehensible goals, they acted logically and dealt reasonably. They knew the value of everything and knew the value of giving value. Their love of money was, as far as Vivian could tell, the love of a numerical system which could be accurately and coherently applied to nearly all things. Humans dishonestly insisted they could never put a price on love or a child's safety or peace of mind when it was patently clear that people could and did. That's how smoke alarm manufacturers made money. Mammonites knew the value of love, safety and peace of mind. And they drove a hard bargain.

Xerxes Mammon-Mammonson, chair of the school governors, had a calculating gaze. Vivian felt he was constantly evaluating her, adjusting his estimation second by second. His undeniably handsome face had a certain simian aspect to it and his skin was a fascinating blend of craggy, rubbery and leathery, as though he was a veteran Hollywood icon appearing in the latest adaptation of *Planet of the Apes* and had walked out halfway through having his makeup done.

Vivian had been brought before him in a staff meeting room resembling a corporate boardroom. Two other Mammonites sat beside him. He had made her wait while he unhurriedly finished his conversation with them before turning his attention to her. He did not invite her to sit and she didn't ask.

"Do you think I can't see what you're up to?" he said.

"I don't think that, Mr Mammon-Mammonson," she said honestly, having never given the hypothetical, cryptic and meaningless notion any thought. "What am I up to?"

Xerxes's gaze ran up and down her as he made a silent tally of her worth.

"You come here. Into this place. Onto this land. And you seek to disrupt the education of our young with your fake stories of missing school children and murder most foul."

"We are conducting an investigation. I do not concoct stories. I do not have the talent for it."

Xerxes chuckled.

"I can see through you. You know it. Don't feel stupid or insecure. I'm just more intelligent than you. It's not your fault."

"Thank you," she said because there was nothing meaningful to be said. "Perhaps then, given that you are so intelligent, you could help me understand. We found some remains and some belongings. You know where?"

He nodded with ponderous and magnanimous slowness. "In the Anchor facility, the chambers dug for our mother when she last incarnated in this city."

"And which *Yoth Mammon – schluri'o bento frei*," she added reverently – "vacated decades ago. Those tunnels should be empty."

Xerxes smiled. It was a broad self-indulgent smile, like that of a flatulent infant.

"We have re-opened them. We are putting them to good use and making them ready for her return."

"With the greatest respect, they are not yours to re-open or use."

The school bell rang for the end of day. Xerxes held her gaze and his tongue until it had stopped.

"With the greatest respect?" he said. "I won't tolerate any employee talking to me in such tones."

"How fortunate that I am not one of your employees then," she replied.

He shook his head.

"You work for the consular mission. The consular mission works for the *em-shadt* Venislarn. Ergo."

He opened the leather-bound document wallet on the table in front of him. A polished zombie knife, all spikes and sculpted curves sat inside it. He picked it up reflectively, looping his elongated fingers around the haft.

"You are mine," he said. "But I don't think you are worth keeping."

44

When the bell had rung for the end of the school day, Nina observed the class as it broke up and left. Nina understood people. She understood the meaning of a passing gaze, the power of a single word. She could spot a conniving bitch or a cheating boyfriend across a crowded room. In this room, power and influence circled around the pig-tailed Yang girl. As she packed away her pencil case and tucked some sort of misshapen Venislarn plush toy under her arm, others watched and waited. But Yang's attention, subtle though it was, was fixed on the boy, Croesus.

So, when the class departed, Nina surreptitiously drifted out into the playground with the flow of sharp little Mammonite children and kept an eye on those blonde pigtails. But Yang did not go with the greater mass of students towards the front gates. She turned right, towards the rear playing fields. There were a couple of other students with her and – ah – her arm laid possessively across the shoulder of Croesus Smith-Mammonson. It was not the arm of friendship nor juvenile romance. This was the guiding arm of an arresting officer, of a gangster leading an incompetent underling into a basement where only baseball bats and concrete boots awaited.

Nina kept her distance, hugging the cover of the all-weather pitch fence as she followed the four youngsters. They were making towards the edge of the woodland that backed onto the school. While she waited for them to move on, she hunkered down beneath a tree (it didn't have conkers or acorns or apples on it so she had no idea what kind of tree it was) and texted Vivian to let her know what she was up to. She also took a selfie, posted it on Snapchat and sent Rod a picture of a cute spider in a hat before picking herself up and making towards the break in the fence the children had gone through.

One of the spiked uprights on the fence had been unscrewed and tilted aside, to create a space large enough for a child, or an uber-petite sex kitten, to squeeze through. For a moment, Nina considered that it was unlike the super-professional Mammonites to allow such vandalism to go unrepaired but, then again, they weren't the kind to wrap their offspring in cotton wool. If one of

45

them was stupid enough to go wandering the dark woods, that was their lookout.

There was a faintly discernible path, a shoe-thin line of brown earth between the ferns and brambles. The thin, slick-barked trees (no conkers, acorns or apples here either) created a broad and almost total canopy that reduced the light level to a wintry gloom.

Nina listened and heard voices some distance ahead. She crept forward, her attention split equally between the voices and making sure she didn't step on any noisy twigs (if cinema had taught her anything, it was that forests were full of treacherously noisy twigs). What she wasn't looking for and failed to notice were two youths in army cammos. The first she knew was when something sharp jabbed into the small of her back.

She turned and nearly disembowelled herself on the lad's bayonet.

"Don't move, you *adn-bhul shaska.*"

Nina blinked.

"You kiss your mom with that mouth?"

The Mammonite girl raised her rifle, placing her bayonet inches from Nina's chest.

"Our mum isn't here."

"Yeah. If I was your mum, I'd abandon you in the woods too."

The lad put two fingers in his mouth and unleashed a migraine-inducing whistle. There was a rustle in the foliage and Yang, Croesus and two other adolescent Mammonites appeared. All four were smiling. The threatening power dynamic Nina had seen between Yang and Croesus in the playground had vanished. They stood shoulder to shoulder now as friends. It had been a lie, just for Nina. And she'd fallen for it.

"I should imagine that you're all wondering why I've summoned you here?" she ventured.

"Summoned? Us?" sneered Yang.

"Absolutely," said Nina. "I'm doing the old detective thing. You know, like Miss Marbles, where I reveal who did it. And, um, what it was they did."

"She's *adn-bhul* crazy," said the army cadet boy.

"And I've already spoken to you about your language, you *bhul-tamade pabbe*-sucker." She gave them her best stone-cold bitch stare. "You think this was a trap? You think I've fallen into your trap? Nah, this is where I point the finger and you get to plead for forgiveness."

It wasn't working. She could see from their faces it wasn't working.

"That wasn't Croesus's satchel we found, was it?" she said. "It was your teacher's. Your old teacher. What was it? Did she give you too much homework? Did she forget to give you a gold star? That's why you killed her."

Yang shook her head.

"Kim. *Sperr felai p'at umlaq.*"

Nina tried to duck but the army cadet girl was quicker, reversing her rifle and slamming the stock into Nina's temple. It hurt. It really bloody well hurt.

The chair of Thatcher Academy school governors stood, knife in hand. And Vivian stood her ground. In her pocket, her phone buzzed.

"You are not going to kill me, Mr Mammon-Mammonson," she said.

"That's wishful and delusional thinking, Mrs Grey," he grinned.

"Not at all," she replied. "And I will give you three reasons if you are prepared to listen."

"Three reasons," he said.

It was a simple ploy on Vivian's part. He could kill her if he wanted. He was notionally within his rights. But Mammonites liked numbers and they liked order. They couldn't resist a list.

"One," she said, "I no more work for you than Miss Cook-Mammonson works for me."

"I don't work for you," said the headteacher defensively.

"Of course, you don't," said Vivian, "even though my taxes pay your salary and you are ultimately employed by the government that I voted into power."

"Hardly relevant," said Xerxes.

"Two," she continued, "I am extraordinarily valuable to you."

He arched an eyebrow at her.

"If I can be this calm, collected and authoritative in the face of death," she said, "just imagine how effective I will be when I'm pleading for your life."

He paused at that. Xerxes said nothing but spread his arms wide for Vivian to go on, to explain herself or to hang herself with her own words.

"By contract, the children of *Yoth Mammon* have been given the village of Dickens Heath. Boundary lines have been drawn, the extent of your power set," she said.

"You don't tell us what to do," said Xerxes.

"Quite right. I don't. *Yo-Morgantus* does." She saw doubt flicker in his eyes. "My colleagues are currently seeking out and destroying any *Dinh'r* currently residing in the Anchor tunnels. You knew that was where we found the remains. That probably means that you – collectively you," she said, drawing the headteacher and the two silent governors into her accusation, "are responsible or at least complicit in them being there. I could speculate. A ritual? Death as sport? Maybe just a way of disposing of those who simply don't cut the mustard."

"How we treat our own kind or any humans we come across is our business, Mrs Grey," said the headteacher. "The Anchor facility is not under your jurisdiction."

"Nor yours. As I said, your authority extends to the boundaries of this village and it is *Yo-Morgantus* who holds power in the Venislarn court. He rules this city and I do wonder how he will respond to the discovery that you have been breeding *Dinh'r* and engaging in unauthorised activities beneath his city streets."

"*Yo-Morgantus* is nothing," blurted one of the governors.

"Nothing?"

"A petty princeling beside our royal mother."

"Yes, but she's not here," said Vivian. "I'm not overly certain where *Kal Frexo leng*-space is, but I think it is quite a long way away. And even if *Yo-Morgantus* is, and I quote and will recite when asked, 'a petty princeling' and we humans mere

48

peasants, you are still nothing more than, what, knights or barons in his court."

Xerxes Mammon-Mammonite inhaled deeply and made a deeply dissatisfied noise in his throat that was probably meant to sound like a growl but which sounded more like an asthmatic vacuum cleaner.

"Not peasants. Livestock," he corrected her.

"Fair enough, if that is our place in the order of things. But, to return to the all-important point three, this particular piece of livestock is the only one who might dissuade her colleagues from telling your current master what you have been up to." She took her phone out of her pocket. There was a fatuous text from Nina. "Ah, a communication from one of my colleagues now."

"You lie," said Xerxes.

"Not at all," she said truthfully.

"When our holy mother returns..." warned one of the governors.

"Is that going to be in the next twenty minutes?" Vivian asked. "I would guess that is approximately how long you have."

Xerxes approached her, the knife still raised. The jagged blade looked foolishly impractical but Vivian did not doubt its ability to inflict life-ending injuries. Xerxes, reeking of cologne, twisted it to catch the light.

There was a knock at the door behind Vivian and a Mammonite woman entered.

"Sorry," she said bashfully. "I was just tidying up. You wanted to see me. I didn't know if you wanted me to..." She looked at Vivian and the knife. "Maybe you're busy."

"Ah, Miss Carter-Mammonson," said Xerxes, suddenly full of avuncular cheer. "This has direct relevance for you."

"Oh. Then shall I...?"

"That's it. Close the door. We need to address the problem of your low scores."

"It's been a tough week, Mr Mammon-Mammonson."

"The progress data for your year seven English group is very alarming," said the headteacher, flicking through her tablet.

"There are behaviour problems in the group," said the teacher.

"Which would be remedied by better teaching. Pupils who are entertained do not misbehave."

"I'm not sure it's possible to make *The Fountainhead* entertaining."

Xerxes slapped his heart as though shot. "Are you blaming your poor classroom management on Ayn Rand's writing?"

The teacher struggled to find a meaningful response to the question.

"I'm only a supply teacher," she said weakly. "I haven't been given much of a chance."

"Good teachers don't need a run up," said the headteacher.

"Now," said Xerxes, "here's the rub. Mrs Grey here" – he waved the knife at Vivian – "has informed us that it would be improper for us to cart your sorry ass off to the *Dinh'r* pits to face trial by combat."

"Oh?" said the teacher.

"We can't give you a final opportunity to redeem yourself, to attain personal glory for yourself or provide psychic nourishment for our holy mother's intimate fauna and some entertainment for your betters. Apparently, it is 'unauthorised.'"

"Right," said the teacher who couldn't see where this was going. Vivian could.

Xerxes put one hand on the doomed teacher's shoulder and tightened his grip on the knife with the other.

"Isn't she a spoilsport?" he said.

The teacher's mouth was open to speak but she didn't even get the chance to do that.

Rod rolled up the dollar note and slid it into the gap between the lock and the cage doorframe. He pulled the button from his jacket cuff, unspooled the thread and tucked it into the end of the rolled dollar.

"To a casual observer that would look like the actions of a crazy person," said Morag cheerfully.

"Is this some sort of James Bond thing?" said Colin.

"Cordite-infused dollar," said Rod. "Thread laced with black powder."

"I thought you had the explosives in your sand timer thingy," said Morag.

"The sand timer explosive is francium. Twenty-yard blast radius. Minimum. This will be much more controlled." Rod gave the woman in the cage his most reassuring smile. "Nicoleta. I need you to move to the rear of the cage and crouch down. It's going to be noisy."

The young woman did as instructed, disappearing into the gloom at the back of the cage. Rod waved Morag and Colin back, lit the fuse and joined them some distance away. Five seconds later, the lock flared with sun-bright light and then popped with a harsh metallic toink!

Keeping his hands far from the superheated lock, Rod flung the door open. It caught the giant cow bell as it opened and sent the clapper rattling with a dull atonal sound. Nicoleta burst from the cage and slapped her hands to either side of the bell to silence it.

"No," she said tremulously.

"What?" said Rod.

"They come," she said.

"Eh?"

Morag slapped his arm and held up a finger to indicate he should listen. From the low arches near the arena floor, the sound of dripping water had been replaced with a rustling sound. Like leaves, albeit huge leaves, with steel piton feet and bigger mandibles than any insectoid on earth.

"That's the dinner bell," said Morag hoarsely.

"What?" said Colin.

"Let the games begin," said Rod sourly. "Time to run."

As Morag shoved Colin ahead of her, Rod grabbed Nicoleta's hand and dragged her along the stone step and towards the tunnel by which they had entered.

The first *Dinh'r* – the first of dozens – squeezed spongily out of the burrow-like arches before the four humans were halfway round the arena.

"Spiders!" yelled Colin.

"We noticed!" yelled Morag in reply.

Rod did a double-take.

"You can let go of the broom!" he said to Nicoleta, wrested it from her grasp and hurled it down at the nearest critter, where it bounced off its cushiony thorax.

"We have to pay for broom ourselves," said the cleaner.

"Aye, you need a better job," said Rod.

"This better than the school," said the cleaner, panic in her voice. "Cannot go back there. Teachers bad. Children even more bad."

The *Dinh'r* rippled up the steps as their prey reached the exit tunnel. There was no door for Rod to pull shut behind them. He was the last through and turned on the nearest pursuers. He took aim. The pencil torch on the Glock barrel picked out a pair of intricate silver-pink eyes. The eyes swirled, loomed large. Rod felt his mind teetering on the lip of something, a pull against him like the torrent above a waterfall.

He turned his head aside and fired blindly. He hit something.

As he made to run, something wet and cold latched onto his gun hand. The creature had its maw wrapped around his gun, his hand, his whole forearm. Mandibles like crooked chisels came down upon his arm to strip flesh from the bone.

With no direct input from his brain, Rod's finger pulled the trigger repeatedly. The creature bucked and shook as bullets tore through it and exploded from its soft body. The *Dinh'r*'s thrashing and Rod's considerable desire to save both himself and his arm tore them apart. It was only while he was sprinting away that he realised that he had left his pistol inside the dying creature. He shook the mucosal slime from his hand.

"Still stinks of prawns," he spat.

"Come on!" Morag shouted.

Torchlight blinded him and suddenly he was splashing through shallow puddles.

Morag was waiting for him. Somewhere ahead, Colin the engineer and Nicoleta the cleaner were making their escape. Morag spun a valve wheel on a nearby pipe. Water sprayed out from beneath the wheel.

Rod gave her a look.

"They might be afraid of water," she said.

"Incy Wincy Spider?" he said.

Shapes tumbled and rustled in the dark behind them. They ran.

"I lost my gun and torch," he said.

"That was careless," she said.

Behind them, the tone of the spraying water changed as the *Dinh'r* pushed through it.

"Okay," panted Morag. "Not afraid of water."

"No, but…"

Rod found his keys and snapped the little hourglass key fob from its chain. He violently depressed the top to break the vacuum seal, paused, turned and threw it as far back towards the *Dinh'r* as possible.

"What was that?" said Morag.

"Two grams of francium. It can react explosively with air. But it really hates wa–"

The explosion was a bright flash and a low boom, loud enough to clear sinuses and make ears bleed. A wall of pressure nearly tumbled them from their feet and then, in the ringing silence as they helped one another onwards, the water surged around their ankles. Morag yelled.

Something huge and spongey bashed against Rod's leg, a dead *Dinh'r* surfing the wave. They sprinted on through ever-deepening water.

In the bouncing light of Morag's torch, Rod could see a door ahead. Colin stood on the other side, clearly poised to slam it shut and throw the bulkhead bolts. Morag was through first with Rod close behind.

Water was already pouring over the lip of the door as Colin closed it and span the locking wheel.

"What the hell happened?" shouted Colin.

"What?" said Morag, waggling a finger in her ear.

"Explosion ruptured the pipes," said Rod. "I should think the water table's going to rise with a vengeance now."

As he said it, he noticed that water was pooling about their feet already. It wasn't coming through the blast door but from elsewhere. From conduits in side corridors? Rising through cracks in the concrete?

"I think we need to find an access ladder," said Rod.

"I think we need to find a ladder, don't you?" shouted Morag.

They tied her to a tree.

Nina had been tied to a tree before but that first time had been a lot more fun and there had been safe words and alcohol and a much lower chance of the night ending in savage murder. Right now, she was being kept alive by the children's indecision.

"I think we should eat her," said young Croesus for the third time.

"It's pizza for tea tonight," argued the army cadet girl.

"I'm not saying we eat all of her," he replied.

"We should hold her for ransom," said the army cadet boy, sitting on a fallen log and resting his chin on the muzzle of his rifle.

"And do a deal with the humans?" said pig-tailed Yang.

"They'd give us several grand for her," said the boy.

"Human money," said Yang. "No. We kill her and leave her body as a warning."

Yang stepped towards Nina and licked her teeth.

"Who's going to video it?" asked Nina.

Yang frowned at her, like she was some kind of worm: a worm that had learned to talk but a worm nonetheless.

Nina tried to shift her position. The movement made her head pound; the rifle butt had left her with a localised but astonishing pain in her temple. She didn't know if she was bleeding. She hoped she was bleeding. What was the point of getting hurt if it didn't leave a cool and colourful injury?

"Someone's got to video it," she said.

"Why?" said Yang.

"If you don't video it, no one will know."

"We'll know."

"And when people find the body," added one of Yang's cronies.

Nina laughed. "Not much of a marketing strategy, is it? Look, if it's not online, it didn't happen. Rule number one."

"Like on Facebook?" said Croesus.

"Facebook? Sure, if you're an ancient. Facebook's for mums and dads and sad loners called Emily who post pictures of their dinner and who will one day be eaten by their own cats."

"I don't have Facebook," said the army cadet girl.

"Who's Emily?" said Croesus.

"A sad and lonely *glun'u* who tangled with the wrong bitch and will one day be eaten by her cats. Pay attention."

The army cadet boy nodded sagely.

"We could put it on YouTube and get money from advertising."

"There we go," said Nina. "See? A man with an eye on the future."

"Fine," said Yang. "Prester, get out your phone. I'm going to do her."

Nina was shaking her head.

"What?" demanded Yang.

"You can't just do it," said Nina critically. "You never heard of foreplay?" She looked at the pre-teen. "No, probably not. Um, if you're going to do this then… Look, Prester hasn't even started filming."

"I'm just deleting stuff to make room," said the army cadet boy, fiddling with his phone.

"You don't just leap in," said Nina. "You don't give the viewer thirty seconds of footage that's one hundred percent money-shot. Tease and reveal. Tease and reveal. Here, I've…" She struggled against the cords that tied her to the tree. "I've got this brilliant video I shot on my phone. It's just a dog falling into a canal but it's… well, you just have to see it."

"I'm not untying you," said Yang.

"Actually," said Croesus, "I'd like to see the dog falling in the canal."

"Oh, and I've got this amazing picture of a cute spider in a hat."

"Spiders don't have hats," said Yang.

"Right, I'm ready," said the army cadet boy.

"But we are going to watch the dog video, aren't we?" said Croesus.

"We've got time," said Nina.

"But it's pizza tonight," said the army cadet girl. "We need to go home."

"We do this first," insisted Yang.

"No," said Vivian loudly, behind Nina and out of sight. "You are going to untie Miss Seth and, as your friend suggests, go home."

Vivian entered the rough clearing, trampling brambles. She held out a twenty pound note between her hands. The army cadets already had their rifles raised and aimed.

"Who are you?" demanded Yang.

"My name is Mrs Grey. I work with Miss Seth. And you need to let her go."

"You can't tell us what to do," said a girl.

Vivian's expression was stony.

"I certainly can and I am. Now, luckily for you, I don't yet know who you are. You can walk away from this."

"They killed their teacher," said Nina. "It's her remains in the tunnels."

"No, they didn't. The teacher – several teachers probably – were killed by the head and the governors and other upstanding members of the community and," she added with a stern look for the children, "they are in a lot of trouble."

"But you lot don't get to tell us what to do," insisted the girl. "Not here."

"Here?" said Vivian. "In Dickens Heath?" She looked up, down and around herself. "But we're not in Dickens Heath. Your land is approximately twenty metres that way. This, here, is not your territory."

"No, it is," said Yang, but without conviction.

"Lines on a map, bitch," said Nina.

The mood of the group had switched. Suddenly the idea of going home for pizza seemed more appealing.

"But who would know?" argued Yang. "We kill them and drag them over there."

"That would be dishonest," said Vivian. She stepped towards Yang, the twenty pound note held out before her.

"What?" sneered Yang. "You going to bribe me? With twenty measly quid?"

"No," said Vivian and tore the banknote in two.

Yang reeled. A girl gasped. Prester nearly fell off his log.

"What...? What did you do that for?" said Yang.

Vivian had another banknote in her hand.

"You will untie Miss Seth and let her go."

Yang stammered. "No one would... Why would you...?"

Vivian tore the second note in half.

"Stop it!" yelled Croesus.

"I'm going to be sick," said the army cadet girl.

Mammonites worshipped money. Value was the sea they swam in. It was life to them. Vivian tearing up banknotes was the Mammonite equivalent of repeatedly punching a kitten in the face.

The army cadet boy fumbled with the cords that tied Nina.

"Thank you, Prester," she said.

"Now go home," said Vivian, another banknote in her hand.

The Mammonite children fled from the deranged woman. Nina brushed leaf mould and bark from her clothes.

"Are we actually outside Dickens Heath?" she asked.

"I don't know," said Vivian. "You owe me forty pounds."

Nina scooped up the ripped notes.

"You can Sellotape them back together."

"But I'm not going to."

Vivian led the way out of the woods.

"You could have used fivers," suggested Nina.

"You can't tear the new five pound notes. They're plastic."

"You could try," said Nina. "Anyway, you stopped me getting a muffin earlier. So that makes us even."

"No, it doesn't, Miss Seth," said Vivian.

Nina sighed and took out her phone.

"Maybe a picture of a cute spider in a hat could change your mind."

"No."

"I bet Rod thinks it's funny."

"I think," said Rod, quietly contemplative, "I will be happy if I never see another spider for as long as I live."

Morag heard him. He sounded like he was speaking from the bottom of a tin dustbin but her hearing was at least returning.

Nicoleta clung to the ladder, eight rungs above the rising flood. Morag, Rod and Colin stood shin-deep in water. While Colin spoke on the chunky, wall-mounted telephone, Morag swept her torch back and forth across the tunnel and Rod inspected the scratches the gun-swallowing *Dinh'r* had gouged in his arm.

"Access fourteen," Colin said. "Yeah. It won't open from the inside. Five minutes? Okay."

He put the phone down.

"It'll be about half an hour," he said.

"Good," said Rod. "I'm surprised the water is rising this fast."

"If the Venislarn messed with local space-time down there," said Morag, "who knows what reservoirs they accidentally tapped."

"Let the wriggly bastards drown," said Rod with feeling.

Morag looked at his wounded arm.

"You'll have to go to the hospital with that."

Rod groaned.

"At least you might accidentally bump into that cute doctor you fancy," she said.

"What cute doctor?"

"You know the one."

"I'm sure I don't, thank you," he said.

It wasn't possible to see him blush in the dark. Morag didn't need to.

An hour later, with the water approaching their knees, they heard the *clunk* of a manhole cover being shifted.

"Up, up, up," said Rod, shooing the others toward the ladder and then rapidly bringing up the rear.

It was evening in the world above. Rod looked about. They had come up near Millennium Point, practically in the shadow of the old Curzon Street station building. A trio of police cars were parked nearby. Paramedics guided Nicoleta to an ambulance.

Rod clapped a hand on Colin's shoulder.

"You did a right good job down there," he said. "Above and beyond."

"I won't lie," said Colin. "I think I'll need a big drink and a long sit down."

"Watch some *Downton* on catch-up."

Colin gave him a wry look.

"Maybe so."

Rod's phone buzzed in his pocket as it reconnected with the world.

He shook out his wet trouser legs and looked at his one message, from Nina.

"Shall I come with you to the hospital?" asked Morag.

Rod tilted his head. "Probably best if you did. You should get checked out."

"I didn't get bitten."

"Aye," he said, "but the thing with francium, it is a bit radioactive."

"A bit radioactive?"

"A wee bit."

"God damn you, Rod Campbell. I had plans for tonight."

He showed her his phone.

"Maybe a picture of a cute spider in a hat will cheer you up," he suggested.

Morag punched him.

Tuesday

Once she realised she was going to be late for work, Morag decided to enjoy the experience. She stopped *en route* from New Street Station to the Library to pick up a hot drink and a breakfast roll and ate half of it while watching the cranes over the Central Library demolition site. Then she cut through the dodgy underpass of Fletchers Walk into Centenary Square and strolled toward the Library of Birmingham.

The Birmingham consular mission to the Venislarn was housed in a purpose-built confection of glass, gold cladding and vast interlocking magic wards forged from a tungsten-magnesium alloy with a selenium core. The building did a sterling job of masquerading as the city's largest public library even though some might question why so much of the huge building was clearly inaccessible to the public.

Morag stuffed the uneaten half of her breakfast roll in her jacket pocket as she entered the Library through the concourse. She circled around to the bank of lifts behind the ground floor coffee shop and swiped her ID against a blank piece of wall, then stepped into the lift and pressed for the seventh floor.

"Hold the door!" called Lois Wheeler, scuttling over in impractical heels.

Morag did as instructed and the office receptionist clattered in, all chunky jewellery, bust and bustle.

"Ta, bab," she said.

"Not like you to be late," said Morag.

"I'm not. I was sent down to find you. You weren't answering your phone."

"Dead battery," said Morag. "Spent half the night at the restricted ward and forgot to plug it in before bed. Sent to find me?"

"Vaughn demands your company."

Morag snorted. "Vaughn? Demand?" The consular chief was a virtual ghost and an actual recluse. He was like the after images you get from staring at the sun. He was clearly there but it was impossible to pinpoint him with any clarity and if you stared at him he'd slide off to the corners of your vision. The idea of him demanding anything was absurd.

But Lois wasn't joking.

"Well, he can go boil his head if he thinks I'm going to run for him," said Morag. She pointed at her forearm and the cotton balls taped along it. "That is for the general antibiotics they gave me. That one is the antimicrobial something or other. And that one is for the *pyam'n sree* anti-parasitics, even though I didn't get bitten by one of the bastards."

"And what's that one?" said Lois, pointing at a red mark on her wrist.

Morag licked it.

"Red sauce. I had a bacon bap. What's he worked up about anyway?"

"You know he's been going on about the likelihood of a ministerial inspection after the whole" – Lois did a complex and sound-effect laden pantomime which was apparently supposed to convey a train crash, a rampaging god monster, a fight in a chocolate factory and all the other events of three weeks ago that had left two consular employees dead and two injured – "you know, thing."

"I've seen the e-mails. He now wants to talk about it, huh?"

"There's someone from the ministry here."

Morag paused.

"Right. So, he wants everyone in and everything spic and span. I get it."

Lois wrinkled her nose.

"The ministry feller wants to talk to you."

"Me? Why me?"

"Like they'd tell me that, bab," said Lois and then tutted. "You've made me hungry now."

"Because I mentioned bacon?"

Lois leaned in and sniffed at Morag's jacket.

"You smell of it too."

"Gee, thanks."

"No, not in a bad way," said Lois, taking hold of Morag's arm so she could get a proper nosefull.

Professor Sheikh Omar had for many years used the rib bone of an alligator as a letter opener – not because it was imbued with special properties or esoteric powers, but simply because it amused him. In recent months, he had been receiving more handwritten mail. This ought to have been a diverting novelty in an age when incoherent email, dashed off in a trice, was the norm. But, he'd found that the letters conformed to a depressingly predictable pattern. They would be written in coloured ink on material that varied from homemade vellum (crafted from the skins of family pets) to lumpy mats of plant (and, perhaps, insect) fragments embedded in recycled paper pulp. The intention was always to create a sense of uniqueness and power, but Omar found them unimaginative and more than a little unsavoury. Maurice knew to bring him the tongs when one of these appeared in the post.

He sighed and opened the latest handwritten letter, which was from someone called Jeffney Ray. The name was familiar. Omar had published *Venislarn: A Language Primer* as a convenient source of income. The textbook had proven a useful resource for students, but an unforeseen consequence was the correspondence from those who had bought it, expecting not only to become fluent in the language of the Venislarn after quickly flicking through its pages but also to have the expertise of the author at their disposal for anything relating to the Venislarn. Omar knew that his readers paid handsomely for the book, but that was more to do with the nature of the illegal sales channels where they found it than his own modest profiteering. Omar operated a three strikes system, and Jeffney Ray was now on his second strike.

>   *Dear Professor,*
>   *Can you tell me if theys a market for elderly women in Fish Town as consorts or sex slaves? My mom is asking too many questions about my business operations. Her*

eyesight is quite bad so I might be able to tell her it's
assisted living.
    Yours
    Jeffney Ray

Omar shuddered. Not at the callousness of the question but at the appalling grammar. He used the tongs to drop the offending object into the waste paper basket and hoped that he wouldn't be hearing from Jeffney Ray again.

Rod woke from unpleasant dreams with a sharp intake of breath and was reaching to throw off his bed covers and leap at the intruder in the room when he realised who it was. Kathy Kaur, the restricted ward duty doctor, put down the sketch papers she had taken from the bedside table.

"Sorry. I was just looking. I didn't mean to wake you."

He gave a little shake of his head. All was forgiven.

"I've very sharp hearing," he said. "Even the rustle of paper, I'm – whoosh, like a shot. Ears of the hawk, me."

She shrugged.

"I mean, I have spent the last ten minutes checking your drips, writing on your chart, generally clattering around the place and" – she gave him a playful waggle of her perfect eyebrows – "you know..."

"Watching me sleep?"

"No. What? No, that sounds insanely creepy, Campbell. What kind of doctor has the time to stand around watching their patients sleep? I've been waiting for you to wake up."

"So, what was all that eyebrow business for?"

"Well, it's not code for 'I like to watch you sleeping' is it?"

"You confused me," he said.

"And that's the way I like you," she grinned.

Rod was in a private room on the restricted ward. His left arm had a cannula and drip taped to it. His right was patched with gauzy dressings where the *Dinh'r* had bitten him. The light behind the blinds told him he had slept in late.

"What are these?" Kathy touched the sketches on his bedside.

"Summat from long ago." He picked one up. It was a failed rendering of an irregular, vaguely beast-shaped jewel he had seen for only a few seconds many years ago and which he had glimpsed again in a *Dinh'r*-induced vision the day before. He had sketched them in the wee hours when bad dreams and then insomnia had a hold on him. "A magic stone," he said. "Supposed to grant your heart's desire."

"Really?" she said.

"Your eyebrows are doing that thing again."

"Are you fixated on my eyebrows?" she said.

"No," he said.

Rod could honestly say, despite Morag's nudge-nudges and wink-winks on the matter, that he wasn't at all fixated on any part of Kathy Kaur. A more honest bit of him might acknowledge that his fixation was evenly distributed around all of Kathy Kaur's parts. An even more honest part of him might concede that he was happy to fixate on any one of a broad number of attractive, funny and smart women, particularly since he had neither the time nor the social skillset to do anything about any single one of them.

"Is this magic stone meant to look... wonky?"

"Yes. It was a red piece, like a ruby."

"I've seen something like this before," she said.

"Where?" he said, sitting up.

She scrunched up her face, going up in the funny stakes, down in the attractive stakes and apparently trying to squeeze out some extra smarts.

The moment Morag knocked on Vaughn Sitterson's office door it opened, Vaughn turned away from her and gestured to the slender man drinking tea in one of the low seats. Vaughn, the ghostly recluse of a consular chief, did not do physical contact, eye contact or any specific acknowledgement of other people's existence.

"And here she is now," he said, apparently addressing a patch of carpet by the man's feet. "Morag Murray, investigator for response team A." He angled round towards her, his gaze not making it much past the edge of the door frame. "Jonathan Cattress of the Foreign and Commonwealth Office's Audit and Risk Committee."

The slender man stood.

"Glad you could join us, Ms Murray," he said.

Cattress had a posh southern accent, a limp handshake, gold cufflinks and what appeared to be a public-school tie. But Morag wasn't quick to judge him. She would bide her time before declaring him an effete, toffee-nosed Sassenach.

"Come to inspect us little people on the front line?" she said.

Cattress made a lingering noise in his throat as though his super-plummy tones needed a good run up to get started.

"Not an inspection as such," he said. "That will be conducted by a full team, my dear. Consider this a pre-inspection inspection, if you will."

"And I shall," said Morag brightly, who had no idea why she was there. "Mr Sitterson, is there something you needed me for, in particular?"

Vaughn, who had managed to slide behind his desk and take cover behind a sheaf of papers, looked up towards her but only got his gaze as far as the filing cabinet by the window.

"Mr Cattress needs a tour of our facilities."

"Oh. And?"

"And I thought," said Cattress, "that as a relative newcomer, you might be best placed to introduce me to the esoteric mysteries of this provincial outpost."

"I do have work to do," Morag said to Vaughn. "A number of house calls to members of the public I didn't get to do yesterday."

"And I thought you disliked so-called Crackpot Monday," said Vaughn. "House calls can wait."

"Apparently so," said Morag. "Well, Jonathan, it looks like I'm at your disposal. Where would you like to start?"

"Your records and storage facility. The Vault I believe it's called."

Rod watched Kathy Kaur's face-scrunching attempts to remember where she'd seen the blood-red jewel fail to work.

"It was in a picture," she said, lamely.

"Ye-es?"

"Nope. That's all I've got. Maybe I saw it while swotting up."

Rod frowned at her.

"For the job application," Kathy explained. "The tech support role in the Vault."

"You're going for Ingrid's job?" he said.

"Well, it's not her job now, is it? You don't think I should go for it?"

Rod chose his words carefully. In his experience, telling women what they should or shouldn't do rarely ended well. "I would have thought a doctor such as yourself would have better things to do than poke forbidden books and ancient relics in our basement."

"I know my *pessh khol-kharid* from my *pesco llarith*. There's no other job like it. They're making their selection for interview today and I wondered if you" – she gave him her best smile – "had any inside knowledge on who they're taking forward."

"Ah," he said. "You wanted to pick my brain. And here was me thinking that you were just here to add a little sunshine to my life."

"I can do both," she said.

She came close and inspected the dressings on Rod's injured arm. She made a noise of approval at what she saw.

"I don't think you're going to lose the arm. Or have intestinal Venislarn parasites interrupting your evening meal."

"Shame. It'd be nice to have company."

"How's the pinkie?" she said.

Rod showed her his left hand. She brushed her fingertip over the very pink nub of his severed finger.

"I was thinking of getting a prosthetic," he said.

"A false pinkie?"

He gave a facial shrug. "I was thinking there'd be just enough room inside for a gas-propelled grappling hook and a spool of high-tensile wire. What's your handwriting like?"

"Why?"

"Vivian Grey."

"The ice queen?"

"Aye. She's doing the shortlisting. Knowing her, she'll bin any applications with scruffy writing. It's a doctor thing, isn't it? Part of the training to write indecipherable prescriptions."

Kathy patted his healing arm. "No. My handwriting is beautiful and rounded."

"Not too beautiful though?" he said. "Not a bit girly? Cos she doesn't like that either."

"Well, I don't do little hearts above my 'i's if that's what you're asking. Here, I'll show you and you can rate my chances."

She picked up one of Rod's sketch sheets and then tapped her breast pocket for her pen. She then looked around on the trolley and the bedside unit.

"Balls. Where did I put it?"

"I'm afraid I was asleep while you were clattering around," said Rod.

"The number of things that go missing round here," she muttered.

"People building a better life for themselves by stealing office supplies," he said.

She gave him a dark look.

"It's not just office supplies," she said and her eyebrows weren't waggling so he couldn't tell if she was joking.

"Things go missing in every workplace," said Rod. "Taken home. Fallen down the back of the desk. Surgeons are famous for losing things inside their patients during surgery."

"Not whole rooms," said Kathy.

"Pardon?"

Kathy looked uncomfortable.

"It's not something we talk about. Some people here refuse to believe it but some of us are convinced that some doorways, some corridors and even some rooms have simply vanished."

Rod stared at her eyebrows for any sign of playful wiggling.

"I'm not making it up," she said.

Rod threw back his covers and swung his legs out of bed.

"Show me."

Morag and Jonathan Cattress were waiting at the lifts when a door dinged open and Vivian stepped out with a cheerful-looking border collie on a lead.

"You been rounding up sheep?" said Morag.

"I have not, Miss Murray," said Vivian plainly.

"Ah," said Morag and then, because it was clear Vivian wasn't about to volunteer any further information, "because you do appear to have a dog with you."

"I do," said Vivian, and with a "Come on, Ruffles" she led the dog away.

Morag swiped the hidden card reader in the lift and she and Cattress descended to the basement level of the Library.

"So, what's your Abyssal Rating?" she asked the Foreign Office man.

"What is an Abyssal Rating?" said Cattress.

Morag blinked. "Abyssal Rating. The scale of how much fucked up – I mean, messed up stuff you've been exposed to. Maybe your department have a different name for it."

"I don't think so. What is it for?"

"For? There's some, hmmm, challenging stuff in the Vault. The mind can only take so much."

"I'm sure I have sufficient strength of character," he said in tones of one assuring a child that, yes, Father Christmas did exist.

The doors slid open on a corridor of white tiles. Two Library security guards, pistols holstered, stood before the glass airlock entrance to the Vault. Morag waved at the CCTV camera in the corner and then the guards.

"Malcolm. Andy."

She typed a code at the door panel and the first glass door swung open.

"This guy's with me," she said, as they went through. "Apparently he doesn't need an Abyssal Rating." Malcolm's eyes widened but he said nothing. "If I need you to come in with a bucket and a mop, I'll holler," she said.

Cattress did not deign to comment until they were through the second door and it was closed behind them.

"I do understand there's a certain need for humour in the lower ranks, Ms Murray," said Cattress, "but I hope you don't intend to play me for a fool."

"Wouldn't dream of it," she said.

"And this is the Vault, is it?" he said.

White aisles stretched away to distant walls. Pristine cabinets and spotless shelves housed books, artefacts and objects that defied definition. It looked like a museum designed and run by an OCD cleanliness freak.

"It is," she said.

"It's considerable in size."

"But not considerable enough. We are finding items every week that can't simply be stored at the Dumping Ground."

"The Dumping Ground?"

"The, um, Venislarn Material Reclamation Centre. In Nechells. North of the city."

"But this is where Dr Ingrid Spence worked?" said Cattress.

"Yes," said Morag, suspecting instantly where this line of conversation was going. "They're interviewing for her replacement this week."

"Yes," he said. "Did you know her well?"

"No," said Morag.

"But you were present when she died."

Bingo. This was what it was about. This was why he wanted to speak to her.

"I was there," she said. "Do you want to know what happened?"

"I am more interested in the whys and wherefores, the sequence of events that led to her death."

"It was about funding," said Morag honestly. "Money. Regional bodies receive their funding in line with the perceived need."

"This is the ToHo formula I've heard mentioned."

"Correct," she said. "The more incursions we have, the more money we get. Ingrid knew that we were underfunded and took the logical but mad-as-a-bag-of-spanners decision to engineer two incursions in the city. The first resulted in a lot of collateral damage and there were fatalities. The second claimed Ingrid's life."

"Yes, yes," said Cattress, intrigued. "There are these so-called 'incursions'... By which you mean what?"

"Attacks by the Venislarn."

"Yes. And this Venislarn. I've never got a comprehensive grasp on it. All the boffins talk about it in code. I appreciate that they represent a threat but they do – do correct me if I'm wrong – come in a variety of different flavours, yes?"

"Flavours. I suppose so. Don't touch that."

He withdrew his hand sharply.

"Is it fragile?" he said.

"It's the Unapproachable Stone of *Msgoto*."

"Yes?"

"I don't think it's wise to approach it."

Cattress stared at the stone. Morag gestured for them to walk on.

"So," he said in the tones of one going back to square one, "there are these Venislarn incursions. And it's your job to stop them?"

"Hardly ever. We're not permitted to interfere."

"Right. That's some sort of causality issue."

"No," she said patiently, because the alternative to patience was worry. "We don't interfere because the Venislarn will punish us if we do."

"Punish?" He wagged a finger at her. "It's that kind of obfuscation that I'm struggling with. I understand that your organisation detects these apparent incursions, which I assume occur on some sort of quantum level, and then, even though they are patently dangerous, your role is to simply monitor them until the wave function collapses or whatever."

Morag stopped amid a cluster of cabinets containing the skin casings of a Kobashi at each of its four life stages.

"Time out," she said. "We need to straighten this out."

"Absolutely," said Cattress.

"What is it that you think we do here?"

"Well, that's what I'm trying to understand. I know you deal with hypothetical matters beyond the ken of empirical science. I've heard a lot of talk about otherworldly forces and intangibles and I've always pictured it as being a bit like those clever eggs over in CERN, looking through a quantum microscope for their theoretical Higgs Bosun and wotnot."

Morag shook her head.

"How long have you worked for the Foreign Office, Jonathan?"

"Three years. Why?"

"And who briefed you on the Venislarn?"

He laughed confidently. "Oh, our lot prefer to throw us all in at the deep end and see who sinks and who swims."

She could feel her face paling.

"You've not been told."

"I've been told enough. I'm a quick learner, I assure you."

"Oh, the fucking gallus cuntweasels," she whispered.

"In the FCO, one might be hosting Japanese dignitaries one day, exploring the intricacies of Azeri cultural politics the next and dealing with a sticky issue with a British arms dealer who's sailed too close to the wind on the day after that."

She looked about her as though they had suddenly been transported from a malevolently occult storage facility and into a cage of tigers. Actually, a cage of tigers might have been marginally safer. She was in the middle of the Vault with an over-qualified and under-educated Etonian man-child who had no knowledge of the Venislarn and an Abyssal Rating of zero.

"Gods," she said. "We deal with gods."

"The god particle," he nodded, determined to be on board the train of conversation.

"No," she said firmly. "Gods. Not metaphorical. Not hypothetical. Not theoretical. Gods."

He scoffed and tossed his floppy fringe.

"You are trying to play me for a fool, Ms Murray."

She shook her head.

"I think this pre-inspection inspection is over, Mr Cattress. Let's get you back upstairs at once. This way, please."

Nina entered the response team office with a fat bunch of flowers in her hands and, inexplicably, found Vivian leading an alert-looking collie up and down a grid of papers she had set out on the floor.

The dog worked its way along the rows and the columns, casually sniffing and then sat down next to a pile.

"Good boy, Ruffles!" said Vivian in a joyous and enthusiastic tone that was entirely at odds with her usual character and which unnerved Nina more deeply than she could say.

Vivian picked up the pile, momentarily inspected the name at the top and then tossed it in the bin.

"Okay, I'll bite," said Nina. "What's going on?"

"Interview candidate selection," said Vivian. "I would have thought that was obvious."

"It really wasn't," said Nina.

Vivian encouraged Ruffles to do another circuit of the papers.

"Drugs sniffer dog?" said Nina. "Checking to see if any of the applicants are potheads."

"There are many kinds of sniffer dog, Miss Seth. Drugs. Explosives. Cancer. Diabetes."

"So, you're using Ruffles to do illegal medical profiling. Cool."

"I did not say what kind of detection dog he is. What are those? You know I cannot abide flowers in the office."

"Shame. They're for you," she said, weighing the monstrous bunch in her hands.

"For me?" said Vivian disgusted. "They're not from the *samakha* boys in Fish Town, are they?"

"Where would they find flowers? No, these" – she read the card again – "are from Xerxes Mammon-Mammonson. 'To a bold and courageous woman.'"

Vivian sniffed dismissively.

"Yes. You can put them in the bin," she said. "And turn the lights out."

"Why?"

"Everything is twenty questions with you, Miss Seth. I'd appreciate a little obedience."

Nina turned the office lights off. With the blinds closed, the darkness was close to complete. An ultraviolet torch in Vivian's hands played over the application forms on the floor. Three of them had smudges of luminous material on them. One of them was littered with luminous marks and fingerprints.

"I know people can get excited by their job prospects but did he have to jizz all over the form?" said Nina.

"It's likely to be urine. Someone who doesn't wash their hands. And it's a she. Lights!"

Nina turned the lights on. Ruffles wagged his tail. Vivian tossed the three marked applications in the bin.

"The flowers," said Vivian, offering Nina the bin.

"But they're nice. Not as nice as cold hard cash, but it's kinda cute that he likes you."

"Xerxes Mammon-Mammonson does not like me," said Vivian coldly. "He wishes to ingratiate himself with me because he thinks he can use me to further his cause. Those flowers are expensive, which means they are above the threshold of gifts we are allowed to receive. Additionally, the card called me bold and courageous which is a tautological redundancy. And that's unforgiveable. Bin."

As Nina binned the flowers. Vivian gathered up the final seven application forms and brought them to a desk.

"I need to narrow it down to four for interview on Thursday."

Nina idly flicked through them.

"I might have to recheck their hobbies and interests," said Vivian.

"This one is a... phil-a-te-list," said Nina. "Does that mean she likes to sleep around?"

"No, it means she is a stamp collector."

"Snoozeville."

"You would rather we hired someone who was into mountain climbing and skydiving? No, a boring pair of hands is a safe pair of hands."

Nina stopped at one of the forms.

"You've got to be *adn-bhul* kidding me, Vivian," she said with a fierceness that made Ruffles look up.

"What is it?" Vivian looked over at the application form. "Yes. He applied."

"Professor fucking Sheikh Omar?"

"His CV is quite impressive. Did you know he is the only person to survive an encounter with the *Voor-D'yoi Lak* on Shetland?"

"I don't give a monkey's."

"And he was the first to establish the loci of Abyssal impact?"

"By forcing innocent undergrads to watch *bhul-detar* images of Venislarn! I know! I was there! He did it to me!"

"His methods are certainly unorthodox," said Vivian.

Nina clicked her fingers in Vivian's face.

"He is a torturer, a criminal and a planet-sized twat with a first-class degree from Twat University."

"And possibly the best qualified person for our vacant role."

Nina almost suppressed her scream of frustration.

"Can't you see that I'm upset you're even thinking of putting him forward for interview? God damn you, this dog has more human empathy than you do."

"Well, of course he does. Ruffles is a clever dog, isn't he?" she said, stroking the collie under the chin.

Nina pushed herself away from the desk, furious.

"Vivian. Look at me. If you put that man forward, you and I are no longer friends."

"When were we friends?" asked Vivian but Nina was already storming out of the office.

Morag, who was always willing to hold Whitehall bureaucrats in low regard, imagined that Jonathan Cattress was not used to being told what to do, particularly by a Scotswoman in the

75

'service' industries. Apart from during an unpleasant spell as a fag at public school or during some homoerotic initiation rites at his Oxbridge college, he'd probably gone through his entire life never hearing 'no' for an answer.

"I'm not leaving this place until I have the answers I want, Ms Murray."

Morag cast worried glances around the Vault.

"You can have all the answers you want once we're the other side of the entrance and back in the lift."

"Is there something you're trying to hide?" he said.

"Yes! You! There are things in here that would suck your brain out through a straw if they knew what easy prey you are."

"Oh, now you're just talking nonsense, Ms Murray."

Morag held her breath and rage.

"Okay," she said. "I'm going to give you a crash course and then we're leaving."

Cattress simply looked at her, silently inviting her to go on.

"Scientists say the likelihood of there being life on other planets is a near certainty."

"Aliens."

"Who we've not met yet. And quantum physics tells us that there are an infinite number of universes, side by side, filled with slightly different versions of ourselves and goodness knows what else."

"Parallel dimensions."

"Well, the Venislarn are not from another galaxy or another dimension. They're from somewhere else entirely. Yes, they're not actually gods. There are no gods but it's the best word we've got to describe them. Their power is limitless and their plans utterly unknowable. They are here. They have been here a long time. We think. They've certainly inserted themselves into our history but they're not restricted by time in the way we are. They might have arrived fifty years ago, ten years ago. Maybe they will come here for the first time next week and then just insinuate themselves back in time to the present day. We don't know. What we don't know about them would fill a bloody big book."

She took him by the elbow and pulled him a dozen feet towards a large metal safe that had the appearance of a deep sea diving pressure chamber. She pointed through the porthole at the large open tome on the pedestal within.

"That is the Bloody Big Book AKA the Wittgenstein Volume AKA the Book of Sand. It is a book with an infinite number of pages."

"That's ridiculous," said Cattress.

"Isn't it? But it's real. It details everything that ever has happened, is happening and will happen. It contains every other book ever written and translations of them all into every language known and unknown."

"Why is it inside that chamber?"

"For a number of reasons, although the one I find most compelling is that it's a monumental fire risk. Imagine what would happen if you set fire to an infinite quantity of paper."

"Poppycock."

"It's just one of the thousands of Venislarn artefacts we end up collecting, the cultural cast-offs of an alien invasion force."

"Oh, so we're being invaded now?"

"Have been invaded. Past tense. We're pigs in the slaughterhouse and will only realise it when they shut the door closed behind us."

"This is nonsense."

"Listen, pal, you're in an Aladdin's cave of magical wonders and you want to tell me that I'm just making it all up for a laugh. Look. Here. These are the Tiny Blue Innumerables."

"What of them?" said Cattress, peering disdainfully at the smooth semi-precious stones in the display case.

"What of them? Count them."

Cattress sighed petulantly. "Well, there's obviously eight. No, I missed that one. There's... not nine but..."

"'Not nine' is as close as you'll get to an answer."

"No, just wait a moment." He put his finger to the glass as he counted. "Twelve, unless I've counted that one twice."

"They're innumerable, Jonathan. They can't be counted."

"But that's preposterous."

"It's the Venislarn. Look, the one-sided coin of *Ogdru Jahad*. Look, the last extant copy of Ryngu's *The King in Crimson*, the first act at least. Look, at these." She gestured to shelves casually filled with artefacts that had arrived since Ingrid's death. "Out of Place Artefacts, most of them. Impossible objects found in locations they couldn't conceivably be found in. This cube was found inside solid rock. This *pabash kaj* doll was found inside a five-pound bowel cancer tumour."

"A doll?"

Morag picked up the brown sackcloth effigy. "Burmese tribespeople used them to physically entrap their enemies in the body of the doll. All they needed to do was to get the person to step inside a *tcho-tcho Loigor* circle. I could draw one for you if you like."

"Ridiculous," said Cattress and then pointed. "And is this also some magical mumbo jumbo?"

"This? It was found buried beneath Iron Age ruins at Berry Mound near Shirley."

Cattress looked at the vase. It was a simple receptacle in white clay, a rounded square that became squarer towards its fluted lip.

"It's just a vase," he said.

Morag could see that it didn't appear impressive – if Tesco produced a Tesco's Basics vase for £3.99, it would look like that – but she was annoyed now and determined to demonstrate the truth of the Venislarn occupation before marching Cattress out of there, straight back to his parliamentary bosses and giving them a piece of her mind.

Morag picked up the item. It was unpleasantly light, like bird bones. A slow but ceaseless flow of warm air poured from its mouth.

"It's the wrong age to be in an Iron Age fort. We call it a vase but that's only us putting a shape to something we don't understand," she said. She took a pen out of her jacket pocket and dropped it in the vase. It landed with a hollow tap. She then tipped the vase up and two identical pens fell out onto the floor.

Cattress's laugh was hollow and disbelieving.

"Very good." He spun around. "And there are, I suppose, hidden cameras to record my astonishment."

"Try it."

Cattress patted his pockets and, finding nothing, removed one of his cufflinks and dropped it in the vase. Morag peered in and then upended the vase. Two cufflinks fell out into Cattress's hand. His breath caught in his throat.

"A trick," he said. He lifted the vase from Morag's hands and inspected the base. "It's not possible."

"This is the world we deal with, Jonathan."

"No, this is part of some ploy, an agenda that I don't yet fully grasp." He was struggling with his thoughts, barely had any confidence in his own words. "There's a secret compartment..."

She reached out to take the vase back but Cattress stepped out of her reach.

"There has to be an explanation," he said and tapped the vase hard against a shelf to dislodge whatever trickery was inside. Instead, the sharp blow punched a hole in the bottom edge of the vase.

"What the hell!" snapped Morag and snatched the vase from him but the damage was already done.

Whatever one placed in the Berry Mound vase was instantly multiplied and what Cattress had put in it was a hole.

Rod dressed, rolling up his shirt sleeves to hide the tattered cuff destroyed by *Dinh'r* mandibles, and went to find Kathy Kaur in the pathetic cubby hole that served as her office. She tapped at her computer keyboard.

"I had them here," she said. "They've been deleted."

"What have?"

"The CCTV footage files. I started downloading them and saving them after the first doorway went missing. And now the files have gone missing too."

"Are you sure? Let's have a gander."

She gave him a look as he reached for the mouse.

"What? Are you going to find them with your special man-powers?"

He backed off, hands spread to mean he meant no offence.

"Don't bother with the files," he said. "Just show me."

Kathy gave a couple more experimental clicks and then gave up with a growl of irritation.

"I don't know where to start. It's like when you... when a man goes bald."

"I wouldn't know owt about that," said Rod, running a hand through his hair.

"When you go bald, Rod, it won't be full head of hair one day and bald the next. It'll be a hair here, a hair there. And that's how it's been. Pens, paper, patient notes. They go walkies all the time. And then it's a trolley. And then, one day, in a place where you'd swear there was a cleaning cupboard or an alcove, there's just a blank wall. Nothing. If I didn't know better, I'd say people were missing too."

"Really?"

She laughed but without humour. "Mostly agency staff. They come one day and don't come back the next. I mean, all areas of the NHS have a high turnover of staff and they don't have to deal with geriatric *dhosterata*, impossible human-Venislarn hybrids or previously uncatalogued parasites that are resistant to all known medicines."

He nodded. "But have people gone missing?"

Kathy gave it some thought. "We would have noticed, wouldn't we? Wouldn't we?"

His phone buzzed in his pocket.

"Could you rustle up a list of people who have worked here? All the people who have worked here?"

"Is this Rod asking me or the consular mission?" she said. "We haven't reported this as a problem or anything..."

"And a map of the restricted ward. The whole hospital if you can."

He answered his phone. "Campbell."

He didn't get an opportunity to speak further for a full forty seconds and that small opportunity allowed him to ask, "And by 'soulless dried up witch-bitch' you mean...? Uh-huh."

Twenty seconds more ranting, then Rod asked, "And the 'psycho mystic-my-arse creepy-Dumbledore fucker' is…?"

Nina ranted on although Rod could tell she had peaked.

"Yes," he said. "I'm still here. With Dr Kaur. Yes, the one with the… Yes. That's fine, you come over and tell me what Vivian and Professor Omar have done to you and then – yes, apart from the obvious. Okay. Bye."

Kathy Kaur was looking at him.

"What?" he said.

"Dr Kaur. The one with the…?" she asked.

"With the, um, excellent chances of getting invited to interview on Thursday."

"Smooth, Campbell. So smooth."

In the Vault beneath Birmingham Library, something emerged from the mouth of the Berry Mound vase of multiplication. At first it appeared to be a bubble, a milky mirror-coated bubble, like cloudy mercury, but the image it held was not a reflection; it was a distorted view of the Vault, looking out and across to the furthest wall. The bubble seemed to weigh nothing in Morag's hands but as it grew, it threatened to engulf her arms and she hurriedly put the vase down on a shelf.

"What's going on?" demanded Cattress.

"I don't know," said Morag and thought quickly. "It makes a copy of whatever's in the vase. You put a hole in it."

"That's not a hole," said Cattress, waving wildly at the vast bubble.

"A hole's not a thing," she said and then understood. "You put a hole in it. And now when we look in the vase we'd see…"

"Whatever was on the other side."

The expanding mass was not a mirror. It was not a distorted view of what was on the other side. The bubble was a copy of the world, ballooning out like a tumour.

"This is bad," she said.

"I don't like it," said Cattress in a tone of voice straight out of childhood.

The copy-universe folded round and enveloped the vase.

"Oh, crap," said Morag.

A distinct and separate tumorous bubble began to form on the side of the first. The vase was making a copy of the world, a copy that had a copy of the world in it. Tumours upon tumours...

Nina took the train out to the Queen Elizabeth Hospital. The vast hospital complex brushed up against Birmingham University on one side and eclipsed the site of an ancient Roman fort on another. It was home to all the services that a major NHS hospital provided plus the Royal Centre for Defence Medicine, which received all British military personnel injured in action around the world. It also, unbeknownst to the public, contained the restricted ward that dealt with those infected or injured by the Venislarn and those Venislarn who demanded earthly medical attention.

Nina wasn't a fan of hospitals. They were mazes, specifically designed to confuse her. And they smelled of old people. Nina wasn't against the concept of old people but, in her experience, they were casually annoying, daytime-TV-watching, fun-sucking vampires. Funpires.

The upper floors of the hospital split into three lozenge-shaped towers, identical in floor plan so as to confuse the unwary visitor. Nina only made three wrong turns before she found herself on the eighth floor standing in front of the security doors to ward 829, the restricted ward. The security guard wore the simple uniform of ordinary hospital security, but Nina could see the bulge of a concealed firearm underneath the front of his jumper. He inspected her pass and then allowed her to swipe herself inside.

The great curving sweep of the restricted ward corridor formed a single loop. Many of the side wards and rooms were locked and, she knew, would not even open to her electronic pass. The restricted ward was containment for an array of alien diseases and parasites and more than a few hosts who were now beyond even the broadest definition of human. Although she had come here to check up on Rod and vent her spleen at Vivian's decision to invite Professor Sheikh Omar to interview, Nina as always found herself first drawn to a particular side ward, partway along the anti-clockwise turn of the corridor.

The door was locked. Nina peered through the little window. There were five beds, all raised up: Joe, Josh, Kyra, Maryam, and Owen. Their eyes were open but there was no flicker of consciousness in any of them. The five of them were the same age as Nina, give or take a year. They had all signed up for a research experiment organised by Birmingham University's Department of Intertextual Exegesis. None of them had known what they were signing up for but Professor Sheikh Omar had been willing to pay – and even small amounts of money have a certain gravitational effect on young people.

The experiment involved being shown a series of images – some were inscriptions, some were carved scenes or symbols, some were photographs – while wired up to a pulse monitor and an EEG machine. Nina Seth learned three things that day: she learned that the Venislarn were real, she learned that she had a previously unrecorded Abyssal Rating of ten and she learned that Professor Sheikh Omar was willing to drive five young people out of their minds in his personal pursuit of knowledge. Joe, Josh, Kyra, Maryam, Owen.

"I have no mouth," she whispered to them through the glass.

"Yes, you do, you silly dear," said a wobbly voice.

Nina turned. The wrinkled and bent old lady in a quilted housecoat pushed an equally wrinkled and bent finger against Nina's lips.

"That's it there," she said helpfully.

"Back off, grandma," said Nina. She wiped her mouth with the back of her hand and tried not to swallow any old lady germs. "Where the hell did you spring from?"

"Oh," said the old woman with a toffee commercial twinkle, "we came across with the first migration, through the *Kolob* configuration."

"Did you?" said Nina, not listening at all and not caring a jot. "Well, shall we get you back there?"

"Oh, we can't go back," said the old dear. "The stars are gone and the path is lost."

"I'm sure we can try." Nina took her by the shoulders and turned her round, hopefully steering her back to her bed or to someone who she could dump the wrinkled old baggage with.

Rod watched as Kathy drew another tentative circle on the large-scale plan of the eighth floor.

"I'm fairly sure that there was a room there."

"Are you sure, or aren't you?" said Rod.

She looked pained. "Well, yes, I am sure but even if a room had vanished, which is a physical impossibility – only according to human concepts or reality, yes I know – but even if it had vanished, it would still be on this plan, wouldn't it?"

"Indeed," said Dr Zondervan, entering the staff break room Rod had commandeered.

Zondervan was the administrative manager of the restricted ward, effectively boss of the facility and everyone in it. Rod didn't like him and Rod knew that the root cause of that dislike was nothing other than jealousy. Dr David Zondervan was an accomplished doctor and research scientist but looked as if he had just dropped by after crossing the Antarctic unassisted or abseiling down the cliffs of Dover. He had brains, sculpted good looks and action-man credentials; Rod despised him – and despised him all the more because he knew his animosity was entirely undeserved.

"We're seeing you quite a bit round here, aren't we, Rodney?" asked Zondervan. "First that business last month where you lost your finger –"

"Part of my finger."

"– and now your arm. You must stop sticking body parts where they don't belong," he smiled handsomely.

I bet he's had his teeth whitened, thought Rod sourly but actually said, "Dr Kaur and I were looking at a possible anomaly in the –"

"I heard," said Zondervan. "I'm not sure how Kathy's confusion is the concern of the consular mission response team."

"We encounter time-space anomalies surprisingly often."

"I don't doubt that but Kathy, let me put it to you: a patient comes to you with the belief that rooms in their house have been

84

rearranged or with very poor memory of commonplace things. Your diagnosis?"

Kathy wasn't offended or put out by the question.

"Dementia would be a strong contender," she answered immediately, "particularly in the elderly. Psychosis is a possibility, or maybe a developed aspect of schizophrenia. Or something affecting the brain directly, such as CJD or a tumorous growth." She looked at Rod. "There might be a far more mundane explanation for what I'm experiencing, true."

"But haven't others noticed things going missing?" said Rod. He picked up the list of restricted ward staff. "You said that there have been some staff who were here one day and gone the next."

"Sounds like any department of the NHS," said Zondervan.

"Actually, none of them are listed on that print off," said Kathy.

"Is that just a list of current staff?" said Zondervan. "I'm sure we would have noticed if people and rooms just vanished in a puff of smoke. People and spaces can't just pop in and out of existence."

Morag backed further away from the new pocket universe and took out her phone. It was dead. Still dead.

"Your phone," she said.

"What?" said Cattress.

"Phone. Now."

Dazed, he unlocked it and handed it over.

Even in the Vault there should have been a signal, but the phone said 'No Network'. She looked up in surprise. In the secondary world, partway down a corridor and backing away from a copy-universe of their own were a red-headed woman and a well-tailored bureaucrat. The other Morag looked her way and their eyes met. Morag recognised the look in the other woman's eyes; it said, 'You're in big trouble now, girl. Big trouble.'

"Hey!" Morag shouted.

The other Morag waved her own Cattress's non-functioning phone. "They're identical. They're confusing the network."

The other Morag tossed the phone back to Cattress, turned to locate a CCTV camera and waved her arms.

"Who is that?" said Cattress, looking at the other people.

"Someone who's in as much trouble as we are," said Morag.

In the shifting visions around the Berry Mound vase, yet another copy of the world was forming.

Once Nina had gotten her started, the tiny old dear seemed to know where she was going and toddled along the corridor at a high-speed shuffle like a wind-up toy.

"Oh, it's all very nice here," she said, of everything and nothing in particular.

"Uh-huh," said Nina. "You probably remember when all this used to be fields, I bet."

The old woman stopped to give Nina a shrewd look.

"I remember further back than that," she said with a genteel huff. "This one."

Nina helped her through the doorway and into a large private room. At the sight of the armchair beside the coffee table in the window, the woman picked up speed and broke into a shuffling sprint.

"Good," said Nina. She inspected the notes on the end of the woman's bed. "Barbara."

"Yes, dear?" said the woman, lowering herself snugly into her chair.

A ripe, faintly rotten smell emanated from a chest-high unit next to a fridge in an alcove. The unit had a screen and keyboard mounted on top and – with a control panel, serving hatch and a hint of industrial innards – appeared to be part photocopier, part vending machine, part mincing machine.

"What's this?"

"It's my little magic stove, that is," said Barbara. "Anything I want, it makes."

"Anything."

"Anything." Barbara shuffled in her cushion, trying to get comfy. "As long as it's hands or faces."

"Hands...?"

86

"Or faces," said Barbara.

Nina, who was always open to new experiences and held to the principle that it was generally better to press buttons than not, pressed some buttons on the machine. The unit came alive with an expensive-sounding whisper-soft whirr. The screen informed her that Preset C was compiling.

Whilst not being so rude as to tell Rod to bugger off, Zondervan's subtle body language made it clear that Rod was in the wrong place and wasting the wrong people's time.

"You're welcome to take those documents if you wish," said Zondervan, "and, if you do discover something amiss, you're very welcome to drop in on my office. Door's open and all that."

"No, of course," said Rod, instantly apologetic. He had monopolised too much of Kathy's time. "For what it's worth," he told her, "I don't think you've got a tumour or mad cow disease or owt."

"Nicest thing anyone's said to me all day," she replied.

Rod patted Zondervan's arm as he passed him on the way out into the corridor.

"But keep an eye out, yeah? Sometimes weird mysterious crap turns out to be real mysterious crap."

"Will do, bud," said Zondervan.

In the gleaming output tray of Barbara's 'magic stove' something was beginning to form, extruded from the space beneath. At first it was a glistening translucence, then white and then, before it had taken on a pinker hue, Nina recognised it as the shape of a human hand.

"It's 3D printing a hand, Barbara," said Nina.

"I know! Wonderful, isn't it?" said the old woman.

"It's not a plastic hand, is it?"

"Course not, silly dear. I've only had it a few weeks. It was bought for me by... Oh, you know the one."

"Which one?"

"Him. The one in charge. Um." For a moment, Barbara looked very cross with herself.

In the corridor, Rod turned back to Zondervan.

"Oh, and I'm sorry for…"

He stopped.

Zondervan wasn't there. The door to the break room swung slowly closed.

Rod pushed back inside, down the tiny spur of corridor and found Kathy Kaur gathering up the last of the papers.

"Yeah, I'm coming," she said and then looked at him.

"Where's Zondervan?" said Rod.

"He followed you out."

"He did. He was behind me and then…"

Their gazes met. Kathy laughed.

"Real funny, Campbell."

He shook his head and, because he was out of clever options, turned to the walls to just double-check that David Zondervan hadn't snuck through a previously unseen door or through the plasterwork itself.

"You're not joking?" she said.

"No," said Rod.

"Fuck."

He thumped the wall. It was solid.

"Aye. It really isn't a tumour or mad cow disease. Unless we've both got it."

Morag's world had become a kaleidoscope of, well, worlds. Corridors, doorways and shelves abutted each other at unhelpful angles, new realities encroaching on each other as the Berry Mound vase disgorged fresh worlds with the zeal of an over-eager creator god.

As she hauled the stunned Cattress down a corridor in what she hoped was the direction of the exit, Morag could not say for certain which universe they were now in. If they had crossed over then the boundary was intangible and these tumour-worlds were not immediately harmful to visitors.

"You said you were going to raise the alarm," said Cattress.

"I am trying," said Morag, peevishly and dragged him down a side corridor. "It's just that nothing is where it used to be."

"What about the fire sensors?" he suggested, pointing up at the sprinkler outlet on the ceiling.

"Great," she said. "Lighter?"

Cattress stared at her blankly. "I don't smoke."

"Any means of making fire?"

"Well, no. I assumed that you might."

"What? I look like a smoker? You think all Scottish people smoke?"

"No." He paused. "But, generalisation though it might be, I was under the impression that in the north, particularly among the working classes..."

Her glare silenced him.

Ahead of them, in a world that ran at a thirty degree angle to theirs, a red-headed woman and a long streak of nothing in an expensive suit hurried across a T-junction. The man said, "Now, listen here, my good woman," and then they were gone from sight.

"That was us," said Cattress.

"And if you call me your good woman, I'll skelp you good and proper." She opened a cabinet on the wall and took down a short-handled axe.

"I can assure you, I shan't," said the civil servant, eyeing the wicked edge of the finely wrought axe head.

"It's just occurred to me," said Morag setting off again purposefully.

"What has?"

"There's a good reason why we don't allow lighters and matches down here anyway. I think it's back this way."

She ran her hands along the cool wall as she followed the corridor to the over-engineered walk-in safe that housed the Bloody Big Book. Such a valuable and potentially harmful item was encased in more than metal and glass. The door, the frame, even the porthole were all alarmed.

And it was clear that Morag wasn't the only one to have realised this.

Morag and Cattress were already there. Another Morag and Cattress. The other Morag looked up at the newly arrived original Morag and then at the axe in her hand.

"Perfect," she said and gestured to the door.

"Watch your head," said Morag, raising the axe. Then she swung it with more enthusiasm than skill into the glass porthole.

Nina found Rod in a little break room off the main corridor of the restricted ward. He and the duty doctor, Kathy Kaur, were hunched over a table covered in building plans and data print-offs.

"Hey, guess where I've just been," said Nina.

Rod ignored her completely and stabbed at a name on a sheet. "This one too."

Kathy circled the name in red pen and then made a mark on the plan.

"I mean it is traditional to guess," said Nina. "Or you can just say you give up and I can tell you."

Rod spared her a glance.

"We're in the middle of something here."

"Ah," said Nina. "I wondered what old people foreplay looked like."

Kathy Kaur gave her a starkly amused look. "Old?"

"Hey, Kath. Age isn't a number. It's a state of mind."

"Middle of something, Nina," said Rod in what Nina reckoned he believed was his stern voice. It was sweet, really. "People are vanishing."

"Where've they gone?" said Nina, approaching to look at the papers.

"Vanished. Poof!"

"To a gay bar? And that's a bit un-PC, Rod."

Kathy put her fingertips on the plan. "It's happened all around the restricted ward."

"Well, not over here," said Nina, pointing to a looping corridor where there were further crosses and circles. "And less so in these bits. If you folded it out, it'd look like one of those things that's really big in the middle and then slopes off."

"A bell curve," nodded Rod.

"I was thinking of an erection under a bedsheet," said Nina. "But okay. Whatever."

"And the centre of the distribution curve" said Kathy, looking up a room number against another document. "Ah," she said, and then, after some thought, a deeper and more serious: "Ah. The *Koloba*."

"What's that?" said Rod.

"Or Barbara, as I think she's called. Sweet old dear with vascular dementia. Human, but host to a sentient parasite. It's her. She's been causing the disappearances."

"Are you sure?" said Rod.

"Hey," said Nina brightly, "guess where I've just been."

Vivian stepped out of the lift, the application forms of the final four candidates under her arm. A red light flashed above the entrance to the Vault. A piercing alarm whooped close to. Two library security guards stood at the door, peering through, though neither had entered.

"Are you not aware I'm in the middle of an important interview selection process?" said Vivian. "What is happening here?"

"Not sure, Mrs Grey. The CCTV cameras have all gone a bit... wonky. The alarm's gone off by the Bloody Big Book. It's Morag and the government inspector in there."

Vivian looked from man to man.

"And neither of you has been in to check?"

"Well," said one, Andy, a little sheepishly, "we usually wait for the tech support to tell us what to do but, you know..."

"Ingrid is dead and we've not appointed a replacement," said Vivian. "Fine."

She tapped the access code into the panel by the door and it slid open.

"Should we come with you?" said the other, Malcolm.

"Why?" said Vivian. "What help could you possibly be?"

Malcolm straightened up, attempting through body language alone to express the idea that he was a big and beefy ex-military man and was a lot of help indeed. It was difficult to express such a sentiment when faced with Vivian Grey's critical glare.

"Fine," snapped Vivian. "You can come with me. You, go and turn the alarm off. We are now sufficiently alarmed, I think."

Vivian and Malcolm proceeded through the double set of doors. Vivian strode towards the section that housed the Bloody Big Book but came to an abrupt halt. It was as if someone had placed a vast and imperfect mirror across the Vault. Beneath her feet, the corridor continued as normal up to a point and then it broke off utterly to become an aisle of display cases that ran off at a skewed angle, up and off to the left. Someone might as well have sliced the Vault into large chunks and placed them back together again with no concept of accuracy, direction or decency. Ahead, the floor sloped away at a crazy tilt.

"That looks freaky," said Malcolm softly.

"It looks untidy," said Vivian.

Morag came running along the aisle of display cases in the lopsided chunk of Vault. Vivian noted that the woman was as lopsided as the space she inhabited, pulled by a different gravity.

"What on earth has happened here, Miss Murray?" demanded Vivian.

"Cattress broke the Berry Mound vase," said Morag. "And I think it's now spewing out copies of the world."

"And you permitted him to do this?"

Morag paused, put a reflective hand to her chin and then said in a tone that Vivian took to be sarcasm (she wasn't always able to spot it), "Yes, Vivian, I permitted him to do it."

"Where is he now?"

"He went off by himself. Claimed he knew better."

"And what happened with the Wittgenstein Volume?"

Morag pointed up, gesturing at the still ringing alarm.

"The Bloody Big Book? I hope that one of the copies of me that's been created thought to set off the alarm to get you down here. I hope. The alternative is that the Berry Mound vase is trying to make a copy of an infinitely large book and that sound is the universe about to explode under the strain."

"Mrs Grey," said Malcolm and gestured for her to step back. The boundary between the two worlds, the real and the one Morag had so thoughtlessly unleashed, was inching towards their toes.

Vivian took a judicious step back. "So, there are copies of you running around in here?"

"Don't make it sound like a bad thing," said Morag.

"I was just pondering… How do you know that you are the original?"

Morag tapped herself. "I am. I remember. I have memories from before the accident happened."

"Yes," said Vivian, "memories that would have been copied. We need to contain this now."

"Good. Brilliant. How?"

Vivian thought for a moment. "Indeed, it's a shame that you couldn't have saved this little act until Thursday. It would have made a superb interview task for the tech support candidates."

"Yeah, we might need a fix sooner than that," said Morag. "I'm not even sure if it's safe for me to step outside this bubble-world."

Vivian took out her phone and leafed through the application papers under her arm.

"Nonetheless, I think I ought to give one of the candidates a call."

Rod, who considered himself to be a man of action first and a Venislarn-wrangler second (or even possibly third), listened as Kathy and Nina gave him the lowdown on the *Koloba*.

"They were sent over by the *Cha'dhu Forrikler* as emissaries or spies," said Nina.

"They have a physical body but they pick a local host to inhabit," said Kathy. "Not because they need to, like a true parasite."

"But to blend in. They don't like to be naked. It's a symbiotic relationship; host and parasite become one entity: one mind, one purpose."

"Ritualistically, they exist on a diet of emotionally and psychologically significant external representations."

"Eh?" said Rod.

"They like to eat pretty things," said Nina.

"Zondervan purchased a 3D bioprinter for her," said Kathy. "The Kyoto consular mission developed it for the *Koloba* they have there. Offal goes in –"

"And hands and faces come out," said Nina. "It's so cool. You've gotta take a look."

"Aye. Another time, perhaps," said Rod.

"Anyway, the *Cha'dhu Forrikler* never made the trip to earth. Not worth the bother for some reason but the *Koloba* remained."

"They're information gatherers," said Kathy. "Functionally limitless. They're practically omniscient."

"And they know everything," said Nina.

"You have an omniscient old lady in one of your wards?" said Rod. "Okay."

"Obviously, they're not actually omniscient," said Kathy. "The *Koloba's* physical presence is only…" She held out her hands as though grasping a well-stuffed sub sandwich. "You can't hold infinite information in a finite space."

"I've seen a book that'd beg to differ," said Rod.

"The *Koloba* store information by sort of linking their brain to real world," said Nina.

"The *Koloba* integrate the surrounding physical universe into their conscious mindstate," said Kathy.

"That's what I said," said Nina.

"I see," said Rod, who didn't. "And this creature is making people – and rooms, I should add – disappear? How? Is she eating them? Are hands and feet –"

"Faces."

"– faces not providing enough crunchy goodness for her?"

"You don't get it," said Kathy.

"He never does," said Nina. "It's cute."

"The individual *Koloba* draws the physical universe into line with its own conscious mind."

"Okay. Words," said Rod.

Kathy rapped her knuckles on the break room table. "You know this table exists because you can see it, experience it."

"Sure."

"And when you've left the room, you know it's here because you remember it."

"Of course."

"The *Koloba's* omniscience functions by switching that round," she said, rotating her fingers over each other. "As soon as the *Koloba* sees this table, it becomes a physical figment of its imagination. It is stored as a memory in the real world."

"Crazy but I get it."

"And this little nugget of Venislarn trivia has zero impact on the real world," said Nina, "except…"

"Barbara has vascular dementia," said Kathy.

"She's forgetting things."

Rod put his hands on the papers before him, maps marked with places where people and objects once had been but now were not.

"She's forgotten these people," said Rod.

"That's what they've all got in common," said Kathy. "They've met Barbara."

"Bloody hell, Nina!" said Rod. "And you had to pop your head in and say hello!"

"Well, she's hardly likely to forget me, is she?" said Nina. "I mean, just look. Visions of this will keep even a heterosexual granny awake all night."

"You need to get yourself back down there, plant yourself in her field of vision and make sure she doesn't get a chance to forget about you."

"Fine," said Nina with a tut. "But I don't see how this is my fault."

"Because this always happens to you," said Rod and he was angry, angry because he cared and this stupid fearless girl couldn't see the danger she was in. "If there's a big sign that says, 'don't stick your finger in here' or 'don't touch the big red button' or 'keep your hands and legs inside the carriage at all times'… It's always bloody you."

"Come on. That business with the big wheel could have happened to anyone."

"But it doesn't, does it? It wasn't me or Vivian who had to be cut out of the carriage, was it? You don't find Morag making stupid mistakes that put lives in danger."

"You know," Morag said to the other Morag, the one who had swung the axe and smashed the Bloody Big Book porthole, "I think I've had better days."

"You think we're going to get fired for this?" asked the other Morag.

"How many of us do you think there now are?" asked Morag.

"Uncle Ramsay did say that one Morag Murray was plenty enough for any family."

Morag mentally reminded herself that it was normal to be a bit unnerved at meeting a copy of oneself – an identical copy of her current self at that – not least because, despite the existence of mirrors and photographs and such, she spent very little time looking at herself. The sense of strangeness and mild loathing she felt was like – as much as it was like anything – was like the experience of hearing one's own recorded voice played back. This woman, this other Morag, wasn't the Morag she thought herself to be. Her posture was more slouched, her clothing less flattering, her resting facial expression far more irritable. The other Morag was a walking, talking version of every bad selfie Morag had ever taken.

One of the Cattresses poked the other in the shoulder.

"They're solid," he said.

The poked Cattress looked at the point of contact as though he had been violently assaulted.

"Yes, I am," he said.

"He touched me," said Cattress, pointing an accusing finger at the other Cattress.

"Don't whine about it, man," said the accused Cattress. "I've not met a copy of myself before."

Cattress splayed his hand across his chest. "Copy? Me?"

Morag was observant enough to spot both the Cattress's eyes flicking momentarily to the axe embedded in the split-but-not-smashed porthole.

"Easy," she said. "We don't know who's real and who's a copy and we don't even know what that will mean when this is all sorted out."

"You stay away from Jennifer!" blurted out Cattress hotly.

The other Cattress spluttered. "Damn it, man! You're married!"

"So are you!"

"To your wife! And you're welcome to her!"

Cattress made a patting motion. He spoke in the patronising tone that Morag imagined he used on everyone. "Now calm down and let's be sensible. There's only one way that this can be resolved. You will return home and say nothing of this while I take care of Jennifer. It will be best all round if we make a clean break, you must see that."

"How dare you speak to me like that!" the other exploded. Morag guessed that Cattress was not used to being on the receiving end of his own condescension. "If you think you can tell me what to do, you're very much mistaken. I simply will not tolerate it and if you think you can go off with Jennifer and keep that a secret, well you're in for a nasty shock, I can tell you."

Morag looked to the other Morag for confirmation.

"Yes," the other said. "They're arguing over who gets the wife and who gets the... girlfriend?"

"One each. It's amazing they had the foresight to prepare for this situation."

"You think this is a joking matter?" said Cattress, angry, agitated and on the verge of tears.

"Of course not," said Morag. "Let's the four of us keep our shit together and work out what to do next."

"Eight of us," said the other Morag, looking over Morag's shoulder.

Morag turned. Another party of four (two Morags and two Cattresses) was coming down the aisle towards them. One of the

Cattresses had a black eye and the other had a rip in the shoulder of his suit.

"Okay, maybe some sort of timeshare on the wife and mistress might be in order," said Morag.

"Yeah," said the other Morag. "Whatever. I'm having the day off tomorrow. You're gonna come in and cover for me."

"Fine, as long as you deal with that backlog of laundry."

"It's a deal!" said Morag with a thumbs up.

In the little side ward, Barbara Gudge, demented old dear and omniscient emissary of the *Cha'dhu Forrikler* sat in her armchair and looked at Nina, the nurse, the orderly and the administrator who sat across the coffee table from her. As Barbara turned her head, they all leaned to stay front and centre in her vision and, by extension, in existence.

"Smile," said Nina.

Barbara obeyed and gave her a toothy little smile, all dentures and wrinkles. Nina snapped a picture and then messaged it to Rod.

"I don't usually have so many visitors," said Barbara.

"Thought we'd drop in," said the nurse with a big, terrified smile on her face. "Keep you company."

"Oh, you don't have to."

"Oh, we really do," said Nina.

The doorway to the room had been covered with a mobile screen. The world beyond the screen had gone awfully quiet.

"Is it time for *Bargain Hunt* yet?" said Barbara, casting around for her TV remote.

"Or maybe," said Nina, who had chucked the TV remote in the bin after the first time Barbara had asked for it, "we could get to know each other a bit better. You know, a good chat?"

The administrator nodded like a hyperactive bobblehead. "You remember me, don't you, Barbara?" she said. "I'm Lizzy. We spoke last week. I told you about my cat, Loki. You remember?"

"I do. I like cats."

"I have two cats," said the nurse, cutting in with a sudden ferocity, as though having multiple cats would instantly beat a singular cat in the game of staying in Barbara's memory. "Two. Jibber and Marmalade. Two. I have pictures on my phone." She automatically patted her uniform. "Oh, but it's…" She looked forlornly towards the door and then turned to Nina. "Can I go and get it?"

"You can…" said Nina meaningfully, leaving the risks of stepping out of Barbara's immediate presence unsaid.

"Look!" said the administrator, holding her own phone triumphantly in front of Barbara's face. "Loki. My cat. You remember?"

Barbara squinted at it and awwed.

"I don't like cats," said the orderly in his languid Caribbean accent. "I can't stand them."

The nurse gave him a look that was ten percent pity and ninety percent gloating. The man didn't even have one cat!

"On account of the fact," continued the orderly, "that my grandmother – God rest her – was killed by one."

"Killed by a cat?" said Barbara.

The orderly, who, slouched in his seat, legs splayed, looked surprisingly relaxed given the situation, nodded slowly. "Killed her."

"A normal cat?" said the administrator. "I mean, not a tiger or a lion or anything?"

"A big fat ginger tom. Came and sat on her face while she slept. Smothercated her. As God is my witness."

"That's awful," said Barbara.

"My great grandma's sister drowned in a washing tub," said the administrator.

Apparently, dead grandmas trumped cats. The game had changed.

Rod swept the corridors, finding any remaining staff who had not been questioned. Rod showed the picture on his phone to a lab technician who had just emerged from an office with a rack of specimen bottles.

"Have you seen this woman?"

"No," said the lab tech. "No, wait. That's the *Koloba* in room thirty-something, isn't it?"

"And – and this is important – did she see you?"

"That's an odd question."

"Aye. And?"

"No. I think the only times I've ever been in there she was asleep."

"You sure?"

"Yes," said the lab tech suspiciously. "Why?"

"Nothing, that's fine," said Rod, turned away and then turned back. "What's a lab guy doing in an old lady's room while she's asleep?"

The lab tech looked affronted.

"Can't a feller steal Quality Street from an old lady now and then?"

Rod gave him a look that suggested the answer was probably 'no'.

"It's not as though she'll remember," said the lab tech. "She probably thinks she ate them."

Rod found Kathy by the makeshift surgical screen barricades they'd set up to stop anyone going within earshot or eyeline of Barbara's room.

"All off duty staff have been contacted," she said. "One's coming in because she's not sure if she's met Barbara or not."

"Good work, Kathy."

"Why thank you, Campbell. Your approval and validation is all that I crave."

"Sarky. What I don't get is why the *Koloba* allows this to continue."

"It's an involuntary thing. The *Koloba* doesn't know it's obliterating people."

"But it could move host, surely. It could live in a human body that doesn't have dementia."

"Maybe it doesn't know it has dementia," said Kathy. "How can you know that your mental powers are failing when you can't remember what it is you've forgotten? Or maybe it does know but

100

it doesn't care. It's very, very old. Perhaps this is what it wants. Perhaps it's tired of being omniscient." She raised her chin and stared at him with an over-exaggerated gravitas. "Intelligence can be such a burden."

"Are you going to use that line in the job interview?"

"Have you heard something?"

"Sorry, no. But if we manage to save the day here, this will be excellent ammo for those 'Give me an example of a time when' questions they'll be asking at the interview."

"Oh, and speaking of memory. It's the *Azhur-Banipal shad Nekku*."

"Eh?"

"The Stone of the King in Crimson. The picture you drew. I knew it would come to me."

Before long, there were four Morags and five Cattresses by the Bloody Big Book chamber.

"Hey," complained Morag, "what did we do to deserve an extra one of you?"

"She insisted on going off in her own direction," said Cattress dismissively.

"I wonder where I might have gone to?" said another Morag.

"Perhaps to meet the rescue party."

"Perhaps she got out."

Morag looked along the corridor. Baby universes crowded around them, aisles bifurcating, shooting off like wild growths. There was no knowing where the exit now lay. "Lucky her."

"How long are we going to be in here?" said the Cattress with the ripped sleeve.

"Could be a while," said Morag. "Could be days."

"So, we're going to starve then," said another Cattress.

Morag reached into her pocket and produced half a breakfast bacon roll, wrapped up in a paper bag. Three other Morags did the same. Four halves of bacon bap. It wasn't much.

Morag was suddenly struck with a vision of a grim and endless future: tribes of Morag Murrays and Jonathan Cattresses roaming the infinite corridors of a nightmarish museum, scavenging weapons and food from the display shelves, and resorting to murder when the meagre food ran out.

"Is it strictly cannibalism if you eat yourself?" one of the other Morags asked.

"Okay," said another Morag, "we need some way of identifying which of us is which. If only so I don't get paired up with cannibal Morag at any point."

"Hey, you were all thinking it," said cannibal Morag.

"Yeah," said Morag, pulling her hair back into a ponytail. "But you were the one that said it. Right, I'm Ponytail Morag."

Rod and Kathy waited at the lift for the woman who was coming in to sit in Barbara's presence and thus secure her own survival. With her in place, anyone who had ever met the demented, omniscient *Koloba* (and was still alive) would be in the room with her.

Rod and Kathy watched the lift numbers climb.

"You know," said Rod, "when I was a kid – I mean when I was just a tot – I used to think that when I closed my eyes the world just went away. Is that stupid?"

"Yes," she said.

"Right. So, I shouldn't tell you that I also thought I was the only real person in the world and everyone else was imaginary, not really human but like a puppet or summat?"

"Oh, that's perfectly ordinary solipsism. Every child goes through that."

The lift dinged.

Rod had half-expected the lift would be empty, that the woman had been forgotten out of existence between the ground and the eighth floor, but when the door slid open there was a middle-aged woman whose expression was in part worried and in part peeved that she had to come into work on her day off.

"Angie," said Kathy.

"What is this about?" asked the off-duty nurse.

"Do you know this woman?" said Rod and showed her the picture Nina had sent him.

"Barbara Gudge," said Angie.

"And she's met you? She's seen you?"

"Yes. I don't understand."

"This way, Angie, please," said Kathy.

Halfway down the corridor, just outside an office door, a rack of specimen bottles lay dropped and scattered on the floor.

"Bugger," said Rod softly.

"What?" said Kathy.

"The Quality Street thief wasn't as sneaky as he thought."

Vivian met Professor Sheikh Omar in the lobby of the Library of Birmingham. She had expected him to be alone but there was a man standing beside and slightly behind him. They were both well into their middle years but were otherwise a contrasting pair. Omar was tall and imposing, like a vulture. The other man was small and slight, like a vole. Omar was balding but wore it well. The other had immaculately coiffured silver hair that looked like a wig but almost certainly wasn't. Omar looked as if he had seen the world and wrestled half of it. The other man looked as if he would faint in fear if he got so much as a crease in his lilac shirt.

Professor Omar was the head of the Department of Intertextual Exegesis at Birmingham University and, for want of a better description, one of the finest occultists in the city. Vivian surmised that the little man was Maurice, his assistant or batman or sorcerer's familiar or whatever he called him, who she was given to understand was rarely far from his side.

"Vivian," said Omar, smiling.

He had good teeth, she noticed. Not false teeth, not mangled and realigned by unnecessary orthodontics, but a set of well-maintained gnashers. Vivian approved.

He shook her hand, warmly but professionally. "I had expected an invitation but not necessarily so soon. Interviews aren't until Thursday."

"The invitation was for you alone," she said pointedly.

"Oh, Maurice is here to carry my tools." Maurice mutely raised a brown Gladstone bag as evidence. "When I'm working I prefer to keep my hands like my morals," said Omar.

"Unencumbered. Besides, the devil makes work for idle little hands like his."

Vivian traded looks with the pair of them that conveyed her displeasure but said no more.

"Now," said the professor cheerfully, "what is the nature of your current problem?"

Vivian explained as they rode down to the Vault.

"So, my good friend Morag Murray and a fatuous mandarin have endangered all existence with some clumsy handling of the mystical crockery," said Omar.

Vivian felt that such a flippant summary should be worthy of rebuke, but this was an entirely accurate assessment.

"Quite," she said. She opened the first door to the Vault and then paused before the second. "May I be candid, professor?"

"Oh, please do," said Omar.

"You have a reputation."

"One tries."

"As an irresponsible dabbler in Venislarn affairs and a pedlar in stolen artefacts. Once we are through this door, you are to touch nothing."

"Understood, ma cherie. It is true that I, like Nero, am a fisher in the lake of darkness but any suggestion that I – we! – are thieves is nothing but slander. As I have told your colleague Rodney many a time, why would I stoop to theft when there is eBay to service all our needs?"

"Very good. Then you won't be offended if I say that Malcolm here has orders to shoot dead any person caught in the act of theft."

Omar looked at the security guard and the gloved hand that rested on his holstered pistol.

"Such a fine figure," said Omar. "Unquestionable authority made flesh."

Vivian opened the second door. "This way."

She led them along the central aisle that ran the full length of the Vault, which covered a subterranean area far larger than the library building on street level. Vivian strode briskly, Omar maintaining pace easily in long strides. Maurice scuttled along behind, the Gladstone bag tucked awkwardly under his arm as he scribbled notes in a spiral notepad.

"A live Julia Set. The horns of *Raa-ghul Yatz*. The Pohnpei Papers. *Son sleen pat'zhadoi*. Two of them," he muttered softly.

"Eyes sharp, Maurice. Look there, the Begbie Manangel. I always wondered if you lot had removed it from public display or if its disappearance had simply been the work of dull and uncomprehending scrap thieves."

Vivian glanced at the wire mesh sculpture of a headless angel, a Faraday cage for gods.

"Rod Campbell removed it under cover of darkness. It was officially reported as stolen. That list you're compiling…"

"Purely for our records. If we know you have it, then we know if we're being offered a forgery on the open market. Oh!"

This exclamation was directed to the boundary between this world and a much younger world. It was almost imperceptible. There was no sci-fi force field shimmer in the air. There was no mirror-like sheen. The gap between worlds was only visible as a disjointed seam in the floor tiles, a subtle shifting in the angle of the floor, a shelf where half a book abutted nothing at all. Morag Murray sat in a bored slump against an inexpertly carved *Wos'ulin* sacrifice pole.

"Hail, thou that art highly favoured," said Omar.

Morag gave a listless wave.

"Professor. Hi Maurice. Come to rescue me?"

"Blessed art thou among women," said Omar. He looked at the boundary line which was slowly edging outward. "First thing to do is stop this spreading any further."

He mimed rolling up his sleeves.

"Maurice. Pens and the book of apotropaic wards, if you would. Oh, and green tea of course."

"Green tea?" said Morag. "What does that do?"

Maurice had opened the Gladstone bag and removed a tartan thermos flask.

"Settles my nerves," said Omar.

"You don't suffer with nerves," said Morag.

"Green tea," said Maurice by way of explanation.

"I'm hungry," said Barbara.

"I'll get you something," said Paula the administrator with sycophantic urgency. This was Paula who, they had learned, owned a cat; whose great grandma's sister had drowned in a washtub; who had broken both her wrists playing hockey; and who had once stolen a packet of crisps off Chris Evans (although whether she meant the ginger Radio DJ or Captain America was never made clear). "What would you like?"

"Faces," said Barbara.

"Faces?"

"It's okay. I'll do it," said Eunice the nurse (who had two cats, had once held a hedgehog as large as a football and had turned down a date with Jason Statham).

"I am kind of hungry myself," said Marco the orderly (whose grandmother had been killed by a cat, who had accidentally taken two pounds of explosive aboard a jumbo jet and had, as a schoolboy, performed an excruciating rap song to the then Prime Minister).

"I don't think you'll want anything that comes out of that machine," said Nina.

"Nina," called Rod from behind the screens at the doorway.

"Yo," she called back.

"I'm sending Angie through. She's a nurse and she needs to join you. She's fifty percent up to speed with what's going on."

"Does she have any food on her?" said Nina.

"No."

"Stuff some chocolate bars in her pockets. We're getting kind of peckish in here."

"How can we eat at a time like this?" said administrator Paula.

"Cos it's sort of lunchtime," said Nina.

"But we could vanish at any moment."

"Can't think of a better argument for why we should eat now. In fact," she pulled up a takeaway app on her phone, "we ought to go out in style."

The band of Morags and Cattresses made their way through the shifting worlds they had unleashed. Pigtails Morag and No Shoes Morag led the way. Plaits Morag and Left Sleeve Up Morag brought up the rear. The three other Morags they had since encountered were spread out among the eight Cattresses. Plaits could feel the tension building among the men and was sure that her other selves could feel it too. They figuratively circled one another and Morag heard occasional mutters about "the wife" or "the mistress" or "the house".

"When we get out of here," said Left Sleeve, "if we could each only take one item from our old home – before beginning a new life in some far-off city or whatever – what would you take?"

"Most of our stuff is still up in Edinburgh," said Plaits.

"True, true."

"I'd want to take the pictures of mum and dad."

"We could make copies of those."

"Our vinyl copy of Marillion's *Misplaced Childhood*," called one of the Morags from the middle of the line.

"Really?" replied Left Sleeve. "It's not a very good album."

"Ah, but the sentimental value," said Plaits, recalling the secondary school boyfriend she had borrowed it from.

They entered a small gallery, lined with Fox Talbot's antique photographs of the *Kuyuncuk Dras'n-orgh* in Nineveh. It wasn't the first time they had come this way. Or, it wasn't the first version of this place they had passed through. As before, the eyes of dead Venislarn followed them as they passed.

"I know," said a Morag somewhere, "we could all agree to try to get back with an old boyfriend. One each."

Plaits wasn't sure there were enough exes to go round and then did a mental count and was surprised there were even a couple to spare.

"Which one would you take?" said Pigtails.

"Cameron Barnes," replied six Morags in unison.

They were a couple of knowing chuckles and a shaking of several heads.

"Yep, definitely the one that got away," said Left Sleeve.

"There's plenty more fish in the sea," said Plaits.

"You have the fish, I'll have Cameron," said Pigtails.

"I don't see why we should split up," said Plaits. "We could all stick together and form a girl band."

There was a chorus of interested hmm noises.

"That would be a lot of fun," said Left Sleeve, "except that some manager would make us all dress up as Robert Palmer girls and try and get us to pout moodily at billionaires' private parties. We'd spend all our time fighting off sex pests."

"Simple answer," said Pigtails, stepping forward. "I'll be manager. We take the bookings we want."

"Come off it," said another Morag from the crowd. "We have no clue how to be a manager."

"Like we've never blagged our way through something tricky before! Who do we think's harder to deal with, an August Handmaiden of *Prein* or a venue promoter?" asked Pigtails.

"Yeah, do I need to remind you that we killed an August Handmaiden of *Prein*?" said Plaits. "I have a feeling we might not be cut out for public relations."

While Marco the orderly took delivery of pizzas under the screen at the door, Barbara Gudge tore into her lunch of 3D-printed face (a young woman of possibly Japanese descent). Nina, who was exploring the settings on the 3D printer, was impressed at the strength with which the old biddy attacked her food. She didn't use a knife and fork but simply ripped shreds from it with teeth and fingers. Her hands were red with blood, as was the heavy napkin she had tucked into her collar.

"I wonder who it is?" said the newcomer Angie faintly.

"Who?" said Nina.

Angie nodded toward the face.

"There's a database of images," said Eunice. "That's someone's actual face."

Nina was scrolling through the database of body parts on the printer's screen. The interface seemed fairly straightforward. There were settings for importing and exporting data files. And the library was subdivided into easily navigable categories.

"Barbara!" said Nina, pretending to be scandalised.

"What is it, dear?" asked the ancient one, around a mouthful of cheek.

Nina had set the printer to work and, moments later, presented the results to all. It was unexpectedly heavy, must have been at least eight inches long and sat in Nina's hands with a surprising sense of life and warmth.

"What?" said Barbara. "Don't look at me like that, dear. You can't tell me you've never wanted to nibble a bit of sausage."

"You dirty old lady," said Nina, smiling. "Catch, Paula."

She tossed it and it wriggled in the air like a leaping salmon before landing in Paula's lap. Paula squealed. It was a squeal that couldn't decide if it wanted to turn into laughter or tears. Fortunately, Paula opted for laughter.

"Who ordered pepperoni on their pizza?" asked Marco, opening the boxes.

"Eat up," said Nina. "I've just had an idea that will save us all."

Eunice frowned. "Does it involve penises?"

"Not unless you want it to," said Nina. "I'm open to suggestions."

The first Cattress casualty might have been an accident. The second was not.

Perhaps a harsh word had been said. Perhaps the favourite mistress had been mentioned again. Perhaps the cause was a mere slighting glance between men who did not get along. Whatever his reason, one of the Cattresses gave another a shove. This was far from fatal in itself but, unluckily, the shoved man brushed up against the small but well-named Unapproachable Stone of *Msgoto*. As soon as his hand touched its cracked surface, that Cattress was doomed. The only glimmer of consolation was that the vampiric stone had been exceedingly hungry and the man died from blood loss and shock before he could complain.

While others cowered or shouted in fear, some Cattresses took the man's death as a challenge for supremacy, a drawing of battle lines. Before Pigtails Morag could attempt to intervene, there were shouts of, "What the hell did you do that for?" and "I saw that!" and, less explicably, "So, that's how it's going to be, is it?"

"Now, just wait…" began Right Sleeve Morag loudly.

There was more shoving, a feeble attempt at a punch and then improvised weapons appeared. The Cattress who pulled down a long *Shus'vinah* mask from the wall had second thoughts when its wooden eyes turned to look at him: the fire extinguisher hanging next to it would have been a wiser choice. The Cattress now swinging that extinguisher was either stronger than he looked or the Cattress he struck was far feebler – the latter went down with a scream, clutching his face.

And so that violent and deadly skirmish began, the most personal of civil wars, not even brother against brother but man against himself.

The video cameras Nina had asked for were hastily ordered from the electrical superstore just down the road in Selly Oak and were set up on tripods around Barbara's side ward.

"*Don't You (Forget About Me)*, the TV show, take one," said Nina as she started the first camera recording.

"What are we supposed to do?" said Angie.

"Nothing. Anything," said Nina. "It's just recording us."

"Am I going to be on telly?" asked Barbara.

"We all are," said Nina. "It's going to be a new TV channel."

"24/7 rolling coverage," said Marco.

Vivian watched Professor Omar's marker pen produce sigil after ward after glyph in a long arc across the floor at the boundary between worlds. He wrote with economic speed and admirable accuracy. There were a number of devices, particularly certain Venislarn ideograms, that Vivian did not recognise and she made a mental note to ask him about those later. In a few short minutes, his barrier was complete.

"What now?" said the Morag waiting on the other side.

"Well, my dear," said the professor, getting to his feet with a slight click of his knees, "all I have accomplished here is curtailing the outward limit of the effect."

"Eh?"

"The effect is sealed in a bubble. The real world is on this side and the fake iterations are on your side."

"Can I cross over?"

"Ah," he smiled, "therein lies the rub. This side is real, aggressively so now. And now, any of the Berry Mound vase's facsimiles that cross over will instantly cease to exist."

"You mean me?"

"If that's what you are. But perhaps the greater concern is that, in there somewhere, the vase is continuing to produce new realities, yes?"

"How do we stop it?"

Professor Omar gave her a reproachful look.

"You're not a stupid woman, Morag. Think. I should imagine smashing the vase entirely would do the trick."

Morag nodded tersely and hurried off.

Omar turned to Vivian.

"Now, shall we discuss the fee for my services?"

"We can," said Vivian, "but I can assure you it will be a very short conversation."

Rod sat with laptop and phone in the Restricted Ward admin office. On the other end of the phone line was Leandra, part of the consular mission's PR department. Her work entailed building up the wealth of marketing, advertising and 'Keep Calm and Carry On' collateral that would be needed on the day the Venislarn were publicly unveiled. Rod frequently found communication with her a struggle as she seemed to be in permanent orbit around Planet Bullshit.

"I need some video material editing," he explained.

"Gonna have to put that in the 'love to later' box, Rod," said Leandra. "We're very much mid-stroke on the current project. We are focussing on outreach and mutual fact-pooling with the local Venislarn community."

"Really? I just need some video editing and jazzing up. It's for Nina."

"Oh?" said Leandra, interested. "Is it more material for the Tentacular project? We are very buzzed by that."

Tentacular was the name for a boy band Nina had invented in a marketing brainstorming session some weeks earlier. Rod was about sixty percent certain she had only said it as a joke but these millennial youths were so bloody self-absorbed and ironic that perhaps Nina herself couldn't even say whether it had been a sarcastic suggestion or not. Whatever, it was looking increasingly likely that there would soon be a government-funded boy band to be the cute and teen-friendly face of the Venislarn occupation.

"No, it's just some footage of people talking. Some straight-to-camera pieces. It just needs a polish to make it a bit more TV-friendly."

"Guerrilla filmmaking," said Leandra approvingly. "I've always been a fan of Dogme. If only we could marry it to a client-centric virtualisation ethos."

"Aye?" said Rod who had no idea what that meant.

"I think Nina is wasted in the response team. We could really use someone who understands premier cloud-ready technology niches like she does."

"Oh, aye. That's what I'm always saying. So, can you do it?"

Leandra ummed and ahhed on the line.

"Well, I do think we should champion superior best practices, particularly in parallel tasking," she said.

"Is that a yes?"

"Send it over and I'll see what I can get done by end of play."

"Ta," he said and killed the call.

Kathy Kaur had entered the room. She held a large framed picture.

"What do you think?" she said.

Nina's photograph of Marco the orderly had been blown up to four times actual size. Along the bottom of the photograph were the words, "Hi, I'm Marco Richards" in case anyone might forget who he was.

"Well, it's hardly art but it is him, yes," said Rod.

"But shall we do the others like this?"

"Quickly," he said.

Ponytail Morag stopped for a breather in the small anteroom that was colloquially known as the Library of Ignorance. After the Cattresses had taken exception to themselves, there had been bloodshed and chaos and the opening, breaking and touching of items that were not opened, broken or touched by the wise. Ponytail and No Jacket Morag had run after the Cattress who had taken hold of and been immediately possessed by the *Shus'vinah* mask. In the pursuit, No Jacket had fallen and tumbled down into a world that was growing at forty-five degrees to this one and Ponytail had run on and now stood in a quiet room surrounded by volumes of Venislarn scholarship that were judged to be utterly harmless nonsense. The Library of Ignorance was indecipherable but no one cared.

Once she had regained her breath and she could hear something other than the blood pounding in her ears, she realised that there were sounds coming from nearby: a dull tapping and intermittent grunts.

She stepped out of the anteroom and took two corners before finding the source of the noise. The mask-possessed Cattress knelt on the floor, his hands wrapped around the throat of the Morag beneath him. Her feet kicked ineffectually. A tongue, longer than any human's and entirely the wrong colour, poked out of the mouth slit of the oval mask and quivered with excitement.

Ponytail ran at him and gave him a boot in the shoulder that sent the possessed man rolling away.

"Fuck off, you *cuda'nih* hellbeast!" she snarled.

The Morag on the floor coughed.

The masked man came to his feet.

"*Hoh'ch ap rhu-ket Yoth-Thorani*," the mask lisped threateningly in a voice that wasn't Cattress's.

"Yeah?" said Ponytail. "Well, you run to mummy and when she gets here I'll wallop her creosoted arse an' all!"

"And that goes double from me," said the assaulted Morag, standing up.

The masked man hissed angrily and ran off. Ponytail was about to give chase but the other Morag put a hand on her arm.

"We need to find the vase."

Ponytail looked her up and down. "Which one are you?"

The other Morag frowned. She didn't understand the question.

"You're a new one," said Ponytail.

"We've got to destroy the vase. Sheikh Omar's instructions."

"He's here?"

"Vivian invited him."

"Things must be bad." Ponytail thought for a moment. "I think we're only a bit down from where we last saw the vase."

"You lead," said the new Morag.

Rod texted Nina while Marco and Eunice were putting up the final photograph.

Barbara's room now had five large and ever-so-slightly obtrusive new pictures on the wall.

"Oh, that's a nice one of you, Ange," said Barbara (who had finished off her face-shaped lunch, leaving only the ears which she wasn't a big fan of).

"Thank you," said Angie.

"Shall we see what's on TV?" said Nina, wielding the remote. She clicked it on. "Oh, my favourite. It's Paula reads a book or something."

On the screen, Paula the administrator opened a large print Catherine Cookson and began reading.

"Is that you on the telly, Paula?" Barbara asked.

"It is, Barbara," said Paula.

"Oh, you are clever," said the old biddy and then almost instantly, "Is there anything else on?"

Nina tsked. "Hospital cuts, Barbara, I'm afraid. We're down to just one channel. Nina-Paula-Angie-Marco-Eunice TV. 24/7 rolling programmes."

"Fair enough," said Barbara, unfussed. "We didn't have telly in my day, you know."

Her day? Was that in Barbara's day or in the early years of the life of the *Koloba* parasite that lived within her? She couldn't imagine the Venislarn, wherever they were from, having television. Maybe that was why they were such miserable jackasses all the time.

The world, Morag knew, was a mad and incomprehensible place. A whole spawning pool of worlds was madder still. As she and the ponytailed other Morag closed in on the Berry Mound vase of multiplication, worlds bunched together and the madness intensified, any sense of reality, of here, lost its meaning. She could not see the vase ahead; she could only assume they were close because the worlds were packed so densely.

Morag watched only where she placed her feet. Off to both sides, ceilings and tiles and doorways boiled away into their own created spaces.

The Morags slowed as they approached. Shifting to single file, they clasped hands as though they were climbing up a steep slope together.

Worlds crowded in from above. Morag felt the tug of misaligned gravities on her hair. Her ears popped. A warm, dusty friction filled the air.

"This is worse than being drunk," she said.

"A lot of things are," said the other Morag.

Morag reached forward. Her hand entered other universes but did not disappear into them. There was nothing to feel in those spaces but the cool, conditioned air of other Vaults in other libraries. And then her fingertips touched the smoothness of pottery, invisible beneath the torrent of growing worlds.

"I've got it!"

"Then smash it!"

"With what? There's nothing here. Just mad shit."

"It's got to be standing on something! Just... just smash it, you eejit!"

Morag grasped the vase by what felt like its fluted neck and waved it about as hard and as fast as she could. It struck something solid; Morag felt the blow through her hand. She struck it again and shards of the vase gave way beneath her grip.

Nothing happened immediately. Nothing really happened at all except... The worlds around them no longer boiled, no longer pressed and squeezed against each other. Everything simply... drifted.

"Did we do it?" asked the other Morag.

"I think so," said Morag cautiously.

"What now?"

"Now, I think we go and find out if any of us is going to be fired."

Vivian watched the two women approach the border between worlds.

"Two more," she said simply.

Professor Sheikh Omar, who was seated upon a fold-out camping stool and nursing the third cup of tea, looked up from the Vault inventory notes Maurice had compiled for him. Vivian watched him underline an item in red pen before closing the notepad and she made her own note, a mental one, to question him about that later.

One of the Morags had bruises down the side of her neck. The other, the one with the ponytail, appeared unharmed, although both looked tired and less than jolly.

"It's done," said the bruised one.

"The vase is destroyed?" said Vivian.

The Morag nodded. Vivian looked to Professor Omar.

"Then we are done for the time being," he said.

"We do nothing about these aberrant realities?" Vivian asked.

Omar stood and straightened his jacket.

"We are in new territories here," he said smoothly. "If, as I suspect, the Berry Mound vase is part of a *Mexk'nah* stone ship then this is a *tair mz'riz ihssen* effect. The various realities will need to find their balance, align in pressure. When I'm appointed to the position of Vault custodian –"

"If, professor," said Vivian.

Omar gave her a cold little look and then smiled.

"We can leave it for a day or two. Put up some barriers in the meantime. Some yellow tape."

"Oh!" said the bruised Morag in surprise.

She had just noticed Cattress, sat on the floor against a bookcase only feet from her, inside the bubble. His blood-soaked arms hugged his knees. His eyes gazed at nothing. His lips mouthed silent words.

"He's been there for a while," said Vivian.

"The blood..."

"It's his," said Vivian. "And when I say it's his..."

The Morags were already nodding.

"Only the original version of each of you can cross back over," said Omar. "You are not the first Morags to make it this far. None have crossed, not successfully."

"Mr Cattress here is the first of his incarnations to get here," said Vivian. "We suspect he's the only one left."

"Had to," Cattress murmured faintly. "Jennifer."

"Yes," said Omar. "Jennifer?"

"His girlfriend," explained Morag with the ponytail. "So, if we both cross, what happens?"

"One of you will vanish in the wink of an eye," said Omar. "At least one of you."

"Painlessly?"

"Our observations of your previous attempts suggest so," said Vivian.

The Morags looked at each other, thoughts synchronised.

They each took one of Cattress's arms and hauled him to his feet.

"But..." he said softly, too shell-shocked to resist.

"No one wants to stay down here forever," said one Morag.

"There are people waiting for us on the other side," said the other.

"We just step?" Morag asked Omar.

"Just step over," said the professor.

The Morags looked at each other one last time and then, carrying Cattress between them, they stepped.

Plaits Morag, armed with the two glass daggers she had used to scare off a rogue Cattress, poked her head around the corner in time to see two Morags and a Cattress step forward arm in arm. One of the Morags abruptly winked out of existence, like a light projection simply turned off. Cattress, suddenly unsupported on one side, slumped to the ground. The remaining Morag let him fall.

Plaits thought for a second and then understood. Vivian was there. Professor Omar too. There was a line of symbols, unreadable from this distance and angle, along the floor: a barrier that only some could cross. Originals.

"Balls," she said with feeling. "I'm a bloody copy."

It was a gut punch of a discovery. It had been almost acceptable, funny even, when there had been a half dozen of them and none of them had known which of them was real. But, to discover that you were a fake, less than a day old, as significant and as durable as a person's shadow... Well, that was just a steaming pile of shite.

And Omar had painted a magic line that would erase her the moment she tried to escape. Bastards, the lot of them.

"So, that's it," she said grimly to herself.

Plaits took herself away a distance, far from the view of the real-world gits, found a reasonably inoffensive pillar to slump against and sulkily considered her lot.

A strong part of her argued that she wasn't meant to exist, that, despite the thirty years' worth of baggage in her head, she had barely existed any time at all and that she should simply run at Omar's death barrier and have done with it. She stood up, her decision made. She then discovered she still had half of a bacon bap in her pocket. So, she ate that first. And even though it was cold, it was delicious.

"*Bhul*," she swore.

Copy or not, bacon was better than death. She wanted to live.

"Options."

Taking the glass daggers with her, Plaits set off into the maze of aisles and mashed-up worlds, to seek inspiration and make choices. Walking gave her thinking space and, within the hour, she had four basic choices. She could kill herself by stepping into the barrier. She could stay here and hide, try to forage some sort of secret existence in the Vault. She could try to draw the attention of the consular mission staff and throw herself on their mercy (whether they would attempt to free her, destroy her or keep her in there as their pet Morag was debatable). Her fourth option was to free herself, find a way out of these pocket dimensions and back into the real world without crossing Omar's kill barrier.

This fourth option naturally appealed. It offered a return to her old life (albeit one that already had another Morag in it) and it would be done on her own terms. Of course, she had no idea how it could be accomplished.

She explored the copy universes as well as one might without any map or point of reference. There was the possibility that some had expanded sufficiently to include other areas of the Library building or the wider city. She'd be ecstatic if any of them had reached as far as the coffee shop in the ground floor concourse. She could murder a donut or a Belgian bun.

When that exploration proved fruitless, she considered other ways out. She levered up floor tiles and then climbed on a table and pulled down ceiling tiles, hoping against hope to find a way through ceiling or floor into notional levels above or below. Solid concrete and a lack of tools to cut through it put paid to that idea.

In her wandering, she eventually found the remains of the Berry Mound vase. Here, where universes had been vomited out one after the other, the edges between realities were still pressed so closely together that looking in any direction was like staring into a smashed mirror. Nonetheless, with the vase destroyed, there had been a certain amount of natural settling and the epicentre, containing shards of pottery and the shelves of OOPArts where the vase had been stored, was at least a definable space in which she could stand without danger of falling into other worlds.

A practical, physical escape appeared impossible. Calling on the powers of the Venislarn might be her last recourse. She looked at the shelves and, thoughtfully, picked up the *pabash kaj* doll.

Nina produced a roll of semi-transparent plastic with a small ta-da.

"What's this?" said Paula.

"Stick-on glass frosting," said Nina. "You can help put it up. No more looking at people outside the window."

"What's happening to my window?" asked Barbara.

"Nothing, Barbara. It's dinner time now," said Nina. "Come on, what are you having?"

The old lady waddled over to the printer.

"Faces."

"Pick mine," said Eunice. "Go on. Pick mine."

"Have they changed the menu, dear?" asked Barbara.

"Hospital cuts again, I'm afraid," said Nina, pushing buttons. "It's a choice of fried Marco, roasted Paula, Angie au gratin, fricasseed Nina or … Eunice tartare."

In the printer tray, extruded from minced and then reconstituted meats, a face began to form.

"It's beautiful," said Eunice.

"Eye of the beholder, man," said Marco, less than convinced, and began to unroll the frosting.

Vivian took Morag to the office on the seventh floor and insisted on presenting her with a cup of tea. She ignored Morag's argument that she was fine and, if anything, was in need of something stronger than tea. (Morag mentioned a "nasty" bottle of Merlot that she had at home that would apparently "do the trick".) She certainly did not permit Morag to make her own cup of tea; Morag's abilities in that area were entirely deficient. And, because Vivian was a civilised human being and knew some form of thanks was in order, she invited Professor Omar and his assistant, Maurice, to join them.

Four cups of tea. They sat in a meeting room and drank, for the most part, in silence. Vivian chose to ignore the critical eye Maurice gave to the colour of the tea as she poured and the disapproving twist of his lips as he drank. The man was incorrect in his opinions but she had no need to point that out to him.

"Of course," observed Professor Omar, "now that you have untold spare universes in your basement, you will also have additional – dare I say redundant – copies of numerous artefacts."

"Your payment," said Vivian, "is an invitation to interview on Thursday. Nothing more."

"I wasn't suggesting otherwise," said Omar suavely.

"I worried what might happen if the effect reached the Bloody Big Book," said Morag. "A book that contains literally everything and an effect that makes perfect copies. I thought it might be like the unstoppable wotsit meeting the immovable thingy."

"Eloquent as always," said Omar.

"I don't think it would have caused a world-ending event," said Vivian.

"No," Omar agreed. "The infinite obeys the same rules as the finite – more simply sometimes. Infinity times two is still infinity. Likewise, infinity halved. I have thought that one could rip out any number of pages from the Wittgenstein Volume and it would not change its total contents one iota."

"Do not get any ideas, Professor," said Vivian.

"Heaven forfend. Although I would give an arm and a leg to spend an afternoon with that book. Not my arm and leg but definitely whatever limbs I might lay my hands on."

"It is certainly an enlightening read," said Vivian. "I have encouraged Miss Murray to read it although she claims to not have the time."

"It doesn't look like a light read," said Morag.

"A poor excuse," said Omar and then paused to remove a fleck of tea leaf from his lips.

Maurice said nothing but the little man's eyes glittered.

"The dangers of using loose tea," said Vivian unapologetically. "Something always slips through the sieve."

"Indeed, my dear," said Omar. "So few take the effort to use loose leaf these days."

Maurice coughed lightly.

"Yes," acknowledged Omar with an affectionate smile. "Maurice is one of those few. He's a dab hand at reading the leaves too. He could read the lottery numbers in your lapsang souchong."

Maurice made demure noises.

"No, not at all," said Omar. "In tea, truth."

Plaits sat cross-legged on the floor and twisted the Rubik's Cube of *Prein*. The glittering symbols shifted as she turned the sides. She considered herself a fair student of the language of *aklo* and was ninety percent confident of what would happen if she rearranged it into the correct config–

A pinpoint of wan blue light appeared in the air before her and rapidly expanded into first a disc and then a lightning-bounded tunnel.

Eighty percent confident.

There was a screeching howl like the badly-oiled gears between worlds crunching against each other and then, out of the vortex of sickly light, stepped an otherworldly horror.

"Rhon-ada-ho, et glad muise!" it – he – gloated in wet-throated triumph.

"Wow," said Plaits, stepping back to take it all in. "Just wow."

"Gue-am-bhun, muise!"

"No," said Plait. "I mean, 'wow, what the hell have you got going on here with your look?' You've got the crab claws and the gazillion legs and –"

"Pad veri-klu svet Prein!"

"Oh, I know you're part of the entourage of *Prein*, but then you've also got the chains and the blades embedded in your flesh and the whole 'oops, I'm sorry, you've caught me halfway through an autopsy' thing and –"

"Cud vadu ib fenq muise!" he roared, waving a tattooed tentacle-leg-frond at her.

"I may be just a bloody mortal but at least I don't look like a rebellious teen trying too hard to get a reaction. Seriously, who needs that many penises? What's your name?"

"Se'ad u Qulsteyvan weh Pelk-chromlid."

"*Qulsteyvan* the… Deconstructor?"

"It translates as 'destroyer', morsel," the creature gargled.

"Destroyer? Really? Okay. So, *Qulsteyvan*. Steven. Steve."

"*– weh Pelk-chromlid.*"

"Right. Steve the Destroyer. You're probably wondering why I've summoned you."

"You are an explorer in the realms of pleasure and pain. You have reached the limit of human experience and have now come to us. We have so much to teach you."

"No," said Plaits. "Not that."

"It's too late to change your mind, sweetling."

"I'm not into all that S and M jazz. I had me a boyfriend once who wanted me to bite his boabie during foreplay. Not my thing. I hear his next girlfriend accidentally put him in hospital. No, I'm sorry, Steve, I'm only interested in your big glowing dimension corridor," she said, pointing at the tunnel of light.

"I will take you to realms beyond imagining," he burbled grandiosely.

"I just need to get to Bourneville," she said. "Or a train station. And you're not taking me anywhere."

"I am an angel-demon of the desecrated ranks, gobbet. How dare you defy me!"

"How?" said Plaits. "With that." She pointed at the *tcho-tcho Loigor* circle he was standing in, had landed in. She'd had to paint it in blood, drawn from her fingertip, not because blood was part of the ritual but because there had been no other materials to hand.

The Venislarn monster tried to crane its insectoid eyes round and down to see what she was pointing at. If it had elected to have more eyes and fewer extraneous genitalia it might have spotted the trap sooner.

Plaits held up the little *pabash kaj* doll.

"You can't!" spat Steve.

"I can."

"You wouldn't dare!"

"Oh, I do."

"I am of the entourage of *Prein*!"

"Funny thing that," said Plaits. "I've met you guys before. One of the August Handmaidens of Prein surprised me one time and I put a shotgun in her mouth. Her sister, *Shardak'aan Syu*, swore she would have vengeance against me. And bits of *her* still decorate my living room. You guys, you're all mouth and no troosers. *Hrorzza!*"

In a fraction of a second, the Venislarn had folded in on itself and was gone and, in her hand, the cloth dolly became a little heavier. Steve the Destroyer's tunnel of light remained.

"I will destroy you, fleshling!" cried the doll in a babyish high pitch. It tried to savage her with its sackcloth hands. It tried to bite her with a mouth that was stitched-on thread. It even headbutted her – bless! – gently tapping her fingers with its little wooden eyes.

"So, cute," said Plaits and gave him an affectionate squeeze. "Now, help me redirect this tunnel to somewhere I want to go."

Rod and Kathy assisted the restricted ward caretaker in screwing plywood panels over the small windows to either side of Barbara's door and then in sliding into place and fixing the wood-constructed 'airlock' that insured no one could see out of the room as people were entering or leaving. A more durable and secure doorway would have to be built eventually but this would suffice for now.

"You see, this is what I mean," said Rod, as they held the frame in place and waited for the caretaker to screw it in. "I could get a little prosthetic screwdriver."

"Tiredness has made you speak gibberish," said Kathy.

"For my little finger: an electric screwdriver with interchangeable heads."

"And that's what you think you need? A screwdriver."

"Or some other battery powered device. Whatever the situation calls for."

Kathy gave him a look, one that featured much wiggling of her perfect eyebrows.

Once the caretaker had it all screwed down, Nina was the first to use the airlock.

124

"And back to the real world," she said, audibly relieved.

"The others not coming out yet?" asked Rod.

"Don't think they're ready to put their faith in my brilliant plan."

"It was a brilliant plan," Kathy agreed.

"Pictures of us on the wall. Nothing but us on the telly. Nothing but our hands and our faces to eat. I've told them all that they can spend as much time as they like in there. Well, no one else is going to be doing Barbara's meals and cleaning. I think Paula is already eyeing up a corner for her desk."

"Aye, you done good, kiddo."

"Enough to deserve a drink from a grateful colleague?" Nina asked.

"Another night," he said. "Tonight, I just need to sleep."

"Tomorrow night it is, then."

Rod looked to Kathy, a question on his face.

"Hey, the more the merrier," said Kathy. "I'm just going to get my coat," she said and went off to find it.

When Rod looked back at Nina, there was a curious look on her face. He'd had enough of women giving him meaningful looks today.

"What?" he said. "Kathy got a text. She's got a place at interview on Thursday. I said we should go get a pint tomorrow to celebrate."

"Oh, okay," said Nina archly. "So, it's not cos you fancy the doctor with all the curves?"

"I don't know what you —"

"You know it's all corsets and underwiring under there. When you take it all off, she'll be like that tub of gloopy goo that Vivian uses to clean her keyboard. You'll see the edges of her seeping across —"

"I'm not going to take it all —" Rod lowered his voice, realising how loud he was speaking. "I'm not going to take it all off."

"Have you forgotten how it's done? I could send you a link to some videos to remind you."

"Nina," he said in his sternest voice (which only made Nina smile), "it's just a drink."

"Okay. I understand. Cos I thought you had a thing for someone else anyway."

"Who?"

Nina put her hands on her hips and, in something that might have been an attempt at a Scottish accent, said, "Och aye, Rod. Come away wi' me to my highland glen and we'll drink Irn-Bru and eat deep fried Mars bars."

"Shrek?"

Nina smacked him in the chest. "That was clearly an uncanny impression of Morag."

"That was meant to be Morag?"

"Meant to be? It was. You put us side by side and I did that, you wouldn't be able to tell which of us was which."

From Bourneville train station, through the leafy suburbs and to her flat in a subdivided house on Franklin Road, the real, the one and the only Morag walked on autopilot. She had her key in the door before she came to and realised where she was.

Richard, her downstairs neighbour, stood in the hallway waiting for her. He often waited for her to return from work. It wasn't a creepy thing; it was more that he was like a dog (a dog with a big bushy beard and a penchant for ugly checked shirts) that couldn't rest until everyone was back home.

"You're late today," he said.

"Long day," she said.

"What's that on you?" he said and pointed to two smeared bloody fingerprints on her blouse.

"Um. Red sauce," she said.

"Red sauce, of course," he said. "I cooked pizza. You like pizza."

"I do," she said. "Can it keep? I'm –" She gestured to the stairs. "I'm going to get changed and have a little lie down first."

"Are you unwell?"

"I'm fine. I just don't feel myself today."

She climbed the stairs slowly. One of the vicious cats that belonged to Mrs Atraxas on the top floor lay on the middle landing, giving her an evil look.

"Just try it, cuddles," she said warningly and stepped over it to get to her door.

Inside, she immediately kicked off her shoes and threw her jacket aside. In the bedroom, she put her dead phone onto charge and then went to get a shower. The phone was ringing as she came back in, towelling her hair dry. The caller ID was a blast from the past. She didn't hesitate in answering.

"Cameron Barnes!" she said.

"Morag Murray!" he replied, with mimicked and only slightly sarcastic enthusiasm. "Someone's *teglau* glad I called."

And she was. His Morningside accent was an instant anchor to a past, not too distant, before she had screwed things up royally in Edinburgh and been sent to Birmingham as penance.

"I was just... I was just talking about you today," she said.

"Oh, yes? Who to?"

"Myself," said Morag. "It's a long story."

"Well, maybe you'll get a chance to tell me. I'm in your neck of the woods tomorrow evening."

"Really?"

"Got a job interview on Thursday."

"The tech support role?"

"You know about it?"

"I knew the previous person," said Morag. "Knew, fought, fed to a shape-shifting god."

"Really?"

"Long story."

"Sounds like we have a *wau* lot to talk about."

"I'm looking forward to it."

A movement at the edge of her vision caught Morag's eye. She turned and, for an instant, didn't even recognise the woman and then, with a jolt, she saw that it was herself: herself still wearing the work clothes she had taken off just minutes earlier, herself holding a wide slice of pizza.

"Call you back," she said and ended the call.

She stared at the other Morag.

The other Morag took a bite of pizza. "Richard said you didn't want any."

"How the hell...?"

"I didn't know where else to go."

"And they told you to come here?"

The other Morag gave her a tired smile. Is that what her smile looked like? God, it looked smarmy.

"No one knows," said the other Morag. "I didn't know what they'd say."

"What?"

The other Morag rustled in a carrier bag and pulled out the Rubik's Cube of *Prein* and the *pabash kaj* doll.

"You stole them?" said Morag and then immediately, "You used them? The tunnelling power of the cube to bypass Omar's wards and then..."

"This is Steve the Destroyer," said the other Morag, "of the entourage of *Prein*."

"I will tear your soul apart," squeaked the doll adorably, struggling in the woman's grip.

"Jesus wept," said Morag. "And I thought I had fucked up enough for one day. I break one OOPArt and cause a disaster and now you steal two more and... you!"

"Me?"

"You're a damned OOPArt yourself! You don't belong!"

"Charming, Morag. I'm you."

"You're a... you're an OOPMorag."

"So witty. Are you finished bitching now?"

"Probably not."

"Fine," said the other Morag. "Now, let's open that bottle of nasty Merlot in the cupboard because I don't think I can face any more of today sober."

And Morag heartily agreed.

Wednesday

"We need to decide on names."

"I was trying to sleep."

"I can't. We need to decide on names."

"What's to decide? My name's Morag."

"So's mine."

"We can keep using them both. When I say Morag, I mean you. When you say Morag, you mean me."

"And if someone says Morag and we're in the same place?"

"When are we ever going to show our faces in the same place?"

"I will drag your soul to hell!"

"Shut up, Steve. You're not helping."

"We need names to define ourselves. You were Plaits Morag yesterday."

"I took the plait out."

"You can still be Plaits."

"No. It's a stupid name."

"OOPMorag, then."

"Why do I have to change my name?"

"Because I'm the original."

"Which makes you better, huh?"

"No, it makes me the oldest. I'm Morag. You can be... Morag Junior."

"Junior?"

"Yeah, just Junior is fine."

"I think I preferred Plaits."

"If you like."

"No, I'll be Junior. You can be Senior."

"Hmmm?"

"Old Mother Murray. It suits you. You've already got more grey hairs than me."

"That makes no sense."

"The elderly can often find things confusing."

"Cheeky wee bitch."

"You've only got yourself to blame."

"I will flay the sins from your bones!"

"Shut up, Steve."

Jeffney Ray got up at dawn every day.

He rolled nimbly out from under his Aston Villa duvet, cast his sleep mittens aside and stood in front of the mirror above the hand basin that had been put in when this had been his grandma's bedroom. The smell of grandma still clung to the place, to the fat pillows and the pink, deep-pile carpet, even months after she had gone. Ray had tried to make the place his own – the Villa duvet, his collection of forbidden texts on the window sill – but the old woman's ghost lingered.

As a self-employed and independent dealer in all things occult, he knew that an early start was a positive start on the day. He had once seen an internet meme that read, "The early bird catches the worm, but the second mouse gets the cheese" and it had stuck with him. He'd typed it up on his mom's computer in a bold and dramatic font, printed it off and wedged it in the side of the mirror so he would see it every day. Yes, he was the early bird and, yes, he was that cautious mouse. And today was going to be an especially busy day: door-to-door sales, a trip to Fish Town, then the Black Barge and an appointment at MMI.

Ray looked at his reflection. He ignored the most recent cuts on his face. They were still healing. The old scars were the ones that bothered him most. His mom told him repeatedly that they were barely noticeable but once you saw them, the white web of short scratches was impossible to ignore. His face was more scar than gap, a crazily smashed mirror of a face. Ray set about his morning routine, washing and then applying bio-oils and silicone gel to his ruined face. He hummed his mantra as he rubbed them in: fifty *it-rubs-the-lotion-on-its-skin*s for the bio-oil and fifty *it-rubs-the-lotion-on-its-skin*s for the silicone gel.

Cleansed, Ray dressed. A proper businessman dressed smartly and Ray was determined to look the part. A shirt with metal wingtips. Blue jacket on top. Polished shoes. Oxfords not brogues. That's what the man said. Ray applied a blob of gel to his hair and combed it through. Lots of product. The girls liked that. Looking neat, looking sharp. He pocketed his comb, checked he had his Travel West Midlands bus pass, packed his clipboard, his notebook and his copy of *Venislarn: A Language Primer* in his briefcase and slipped down the stairs and into the kitchen.

His mom was at the kitchen sink, smoking a fag and staring mindlessly out across the garden. Ray got his probiotic yoghurt drink from the fridge and gave her a peck on the cheek.

"You smell nice," she said absently.

"That's the lavender-scented facewash."

She came back to the here and now slowly. She looked at his suit and the briefcase.

"Where you off to?"

He waggled the briefcase. "Sales don't make themselves."

"They are paying you, aren't they?" she asked. She had asked it before.

"And how!"

"Don't let them take advantage of you, Jeffney."

"God, mom."

She looked back to the window. "Weren't you going to take that shed down for me?"

He tutted at her. "I've got to clear some things out first, mom. I'll deal with it."

"Right," she said and went back to smoking her fag.

Morag Junior (previously Plaits Morag, previously just Morag or perhaps nothing at all depending on one's perspective) made tea and toast for the pair of them in the morning. It was a reconciliatory gesture. Turning up on one's own doorstep unexpectedly would come as a surprise to anyone and perhaps she, Junior, had misjudged how Morag Senior would react. A settling in period was needed. Bridges needed to be built.

While Steve the Destroyer ran around on the kitchen counter looking for weapons he could a) use to disembowel her and b) lift in his tiny cloth hands, Morag spread thick marmalade and poured the tea. As she added milk, she dithered over which cup she would give to Morag Senior. Of the two that were clean, one was perfectly adequate and the other was her favourite mug with the ducks on it. She was naturally inclined to give the duck one to herself but she was trying to be nice so she should give it to Morag Senior *but* Morag Senior would instantly know what the gesture meant and thus it would be crass and obvious.

Morag Senior walked in, scooped up the duck cup and sat at the fold-leaf table to eat her toast.

"Helped yourself to my wardrobe, huh?" she said, nodding at Junior's clothes.

Junior bit back the reply that they were her clothes too.

"I couldn't wear yesterday's clothes."

Senior nodded.

"True. But I don't think I'm happy about it though. You need your own clothes."

Steve the Destroyer ran along the counter, a chopstick held overhead like a spear and tried to impale Junior's hand as it rested on the counter. The chopstick bounced off Junior's skin. The force knocked Steve the Destroyer from his feet but he came up in a fighting stance.

"Stop it," she said.

"You will suffer the death of a thousand blows, gobbet!" he squeaked.

"That was a poke, not a blow."

"The death of a thousand pokes!"

Junior picked him up, put him in the microwave and closed the door.

"Today, you can sort out my clothes," said Senior.

"You're giving me chores?" said Junior.

"You have other plans? Get all the laundry done and then make two equal piles. One for you, one for me."

"And then you pick which one you want when you come home. Sounds fair. You want me to cook dinner too?"

"I've tasted our cooking," said Senior. "Besides, I've got dinner with Cameron tonight. But if you're having the day off work, you could do some other jobs."

"Like what?"

Senior looked at her. "You're me. You know what needs doing."

"We need to buy some new towels. And there's that art print in the shop you fancied."

"You're picking jobs from the nice end of the list there."

"I could change the bedsheets. You hate doing duvets."

Senior shook her head.

"What then?"

"We promised Richard we'd help him with his jigsaw."

"God, no."

"You told him it was an intellectual challenge and, I quote, 'I'd love to help finish it'."

"Do I have to?"

"And, on top of that, we've been promising to –"

"No. Not that," said Junior loudly and forcefully.

"You don't know what I was going to say."

"I'm not doing it."

"Mrs Atraxas lives upstairs all by herself."

"Don't care."

"And when did we last go round for a coffee?"

"That stuff's not coffee."

"It's just a drink and –"

"A million photos of her cats in knitted bonnets."

"Yes. Take a bullet for the team."

Junior bit her toast miserably. She opened the microwave and released Steve the cuddly Destroyer.

"Kill me now, Steve."

The doll did a little dance of glee and went off in search of weaponry.

Rod and Vivian sat in traffic in one of the Queensway tunnels. Attempting to drive from the Library of Birmingham out to the housing estates of south Birmingham during morning rush hour was an almost pointless exercise. They now sat in the green-grey light of the tunnels, breathing the fumes of all the other vehicles in the two-lane queue.

If Rod had his way, they wouldn't be there at all. Mr Canal-Bike had called the police with further tales of bicycles mangled by canalside predators. Rod was happy to ignore such time-wasters. Vivian, however, was quick to remind him that aquatic incursions fell under the response team's specific remit and they were obliged to attend. Rod had told her that she was welcome to attend. Vivian had assured him that she would do so, and then insisted that he drive her there so she could read *en route*.

"Look at this," said Rod, gesturing to the traffic.

Vivian looked.

"Yes," she said and returned to her papers. Traffic jams were none of her concern. They merely gave her more time to read.

Rod tried some meditative breathing. In through the nose, out through the mouth.

"Stop that," said Vivian.

"Breathing?"

"Breathing like that."

Rod grimaced and held his tongue.

"You know, perhaps I shouldn't even be driving or owt with this arm," he said, gesturing to the dressings invisible beneath his shirt and jacket sleeve. "That *Dinh'r* near had my arm off."

Vivian regarded the arm in question.

"Did the doctor say you could not drive?"

"Not as such."

"No."

The car in front inched forward a fraction. Rod inched forward too. His thoughts were now on doctors, one doctor in particular.

"I'm meeting someone for drinks later."

"Yes?" said Vivian, uninterested.

"I'm wondering what to wear."

Vivian lowered her papers. "Are you likely to spill some?"

"That's not what I..." He shook his head. "I'm wondering what I'm meant to wear if I'm meeting someone. I dress smartly for work."

"I approve."

"But I can't just dress smartly again. That's just me turning up in my work clothes."

"But you have more than one suit, do you not?"

"Four. Three for work and one for funerals. I'm not wearing my funeral suit. That would send out the wrong signals. Vivian…" He paused, knowing he was heading into dangerous territory. "If you were meeting someone, a man, for a date, what would you want him to wear?"

"I do not date, Rod. I have never dated. Nasty American invention. In my day, one had dinner or met in some other social situation. There was no need for a special word for it."

"Yes, but when you went out with Mr Grey, back when, you know…"

"When he was alive, Rod. Yes. Don't be coy. I do know he's dead. There is no need to break it to me gently."

"But what did he wear?"

"He wore the clothes I bought him."

"And those were?"

"Suit trousers, jacket and a shirt."

"No tie?"

"It depended on the social event."

"So maybe I should just take my tie off," he said and then sighed. "I think what I'm meant to wear is smart casual."

Rod's phone, tucked into the satnav holder on the dashboard, rang. Rod tapped the answer icon. "Campbell."

"Hi bab, it's Lois," said the office receptionist on speaker. "Are you at the call in Aston?"

"Stuck on the A38," said Rod. "So, no."

"Are you close to Ludgate Hill?"

"By the canal?" They were only twenty yards from the tunnel exit and the slip road that could take them off via Livery Street towards the Jewellery Quarter. "Very close. If we can get out of this traffic."

"The police need back up with an incident, a Mammonite caught trying to kidnap a local."

"We can probably be there in ten minutes."

"I'll let them know you're coming."

"Ta."

The call dropped. Rod inched forward again even though the car in front hadn't moved.

"What is smart casual?" he said.

"An oxymoron," said Vivian, "and an abomination."

The number 6 bus took Ray from Shirley up the Stratford Road to the city. Ray sat on the upper deck and read his Venislarn primer.

"*Skeidl hraim yeg courxean. Oyo-map-ehu merishimsha meren'froi.* Do not kill me, honoured friend. I was only admiring your beauty. *Meren'froi. Meren'froi.*"

He rolled the alien word around in his mouth and ignored whatever glances the other early commuters threw his way. The lone wolf did not care for the opinions of sheep. A girl across the aisle watched him. Ray reckoned she was a five, maybe a six. She was giving him filthy looks. He knew what she wanted. *Dream on, girl*, he thought.

In his briefcase, Ray had a folded map of the city on which he had crossed off the streets he'd already covered. When he'd first started this sales racket, he'd worked his way up the Stratford Road, through Hall Green, Sparkhill, Sparkbrook and into the city centre via Deritend and Digbeth. From there he'd experimentally branched out into different areas. He quickly found that although it was quicker to cover the cheaper areas of town (in tower blocks, it was less than five seconds from one door to the next), he'd convert more knocks to sales in wealthier areas. Ray was peddling an offer that was too good to be true and the wealthy were likelier to fall for it. They spent their lives expecting something for nothing, why should it be any different with their phone and broadband?

Today, Ray continued to work his way through the big old houses where Edgbaston ran up against the ring road and Five Ways. The first knock of the day was always the hardest. A salesman didn't get a chance to warm up; he had to hit the ground running. As he crunched up the short gravel drive, he reminded himself: he was the early bird, the cautious mouse, top dog, a lone wolf. Frankly, Ray was a lot of animals. He didn't have to settle for just one.

Knock, knock.

The man holding the slice of toast who answered the door was young, perhaps only a handful of years older than Ray. Good. The young and wealthy were the best marks of all. The young thought they had a handle on the world and were immune from tricksters and con artists. Not that Ray was a con artist, he delivered exactly what he promised. The terms and conditions were quite precise.

"Good morning, mate. And it is a good morning, isn't it? Tell me, are you happy with your current broadband provider?"

"We've got Sky," said the man, already closing the door and putting the toast to his mouth.

"Because I can get your telephone and broadband down to a fiver a month," said Ray quickly.

The door stopped.

"Five pounds?" said the man.

"Five pounds, mate," said Ray. "Five of your English pounds."

"For both?"

"For both."

"Everything?"

"Everything." Ray brought his clipboard round to show him. "I can show you the details, all protected by the Direct Debit Guarantee. You can cancel at any time."

"And it will only cost me a fiver?"

"And maybe your soul," said Ray and laughed because it was funny.

"What am I supposed to do?" said Vaughn Sitterson.

Morag Senior looked up from the text alert on her phone and gave the consular chief a blankly enquiring look but it was a pointless gesture. Vaughn never looked at her face. He'd probably struggle to pick her out of a line-up. He could never be called to identify her corpse if the Venislarn eventually killed her.

"We have a foreign office representative in the restricted ward who screams constantly when he's not sedated," said Sitterson, flicking between windows on his computer. "We have all manner of topological irregularities in the Vault. And we still have a case to answer to the ministry for that nasty business with Ingrid Spence and the release of *Zildrohar-Cqulu*."

"I'm sure they've got spare bods they can send up here when they want that case answering."

"Are you making light of what happened yesterday?"

"No," said Morag, feeling in her voice a tone halfway between cheery indifference and indignation. "I am acutely aware that our ministerial overlords sent us a public school dweeb whose ignorance, arrogance and sense of entitlement were the primary causes of an incident *in which nobody died*."

"But the fact that he was even able to break such a hazardous artefact –"

"One we collected only this month – one among several artefacts that seem to have randomly appeared in the city recently – and which no one has been able to properly assess or catalogue. And that would be an issue for the new tech support person, wouldn't it?"

Vaughn made a thoughtful noise, toyed with a pen and looked at his computer screen.

"Am I being fired?" asked Morag.

"Of course not," said Vaughn at once.

"Am I being formally disciplined?"

His eyes moved towards her but his gaze skirted her face at the last moment. The man was being an absolute flirt.

"Let's consider this an informal formal warning, shall we?"

"Very good, sir."

Morag stood and left, pausing only at the door to glance back at her boss – just to see if he dared look at another human when their back was turned. Not today.

She looked at the text. It was from Cameron.

TRAIN ARRIVING AT NEW STREET STATION. 7:10PM. DINNER PLANS?

The customer filled out the paperwork on the doorstep. He didn't invite Ray in. People almost never invited him in, even when they were buying. The customer – Edward Winters, 36 Harborne Road, B15 3DH, mainly uses internet for streaming television, doesn't use the landline phone at all – let Ray stand on the driveway while filling in the forms and eating his toast. Ray didn't know if people didn't invite salesmen in at all or whether it was just him. He had noticed the way some had looked at his face, his scars, with involuntary but unmistakeable revulsion. Many refused to shake his hand, even when the deal was done. Of course, the looks he got from women were something else. Some of those cougars and stay-at-home milfs, they were just itching to drag him inside, to –

"What's this bit?" said Ed, flipping to the next page which had an intricate printed border and a hologram sticker in the top corner. "*Kaha-aid lo…ax…rid…?*"

"*Kaha-aid loaxridi kurm-rhovi chedian.* It's all just legal speak, mate. There's a plain English version underneath." He craned forward as though to read it, even though he knew every word. "You need to sign this document to get your discount. It allows my company to offer you a reduced rate in exchange for key intangibles –"

"Sure, sure," said Ed, already signing.

"And you've got to sign again at the bottom, there and there, to indicate that you agree to the terms and conditions of the sale and have freely consented to the sale in full knowledge that –"

"Done," said Ed and passed the clipboard back to Ray.

"Thank you," said Ray. He tore off the relevant carbon copies and information sheets and passed them back to Ed. "You'll receive a new router in the post in the next three to five business days and can make the switch over from then."

"Great," said Ed and shut the door.

Ray walked back to the pavement and, leaning his briefcase against the brick and wrought iron wall at the edge of the property, sorted the broadband paper work and the 'intangibles' certificate into separate folders. There were fifty completed certificates in the folder. Nearly enough to make some purchases and pay off some debts at the bank.

"Onwards and upwards," he told himself and, with a click of the briefcase catches, he continued up the Harborne Road.

Rod parked on Ludgate Hill and looked up at the apartment block.

"I've been here before."

Vivian paid him no mind and walked past the police car parked at the entrance. Rod followed, as Vivian mounted the stairs. On the fourth-floor landing, two police officers casually blocked access to the top floor. She presented her identification and led the way through.

"If you need us to slap him in cuffs, just say," called one of the cops after them. "Another couple of lads are in the flat."

The Mammonite was on the fifth floor, standing outside a flat door. He had a sharp suit, a clipboard and a bright smile that was a few degrees skewed out of normal. He looked like a badly photocopied car salesman.

"Who are you?" he said.

"We are from the consular mission. I am Mrs Grey. This is Mr Campbell."

"I expect better co-operation than this."

"Than what?"

"Mammon-Mammonson Investments does not expect to have its employees' valuable and billable time wasted."

"We have yet to see whose time is being wasted," said Vivian. "I can assure you, I too have better things to do."

"I know this flat," said Rod.

"Yes. Thank you for your idle reminiscences, Rod," said Vivian.

The Mammonite passed her a sheaf of official looking paperwork. "It's all there. Black and white."

Rod knocked on the door. "Annie?"

The door opened immediately. The detective inside looked Rod up and down and let him in.

Annie hadn't gotten much further with unpacking her boxes since he was here on Monday, but she had escalated her attack on the rotten prawn smell. The air was now a malodorous riot of scented air fresheners, plug-in aromatherapy diffusers, perfumed candles and patchouli body spray.

Annie sat on the sofa, her face the pink and white marble of a woman who had cried herself out some time ago.

"Hi Annie," he said.

Her face lit up as she recognised him. It was pitiful really.

"Detective Campbell..." she said.

"I'm not with the police, remember?"

"I don't know what's going on," she said miserably.

"We'll find out," he reassured her. "Whatever's going on, we'll get to the bottom of it and straighten it out, all right?"

Annie sniffled and dabbed her nose with a wadded tissue.

"Thanks for calling us in," Rod said to the detectives.

The women looked at each other and then at him.

"We didn't call you," said the older one.

"No," said Vivian, entering the flat with a single sheet of browning, parchment-like card in her hand. "Mr Watts-Mammonson called us. To help retrieve his rightful property."

Vivian looked at Annie. Annie put the tissue to her mouth.

In the flat, Morag Junior put Steve the Destroyer on sock sorting duty.

She would have cursed her other self for allowing a two-and-a-bit week backlog of laundry to build up but who could she blame but herself? One load was washed and dried, a second load on a rinse cycle. Meanwhile, she began the sorting of clothes and shoes to be divided between the two Morags. It was an exercise in personal psychology. Clothes she didn't think she had any affection for took on new meaning. Even the placing of a vest top or a pair of knickers on one of the two piles tipped its favourability one way or the other. This pile got the cheap but beautiful top from New Look. This pile got the slobby fleece that she simply loved lounging around in.

"This sock has no partner," said Steve, emerging from beneath the clothes pile with a grey ankle sock.

"There's some other grey ones there," said Junior.

"The weaves of the cuffs do not match."

"It's close enough."

"No. No. It will not do!"

"Is the entire entourage of *Prein* OCD?"

"The cuffs do not match!" declared the rag doll passionately and dived back under.

The world was bent in mysterious ways. As an initiate into the great secrets of the world, Jeffney Ray knew this.

An innocent canal boater or bargee could take their craft out from Birmingham city centre and after negotiating the steep set of locks that ran behind the BT Tower cut down through the relatively short Warwick and Birmingham Junction canal and not see anything more remarkable than an abandoned warehouse or a pair of nesting geese. Yet, at the same time, a person who could find this hidden alleyway or make a shortcut through that particular building, would come out onto the towpaths of a Warwick and Birmingham canal that teemed with Venislarn life.

Ray might have been a player but he trod carefully along the side of The Waters. Large unblinking eyes watched him from behind boarded up windows, from hidden eyries and from just below the surface of the water. The *samakha* were subtle and unhurried creatures but that didn't make them cowards. Ray had heard more than one story of a human who had stepped too close to the canal or a dark doorway and a powerful, webbed hand had silently pulled them in, never to be seen again.

Like fifties B-movie monsters, the *samakha* had a fondness for human women. Bedraggled girls in mouldy leggings or tattered skirts were the only figures in full view this morning, carrying their shopping in homemade string bags or dragging their ugly and scaly offspring behind them. At some point, each of them had probably been pretty, and happy to legally sign herself over to the fish-men. That all changed soon enough. Ray didn't have a girlfriend – he hadn't yet decided on which lucky girl he would bestow that honour – but he wouldn't touch one of these stinking fish-wives. Not unless she really wanted him to.

The buildings on either side of The Waters were covered in ad hoc extensions; roof gardens, wood-made balcony flats and rickety rope bridges sprouted out like fungal growths. Most of the locals lived in the damp vertical shanty town. To occupy an actual bricks and mortar building was to hold considerable status.

Ray crossed one of the more stable bridges – The Waters was no ordinary canal: gods swam in its bottomless depths – and approached a doorway above which a neon sign fizzed and crackled dangerously.

Ray guessed that the tables in this café had been ripped out of some human takeaway shop during a refurb. Now, full of damp, they were swollen and warped, their chipboard undersides slowly disintegrating. Behind a glass counter, southern fried chicken pieces and congealed slices of pizza sat beside raw and anatomical *samakha* delicacies. The half-breed proprietor prepared foods behind the counter, paring kebab slices off the rotisserie and then dissecting some unidentified green crustacean with the same knife. The place stank of wood rot and shellfish. It was a classy joint by The Waters standards.

Tony T and his lieutenant, Death Roe, were the only customers in the café.

"Wassup Tony," said Ray. *"Yo-cyo l'eaufin sheem-pika, oy?"*

Death Roe snorted Pepsi Max out his gills.

"What's that you say?" said Tony T, not looking up from his bowl of Rice Krispies.

"I said, wassup, Tony," said Ray.

"You said, *'Yo-cyo'. Yo-cyo?"*

Death Roe gave a 'ggh!' of a gill gasp. "Does Tony look like a bitch to you?" he asked, his dangling barbels quivering.

Damn! Venislarn female pronouns! Ray thought quickly.

"Yo... Yoth-cyo..."

"Adn-bhul makin' it worse, dog," said Tony. "Sit."

Tony T was the leader of the Waters Crew. He and his boys were all half-human. The Waters Crew was the most influential of the *samakha* gangs, bad boys with baseball caps on their fish heads, flick knives down their codpieces and spinning rims on their pimped-up coracles. They didn't have any real power on The Waters. It wasn't even that the true *samakha* and their god-father, *Daganau-Pysh*, tolerated their antics. The true *samakha* didn't understand the Waters Crew's wannabe gangster antics. As far as they understood, the gangster boys were just kids playing at being human.

"Have you got the goods, Tony?" said Ray, taking a seat.

Death Roe put a tatty carrier bag on the table. Its loose contents settled and threatened to roll out. Tony T took out a dried brown casing the size and shape of a tennis ball.

"Don't know what the *bhul* you want 'em for. These eggs are dead," he said.

"Then I'm sure you won't want much for them."

Tony T tried to give him a shrewd and suspicious look but it was a hard look to pull off with eyes four inches across and no eyebrows.

"Either you're a dumb *zek'ee* an' I should just toss your ass in the canal or you're up to something. Ggh! What you want them for?"

Play it cool, Ray, he told himself.

"Are you selling, mate, or do you want my life story?" he said.

Tony T threw his spoon down in the bowl. Death Roe casually pulled out an angler's knife.

Ray opened his briefcase and took out the certificates he'd got signed that morning.

"Soul cash?" said Tony T. "What do I want with that? Ggh!"

"It's hard currency," said Ray.

"Don't need it, dog. I got bitches I own, body and soul. I don't need more. You – ggh! – you know what I want."

"What you want, I can't get," said Ray.

"Some *adn-bhul* fixit man you are," sneered Tony.

"Oh, you misunderstand. I could get you the tickets to Gorgons Gentlemen's Club. I could get you a private booth with a pre-paid dance from the hottest girls. But they'd turn you away at the door. They do have a dress code."

"I can buy shoes," said Tony.

"I think the dress code probably includes no fish."

"That's racist *muda*," said Death Roe.

"*Bhul*. It's like MLK – ggh! – never happened, man," said Tony. "You're wasting our time, *crik'hu-chat*."

Death Roe pressed the point of his knife against Ray's inner thigh. One short stab and Ray would bleed to death all over this stinking café. He laughed. (Not nervously, no.) He laughed to show he wasn't afraid.

His mouth had gone dry. He turned to the guy at the counter. "A bottle of Boost, mate."

"No Boost," said the proprietor thickly. "Pepsi?"

"Whatever," said Ray. "As long as it's sealed and you've not touched it."

The proprietor slouched over to the chiller unit on feet that flapped like flippers.

"Now, what I can give you..." said Ray, dipping back into his briefcase. "A choice." He held out an envelope in one hand and a slim box in the other. He looked pointedly at the knife against his leg. Death Roe withdrew it slowly. "A choice. Tickets to a Broad Street night club that has very low lighting and no dress code, plus some two-for-one vouchers for fishbowl cocktails."

Death Roe twitched. The big guy was interested.

"Or a couple of the latest Samsung phones," said Ray.

"They the ones that *adn-bhul* explode?" said Tony.

"Yes, they are."

"You trying to sell me defective shit?"

Ray shrugged. "There aren't many guys who have the balls to use a live hand grenade as a mobile phone."

Tony T laughed: a wet honk, like a goose drowning at the bottom of his wide, piscine throat.

Death Roe pushed the bag of eggs across the table to Ray.

Annie gave a whimper of fear when Vivian invited the Mammonite into the flat.

"Please contain yourself, Miss Castleton," said Vivian.

"I have a gag somewhere," offered Watts-Mammonson.

"You stay right there," said Rod, shifting his stance to emphasise his position between the Mammonite and the terrified woman.

Watts-Mammonson raised a phone and took a photo.

"Your name," he said to Rod curtly.

Rod opened his mouth to give it but Vivian spoke first.

"His name is not germane to this matter," she said. "We are here only to discuss the contract you have with this woman."

"Contract?" said Annie.

Vivian presented her with the parchment-coloured card. It was covered in dense legalese text. There was a hologram sticker in the corner.

"Is that your signature on the bottom?" she asked.

Annie stared at the document.

"There is no doubt regarding the signature," said Watts-Mammonson. "We don't make mistakes."

Rod scoffed and made sure the Mammonite caught his eye as he did. However, he'd already spotted the sheen on the signatures on the document. There was a constrained restlessness in the ink, like a Magic Eye picture aching to pop into existence. No, there'd been no mistake.

"What is this?" said Annie.

"A bill of sale for key intangibles," said Watts-Mammonson.

"Key...?"

"Your soul," said Rod.

"My soul? But this was just some terms and conditions thing," said Annie, her voice fading. "I didn't know..."

Watts-Mammonson stepped forward to point at the document. Rod turned his whole body – and it was a considerable body – to block him.

"Touch me and bad things will happen," the Mammonite snapped before shaking his finger at the contract. "Annie Castleton has signed to say she has made a sale in full knowledge of what she has signed up for and that she understands all aspects of the terms of our agreement."

"I just signed it," said Annie. "The man said I needed to, in order to get my discount."

"Discount?" said Rod. "What man?"

"Mr Watts-Mammonson," said Vivian, "are you aware of the Consular Conventions on Trade and Exchanges?"

"I am."

"We have a clear process of interviews, consultation, assessment and counselling of any individual who wishes to sell their body and slash or soul to another."

"It is very clear," said Watts-Mammonson. "Admirably transparent."

"Thank you. This woman has not been given access to any of the above. She is not on our records."

"No," the Mammonite agreed. "But the convention is merely a convention. It is not legally binding."

"No," Vivian conceded, "but if this woman signed the agreement with a registered human agent then they themselves have to agree to abide by our conventions."

"And that's an issue for you and the human agent. I'm merely in retrievals, Mrs Grey." The Mammonite smiled smugly. Mammonites did smug well. A smug smile on this one made him look like a toad who had caught all the flies.

"This is legally binding?" Rod asked Vivian.

"It is," she said.

"But I didn't know," Annie pleaded. "I don't understand."

"But you signed to say you did understand," said Vivian.

"But I didn't understand that bit either. I didn't read it."

"Ignorance is no excuse," said Watts-Mammonson.

"Come on," said one of the detectives. "We all do it. Click next, next, next, accept terms and conditions."

The Mammonite gave the detective a most curious look, disdainful yet avaricious. The creature's fingers twitched over its clipboard as though it longed to get the detective's signature on a contract there and then.

"Okay," said Rod. "Is there anything we can do to resolve this? Vivian?"

"It's entirely legal and above board," she replied. "Our best hope is to take it up with Ms Castleton's creditor, Mammon-Mammonson Investments."

"I'll be heading back there once I've got this one in the van. I'll be full up then," said Watts-Mammonson.

"Van?" said Annie.

"Full?" said Rod.

Nina did a drum tattoo on the edge of Morag Senior's office desk and blew an imaginary trumpet.

"Black Barge!"

Morag looked at her. "Um...?"

Nina blew her pretend trumpet again and even did some finger wiggling.

"Black Barge!"

"Ye-es. You said."

"Just heard it's arriving today," said Nina.

Morag turned to Nina.

"Yes. Now, either you're referring to some racially-dubious form of Sumo wrestling or –"

"It's the Black Barge. It's here. Didn't you have Black Barge up in Scotland?"

"Clearly not."

"Oh," said Nina, surprised. "Well, it's this barge and it's black."

"Yes, I had decoded that aspect of the name."

"And it turns up, whenever it likes, to resupply and trade at the canalside. Usually once or twice a year."

"Ah, okay. We had the Penury Market. Maybe a similar thing. And whose barge is it?"

Nina opened the fruit salad Morag was going to have for lunch and stole one of the grapes.

"It's dedicated to *Yoth-Qahake-Pysh*, Goddess of the Deep. The barge comes with *Yo-Morgantus'* permission but it isn't under his jurisdiction."

"Like an embassy?"

148

"Perhaps. It means that local chancers and bell-ends flock to it in the hope of buying items that are strictly non-legit."

Morag gave this some thought.

"You want to go down there and try to bust Professor Sheikh Omar for buying illegal shit," she said.

Nina gave her a spooky look and waved her hands in a witchy fashion.

"Psychic! It's true what they say about the gingers: cursed and blessed in equal measure." She grinned. "Also, there's a nice pub near to where it moors up and we can probably put the drinks on expenses."

Watts-Mammonson flung open the rear doors of the nondescript van he had parked outside the apartment block. One of the detectives swore colourfully.

The interior of the van had been partitioned into cages, ten of them, and all but one of them were occupied. In spaces that were too narrow to sit in and too short to stand in, men and women squatted in shackles. They were of various ages and a range of ethnicities, almost as though he was aiming for demographic diversity. Some were in their night clothes, one was in a business suit, another in his lollipop man jacket. All were gagged, but that didn't stop them crying out and pleading wordlessly.

"Oh, God," said Annie.

"Get them out," said the detective.

"Be quiet," said Vivian.

"Get them out! Now!"

Watts-Mammonson bristled. Vivian was sure the Mammonite carried a weapon about him somewhere and would use it if he was prevented from carrying out his lawful business.

Vivian turned on the detective. "You will be silent or you will leave."

Rod stepped in. "This is above our pay grade, yours and mine," he said calmly to the detective and, by extension, to all the police officers. "Let's give them some space while Vivian deals with this."

Rod ushered them back a few paces. Vivian had little respect for Rod's skills beyond the merely practical but he seemed to have the common touch with a certain type of person. It might be his background as soldier of the lower ranks. It might be his unsophisticated northern manner. She neither knew nor really cared, so long as the big lummox stopped the police officers from doing anything foolish.

"The paperwork's all here," said Watts-Mammonson. "You're free to check it."

"I shall," said Vivian. "I will take copies of it all when we are back at your office. We will follow you there."

Watts-Mammonson shrugged. It was an odd-looking gesture, as though his shoulders weren't quite in the right place.

"We'll just get this one loaded up."

With snake-strike speed, Watts-Mammonson grabbed Annie's wrist and pulled her towards the last cage. She shrieked.

"Don't let him do this!"

"You will need to comply, Miss Castleton," said Vivian firmly. "For the time being."

"No!"

Clothed though he might have been in a human body, the Mammonite was much more powerful than Annie and a palm to her stomach lifted her up bodily into the van and the cage. Annie screamed.

"Fuck's sake," muttered one of the police, sickened.

"It's okay, Annie," said Rod, which Vivian knew to be a pointless and bare-faced lie. "We'll do all we can."

Watts-Mammonson effortlessly tucked her kicking feet into the cage and closed the grille.

"Bastard!" the woman screamed. The scream was utterly cut off by the shutting of the door. The soundproofing was more than good; it was uncanny.

Watts-Mammonson inspected a scratch that had appeared on the back of his hand.

Vivian turned to Rod. "We will accompany Mr Watts-Mammonson to his offices. We will need to discover who has duped all these foolish people."

"You don't think it's these guys?" he said, jerking an angry thumb at the Mammonite.

"No," said Vivian. "This all seems too... dishonest. The Mammonites are many things but they are truthful in their dealings."

Watts-Mammonson held his phone over his scratched hand and took a picture.

"I will need the pair of you to sign statements," he said.

"What for?" said Rod.

"There's a claim to be made. You witnessed that woman assaulting me."

"As you forced her into your van," Rod pointed out coldly.

"Our staff should never have to tolerate abuse from clients or property."

"Can you believe this bastard?" muttered Rod.

"Yes, I can," said Vivian.

"You're not coming with me," said Morag Junior.

"But it is dark in there," said Steve the Destroyer. "I do not like it."

"It's better than what I'm going to have to put myself through. Trust me."

"You are a *shat-qoi* fiend, fleshlet!"

"Look, there's half a garibaldi in there. You can have that while I'm gone."

"What is garibaldi?"

Junior popped the doll in the biscuit tin, sealed the lid tightly and with the heavy heart of a woman going to the gallows, walked upstairs to the second floor and flat three, the home of Mrs Atraxas. Mrs Atraxas was just an old woman, perfectly harmless and hospitable. At the same time, having spent too long in her own company and that of her cats, she was sufficiently peculiar that, before meeting her, Morag had been convinced she had a Venislarn god for an upstairs neighbour. Morag had, in truth, put off this neighbourly visit far too long but that didn't stop Morag Junior despising Morag Senior for putting it on today's to-do list.

A huge black log of a cat by the name of Pascal lay across the landing in front of the door to flat three. He opened one evil eye and within the mass of black fur, white claws slowly slid out.

Junior realised she should have worn her knee-length boots and immediately wondered if she'd put them on the right clothes pile.

Junior leaned over Pascal, slowly, gingerly, treating the beast like a furry landmine and knocked. There was a shuffle and a series of clumps from within and then the door was opened by a short, lopsided thing with a head that looked like a giant, polished walnut surmounted by a pile of white cotton-wool.

"Yes?" said Mrs Atraxas.

"It's me, Morag. From downstairs."

The woman had to crane her neck up just to meet Junior's eye.

"You have come for the hair cutting."

"No, Mrs Atraxas. Morag. From downstairs."

"Ah. You'll be wanting to come in for a drink." Mrs Atraxas's somewhat unplaceable European accent made the sentence sound like an exercise in grammatical mutilation.

"A coffee would be lovely," said Junior.

"I do coffee," said Mrs Atraxas.

"That's fine."

"I don't do tea."

"Okay."

"I don't understand it."

"Of course."

The old woman wheeled around, pivoting on her walking stick, and led the way into a fusty flat carpeted entirely in cat. Junior eyed Pascal cautiously as she stepped over and followed.

Jeffney Ray arrived at Gas Street Basin shortly before the Black Barge. The canals leading into Gas Street Basin were a world away from the grim squalor of The Waters. As part of Birmingham's endless transformation, there had been a spate of redevelopment along the basin in the past couple of decades. New buildings had gone up, old buildings had been refurbished and dour waterside pubs had been abruptly designated as listed buildings and imbued with a hitherto non-existent historical importance and charm. Now, the towpath from Broad Street to the Cube was crowded with bars, gentlemen's clubs, restaurants and sandwich shops which Ray could not afford to frequent.

Ray wasn't interested in such things. He was interested in a short spur of canal across the water, one which was only accessible on foot via a narrow wrought-iron bridge. As he crossed, Ray could see the Black Barge emerging from the Broad Street tunnel.

The sight of the Black Barge sent a shiver of excitement through Ray. He might tell himself – and rightly so! – that he was a major contender, an occult force to be reckoned with, but sometimes he felt a nagging doubt: a sense of inferiority, that he was nothing but a stupid young man who still lived with his mum and that all *this* – the soul cash trading, the deals with Venislarn – was just the antics of a toddler paddling around in the shallows of a huge murky pool. The appearance of the Black Barge – invisible to the eyes of many, a mystery to all but a few – proved that Ray was one of the big boys, a true player.

At a distance, the Black Barge looked like any other boat on the canal. Closer to, it revealed itself to be a drab soot-grey: neither the true black of its name nor jauntily painted like many of the touring barges that moored up at Gas Street. Closer still, and its alien origins became obvious. The beams and uprights around the windows were of no ordinary wood. They looked organic, excreted rather than cut, as if they had been regurgitated layer-by-layer by some nest-building insect. And the windows themselves were translucent but not transparent, as though they were made of paper or a rough membrane.

As the barge drew up to the towpath, Ray observed other parties moving in. A redheaded couple strolled slowly towards the barge. A bundle of sticks in the shadow of a wall unfolded into a spindle-limbed *presz'ling*. Something mostly without form pressed itself against a window in the building on top of the Broad Street tunnel and peered down. Ray hung back a little – the early bird catches the worm but the second mouse gets the cheese – and waited for the right moment to go aboard and inspect the wares.

153

The bargemaster, a fat slug of a man dressed in little but dirt and leathers (and the fine chain that bound his ankle to the boat), stepped onto the towpath. A tall, willowy figure followed him. This wasn't one of the crew, Ray could see that. A paying passenger then. The figure's pale, sand-coloured robes hung about it, crisp and mottled like autumn leaves. Its bald head was as white as candle wax. The creature's hands, white too, were stained black at the fingertips. The overall impression was of such frailty that Ray was about to dismiss him as some old and useless git, and then he saw the thing's forehead and the mark upon it, a brand-like indentation in waxy flesh.

Ray shivered with sudden recognition.

"Fuck," he whispered.

"You talking to me?" said a man who happened to be passing.

Ray looked at the guy in the broad-brimmed hat. He was another dealer. Strange Ken or Mystic Trevor or some name like that.

"You know who that is?" said Ray, gesturing subtly at the robed figure now walking slowly along the towpath.

Mystic Trevor (or was it Magic Ian?) squinted. "No."

"Oh. Me neither," said Ray with his best smile.

"Fucktard," said the dealer and moved on.

Ray hadn't told the man because knowledge had value and shouldn't be shared for free. But he could have told him. He could have said, "that there is a *be'ae tyez*, one of the Carcosan word mages, the most powerful casters in existence. And he's here in Birmingham."

Ray moved out of the way as the *be'ae tyez* shuffled close. Ray looked aside and bowed his head. The creature's dry, dusty stink filled his nostrils

Ray held his breath and wondered what he could gain from this new knowledge.

Mammon-Mammonson Investments occupied a six-storey cuboid building of white stone on Great Charles Street, in that slice of city centre that had once been the city's pounding financial heart and was now little more than a high-rise buffer between the New Street shopping area and the A38 dual carriageway that split the city from north to south.

Rod followed Watts-Mammonson's van down a steep ramp into a basement car park. Rod wasn't a big car fan – in his book, the pinnacle of vehicle design began and ended with the British Army Land Rover – but he could recognise the level of wealth on display in these parking bays. It wasn't a large car park but it possibly had the highest cash value of contents of any in the city.

"Gaudy, isn't it?" said Vivian, giving an Aston Martin a critical sneer.

"Aye," said Rod.

"Vulgar," she said.

"Oh, aye."

"I wonder what it's like to drive one."

The van pulled up just beyond a well-lit set of automatic doors. Three Mammonites stood waiting in a perfectly spaced line, hands at their sides, like the dullest mannequins at a gentleman's outfitters.

"This will be for us," said Vivian. "Watts-Mammonson will have called ahead."

They stopped and got out. The middle suit gave them a big smile. Whatever discrepancy there was in the Mammonite attempts to mimic humans, it was only made worse when they smiled. This one looked like the victim of a botched teeth-whitening procedure.

"Mrs Vivian Grey," he said, as though greeting an old friend. "And Mr Rod Campbell. Welcome. Welcome. Strong, manly shake you have there, Rod. I've been appointed to show you around and service your needs."

"Is that so?" said Rod.

"My card." He whipped a business card from his top pocket and passed it to Rod:

TRUMAN LODGE-MAMMONSON
MAMMON-MAMMONSON INVESTMENTS
GREAT CHARLES STREET, BIRMINGHAM

The card had a surprising weight to it.

"It's nice, isn't it?" said Lodge-Mammonson. "Have them made by a little artisanal printer in Milan."

"Right," said Rod, turning the card over.

"That font is Silian Rail."

Rod ran his finger over the metallic border. "Is that...?"

"Gold, yes," said the Mammonite matter-of-factly. "Just a microplating but it makes it look classy. Sharp. Don't you think? Chet here will park your... vehicle."

Rod held out his keys to the Mammonite. Chet looked at them like he was being offered a severed head but took them anyway.

"Come on in," said Lodge-Mammonson with a head jiggle. "Let me give you both the grand tour."

"We are purely interested in the humans you have captured," said Vivian.

"Ah," said Lodge-Mammonson with a wave of a finger. "Collected. Don't worry, we'll get to them soon enough." He beckoned them into a lift of glass and mirrors. "But let's go see where the magic happens."

The lift took them up to the first floor.

"Up until 1987 and the computerisation of all trading in the United Kingdom, this building was home to the Birmingham Stock Exchange," said Lodge-Mammonson. "Stocks and shares in the armouries and engineering works on which Birmingham was built were traded here. We at Mammon-Mammonson Investments have great respect for history and felt that nowhere else would do for our corporate headquarters."

The first floor was one enormous office area. A screen filling the far wall crawled with the esoteric codes and numbers of financial data. The outer spaces by the tall windows were lined with desks and computer screens at which sat Mammonites in pin stripes, ugly ties and those shirt sleeve armbands (that Rod had never seen on anyone but croupiers and steampunks). The room buzzed with a dozen conversations. It was, Rod guessed, no different from the workspace of any financial institution – apart from the enormous mosaic of *Yoth Mammon* set within a ritual magic circle that spanned much of the floor, of course.

"Wow," said Rod. "That's... vivid. A lot of red and pink and..."

"It's a mostly stylised depiction of our holy mother. It's hard to truly encompass her scale."

"Yeah, and those teeth..."

"The green marble hardly does them justice," said Lodge-Mammonson. "But it's a constant reminder of why we're here." He gestured onward. "We trade in stocks, shares and international currencies for her greater glory, *schluri'o bento frei*. The very lifeblood of the world's economy flows through here. It's a great honour, for us all and for me personally, to serve our mother and help build this great nation we live in."

Rod waved his hand at all the machines.

"But what do you actually do?" he said.

"We buy and sell. We invest. Without the kinds of financial services we offer, businesses wouldn't have the capacity to expand and grow."

"Gotcha," he said, nodding. "You're like a bank, lending people money."

"Well, no," said Lodge-Mammonson. "Although we have loan arrangements with some individuals and do trade in bonds, we are not a lending bank."

"A building society then."

"No. We invest. We buy up companies, or shares in them."

"And do what?"

"Do?"

"Once you've bought them."

"Well, our investment and the price we buy the shares at shows confidence in the company which gives others confidence in the company so people might also want to buy shares or do business with the company. And so, the company grows."

"But you've done nothing, apart from buy up bits of companies?"

"The right companies," said Lodge-Mammonson.

"I see," said Rod. "Got it. It's gambling."

"Well, no…"

"It's just backing the right horse."

"There's a lot of mathematics behind what we do."

"You've got a system. Sure."

"It's not a 'system'."

"But you've got a method of working out which companies to pick."

"Our expert team has a keen understanding of what investments to make."

"I think that's called a system."

The Mammonite looked helplessly at Vivian.

"I'm afraid you're dealing with a northerner, Mr Lodge-Mammonson," she said. "Not only are they mostly red socialists, but few can comprehend business models that don't involve digging things out of the ground." She looked at the giant screen of share prices. "It occurs to me that you might be privy to certain insider knowledge," she said, "as part of the *em-shadt* Venislarn."

"One can't help but pick up certain titbits," he conceded. "The sinking of the Ranger Four oil platform by *Kozzoth Ek'en* earlier this year and the sudden fall in fortunes of a certain energy corporation had no impact on our clients' portfolios. But a surprise turns of events – say, the destruction of a chocolate manufacturer's principal factory in the UK by an awakened and understandably angry *Zildrohar-Cqulu* – are beyond our prognostication skills."

"Yeah. Our bad," said Rod, holding up a hand.

"And you aren't just trading in… earthly commodities," said Vivian.

"There are currencies beyond the ordinary," agreed Lodge-Mammonson. "Ones that mortal men are either unaware of or unwilling to trade in."

"Indeed," she said. "I think we'd like to see the prisoners now."

Lodge-Mammonson gave her a frank and deliberately uncomprehending look. "We hold no prisoners here, Mrs Grey. We hold stock. We hold collateral. We hold business capital. No prisoners."

"The humans," said Vivian.

"Oh, them," he said. "You should have said. This way."

Mrs Atraxas pushed herself out of her armchair with considerable effort. Cats on shelves, window sills and the top of the Welsh dresser followed her with their eyes as she rocked back and forth and eventually up onto her feet.

"You have finished your coffee?" she asked.

Morag Junior glanced at the tall mug on the ornamental table next to her. The thick and certainly aromatic slurry in the mug had not magically disappeared. However, an industrial-looking grey scum had formed on the surface.

"Yes," said Junior. "Finished. Definitely done with it."

"Good," said Mrs Atraxas. "Now it is time for the hair cutting."

The woman waddled off into the kitchen, pushing lazy moggies aside with her foot as she went.

"Mrs Atraxas?" said Junior, standing. "I don't know which of us you think is having a haircut but that's not why I'm here. Oh."

Mrs Atraxas stood in the kitchen doorway, wearing a pair of oven gloves and holding a disgruntled looking long-haired cat. It twisted and contorted in her grip and bit savagely at the gloves. Mrs Atraxas thrust it at Junior.

"You pin it down. I will do the hair cutting."

"I don't have any gloves," said Junior.

"Oh, I think you should wear gloves," said Mrs Atraxas sagely.

The interior of the Black Barge was larger than the exterior, not wonderfully and magically so, it just was.

The bargeman and his band of filthy mute underlings had unloaded much of their stock onto the towpath. The *presz'ling* and a loitering *Shergai apmaisier* collected what was theirs and the *apmaisier* loaded several bundles onto the back of a beast of burden that seemed to be mostly arms and hands. Jeffney Ray followed Mystic Trevor and the smattering of other speculative browsers on board and down into the hold.

The walls were slick with damp, knobbly with inexplicable calciferous build-up. The floor was so dark as to be invisible but soft and silent underfoot. Worn rails stretched the length of the ceiling, securing the hooped ends of the barge slaves' chains. Every wall was lined with ridged shelves crammed with treasures. Junk shop boxes, welded into place with nacreous cement, overflowed with a miscellany of trinkets, effigies, preserved bones, shards of unknown material and fragments of sculpture that hinted at a horrible whole. Rot-blackened baskets held bundles of dried plants or smoked meats. Stacks and slim recesses housed books, scrolls, inscribed plates and inked hides.

Nothing was locked away. Neither the bargemaster nor his scabby team kept watch. Simply: no one stole from the Black Barge. No one had told Ray why this was but he had never questioned it. He was wary of the Black Barge – frightened? No, of course not – and, besides, he knew better than to even touch items he did not properly understand.

He was looking for something in particular and when he failed to spot it, he whistled to one of the barge slaves. She shuffled over to him, dragging her ceiling-mounted chain with her, and gave him a questioning look. She was a filthy looking bitch, maybe the same age as Ray but no tits or nothing. Even if she scrubbed up, she'd be lucky to get any attention from Ray, not unless she really begged.

"Darling, *li'renqor ist khei-ba drel*?" he asked.

She frowned.

"*Khei-ba drel*," he said.

She shook her head. He sighed.

"*Tuf? P'ye nav tre-cha soi p'ye nav ren'chlo?*"

She shook her head again.

"Christ's sake, love," he said. What was the point of having mute slaves if they couldn't answer simple questions? Rubbish customer service was what it was.

Her chain rattled as the bargemaster yanked it. The dirty little scrubber scuttled away and the greasy lump of a man waddled over.

"What?" he said.

"Li'renqor ist khei-ba drel?" asked Ray again.

"English," said the bargemaster.

"You don't speak Venislarn?" said Ray.

"You don't," said the bargemaster, wiping his nose on the back of his hand. His voice had a light European accent. Dutch or Danish or something, from one of those countries Ray would be flying over on his luxury sunshine holidays when he'd finally made it big.

"I asked if you have any *khei-ba drel.*"

"What you asked and what you wanted, two different things," said the bargemaster. "How much do you want?"

Ray held out his hands. How big was the last bag he bought?

"A pound?"

"Half a kilo," said the bargemaster, sniffed and slouched off.

Ray waited and idly watched the scabby girl slave going about her chores. God, yeah, she'd have to beg him if she wanted a bit of Ray.

Nina clicked her finger.

"You've had sex," she said.

Morag Senior stopped at the foot of the humpbacked bridge and looked at her colleague. Nina had a can of Lynx deodorant and a Boots sandwich meal deal in a little carrier bag. Morag had no idea why she had insisted on buying them on the way.

"Yes, I have had sex," said Morag. "I am a woman very much on the depressing side of thirty. It's a reasonable assumption that I've done the nasty at some point in the last couple of decades."

"I don't mean you've ever had sex."

"But I have."

"I mean, there's a spring in your step."

Morag looked at her feet as though there might be a tell-tale sign in her practical heels.

"A spring?"

"A spring. And I figured it was because you'd shagged someone."

"Ha. Fat chance. It's been" – she did a mental totting up of days – "a good few weeks."

"I thought you and your weirdy-beardy neighbour were…"

Morag gave her a wry smile. "Richard. God, no. He's lovely but that's a very special relationship."

She wondered briefly whether Morag Junior was keeping to the bargain and making the social rounds of her neighbours. Richard was truly lovely company but romantic material? Hell, no.

Nina hummed in thought.

"Not sex, then what is it?" She clicked her fingers again. "Your bagpipes have come back from the cleaners."

"No, but that would make a great euphemism. I guess I'm just happy today. Lord knows why. Another day on this doomed fucking planet. Actually…" She looked at Nina askance. Nina was too young and indiscreet to be an ideal confidante but Morag was still the new girl in town and had a limited supply of friends. "Okay, there's this guy."

"I knew it!" said Nina, leading the way onto the canal bridge. "My spring-in-the-step spotting, sex detecting senses never lie."

"We haven't had sex. Well, not in years. He's an old boyfriend. Works for the consular mission. He's coming down from Scotland today. And I'm really looking forward to seeing him."

"Gonna rekindle some of that old tartan magic, huh?"

"Would you quit with the casual racism, Nina?" said Morag.

"Sure. I'll just stick to ginger jokes. Speaking of which, there's a couple of your brethren over there."

Morag craned her neck to see over the brow of the bridge. Down on the spit of towpath on the other side, a very loose group of people milled around a moored barge, most doing their best to pretend the others didn't exist. Standing off to one side were a man and a woman, both natural redheads.

"*Yo-Morgantus'* representatives," said Morag. "Are they gonna cause a ruckus?"

"Doubt it."

Morag looked at the Black Barge. It was a barge as designed by HR Giger, as though a short-sighted facehugger had forced itself upon Boaty McBoatface and this was what had burst forth.

"It's not black," said Morag.

"Yeah," said Nina. "But Grey Barge... just sounds naff, doesn't it? Right, let's go have a quick poke around and then get some drinks. Reckon it's gonna be a sunny day."

Inside the Black Barge, Ray waited patiently for the bargemaster to return. A pod hanging from the ceiling drew his eye. It was hard to tell if the brown, vaguely diamond-shaped thing was a manufactured ornament or some sort of dried seed casing. Ray reached out a finger to poke it. A bat wing unfurled and a small, sleepy tentacle extended to meet Ray's finger. He drew it back quickly.

"Maybe not," he told himself.

In a wicker basket on a shelf were little plastic baggies, tied off with elastic bands. The contents looked like rice paper squares, painted with intricate ideograms. They looked achingly familiar.

The bargemaster rolled back, a linen bag in his hand. "Half a kilo."

"Great," said Ray and opened his briefcase. Of his sheaf of soul cash notes, Roy offered him four. The bargemaster took five and then spat on his hand to seal the deal.

"I'm not shaking that, mate," said Ray. "What are these things?"

The bargemaster looked at the baggies of rice paper squares.

"Summoning runes of *Kal Frexo*," he said simply.

"Un-uh," said Ray. "The runes are lost. Even I... I mean, everyone knows that."

"Not all of them."

Ray still didn't understand. "And what do they do?"

"Party. Rave," said the bargemaster. "Put under tongue and you will see."

"Ah." Ray grasped it. What were LSD and shrooms for if not summoning alien visions? He was taking Tony T and his crew to

Broad Street clubland that night and he knew exactly who he could sell this kind of shit to. "I'll take a bag."

The bargemaster tugged at two soul cash certificates.

"I can't pay that," said Ray. He did a quick mental recount. He needed all the remaining notes to make today's payment to MMI. "Cash price."

"Euros?"

"Pounds."

The bargemaster made a gargling throttle sound of displeasure. "Three hundred."

Ray groaned inwardly. The price wasn't unreasonable – he could already see himself making a two-hundred percent return on the rune papers – but he didn't have that kind of cash on him. But he would after tonight and he reckoned he could make a tidy little profit on a piece of information he'd just picked up…

"A loan," he said.

"Loan?" said the bargemaster.

"Twenty-four hours."

"Collateral?"

Ray sighed. The bargemaster smiled. He stamped his foot to rattle his chain.

"Ten years."

"Make it a hundred," said Ray, bouncing the git's smile right back at him. "I'll have your money."

Morag Senior nodded to the two gingers. Part of her felt stupid for doing it, like they were all part of some Great Ginger Conspiracy. But she knew the court of *Yo-Morgantus* and she was known to them. Half a mile down the canal from here and just about visible over the rooftops was the Cube: a huge tower of glass and irregularly shaped cladding, like a titanic greenhouse that had been repaired with Duplo bricks. For the most part, it was offices and apartments for those who felt that being in spitting distance of the fashion boutiques, wine bars and eateries of the Mailbox was worth the sky-high rents. However, the top two floors were home to the Venislarn court in Birmingham, a hodgepodge of humans, eldritch gods and unspeakable horrors that would have sent

164

Hieronymus Bosch running for his paint set. And, sitting above all of this, both figuratively and literally, was *Yo-Morgantus,* whose physical form in this world was a suppurating sea of flesh, both featureless and infinite in form.

Parliaments and councils and the apparatus of civilisation could pretend what they liked but Birmingham was *Yo-Morgantus*'s plaything and he was its absolute monarch. His eyes and ears and mouth in the city were the ginger slaves who had sold themselves into his service. *Yo-Morgantus* had a fondness for redheads, much like a lion has a fondness for crippled zebras.

"Just observing?" said Morag.

The ginger woman gave her a piercingly unpleasant look but said nothing.

Nina tapped Morag in the ribs and pointed to a round fellow who had the doubly alluring qualities of wearing only leather (and not enough of it) and having grease-smeared sweat flowing over the portions of his body not covered with leather (of which there was definitely not enough).

"The bargemaster," said Nina.

"What's the chain for?"

"He's property of the boat, just like all the people on it. Let's go have a chat."

A slender youth in a suit that screamed spiv and with a face so covered in scratches he might well be using glass as a face scrub stepped out of the boat, looked at his phone and with a "twenty-four hours, mate" for the bargemaster, headed toward the bridge. He leered at Nina and Morag as he passed and made no bones about letting them know he was looking at them.

"Ugh," said Nina, not bothering to keep her voice down. "You see that? Being an absolute fox is a burden sometimes, you know."

"He could have been looking at me," suggested Morag.

"Even pervs have standards, grandma."

"Sorry. He's your boyfriend. I understand. He's all yours."

Nina sniggered and went up to the bargemaster.

"Sven," she said.

The bargemaster grunted in non-committal greeting.

Nina held out the Boots bag.

"That's an all-day breakfast sandwich and salt and vinegar crisps for you."

The bargemaster took the bag, removed the can of deodorant, twisted the cap, sprayed and sniffed.

"That's Lynx Apollo," said Nina.

The bargemaster nodded approvingly. "What is the smell like?" he asked.

"A teenage boy on the pull," said Nina.

"Desperation," said Morag.

"One step up from basic BO. How's tricks?"

The bargemaster shrugged, sprayed himself liberally and waved for them to come aboard.

There was an unsettlingly organic quality to the Black Barge, Morag decided. Its *Alien*-themed construction aesthetic extended to the interior, where even the fixtures and fittings seemed to have been formed through unnaturally natural processes. Morag felt as if she was entering a cave. No, that wasn't it. She felt as if she was entering the dried out and mostly consumed carcass of some long-dead monster. Maybe she was.

Nina flicked casually through the wares as she followed the bargemaster. Morag poked desultorily through *Aden-schnat* pods, a pot of collected *lamisal* needles and what looked like some shoddily forged *pongroi* shaving discs. She stood next to a man who was inspecting a sleeping *bondook* shambler. It dangled by a single tentacle from a ceiling bar and had its fine membranous wings wrapped about itself.

"Ah. They're cute when they're that age," she said.

The man gave her a haughty sneer. "Who are you?"

Morag showed him her consular mission ID badge. As a supposed joke, Lois the office admin had printed it with a picture of the Marvel superhero Black Widow instead of an actual picture of Morag. After a month on the job no one had yet spotted this discrepancy. Morag didn't know whether to be offended or flattered.

The man took one look at the ID, dropped the snooty look, tipped his hat to Morag and made swiftly for the exit.

"There's no point running, Mystic Trevor," Nina shouted after him. "We know where you live. If you can call it living, eh, Sven?" she said to the bargemaster.

Morag wandered over to them, inspecting items as she did. There wasn't much on display to get excited about. There was a door and some stairs at the far end of the hold. Perhaps all the juicy goods were held through there.

"So where have you come from this time?" said Nina.

"Utrecht," he said. "Alappuzha. Hali. Liverpool."

"Any particular goods you've brought in that I should be aware of?"

The bargemaster gave a genial shrug.

"You are such a flirt, Sven."

Morag saw a pile of papers, held down by a seemingly mundane conch shell, and happened to catch the writing at the top.

"You trade in souls, do you?" she asked. "Humans?"

She looked back along the hold at the filthy boat hands. She realised that the nearest girl was wearing the utterly destroyed remnants of a pair of Converse sneakers.

"Soul cash," he said, sliding the pile out of view. "Only used for payments."

"Really?" said Morag. "Because that address on the bottom was a Birmingham address. And it was dated only this morning."

Nina made a very childish ooh. "Has someone just paid you in souls, Sven? Fresh ones?"

The human captives were on the third floor of Mammon-Mammonson Investments.

Mammonites held *things* in high value, and value was life itself to them. Humans in general had little value. Humans were ephemeral, unpredictable and frequently useless. (This was a viewpoint that Vivian supposed she and the Mammonites shared.) However, humans *as property or collateral* could have considerable value, so the Mammonites treated their human property with, if not respect, at least with care.

They weren't locked away in cells; they were exhibited. Lodge-Mammonson led Rod and Vivian down a long, marble-floored corridor lined on alternate sides with glass-fronted recesses too narrow to qualify as alcoves but deeper than museum cases. In each recess stood a solitary man or woman. The collection was a representative sample of the city's adult population. Vivian recognized the architect's intent in the broad offset between niches and sightlines that always led to blank walls: exhibits were to viewed in isolation (and they were never to view each other). There were at least thirty people along the corridor but whoever stood there, stood alone.

Rod found Annie Castleton. The young woman gazed passively out from behind the glass, not a flicker of recognition for Rod: zombie eyes in a tear-stained face.

"You've drugged them?" said Rod.

"We wouldn't want to taint them," said Lodge-Mammonson.

"Taint?"

"A simple invocation of *Ka'teriah Ba*," explained the Mammonite. "Keeps them docile."

"Allows for convenient storage," agreed Vivian. "And stops them resisting when you draw their blood." She pointed at the tell-tale plaster and needle mark in the crook of a man's arm and then again at another.

Lodge-Mammonson's expression was initially sharp but almost instantly touched with self-recrimination.

"Why would Mammon-Mammonson Investments wish to take people's blood?" asked Vivian.

"It would be unprofessional for me to disclose details of confidential business practices," said Lodge-Mammonson.

Rod pulled out his phone. It was buzzing.

"Campbell," he said and drew away from the others to speak but then said with deliberate loudness. "Soul cash certificates? Guaranteed by Mammon-Mammonson Investments? You don't say."

"Why are you using that silly voice?" said Nina, on the phone inside the Black Barge.

"Because we are currently at Mammon-Mammonson Investments," said Rod, "probably working the other end of the same case. Someone's not been playing fair. They've been buying up the bodies and souls of gullible idiots who don't read the small print."

"Life's too short to read small print."

"And there are lots of people here who are paying the price. I think we need to find who's doing this."

"Let me ask some questions," said Nina and ended the call.

"So, who gave you that soul cash?" Morag asked the bargemaster.

His pudgy face produced a reproachful expression.

"There's no client confidentiality," said Morag. "You're a shopkeeper, not a lawyer."

"I don't know him," said Sven.

Nina flicked through her phone and held up an image of Professor Sheikh Omar.

"This guy?" she said.

"No," said Sven. "Not Omar. Young man. Ugly boy."

"Ugly boy?" said Nina. She hitched a thumb over her shoulder towards the exit. "You mean that guy with a face like a roadmap of Britain?"

Another shrug but this one conceded she might be right.

"His name?" said Morag.

"I don't know."

"Are you lying to me, Sven?" said Nina. "I don't like it when my friends lie to me."

"Friends?" he said.

Nina snatched the can of deodorant out of his hand. He looked genuinely crestfallen.

"You don't deserve this," she said harshly. "I thought we had something, Sven. A little thing called trust. I want to know who he is, what he was doing here. Did he buy anything, Sven? What did he buy?"

"Just some *khei-ba drel* and some runes." Sven gestured dismissively to a basket packed with plastic bags.

"Khei-ba drel?" said Nina. "Fish seed?"

Morag had picked up one of the plastic bags. "You sold him some of these?"

169

"Yes," said Sven and cautiously held out his hand to take the deodorant back.

"Have you sold any others since you've arrived?"

"No."

"What are they?" said Nina.

"A real bad trip for anyone who takes them," said Morag. "A batch of these did the rounds of Edinburgh pubs and clubs last year."

"They're drugs?"

"More like encoded imagery and spells."

"And people died?"

"A couple," said Morag. "Three people were never found."

"Where did they go?"

"On a bad trip," said Morag.

"Bad Sven. Naughty Sven," said Nina. "Where did you get them?"

"Payment for passage. Private client. It is just business," he said.

She sighed heavily but tossed the deodorant back to him. "I can't stay mad at you, can I? But I'm taking some of these runes for analysis. Drink time," she said to Morag.

Up on the towpath, Nina multitasked, giving threatening glares to any individuals making for the Black Barge while simultaneously messaging Rod what few details they had uncovered.

"Are we going to get some calls about these rune drug things?"

"*Kal Frexo* runes. Probably. Of course, there's a bigger question to answer."

"Yeah?"

"Like, why do you have a picture of Professor Sheikh Omar on your phone?"

"For obvious reasons."

Morag gave her a questioning look.

"I've got a whole collection of pictures of clunge monkeys I have known and hated," said Nina, "to show people at times of need." She flicked through, showing Morag. "He's a git. He's a fucker. He's killed and dismembered six old ladies but no one can prove it. He's a twat. She's a sad loner who tangled with the wrong bitch and will one day be eaten by her own cats. He…"

"That's a picture of a cute spider in a hat," said Morag.

"I think I put it in the wrong folder."

"Not your arch nemesis then?"

"No." Nina, at the apex of the narrow humpbacked bridge, looked around. "I'd have thought Omar would be here by now."

"Maybe he's not coming. Even evil wizards take a day off now and then."

Truman Lodge-Mammonson consulted his phone.

"Ah, Mrs Grey," he said. "You have an appointment with Mr Mammon-Mammonson himself in five minutes time."

"I made no such appointment," said Vivian.

"He did," said Lodge-Mammonson.

Rod saw a twitch on her face. Vivian didn't like being ordered around. No one did. But Vivian made sure people knew she didn't like it, in meaningful and memorable ways.

"I do wish to speak to him," she admitted.

"Then let's go see the man," said Rod.

Lodge-Mammonson's expression clearly displayed the embarrassment of having to deal with the socially inept.

"The appointment is for Mrs Grey," he said. "Not you, sir."

"Xerxes Mammon-Mammonson and I have met before," Vivian explained.

"I'm not right happy about this. These blokes are dangerous," said Rod.

"Are you making an accusation?" said Lodge-Mammonson.

"Paying a compliment," said Rod.

"Oh?" said the Mammonite. "I have a customer feedback form if you'd be willing to offer some formal feedback."

"What, like 'these fellers are dangerous, five stars'?"

"Very much so."

"Insane," Rod muttered and looked at Vivian. "You'll be all right?" he said and then realised it was Vivian he was talking to.

"Stupid question. I'll head back to the office. Call me if you need a lift. Or backup."

With a final gaze at poor zombified Annie Castleton in her glass cage, Rod made for the stairs.

He read the flurry of messages from Nina as he walked down. Soul cash certificates exchanged for alchemical powders and dodgy runes. It was like someone was just trying to make more work for them.

Rod was not a man for strong words but this fool, playing with the lives and souls of the innocent and poking things best left un-poked, roused strong feelings.

"Git."

Jeffney Ray didn't like the way the Mammonite on the front desk at Mammon-Mammonson Investments looked at him. Who was he to look down his nose at him? Didn't he and MMI have a contract? Weren't they business partners?

"I need to see Mr Lodge-Mammonson," said Ray, stabbing at Lodge-Mammonson's image on the ostentatious portrait of the board of directors that hung behind reception.

"He is not available," said the receptionist smoothly.

"Make him available. I have a payment for him on an agreed debt here." Ray put an envelope of soul cash certificates on the edge of the counter.

"I can take them," said the receptionist.

On the surface, this might have seemed a perfectly reasonable request – Ray had one more call to make that day and he could be off and away in seconds if he handed it over – but there was a principle at stake, a matter of prestige and honour.

"I'm not letting you have them," said Ray, sliding the envelope out of reach.

"I will put them directly in Mr Lodge-Mammonson's hand," said the receptionist.

"I don't trust you to."

"Are you saying I am a liar?" said the receptionist with slow deliberateness.

"I'm saying that, if you don't change your tune, mate, we're either taking this to Mr Mammon-Mammonson himself or we're taking it outside."

The Mammonite put a large hunting knife on the counter. He didn't make a thing of it. He didn't even look at it while he did it.

"Mr Mammon-Mammonson is not available either," he said.

The receptionist looked back over his shoulder. A big man – even from across the lobby, Ray could see he was a human man – was coming down the stairs, talking distractedly on his phone.

"Would you like to take this up with the gentleman from the consular mission?" suggested the receptionist.

The big man took a turn at the foot of the stairs and continued down to the basement.

Ray gave the uppity receptionist a cold stare, to let the *bhulgen* know that he'd just had a narrow escape.

"Directly in his hand," he said, pushing the envelope at the Mammonite, and left swiftly before he could reply.

Richard wrapped a plaster around Morag Junior's index finger.

"I think that's enough plasters now," she said.

"Yes, I think so," he agreed.

Junior's hands had seven plasters on them, covering the scratches and the one considerable gouging that Mrs Atraxas's long-haired cat had given her.

"Did the cat need a haircut?" Richard asked.

"Certainly didn't want it," said Junior. "I think she was actually harvesting fur for, um, knitting."

"I didn't know you could knit with cat hair."

"You can try."

"Chocolate?"

Richard offered Junior a plate on which he had laid out segments of Terry's Chocolate Orange in a decorative pattern. Richard had a thing for chocolate oranges. Someone had once told him that he would like them. So he did. Many of Richard's lifestyle choices had been made out of an uncontrollable need to please others. It explained such diverse choices as the soft floral

173

furnishings in the flat, the Jeffrey Archer novels on the bookshelves, the big hipster beard, the lumberjack shirts, the bagpipes in the corner and, most recently, Richard's decision to drink kale smoothies at any opportunity. It was also the reason he and Junior were currently tackling an enormous jigsaw: the result of her off-hand comment about puzzles.

"I've sorted out all the water bits," he said.

"What do you want me to do?" she asked.

"Maybe find all the bits of the side of the boat."

She looked at the picture on the box. It was a painting of a canal boat, bedecked in flowers, gliding serenely past a country pub with a thatched roof while swallows swooped in the sky above. Junior, always an art critic, judged it to belong to the school of horribly twee and nostalgic art. It was the kind of thing Hitler would have approved of.

"Bits of boat," she sighed. "Right."

"Do you like canal boats?" he asked.

She had visions of him going out and buying a barge or booking them both on a boating holiday if she gave the wrong answer.

"No, I do not, Richard."

Xerxes Mammon-Mammonson, chair of governors at Thatcher Academy and managing director of Mammon-Mammonson Investments, had an office that Vivian judged to be far bigger than one individual could possibly need. Mammonites were not wasteful creatures and tolerated conspicuous consumption of wealth only when it contributed to something of even greater value. Vivian couldn't guess how much rent per square foot this office demanded but Xerxes Mammon-Mammonson must have thought it was worth every penny. The same must have gone double for the eight-foot portrait of himself that stared down from the wall.

Xerxes stood at the broad office window, gazing out over the city with his hands clasped behind his back, his legs spread, the very image of a general observing his troops, an emperor surveying his lands. It was a calculated pose and the Mammonite held it even when the door clicked closed behind Vivian and she was alone with him.

She decided she wouldn't be the first to speak. If he wanted to stand there, trying to send a message with his power pose, she wasn't going to stop him. On a nearby table, quite incongruous in the corporate setting, was a plush stuffed toy. It looked like the invention of a demented and colour-blind seamstress but Vivian had actually seen a toy very much like it in a meeting with the consular mission's marketing gurus, Chad and Leandra: one of the Venislarn-themed plushies they had commissioned to make the Venislarn "more relatable" when revealed to the public. Vivian was unaware that the prototypes had gone into full production. She picked it up and gave it a squeeze. It was, she deduced, supposed to be a cute and cuddly representation of the water god *Daganau-Pysh*. The real *Daganau-Pysh* didn't have jolly pink tentacles with laced edges.

"It is for my daughter," said Xerxes and turned round. "Assuming she gets top marks on her English project."

"I believe education is its own reward," said Vivian.

Xerxes grinned, folds forming in his leathery, albeit handsome, face.

"I couldn't agree more, Mrs Grey. Which always makes me wonder why the government gives it away for free."

"Because an educated populace is more profitable than an uneducated one."

"You have the soul of an accountant," said Xerxes.

"Thank you," said Vivian.

He crossed the room, held his hand out for the toy and set it down on the table.

"How much does the consular mission pay you?"

"It's not very British to discuss something as vulgar as money, Mr Mammon-Mammonson."

"I could pay you more."

"Why would you do that? The last time we met, you threatened to gut me. Yesterday, you sent me flowers. And today you offer me a job? I believe that would be described as mixed messages."

"Did you like the flowers?"

"I have never understood the point of sending recently killed plants to someone as a sign of affection. I have never understood the point of flowers as a gift at all."

"They are colourful and decorative, Mrs Grey. They are attractive."

"That's because they are trying to draw attention to the plant's organs of reproduction. They are the vegetable equivalent of a push-up bra."

"Or a vajazzle."

"Indeed."

He looked her in the eye for a long second with the critical appraisal of a horse trader counting teeth. "I would like to understand you better," he said.

"Me or the consular mission?"

"I would like to understand the relationship here, how you perceive it. You and your colleague came here because of a small number of human souls that legitimately belong to this company. Two days ago, you raided a place of education with objections to Mammonite cultural practices."

"We visited the school, searching for a person we believed to have been killed by illegally kept *Dinh'r*."

"Do you hate Mammonites, Mrs Grey? Are you prejudiced against us?"

"Prejudiced, no."

"Then why do you do what you do? Are you driven to save the lives we take? Doesn't the world have bigger problems than the globally insignificant goings on of one financial institution or one tiny community in its village ghetto?"

"I do not do what I do in order to save lives," said Vivian. "If I wished to save lives I would go to Africa and dig wells and lay tarmac roads. Better still, I would get the highest paid job I could and use that money to pay others to dig wells and lay roads. I do not know how many people there are on the planet so how can I care if there are seven billion and one people or seven billion and two? We are overpopulated as it is and I am sure the quality of life of every living thing on earth would rise somewhat if three or four billion people just quietly died and freed up some space and resources. I have no interest in saving lives.

"Similarly, I have no especial love for my species. Psychologically and physiologically, we're horribly flawed and we only hold our dominant position because of one or two quirks in our evolution. Even if we weren't doomed by the coming Soulgate, even if we did not wipe ourselves out with environmental degradation, even if we survived the unavoidable death of our sun, my species could not continue for more than a million years or so. Because, by that time, it would have evolved into another species, one that would look upon us with the same detachment and disdain with which we regard our primate ancestors."

"You are a nihilist, Mrs Grey," Xerxes laughed.

"A pragmatist," she said. "There is one governing factor in all human life, in every decision ever made: pain. We suffer. We don't wish to suffer, physically or otherwise. We experience our own pain and, vicariously, the pain of others. I do what I do to ease humanity's suffering. If you presented me with a magic button that would instantly and painlessly kill every other human being on earth, I would press it now without hesitation."

"Every *other* human being?"

"The knowledge that one is about to die, at this instant, now, is also a form of suffering."

"I could arrange for you to be painlessly killed at some undisclosed point in the future, if you wish," offered Xerxes.

"You are very kind but I have a job to do. I am not interested in the individual suffering of those people you have imprisoned."

"Stored."

"They are victims of their own cupidity. My concern is with humanity, the flock as a whole. The end of the world is coming. We have a plan for humanity. It's not a nice plan but it's the best plan we have. This." She gestured behind her and away, figuratively towards the imprisoned humans. "It's not part of the plan."

"A mere handful of people," said Xerxes.

"It's the thin end of the wedge," said Vivian. "Like dress-down Fridays, buy-now-pay-later offers and the words 'no offence but', it is a bad precedent and the thin end of the wedge."

Xerxes inhaled and slapped his chest reflectively.

"I appreciate your honesty, Mrs Grey."

"I'm sure you do," she said.

"I believe in a plan too," he said. "At the bottom is a row of numbers – large numbers – and the return of our glorious mother to this world."

"I see."

"And I strongly suspect our plan and your plan will come into conflict. Sooner rather than later."

"I suspect the same."

"I wonder what will happen then."

"One of us will be deeply disappointed, Mr Mammon-Mammonson."

By late afternoon, Rod was back in the consular mission offices in the Library of Birmingham and trawling through CCTV footage of Gas Street Basin and nearby Broad Street. It was a task that he threw himself into with considerable gusto, partly because he enjoyed the opportunity to play armchair detective (well, desk chair detective) but also partly so he could drive the text he'd just received from Kathy from his mind. Local police and business CCTV covered the city centre with an almost complete blanket, one that only became truly patchy and tattered as the city spread out into suburbia. Rod had heard pub philosophers debate the morality of electronic surveillance, often accompanied by the cry that the UK had more CCTV cameras per capita than any other country in the world and that Big Brother was truly in charge. However, in Rod's opinion, these beery defenders of civil rights undid their own argument by constantly posting their pictures and personal information on social media.

Fifteen minutes of searching found the man Nina had identified. Even on the image gleaned from a CCTV camera fifty yards away, the young man's facial scars were clear. And even though Nina's description hadn't rung a bell, Rod realised that he had seen that face before.

He called Nina.

"Yo," she said.

"I've met him."

"Who?" said Nina.

"The man on the – Are you in a pub?"

"Might be."

"Drinking? In the afternoon?"

"YOLO. Morag and I are planning strategy for her big date tonight."

"We are not," said Morag's distant voice. "It's not a date."

"Whatever. We're just sat outside the Tap and Spile, soaking up some rays and bitching about the general lack of hot men in the world."

"We are not," said Morag.

Rod flicked the virtual wheel on the CCTV viewer program to bring up the live feed.

"There you are," he said, finding the two women at a Parisian café-style table squashed between the towpath and the wall of the pub.

"There...?" On the screen, Nina looked up at the camera. "How many fingers am I holding up?"

"Two. Now one. I'm making a recording of this and e-mailing it to your mum."

"The word is 'mom' Rod, you're in Birmingham, remember? Anyway, my mom: it's Instagram or nothing. So, what did you find out? About the guy?"

"I saw him on Monday morning. Just after I visited Annie Castleton. He was going door to door..." He closed his eyes to draw back the memory. "Selling broadband. You know, am I happy with my supplier and all that nonsense."

"That's how he's getting people to sign themselves away."

"Looks it. I've got him on camera. I'm going to try to see where he went."

179

Ray could have been a uni student. You know, if he'd got the A-level grades. Or the GCSE grades before that. Or if he'd parents who would help shoulder the lifelong, crippling debt university brings, or encourage him to pursue an academic route, or even show him that such a route through life existed.

University was something that happened to other people and, as he crossed the campus green of Birmingham University, Ray felt more of an outsider than he did among the *samakha* of Fish Town or the Mammonites of Dickens Heath. Ray stalked beneath the shadow of the huge clock tower (which looked like it should be home to an evil sorcerer in Ray's opinion), hating every one of the students he passed. That one looked like a smug public school wanker. That one was a gormless twat. That one was clearly frigid. That one was probably a slut.

He had come to the university to find a genuine sorcerer but this one didn't live in a red clock tower, he had an office in the Faculty of Arts building. Ray knew however, that this afternoon, he would be found elsewhere.

Ray walked out from the green, down towards the South Gate. Just before the university grounds came up against the wide Bristol Road, he took a shortcut through a fence and entered a walled area with a small, windowless brick building at its centre. There were no identifying signs but it had the air of a pump house or maybe an old electricity transformer station. Ray had only recently heard of this place and he had never visited before. The sorcerer Ray had come to see had a secret cave, not a tower, for this simple building was the entrance to a mine. The mine had been dug by students in decades past, when mining was a university course and Britain trained its brightest and best to plunder the mineral wealth of the empire.

The door was a sturdy and featureless slab of grey. There was no exterior door handle, only a simple keyhole.

Ray hesitated. Should he give it an experimental push? Or just knock?

He reached out a hand. The door swung open as he did.

"Maybe I put a curse of *obzad melichu chad'n* on the door," suggested Professor Sheikh Omar as he stepped out, "one that would kill you the moment you touched it."

"I'd know the counter-curse," said Ray.

Omar closed the door behind him. Something clicked shut. "You are not a student here."

Ray cracked his knuckles.

"Is there anything this place can teach me?" he said casually.

"I certainly have nothing further I want to teach you," said Omar.

"That's cold, man," said Ray. "I remember a time when you were only too happy to be my mentor."

"Mentoring is not part of the deal when you buy a book, Jeffney. Happy to take your money, but that is the end of the transaction. You've been rather too slow to realise this."

Ray produced his copy of *Venislarn: A Language Primer*.

"I've still got the book, professor."

Omar adjusted his black-rimmed glasses to look at it properly.

"What do you want, Jeffney? A refund? I don't know how you found this place and I've no intention of asking. All I wish to do is go home and curl up on the chaise longue with a naughty book and something indulgently chocolatey."

"I've got some news for you," he said.

"What?"

"News is always worth something."

"Not today," said Omar, stifling a yawn. "Now, be a good chap and either tell me or piss off."

"A hundred quid."

Omar shook his head wearily, took a Parker pen from his shirt pocket, scribbled something and showed it to Ray. It slammed Ray right between the eyes, like a physical punch. Ray stumbled in pain and went down on his knees.

"No defence against that one, eh?" said Omar. "What about this one?"

Omar held his hand out, turned it once to hold up three fingers, turned it again to hold a finger and a thumb in a crescent

181

moon, turned it a third time to make a fist and Ray found he could no longer breathe.

"No?" said Omar. "Sorry. Tiredness makes me cranky. And cruel."

He approached Ray.

"Now, let me guess, Jeffney. You were at Gas Street Basin this morning when the Black Barge arrived? And you saw a figure disembark. Perhaps you managed to dredge up from your memory that it was one of the *be'ae tyez*."

Jeffney nodded but could only produce a strangled croak from his throat.

"And you perhaps recall something of what you learned from my book. You're thinking that the arrival of a Carcosan word mage is significant. It would only be here if it had been summoned. As the young people might say, something is about to go down, yes?"

Ray clawed at his mouth, at the invisible blockage in his airways. Omar crouched in front of Ray.

"And, for some reason, you thought it likely that I would be interested, that I would care, that I'm some sort of cosmic gossip-monger. Yet, it never occurred to you that, if such information was valuable to me, I would have my own means of finding it out."

Ray's chest burned. His jaw worked as he choked, as though he could somehow chew his way free of suffocation.

"You are a stupid and shallow boy, Jeffney," said Omar. "Things will end very badly for you. A kind man would now probably say to you that he regretted ever introducing you to the smallest mysteries of the Venislarn. Do you know what I think?"

Ray shook his head, not because he didn't want to hear, but because he was afraid he would be dead before Omar was done.

"I think I should just put you out of your misery," said Omar. "I could do that." He pursed his lips, giving it some consideration. "But then I'd have to dispose of your worthless corpse and my back isn't what it used to be. And then we'd have your mother weeping on the local news and your despicable face and some earnest police inspector appealing to the public for information and..." He sighed, exhausted.

Omar flicked his wrist and air rushed back into Ray's lungs. Ray heaved and spat, tears in his eyes and spittle across the ground.

"In future," said Omar, "if you come across some exciting titbit, please feel free to keep it to yourself."

Ray coughed and nodded.

"Because I have my own eyes and ears, Jeffney Ray, my own ways of finding things out."

"Scrying," said Ray, wheezing.

"It's called a mobile phone. And at the other end is a man called Magic Trevor."

"I thought it was Mystic Trevor."

"I will call him the Great Ali Bongo if I like, boy, because he is mine. Do not think you know me or can even comprehend my powers. Do you know the story of the blind men and the elephant, Jeffney? Five men each feeling part of the elephant and thinking he understood what it was? That's you, Jeffney. You know why? You know what happened?"

"Is it because –"

"They got trampled to death. Because they were blind and it was a fucking elephant. Now, look at me." Ray instinctively kept his head down. *"Degr ud kissaq!* Look at me, Jeffney Wilson Ray!"

Red-faced and quaking, Ray raised his head. Omar traced a pattern in the air with his fingertips.

"You will forget this conversation, Jeffney. You will forget that you came here. And tonight, you will go to bed without a care in the world but you will forget to put on your darling mittens –"

"No…"

"– and you will scratch your face to royal buggery in your sleep."

Omar made a final gesture and turned away.

Ray watched him go and then (after a moment of panic in which a fading, horrified voice cried out inside him) wondered what he was doing outside a weird little building. Was it a pump house of some sort? And why was he kneeling in the dirt? Ray stood, confused, brushed himself off and left.

At the canalside pub, Morag Senior put up with Nina dividing her time equally between messaging Chief Inspector Ricky Lee on her phone and dispensing unwelcome dating advice. Nina was ostensibly texting Ricky about the potential threat of the rune drugs but she was sending far too many messages for it to be just about that. Nina was an incorrigible flirt and Morag had met Ricky Lee and reckoned he'd be the kind to flirt straight back.

Morag kept an eye on the Black Barge and sipped her drink. Mystic Trevor had snuck back to the Black Barge when he probably thought Nina and Morag weren't looking. Now he was coming back across the narrow bridge.

Nina got up from their pub table to block his path.

"Woop, woop. That's the sound of da police, Trevor."

The occultist heaved a weary sigh.

"You're not the police."

"Nah, we're way worse. Open the shopping bag."

"I don't have to do what you say."

"Don't make it difficult," said Morag. "We're just doing our job."

Trevor put a hand on his tatty leather shoulder bag. He probably thought it looked like the grungy bag of secrets of an itinerant wizard, but it just made him look like an art teacher. In fact, Mystic Trevor was generally rocking a middle-aged-art-teacher-having-a-midlife-crisis vibe. The scraggy beard, ornate silver earring and wide-brimmed hat completed the look.

"You are messing with forces beyond your ken," he warned.

"Don't you bring my ken into this," said Nina. "Open it."

He looked along the towpath behind Nina, perhaps considering running. Mystic Trevor didn't strike Morag as the type who enjoyed running for more than a few seconds. He opened the bag.

"The barge isn't under your jurisdiction," he said. "I can buy what I like."

"Until you step off the barge," said Morag. "And then it is our jurisdiction."

She emptied the contents out onto the pub table carefully, item by item.

"Three gold-plate glyphs of *Shandor*. They'll look nice on the Christmas tree. A pamphlet on the habits of the *kobashi*. A pipe and tobacco."

"Not tobacco," said Nina, inspecting it. "Gandalf's moved on to the hard stuff."

"It's for my joint pain," said Trevor.

"Joint, yes," said Nina.

"A vial of *rehpat viarr*," said Morag.

"Truth potion?" said Nina.

"It's legal," said Trevor.

"Yes, but this isn't," said Morag, gingerly lifting out a much-scratched Tupperware box with airholes punched in it. "You bought the *bondook* shambler?"

Inside the box, the juvenile bat-octopus-anemone-squirrel thing stirred in its sleep.

"What were you going to do with that?" said Nina.

"Keep it as pet. Train it," said Trevor.

"To do what?" said Morag incredulously.

"Sit on my shoulder. Whatever."

"And then suck your brains out through your ears?"

"You've got to lay off the weed, Trevor," said Nina. "We're confiscating this, this and this."

"I paid three hundred for that!"

"The weed or the shambler? Either way, you overpaid. Go on. Clear off."

Mystic Trevor stuffed his belongings back in his bag and then hesitated. Maybe he was trying to think of a way to undo the last few minutes. Maybe he was searching for a biting remark or witty rejoinder. Whichever, it wasn't forthcoming.

"Jesus, Trevor," said Nina, "stop standing there like a creepy uncle."

The miserable occultist shuffled off.

"What a stupid arse," said Nina thoughtfully.

Morag picked up the plastic box and the snoozing horror within.

"These things are huge when they're fully grown."

"They've got a pair up at the Menagerie in Dudley. We can store it in the Vault for now and then get one of the hauliers to take it up to Dudley tomorrow."

"Okay," said Morag and drained her drink. "A walk back to the office then."

She saw Nina pocket the cannabis and the *rehpat viarr*.

"Got plans for those?" Morag asked.

"Maybe. I'm going to meet up with Ricky Lee. See you tomorrow?"

"Every day is a gift," said Morag, gave her a wave and headed off.

Her phone rang as she walked through the Broad Street tunnel. She tucked the *bondook* under one arm and answered.

"What was in the vial she took off Wizard Dave?" said Rod.

"Mystic Trevor," said Morag. "You been spying on us all this time?"

"Spying. Wishing I was at the pub. I tried to locate that scar-faced git but lost him somewhere near Centenary Square."

"It was a truth potion."

"God help us all. Hey, you're a woman."

"Keen observational skills there, Rod."

"I'm meeting someone for a drink after work today – a woman – and, before you go all Nina on me, it's not a date. It's just a drink."

"Kathy Kaur. Nina mentioned it."

"She's texted me to ask where we should meet up."

"Okay."

"What does she mean?"

Morag headed towards the stone steps by the Brindley Place bridge.

"Well," she said slowly, "I think it means she wants to know where you want to meet her."

"But what answer should I give? Where'd be the right place to take her?"

"Ah, I see," said Morag. "Because we women all get together once a week to discuss everything and I should know the answer."

"Fine. Be that way."

Morag laughed.

"It's a drink. Anywhere will be fine," she said and immediately changed her mind. "Not a real ale pub."

"I was thinking of the Wellington."

"Is it a real ale pub?"

"It serves real ale."

"Does it have a range of taps of beer with names like Worcester Wench and Old Dirigible, perhaps with little notes underneath explaining whether it's hoppy or yeasty or got, I don't know, citrus notes?"

"It might," said Rod cautiously.

"It's a real ale pub. I'm going to go out on a sexist limb here and say that no woman in the history of the world ever has liked real ale."

"Harsh and untrue," said Rod.

"And in a recent survey I've just invented one hundred percent of women say that listening to men talking about why real ale is great is the most boring thing ever."

"You and I talk about real ale."

"No, Rod," she said. "You talk about real ale and I pretend to listen because I don't want to hurt your feelings."

"Ow. You've cut me deep. So, a wine bar or something?"

The *bondook* rolled over, shifting its weight in the box. Morag juggled it back into position.

"Seriously? Those are the two options? It's either real ale pubs or wine bars? Christ, man. Just go somewhere nice."

"Like where?"

"A pub. A bar. There's enough to choose from. What was that place under the hotel on New Street?"

"Bacchus?" he said.

"Go there."

Her phone buzzed with a text message.

"Do you think it's nice enough though?" said Rod.

She glanced at the message. It was Cameron.

MANAGED TO GET AN EARLIER TRAIN WHEN WE CHANGED. NEW ST AT 6:30. HAPPY TO WAIT.

"*Muda.*"

"Sorry, I was only asking for advice," said Rod's tinny voice.

"Not you," she said. "I've got to go, Rod. Plans of my own."

She crossed the bridge to the ICC as she dialled her home phone number.

Morag Junior offered the open bag to Steve the Destroyer. "Nacho?"

Steve the Destroyer took one of the triangular crisps and, because he had no mouth, not a proper one, he just stared at it. He sat on the arm of the sofa next to Junior.

"And the idea of this television show is to guess answers to questions?"

"The answer that the fewest people have guessed in their survey. And if they get a pointless answer – one that no one has guessed – then extra money goes in the jackpot." Junior slurped her beer. "This round is countries that end in the letter 'n'."

"*Yantuvan,*" said Steve. "*Ower'een.*"

"I don't think the programme makers will have heard of those."

"Then it is pointless and I win!" declared Steve.

"It has to be countries they've actually heard of. They wouldn't allow those answers."

"Then I will find this quiz man and I will drag his worthless carcass into the flames of hell!"

"That's the spirit."

The landline phone rang. Junior passed the nachos to Steve but kept hold of the beer as she went to answer it.

"Yemen," she called to Steve and picked up.

"Right, listen carefully," said Morag Senior.

"And hello to you," said Junior.

"I haven't got time. Suddenly everything's happening at once. We've spent half the day on the trail of some scar-faced dealer in *Kal Frexo* runes. I've got a baby *bondook* to take to the Vault before I can head home to change and Cameron's train's coming in at six-thirty now, not whenever it was."

"Where'd you get a baby *bondook*?"

188

"No time," said Morag Senior.

Junior could hear the woman panting as she walked and talked. Actually panting. Was she really that out of shape?

"I'm going to wear my gold top and my khaki pedal pushers. I want you to check they're washed and wearable by the time I get in."

"Yes," said Junior, "but they are in different piles."

"Oh, you sorted things?"

"I did everything on your list. I took a bullet for the team." She looked at the plasters on her hands. "A hail of bullets. Steve and I are just kicking back now. A bit of *Pointless* and some spicy nachos."

"Yemen!" yelled Steve victoriously from the lounge.

"I bought those nachos for me," said Senior.

"So did I," said Junior. "Look, if you're going to be late, I can step in and meet Cameron."

"Not necessary," said Senior firmly. "Everything's sorted. I've booked a table at that South American place on Bennetts Hill. It's going to be fine. Just sort my clothes and stop eating my nachos."

"Sure thing," said Junior.

"I'll be there within the hour. Probably."

Senior clicked off. Junior put the phone down and went back into the lounge.

"Five points!" said Steve, dancing on the arm of the sofa and waving his nacho like a pennant. "You are a master of this game, gobbet!"

"Change of plan," said Junior. "That was Grandma Morag. She needs me to go into town and meet our ex-boyfriend."

"Fine, fine," said Steve. "Ha! He said 'Surinam'! It doesn't even end in 'n'! Gouge his eyes out, quiz man!"

"That means it's biscuit tin time for you."

The sack doll dropped its nacho and gave her a look of utter betrayal, an impressive achievement with a stitched-on face.

"But the tin is dark and I want to watch the *Pointless*."

Junior huffed and went to the kitchen. She looked in the fridge. There was a mostly-finished jar of jam. She washed it out in

189

the sink with a torrent of hot water and then dried it as she carried it back to the lounge.

"Here," she said, picked Steve up and stuffed him into the jar. It wasn't quite big enough and his limbs were all squashed up against the glass. He looked like something from an Amnesty International leaflet, or Cirque du Soleil.

"There," she said, screwing the lid on tightly. "The very latest in doll containment with entertainment options included."

She put the jar on the coffee table and rotated it so Steve could see the telly.

"Brilliant!" he shouted.

Jeffney Ray opened the front door. There was the smell of cooking in the air. Wednesday: that meant sausages and potato waffles. He hoped it was tinned peas, not frozen peas. His mom knew he preferred tinned peas. She was at the kitchen sink, staring out of the window and smoking a fag. It might as well have been the same one she had been smoking that morning. She wasn't like Ray. She wasn't a go-getter with a dream.

"What have you got there, Jeffney?" she said.

He looked at the carrier bag in his hand but offered no explanation.

"How far off's dinner?" he said.

"Ten minutes," she said.

"Tinned peas or frozen peas?"

"Mushy peas."

"I prefer non-mushy."

"It's what we've got."

"I'm just going to tidy some things up in the shed," he said.

"You said you were going to take it down."

"It needs tidying first."

Ray went out across the uneven patio to the shed and unlocked the padlock. It was a big shed, put up by the previous owner. The floor and the lower levels of the walls had rotted away – he wasn't sure how much of the funky smell in the shed was rot and how much was his *lu'crik oyh* – but it was still a sturdy structure and good for a few months yet. Ray drew the door closed behind him. He didn't want his mom looking in and worrying.

There was a single deep rack of metal shelving along the long wall. Ray had arranged his tubs and tanks along the shelves in sequential order. From left to right, there were two tanks – one currently empty, the other teeming with ghostly fry swimming, bobbing and occasionally eating each other – then there were the three tubs. Only one of the tubs was open. In its depths, five – oh, no, only four left now – four fingerlings circled each other. Ray wasn't sure if they were best described as fingerlings or spiderlings or something else. They had fins, they had gills but they had legs, plenty of them, and their eyes were not fish eyes. They were... They were a goldmine. The broadband thing was Ray's day job, the means for paying back his start up loan, but this little operation, the only one of its kind as far as he knew, was going to make him very wealthy and very popular with the right kind of people.

The two remaining tubs had lids on and were weighted down with bricks. He had taped labels to the sides of the boxes. LU'CRIK OYH. HANDLE WITH CARE. The rightmost tub shook violently as the creature within bucked and thrashed. He was ready to go.

Ray scrolled through his phone address book and dialled. As he waited for them to pick up, he carefully emptied the carrier bag of dead *Dinh'r* eggs that he'd bought from the Tony T into the empty tank. Some of the more damaged ones just floated on the surface. Most sank to the bottom, the water lending them a brown conker shine.

"Lee-Mammonson residence," said a refined voice on the phone. "Please note, this call may be monitored for training purposes. My name is Imelda Lee-Mammonson."

"*San-shu*, Mrs Lee-Mammonson," said Ray. "It's Jeffney Ray. I'm calling about your order."

"Mr Ray," said the Mammonite with restrained haughtiness, "I was beginning to think you had forgotten us."

"Fear not. I have your order right here."

"We've not had any word from you at all. I was in two minds about cancelling it."

"Well, you can if you really wish, Mrs Lee-Mammonson. We do have a waiting list."

"The Smith-Mammonsons have had their *lu'crik oyh* for two weeks. The envy of the neighbourhood it is."

"As I say, a waiting list."

Ray opened the bag of *khei-ba drel* seeds he'd bought from the Black Barge – at such an extortionate price, the cheeky fat bastard! – and sprinkled them liberally across the surface.

The Mammonite woman on the line made a terse huffing sound as though that might elicit some response from Ray but he wasn't lying when he said he had buyers queuing up for his hybrid creations. The first of the drifting fish seeds landed on a *Dinh'r* egg. A fraction of a second before they touched, a hair-like tracer of yellow energy sprang between them, a mote of lightning, a quickening of life.

"I can deliver it to you tomorrow afternoon," said Ray.

"And you can assure me it's a prime specimen?"

Ray looked at the angrily shaking box. "Positively jumping with vitality."

"I will be in from one," she said.

"One it is. Good evening, Mrs Lee-Mammonson."

Ray put an extra couple of bricks on top of the Lee-Mammonsons' new pet's box to keep it steady and, seeing that the fertilisation process was already underway on the new batch, locked up and went in for his tea. He'd have to eat quickly. He had *samakha* gangsta boys to entertain tonight and a bunch of psycho runes to sell to a greedy public.

Waiting in the New Street Station concourse, Rod Campbell realised just how nervous he was when he caught himself unconsciously reaching for a pistol that was not there – a gun that was in the gut of a dead *Dinh'r* somewhere under the streets of Birmingham, a gun that he wouldn't be wearing now anyway because he was off duty and firearms weren't regarded as mandatory equipment for dates.

"It's not even a date," he muttered to himself.

How could he be nervous? He'd been on dates before. Okay, not dates as such but, in a past life he had flung himself into the pub and club scene and engaged in those ancient mating rituals that involve necking pints, strutting one's funky stuff and trying it on with every lass in the club until he found one with sufficiently low standards. God, that *was* a past life, he thought. In terms of actual "everyone, this is my girlfriend" girlfriends, it had been more years than he could count on his hands (including the missing finger). How could he be nervous? He'd confronted the very hordes of hell. He'd faced off with a man-eating starfish. He'd taken down mutant toad men. He'd stood in the lair of *Yoth-Sheol-Niggurauth*, mother of a thousand young, and bargained –

Oh, heck, there she was!

Dr Kathy Kaur walked towards him from the platform escalators. She was a vision of – okay, she wasn't a vision of loveliness or anything; Rod was nervous, he wasn't a love-struck mooncalf – but she was a vision of someone who had made an actual effort with their appearance. She was wearing a dress that wrapped over at the waist, hugging her figure in a way that was simple and yet very alluring. Rod had nipped into the office loos, changed into a fresh shirt and ditched his tie.

"Hi, Campbell."

"Kathy."

A wave of fresh panic washed over Rod. It wasn't a date but it was sort of date-ish. Should he give her a kiss on the cheek, Euro-style? Wasn't that what everyone did now? Or was that unprofessional? But they weren't in work. Should he? Yes, no, no, yes, maybe. No.

He leaned in a little and then, as an absolutely nothing gesture, patted her elbow.

She frowned at him with those expressive eyebrows of hers.

"Busy day?" she said.

"Always is," he said.

"Maybe a beer is in order."

"Christ, yes," he said.

Morag Junior rode the train into the city from Bournville and spent the journey peeling most of the plasters from the cat scratches on her hands. She'd left the gold top and khaki trousers on the bed as requested. She might be stepping into Morag Senior's shoes without express permission but she wasn't such a heel as to take the clothes Senior had bagsied. Junior made do with a simple skinny jeans and strappy top combo. She arrived at the station by half six and took the stairs up from the platform.

She had few details of the assignation. Cameron was arriving at six thirty. He was in the city because he had an interview for the tech support job. Morag Senior had agreed to meet him at the station but precisely where was unknown.

She spotted him instantly, hanging around beneath the departure boards. At first, she thought that he hadn't changed at all. He still had that dark, floppy hair. He still had that damned university scarf that made him look as if he was just about to cycle off to lectures or catch a train to Hogwarts. And then she saw subtle changes. He'd got a bit of sun for once in his life, his pale Scottish complexion was now a tanned caramel brown. There was a string of wooden beads around his neck under that scarf and running up between them was a pale pucker-edged scar. Travel had apparently changed him. He saw her approaching.

"I just got a text from you, saying you were going to be delayed," he smiled and planted a firm chaste kiss on both her cheeks, left then right. "*San-shu*, Morag Murray."

"My texts get delayed in the wi-fi or whatever," she said. "I've probably sent you a dozen others that'll turn up later when we're off somewhere else. It's like communicating with a time traveller."

She looked at him, properly looked at him. Cameron Barnes, the one that got away. He'd left Edinburgh eight months before she did and under far better circumstances. He'd taken up a research position in Micronesia or somewhere. It had been the amicable end of their decidedly casual but undeniably pleasant relationship.

"It's been too long, hasn't it?" he said.

"Too long," she agreed.

"I'm booked into a *dei-at rho* hotel which I think isn't far from here. But are you free for drinks or dinner?"

"Or both," she said.

"*Camchai.* Oh, and I got you this. Just a small thing." He pulled from his pocket a small box.

"A present? I really wasn't expecting…" She opened it. Sat in white tissue paper was an ornate thing of translucent white. It was evidently Venislarn in design for, although it was scored with encircling lines, it was impossible to identify if they were concentric circles or spiralling out. It was like a hurricane filled with snow, squashed flat and yet still, somehow, retaining its depth. "It's beautiful," she said.

Cameron lifted it out. It was threaded on a leather string: a pendant.

"It's a *shodu-bon* claim marker," he said.

"What is this? Glass?" she asked as he fixed it round her neck.

"It's mostly mucopolysaccharides," said Cameron.

"What?"

"Orally excreted by the *yon-bun* into these impossible geometries. There."

He stepped back to admire her.

"It's dried Venislarn spit?" she said.

"It's amazing, isn't it?"

"Oh. Oh, yes. It's… something."

Bacchus was a bar built into the basement of the Burlington Hotel on New Street. Rather than attempt to conceal the fact it was in a basement, the Bacchus bar embraced it. Exposed brickwork, dark wood beams and subdued lighting made it look the kind of place where gunpowder plots were hatched or nobles might be bricked up behind the walls.

Rod drank a pint of craft lager. He might have perhaps preferred a pint of the Labrador Stout but, mindful of Morag's mocking, had chosen something that at least looked like a mainstream beer. It was stealth real ale and had taken the edge right off his nervousness. Around the circular booth from him,

Kathy sipped from a bottle of tasteless Generic Beer-Coloured Liquid. Rod congratulated himself on not passing comment.

"So, give us the lowdown on this job I'm applying for," she said.

"There's the job they're going to interview you for and the job you'll end up doing."

"And the difference is?"

Rod turned his pint slowly.

"The job they're interviewing for will be all about cataloguing and categorising the ever-growing quantity of Venislarn materials we discover. Kind of like a scientist who discovers a new element or a new animal species, every single week."

"Ten new species of beetle are discovered every day," said Kathy.

"That can't be true."

"Prove me wrong."

Rod sipped. "In the interview, they'll have you believing that it's all about contributing to our expanding knowledge of the Venislarn horde and providing expert assistance to those of us who have to deal with it head on."

"And the reality of the job?"

"You're like the guys who have to find new ways of storing nuclear waste. New stuff – face-melting glow-in-the-dark stuff – will come in each week and you'll have to find somewhere to put it without being given any actual additional space to store it in."

"How did the last person deal with it?"

"Creative bureaucracy. And creative accountancy."

Kathy drank and gave him a quizzical look.

"As soon as summat turned up at the Dumping Ground or the Vault," said Rod, "Ingrid would put summat else on the back of a lorry and have it sent somewhere else. And with some subtle alteration to the paperwork, make it look like we hadn't sent it anywhere, or had kept some and sent some on so that we'd get budget for storage or whatever."

"I suppose that's easy with some of the unquantifiable stuff you have in storage."

"Right. Like those uncountable blue things," said Rod.

"Tiny Blue Innumerables," said Kathy.

"Them's the ones."

"And the Wittgenstein Volume."

"The what?"

"The Bloody Big Book," said Kathy. "If you sent half of that elsewhere, no one would ever know. It would still be infinitely big."

"Ingrid kept the Vault full," said Rod, "kept half of everything else on the road to here, there and everywhere and made sure we never had our budgets cut. She was clever, I'll give her that."

"She tried to destroy the city."

"Oh, aye. She was mad too. But clever." He shrugged. "We all have our off days."

"Off days? Unleashing city-eating gods counts as an off day?"

"I reckon you'll have had days when you've had enough and decide to cut a few corners."

"Speaking as doctor, I'd have to say that deciding to cut corners is spectacularly unprofessional." She gave him a shrewd look. "This is the point where I have to wonder if you're an undercover tabloid journalist. Or a cop wearing a wire. If you're a cop, you have to tell me."

Rod spread his arms as wide as the booth would allow. "Frisk me."

"Easy, tiger. So, are you a corner-cutter, Campbell?"

"We have to prioritise. Like the tech support job, we can't actually do the job as it appears on the job description."

"Triage," said Kathy.

"Aye. That. I was tempted to cut some corners today."

"How?"

"You ever met the Mammonites?"

She nodded. "The ones who'd sell their grandmother if it'd make a profit."

"And some of them probably have. I could have cut some corners today, solved a lot of problems and even saved some lives."

"How?"

"By shooting one or two of the evil gits."

"But a sense of duty got the better of you?"

"That and I've lost my gun."

"That just sounds careless."

"A giant spider ate it."

"That sounds made up."

"Totally true," he said, picking up his pint. "You can ask Morag. She was there."

"And she's here," said Kathy.

"What?"

Kathy inclined her head slightly. Rod looked. Morag was making her way through the press of people near the bar. She hadn't noticed Rod and Kathy and Rod didn't want her to. This might not be a date but Rod didn't want a third wheel at their table. Whatever she was doing here, maybe she'd take her drink to an entirely different corner... No, Morag turned and glanced their way. There was a moment in which their gazes met blankly. Morag and he could have done the quintessentially British thing of pretending not to notice or recognise each other, to avoid social awkwardness. But Morag clearly wasn't as skilled at it as Rod and her eyes widened in recognition before she could pretend otherwise.

She gave a single wave. That was it. They were committed. She would have to come over.

"Who's that with her?" said Kathy.

"Who?" said Rod.

Morag cut aside from the bar towards them and there was a man in tow, a dark-haired fellow who looked like Harry Potter's dad's stunt double.

"No idea," said Rod.

He took a deep breath and prepared to have his evening rudely interrupted by the diktats of polite society. That Morag looked equally put out by this turn of events was of no consolation at all.

Morag Senior ran up the stairs to her flat. It was a quarter to seven, the train home had spent twenty minutes idling at Five Ways station for no conceivable reason. She'd already texted Cameron once to let him know she'd be late. She wasn't going to tell him how much longer she was going to be late until she had an idea.

She had to get inside, get washed, throw on some clothes and the bare minimum of makeup and then head straight out again. She could do that in ten minutes, fifteen minutes tops.

Keys in the door, twist and in.

"I'm home!" she said.

There was a tinny, muffled reply from the lounge. She went through to the bedroom. There were two neat piles of clothes on the bed. The copy had done at least that. Morag instantly saw that Morag Junior had put the grey cropped trousers and the silk camisole in separate piles which just wouldn't do. The two of them clearly went together. Morag would sort that out when she picked a pile later.

Nonetheless her clothes for the evening were there, laid out separately. Good stuff.

"How was your day?" she called out.

There was no reply.

Morag went into the lounge. The TV was on but the room was empty, no Morag Junior. In a jar on the coffee table, a squished up *pabash kaj* doll turned to look at her.

"Put it on channel two!" demanded Steve the Destroyer. "*Eggheads* is on."

"Where is she?"

"Did you not hear me, morsel? Do it now or I will rend your flesh from your bones!"

"Shut it, Steve. Where is she?"

"She went out, to cover for you."

"She…" Fury rose in Morag, nought to a hundred in under a second. "She went to meet Cameron?"

"She went to meet some man," said Steve.

"Gallus bitch!"

"Now put on *Eggheads* before I destroy you," said the doll.

"Screw *Eggheads*. You're coming with me."

Rod couldn't fault the new guy, Cameron. He'd got the next round of drinks in. Bottles of Beer-Flavoured Liquid for Morag and Kathy, a craft lager for Rod and a pint of something dark, cloudy and mysterious for himself.

"What's that?" said Kathy.

"Labrador Stout," said Cameron. "Produced by a local microbrewery. I love microbrewery stuff and homebrew. It's more authentic, you know?"

"I don't know enough about beers and brewing and stuff to know what I'm buying."

"Try it," said Cameron and slid the pint towards her.

"Morag, you told me that real ale is boring," said Rod, "and that, I seem to remember, no woman in the history of the world ever liked it."

"Interesting stuff," said Kathy, licking a foamy moustache from her top lip.

"And I never said that," said Morag.

"Oh, it must be some other Morag who said it to me," said Rod.

"Must be. So, is it permissible for candidates to meet the night before the interview?"

"You're thinking of weddings, aren't you?" said Cameron. "Well, *say-up havvan isch.*"

"Huh?" said Rod.

"May the best candidate win," Cameron translated and offered a hand to Kathy.

She gave it a firm shake. "Bring it on."

"There's the third candidate of course," said Rod.

"Professor Sheikh Omar," said Morag.

"A professor?" said Cameron. "Professor of what?"

"Black magic *muda.*"

"And is he any good?" said Cameron.

"Good at what he does," Rod conceded. "But good? Hell, no. Whoever gets this job, we'd rather it was one of you two."

"I'll drink to that," said Kathy.

Cameron raised his glass to her and she clinked her bottle against it.

Rod wasn't a man governed by his emotions. He was a man for one thing. And a northerner too and emotions hadn't been introduced to the north until 1996. He regarded himself as thoroughly sensible and logical and yet... this Cameron fellow, with his well-spoken Scottish accent, random outbursts of Venislarn and his amiable little face and his... his hair, was getting too pally with Kathy for Rod's liking.

"You guys got dinner plans?" he asked as casually as he could.

"You said you'd booked some place," Cameron said. "*Bogota* or something."

"Did I?" said Morag. "Or we can go somewhere else. Pizza?"

"He's come all this way to Birmingham and you're not taking your guest out for a curry?" said Kathy.

"Cameron eat curry?" smiled Morag. "This is a man who used to think that spaghetti Bolognese was unnecessarily exotic."

"Hey, I'm a changed man," he said. "Travel broadens the mind. And the palate. I've eaten curry. I think I have. It was certainly spicy."

"You *think* it was curry?" said Kathy.

"It was in Indonesia. I can't say I was fluent in the local language. The menu was mostly pictures."

"You were in Indonesia?"

"Only *en route* to Pohnpei," said Cameron.

"What were you doing in Pohnpei?" asked Kathy. "You weren't part of the bloop research team?"

"For six months, earlier this year."

"Bloop?" said Rod.

Kathy put a hand on Rod's knee and for an instant he felt a teenage thrill at her touch. "Campbell, we have to take this wonderful man out for the finest curry Birmingham can offer and he can tell us all about it." And with that, the touch of her hand was

201

transformed and Rod knew that he had been friend-zoned like never before.

"But these two have a booking," said Rod.

"But you don't seem fussed about the place," Cameron said to Morag.

"Yeah, but you don't like curry," said Morag.

"I know this great place behind the Old Rep Theatre," said Kathy.

"The Taj?" said Rod.

"They'll have space for four people."

"Oh, we're all going," said Rod, turning a dismayed question into a statement of pleasant surprise halfway through.

"Sounds *pad camchai*," said Cameron.

"Oh, so it's settled then," said Morag in a tone of pleasant surprise that could perhaps have started out as a dismayed question.

They left Bacchus and walked through the back of the Burlington Arcade and round the side of the train station towards John Bright Street and the curry house. The sun had set. The red exterior lights of the Mailbox were visible beyond the A38 flyover, adding a pleasant demonic glow to the light of evening.

Dr Kathy Kaur led the way. Morag Junior looked at the woman's shoes. How could someone walk so briskly in heels that high? Cameron strolled alongside Kathy, and Junior found herself following a short distance behind with Rod. This was not how she had expected the evening to go. A night of wild passion with a former lover had been, perhaps, an unlikely prospect. Morag Senior turning up and dragging Junior into the street to the astonishment of all would have been more probable. But her base bid, her most reasonable expectation, had been of a gently intimate if non-sexual evening with an old friend, chewing the fat and getting all nostalgic about pointless shite. And now even that had been taken from her. She walked close to Rod.

"Sort this out," she hissed.

"Sort it out?" he hissed back.

"You've turned this into a double date!"

"It's not a date!"

"Oh, I'm glad yours isn't a date."

"And yours is?" said Rod. He nodded viciously ahead at Cameron. "Does he know?"

Junior huffed. "Okay. It's meeting up with an old friend, an ex."

"And we're just going out for drinks," said Rod.

"And a curry now, apparently. And no woman goes out for an innocent drink wearing heels like that."

"You mean…?"

"Oh, yeah. She's into you, Rod. Either that or she's meeting someone she fancies later."

Kathy and Cameron were at the corner now, turning left along the back of the train station. Rod and Junior increased their pace to catch up.

"I wasn't the one who changed their plans to make it a double date," said Rod.

"You were the one who suggested food!" snapped Junior.

"To get rid of you two! So we could have a bit of, you know, privacy."

Morag Junior's laugh was hollow and knowing. "So, it's not just drinks then, is it?"

They turned the corner. Their dates (or not-dates) were getting away.

"The night is young," said Rod. "We were going to see where things led."

"They're leading to the Taj bloody Mahal."

"Are you drunk?"

"Wish I was," she said.

He shook his head bitterly and looked down.

"What happened to your hands?"

"Huh?" She looked at the scratches and the few remaining plasters. "I was attacked while helping Mrs Atraxas trim her cat."

"You were down at the canal only a bit ago, confiscating flying horrors from Wizard Tim –"

"Mystic Trevor."

"Whatever – and you were able to nip home, give a cat a haircut and be back in time to meet sexy boy there."

"I'm a woman. I can multitask."

Much of the Library of Birmingham was in darkness. The office staff had gone for the day. The armed security teams patrolled only the lower floors and the bits of the Vault they were permitted access to. Up on the seventh floor, Nina Seth and Chief Inspector Ricky Lee sat on swivel chairs, face to face, knees to knees. Five minutes earlier, Ricky had phoned his wife and told her that he was working late on a case. This was technically true, although he hadn't mentioned he was currently sitting with his occasional fuck-buddy, planning to take alien recreational drugs.

"You are aware that drugs detectives don't spend their time sampling the gear," he said.

"We need to understand the effects," said Nina. "When we get the call, we need to know what we're dealing with."

"No good if we turn up to the scene smashed out of our skulls."

"Sven assures me that the effects only last as long as the rune is in contact with the body."

Ricky turned over the square of paper.

"Drugs that you can switch off whenever you like. Hardly sounds like a worry for us guys."

"Yeah, but some people swallow when they mean to spit," said Nina. "Come on."

She held up her square. Ricky did likewise.

"Three," said Nina.

"Two," said Ricky.

"One."

Broad Street was half a mile of pubs, clubs, bars, casinos, comedy clubs, hotels, fine restaurants, budget buffet eateries and nasty late-night takeaways. On Fridays and Saturdays, the roads were closed to vehicle traffic, not to create an open pedestrian space and street café culture but simply to cut down on the number of drunks getting hit by passing taxis. It was said that Broad Street had everything you could want from a night out, if you wanted cheap alcohol, a fight and a new STD.

Rockerfellers occupied a space at the unfashionable Five Ways end of Broad Street, between a peri peri chicken shack and the Kowloon Casino. It was a popular spot for lost hen parties, uni kids who had already spent most of their student loan in classier places and, tonight, Tony T and the rest of his Waters Crew.

As promised, Jeffney Ray had found them a dark corner and four positively toxic fishbowl cocktails. Recycled beats of the latest dance hits throbbed from recessed speakers and set Ray's teeth on edge. Out on the dance floor, a woman wrapped in a feather boa bopped drunkenly to the music. Tony T spread his arms wide along the back of the long seat, like this was his place, like he was a king come home. Death Roe, Pupfish and Fluke squabbled over who had the bigger cocktail.

"Done good, Ray," said Tony T. "Now – ggh! – round us up some honeys."

Ray laughed, a gentle respectful laugh. Tony T might be a naïve fish-out-of-water but he was dangerous. "I'm afraid that's up to you boys. I've got some product to shift."

"What product?"

Ray dipped into a pocket and held up a single square of paper. Tony T blinked at it.

"Ggh! What *adn-bhul muda* is that?"

"Activated *Kal Frexo* runes."

Tony T gave him a blank stare. Blanks stares came naturally to fish boys.

"They're contact-activated," said Ray. "Stick it under your tongue. Stick it up your nose. Stick it anywhere you like and it'll work."

"Never heard of them." He clicked his wet fingers. "Give one to Pup."

"What?" said Pupfish.

Ray held out the rune paper. Fluke took it and turned to Pupfish.

"Open wide."

"I ain't taking that *muda*."

"Come on – ggh! – that's not what your momma says when guys tell her to open wide."

"Stop dissing my mom, Fluke."

"Ggh! I'll stop dissing her when she stops giving me freebies." Fluke slapped Pupfish in the gills and shoved the paper in his mouth.

Pupfish pouted sullenly.

"It's warm," he said. "It's…" He raised his head and gazed about the room. "Ggh! Are you guys seeing this?"

"Give me one," said Death Roe.

"Only the first hit is free," said Ray, stepping back slowly, tantalisingly. "I'm around all night."

Nina was instantly struck by how shoddy-looking the rune drug effects were. The moment the paper touched the inside of her mouth, the world around her was cast in green and blue light, like the up-lighting used for the baddie in a pantomime, all garish light and deep shadows that would instantly make the audience hiss and boo.

"It's like a bad disco," she said, mumbling slightly around the sliver of paper.

In the unreal light of the other world, projected over and blurring with the office around them, shapes loomed near and lurked in the distance: fibrous tree-like structures, organic lattices of pipes, frill-edged discs. Dewy tendrils waved in a wind that couldn't be felt.

"Like looking at weird shit close up," she said.

"It's like being in an old *Doctor Who* episode. A really cheap one," said Ricky. "'Attack of the Green-Screen Mushroom Men'. What is this?"

"*Kal Frexo leng*-space," said Nina. "Hell."

"I'd have thought hell would have higher production values. Is this place real?"

Nina nodded. Ricky raised a hand to touch a hanging creeper.

"Consensual hallucination. We're seeing the same thing. This is an actual place. The drugs are summoning runes. Part of a ritual. But it's incomplete. It's a window, not a doorway."

206

"So, we can see them but they can't see us."

"They?"

Ricky pointed. Nina swivelled her chair. Figures pushed slowly through the fungal plant-life (and the office wall) towards them. Figures. They were round, not humanoid, and walked on shovel-like appendages that might have been hooves or might have been huge fingernails.

"*Leng*-space residents," said Nina. "Possibly priests of *Nystar*."

"But can they see us?" said Ricky, rising with nervous energy.

The prehensile limbs that sprouted from the creature's tops bent towards them, like daisies towards the sun.

"Logic says they can't," said Nina.

She saw a pair of mouths open in the body of one. They moved in speech but there was no sound.

"Fuck logic," said Nina.

"Is it working?" said Ray.

The pretty girl nodded mutely and smiled.

"Is it E?" her friend asked.

"Something new," said Ray.

The pretty girl's eyes sparkled. She had a pretty face but a body like an ironing board. The friend's body was all hot, slutty curves but she had a face like a bulldog chewing a nettle. One with a beautiful face. One with a hot body. Ray thought it was a crime and a shame. Maybe if they offered do a threesome with him, he'd consider it, but only consider it.

"What's it like?" the bulldog asked as the pretty friend pirouetted towards the dance floor.

"Twenty quid," said Ray.

"Is it E?"

"It's not E."

"We took some E in Magaluf. It was insane!"

"Fucking hell, bitch," he said under his breath and under the thud of the music. "It's not E."

"Twenty?" she said, digging in her purse.

She passed him the cash and Ray pocketed it.

"Put it in your mouth but don't swallow it," he said.

"Like E?" she said.

Ray made fists with his hands and said nothing.

Morag Senior hunched at the bar of the South American street food restaurant, even though attempting to hide was probably drawing more attention to her rather than diverting it away. The young Australian behind the bar finished serving another customer and came over.

"What name was it under?" he asked.

"Murray. Morag Murray," she whispered.

He looked at his till screen. "That booking was for over an hour ago."

"I know. I just want to know where you sat them?"

"And you are?" he asked.

"I'm Morag Murray. It's my booking. I couldn't see them when I came in and I wondered..." She glanced over her shoulder at the stairs leading both up and down to other seating areas.

"But you didn't turn up," said the Australian. "We've given the table away."

"What do you mean, didn't turn up?"

He put ten fingertips on the bar. "You did just walk in, didn't you?"

"Yes, but... When they... It's..."

"You're here *now*," he said, slowly, as though he was talking to a nutter. "You didn't come *then*. No one came *then* because you are here *now*."

"But where did they go?"

The Australian licked his lips and glanced at the bar phone on the wall. It was a coin toss as to whether he was planning on calling the police or an ambulance.

"Where did *who* go?" he asked slowly.

"Eat his skin!" shrieked a tiny voice from within Morag's handbag.

"Did something in your handbag shout 'Eat his skin'?" said the Australian.

"It's just my ringtone," said Morag which, on reflection, wasn't the best answer she could have given.

Morag Junior waved for the waiter to bring her another beer.

"Make that two," said Rod sourly.

They sat side by side, watching Cameron and Kathy have a *fascinating* conversation with one another across the destroyed remains of their starters.

"I'm so jealous," Kathy said to Cameron. "Six months on a research platform in the south Pacific, just you and the elements and the sunken city of *Cary'yeh*, home of *Zildrohar-Cqulu*."

"*Zildrohar?*" said Junior. "I thought he was in the south Atlantic."

Cameron snapped the poppadum in his hand, shocked. "*Muda*. I went to the wrong fucking ocean." And then he laughed. Kathy too. "It was the Pacific, Morag. I'm fairly sure." He grinned and pointed at her. "Your sense of direction. Wasn't it you who got lost in your own apartment once?"

"In the building," said Junior. "Those Edinburgh tenements all look the same. And you shouldn't be a cock about it."

"I'm sorry," he said, hands raised. "Mia culpa." He looked at his phone. "Ah, a text from you, Morag. How long ago did you send that?" He suddenly snorted with laughter.

"What?" she said.

He showed her. The text read, WHERE ARE YOU?

"I'm saying nothing," said Cameron.

"Don't reply," said Junior. "I think I know where you are now."

The waiter came with the beers. Rod downed half his bottle and then asked, "So what was this 'bloop' research you were doing, Cameron?"

"It was the bloop," said Kathy. "You know, the bloop."

"I'm hearing the word 'bloop' a lot," said Rod. "I don't know what it is."

"The bloop. It was a sound. First heard in the late nineties by oceanographers in the Pacific."

"That's right," said Cameron. "A sound like no other, coming from the deep ocean. It wasn't whales. It wasn't seismic activity. Totally *funsa wiar*."

"It was the Venislarn," Rod hazarded.

"Exactly," said Cameron. "A city. A civilisation. A culture far richer and more diverse than any on Earth. But, of course, the really important thing about the bloop is that it might have been the sound of the first Venislarn arriving on our world, the spearhead of their invasion, the great city of *Cary'yeh*, anchoring itself in the depths of the ocean."

"Nah, mate," said Rod. "The Venislarn have been here for decades, hundreds of years."

"But their point of arrival might have been as little as twenty years ago."

Rod straightened himself up in his chair.

"I think one of us is drunk. You can't arrive after you've already arrived."

"Time doesn't apply to the Venislarn the same way it applies to us," said Junior.

"And it might be that the appearance of the Venislarn in *Cary'yeh* called the rest of the Venislarn past, present and future into our world by ontological necessity," said Cameron.

Rod was shaking his head. Junior didn't know what he was on about either but kept shtum and tried to look intelligent.

"It's like the Mathematical Universe hypothesis," continued Cameron. "Our reality has been called into being by the inherent truth of mathematics. Our universe is an expression of mathematical structures."

"Yep, it's definitely me," said Rod, making a show of looking at his bottle.

Kathy smiled at Rod. It wasn't an unkind smile but it was the sort of smile one gave to a stupid kitten that had got its head stuck in a box.

"It's like…" She looked around the table and picked up the little silver bowl of sliced salad. "It's like this."

"Salad," said Rod.

"Right. Nobody ordered it. None of us want it. But, we all know that if you have a curry a little bowl of salad turns up at some point. Ontological necessity."

"I knew there was a reason I hate salad," said Junior.

"You like salad," said Rod.

"Shhhh." She pointed at Cameron through her raised palm. "There's another Scot here. He hears that and I can lose my passport."

"It's true," Rod said to Cameron. "She's gone totally native."

"Gone native in Birmingham," smiled Cameron. "That sounds *gigginin* terrible."

"And what do you mean by that?" said Kathy with a sudden and not entirely affected brittleness.

"Well, it's Birmingham, isn't it?" said Cameron. "I mean, I'm looking forward to working here but it's not like it has much to offer, does it? It's like a standing joke."

He looked from face to face to face.

"Second largest city in Britain," said Kathy.

"More canals that Venice," said Rod.

"More parks than Paris," said Junior.

"Birthplace of the British Enlightenment."

"And the Industrial Revolution."

"And heavy metal."

"And the balti."

"It's green."

"It's friendly."

"It doesn't pretend to be something it's not."

"It's not Manchester."

Cameron clutched his chest as though shot. "Okay, you got me. Birmingham's bloody *camchai*. The next round's on me."

"The meal's on you at this rate," said Kathy. "And we need to order."

Cameron reached over and put his hand on Junior's to get her attention.

"I never realised Birmingham was so amazing. Let's hope I get this job tomorrow."

"Keep hoping," said Kathy as she browsed the menu. "And Birmingham's not perfect."

"No," agreed Rod. "The roads are mess."

"It's too far from the sea," said Junior.

"The council can't balance the books," said Kathy.

"The tunnels make no sense. You could starve to death trying to navigate through the city."

"The accent sounds stupid."

"There isn't a decent tram or underground system."

"It's not Manchester."

The waiter came to take their order. Kathy pored critically over the menu.

"They give these chili ratings but a lot of places they just don't make the food hot enough."

Rod grinned. "Is this some macho thing?"

"Of course, Campbell," said Kathy drily. "I'm trying to prove my manly credentials by eating the hottest thing on the menu. I just like hot food, okay?"

"Well, nothing too hot for me," said Cameron. "Go easy on the new boy."

"You could just join me in a madras," suggested Rod.

"Is that hot?" said Cameron.

"No," said Kathy and Rod as one.

"Yes, it is," said Morag Junior. "He's being cruel and she's got a mouth made of Teflon."

Rod frowned. "Teflon?"

"Yes, as in it won't – I don't mean Teflon, do I? That's non-stick. What's the stuff that doesn't burn?" There were shrugs. "Famously doesn't burn," she said. Responses weren't forthcoming. "Anyway, just stick to kormas and bhunas, Cameron. It'll be a chicken bhuna and keema naan for me," she said to the waiter.

"Spoilsport," said Rod and asked the waiter for another beer.

Rain spattered against the window. The weather had turned.

"So, what made you give up the sunny south Pacific for Birmingham?" said Kathy.

Something nudged Junior's shoe. Nudge, nudge.

212

"I wish I didn't have to," said Cameron. "I was spending every day studying the *Cquluman'i* Venislarn, getting to know them intimately."

"Intimately?" said Rod.

"I made friends, I'm not embarrassed to say it. But the rotation I was on came to an end," said Cameron. "There's a limit to the amount of time you can spend there, due to exposure to gloxym and fuligin. Besides, I had to come home for my mum."

The foot nudging continued. Was it Cameron's shoe? Was he playing footsie?

"Your mum, how is she?" she said. "I always remember how she used to –"

"She died," he said abruptly. "A couple of months back. Cancer."

"I'm sorry."

Nudge, nudge. Okay, footsie was one thing. Footsie while talking about your dead mother was... odd.

Cameron smiled sadly.

"I was with her at the end. It was as peaceful as it could be. As they say, *sa'frei kantutin ai*."

"That's something," said Junior. "Excuse me."

She peered under the table. Steve the Destroyer was trying to hack off her feet with a teaspoon from the pickle tray. She stared at him. Steve the Destroyer stared back with his wooden eyes and continued his savage and ineffectual attack.

"Lost something?" Rod asked her.

"Um, no."

Junior reached down, took hold of Steve and balled him in her fist to conceal him completely.

"I just need to get a moment of fresh air," she said, scraped her chair back and went outside onto the dark side street. The rain was light but unpleasantly cold.

"How the hell did you g–"

A hand grabbed her shoulder and hauled her away from the windows and into the pungent shadows of a commercial dumpster.

"I have spent all night looking for you!" hissed Morag Senior.

"Ah," said Junior.

"'Ah'? What fucking good is 'Ah'? Have you been drinking?"

"Of course, I've been drinking," said Junior. "We're having a night out."

"I'd booked a table."

"Change of plans."

Even in the dark, the fury was written large on Senior's face.

"Your gold top looks nice," said Junior.

"This is insubordination," snapped Senior.

"I am not your slave, Morag Murray."

"No," Senior snarled. "No, you're like the bloody annoying twin sister I never asked for. Take off your jeans and top."

"What?" said Junior, thinking for a thankfully brief instant that her doppelganger wanted to have angry sex behind a dumpster.

"I'm going in," said Senior. "Give me your jeans and top."

"But I thought you wanted to wear that gold top and khaki pedal pushers?"

"Yes, but if I come out wearing one set of clothes and go back in wearing another, that might draw some suspicion."

"You think men actually notice what we're wearing?"

"The men will only take notice if I go in there naked, but Kathy will spot a change of outfit."

"Here. Hold this," said Junior, handing over the struggling Steve as she undressed. "And what am I supposed to do?"

"Go home. Go elsewhere. I don't care."

"I'm down to my last three quid. *You're* the one with the purse."

Senior growled. There then occurred a complex back-and-forth, like the world's most boring juggling act. Senior took her purse, phone and keys out of her handbag and thrust them at Junior. "No, I need that," she said, took the purse back, gave Junior Steve to hold, removed a twenty, and passed it to Junior. Junior took the twenty and gave Senior the top and the jeans (with Steve wrapped inside). Senior stuffed Steve in her purse and tried to remove her pedal pushers without revealing too much bottom. "I've seen it all before," said Junior. "And I don't need keys. They were copied by the vase." She passed the keys back to Senior and took the gold top. Senior put the keys in the handbag, surprised herself by finding Steve there, took him out, gave him back to Junior. "I will digest your essence, snotling!" came his muffled cry in Junior's fist as she struggled into the gold top (which had a complicated neck fastening).

"Right!" said Junior. "So, I piss off home while you get to spend the rest of the evening with Cameron."

"Exactly," said Senior.

"I'm just the warm up guy."

"Sure, whatever." Senior straightened her clothing and ran her fingers through her hair. "Is there anything I need to know before I go in?"

"Oh, you'll need this," said Junior and unclipped the pendant around her neck. "Cameron gave this to me. You. Us. A gift."

She helped fasten the congealed spittle pendant around Senior's neck.

"That's sweet of him," said Senior. "What is this? Glass?"

"Sure. Why not?" said Junior and wheeled away, feeling more than a little tipsy now that she was upright and in the cool evening air.

One of the bouncers sauntered over while Ray was surreptitiously counting his cash. The club was near buzzing now. Cheap and nasty drinks were enough to fill the place, even on a Wednesday, and Ray had sold enough of the runes already to pay back the Black Barge in the morning.

"You can't sell that shit in here," said the bouncer.

"It's cool, Naz."

"It's not cool."

"We had an agreement," said Ray and tucked his bulging wallet away.

"I agreed to let you bring your freak friends in," said Naz, looming over Ray. It was some impressive looming, given that Naz was a good few inches shorter than Ray. "I didn't give you permission to sell – what is this shit?"

"It's fine," said Ray. "It's not even illegal."

Naz tapped Ray's chest with the back of his gloved hand, a gesture to cough up. Ray got out his baggie of paper squares.

Naz looked back to the dance floor. There wasn't much in the way of dancing. Boys and girls who should be getting smashed and dry humping each other in the darkest corners were swaying too slowly for the music, their hands raised as though playing with the light.

"This acid?" said Naz.

"It's new. It's not acid."

"We still get our cut," said Naz.

"How much?" said Ray.

"Some stupid cow dies on the dance floor, her spinal fluid all dried up by ecstasy, then I need compensation."

Ray had no intention of letting this bouncer get anywhere near his hard-earned cash. Time to move on to another club. Ray offered a rune to Naz.

"Try one."

"You kidding me?" said Naz. "I wouldn't put that in my mouth even if –"

Naz's conditions went unsaid as a scream went up from the dance floor. Naz turned.

Two girls were yelling in panic and clutching at one another. One was pointing across the floor – not at anything actually in the room, Ray knew.

"Get it away!" yelled the other.

"It's just a hallucination," said Ray to no one at all. "It's not real."

One of the girls retched and then spat. A tiny fleck of blue paper hit the floor. She gasped, as though coming up for air. The other girl kept screaming.

"Your fucking drugs," muttered Naz and then stormed towards the dance floor. "Out! Take her out!" he shouted.

And then something did take the screaming girl. It wasn't human. It wasn't visible. It grabbed her by the waist...

Ray could see the indents of something wet and invisible against the girl's thin dress – coils! – and it pulled her back into the darkness.

Suddenly, she wasn't the only one screaming.

Morag Senior stopped at the door of the Taj Mahal, checked her reflection as best she could in the glass, put on a brave face and walked in. She looked round for Cameron, wondering where she had seen him from outside.

Rod was waving at her from a booth. She went over.

Cameron Barnes sat next to Rod's doctor friend, Kathy Kaur. Morag's first thought on seeing Cameron was that he was tanned, looking a bit more butch than she remembered him, particularly with that pale scar running up from his collar to his jawline. Her second thought was that it had hardly been an age since they were both up in Scotland, together.

"Cameron," she said. "Kathy."

They looked up at her and she realised her stupid mistake. She wasn't meeting them for the first time that evening. Morag Junior, the conniving minx had already been enjoying their company for several hours.

"Yes?" said Cameron.

"Can I just say, that it's really lovely to see you both tonight," waffled Morag.

"Yes," said Kathy. "Yes, you can."

Rod gave her a penetrating look. "You've changed," he said.

"Haven't we all?" she said and sat down.

"God, yes," said Cameron. "You certainly have. You've... matured."

"Word to the wise, lad," said Rod. "Never tell a lady she's matured. Doesn't go down well."

"Oh, so am I not mature?" said Kathy. The doctor's eyebrows jiggled coyly. Morag knew some people who talked with their hands. Kathy Kaur seemed to talk with her forehead.

"No," said Rod.

"So, I'm immature?" said Kathy.

"Ah. No."

"*I meant,*" cut in Cameron and Morag realised from his emphasis that he was slightly drunk and that perhaps they were all a bit worse for drink, "that, back in the day, a week wouldn't go by

217

without Morag getting hauled up before Bannerman for some *dolot* mistake or other. And yet, down here, your colleague has nothing but kind words for you."

"Plasters!" declared Rod loudly.

"Is that a kind word?" said Cameron. "It's not in my lexicon."

"I need a beer," said Morag and looked for a waiter.

"That's your beer," said Rod, moving a mostly full bottle over to her. "What I meant was that's what's changed about you. Plasters."

"Hmmm?" Morag hesitated a moment before drinking the beer. By drinking from a bottle that had touched Morag Junior's lips, was she drinking from someone else's bottle or her own?

"You had plasters on your hands when you went outside," said Rod.

"Did I? I did. I did. I took them off and binned them."

"But what about all the scratches?"

"Scratches?" she said. "Yes. They've healed."

"That was quick."

"Yes. Yes, it was. I heal quickly. We're renowned for it," she said, letting the ambiguity of who the 'we' exactly was remain. "I'm like that superhero, you know. The one with the claws and the hair and the super-healing."

Kathy clicked her fingers. "Asbestos."

"No," said Morag authoritatively. "He's not called Asbestos."

"No, that's the thing that doesn't burn. It's famous for it. It's been bugging me for ages."

"Has it?" said Morag, who had no idea what to do with a non sequitur like that.

"If anything," said Rod thoughtfully, "Asbestos would be a supervillain."

"What would his super powers be?" said Cameron.

"Flame-resistant," said Rod, "that's a given."

"The ability to cause lung diseases," said Kathy.

"Turning up unexpectedly during building renovations and being able to close schools and other public buildings for weeks," said Rod.

"I wouldn't mind Asbestos dropping in at our place. Bit of extra holiday," she said. She looked at the menu. "Shall we order?"

They were all suddenly laughing.

"We've ordered," said Cameron.

Rod clapped her on the shoulder. "First day Morag started with us," he said to Cameron and Kathy, "she leapt straight in, hunted down this Kermit-Arsehole that –"

"*Kerrphwign-Azhal*," said Morag.

"Curvy-*Azhal*," he said.

"Just say 'man-eating starfish' if it's easier," said Kathy.

"Hunted it down," said Rod, pressing on unabashed. "Stopped it eating this little boy up at the hospital. Put her life on the line. We came here to celebrate."

"We came here?" said Morag, surprised. "I *was* drunk."

"Drunk and tired. Morag here was so drunk and tired she asked for the bill before we even ate."

As they laughed, Morag waved her hands to calm them.

"Okay. Okay. Enough of making Morag look like a fool. Tonight's not about me." She swigged her beer and gestured across at Cameron. "Hey, how's your mum doing these days?"

The call had come through to Ricky Lee, an incident that could only be described as bizarre at a Broad Street night club. It was close enough to the Library of Birmingham that it was almost quicker for Nina and Ricky to walk there than drive. Ricky drove up the centre of Broad Street, sirens on, his car straddling the low brick island that ran up much of the street. Nina's phone buzzed; a message from Morag.

IN TOWN. FANCY A DRINK?

Nina put a call straight back to her.

"Drink?" said Morag.

"The traditional Scottish greeting. Taxi!" she said to Ricky as a black cab pulled out blindly in front of them. Ricky swerved like a pro.

"Drink?" said Morag.

"I thought you were meeting that Cameron dude for a Highland fling."

"Wordplay. Hilarious." There was the sound of heels on pavement and, more faintly, a stream of high-pitched threats and curses, like a drunken pub fighter on helium.

"I'm actually on a call," said Nina. "Those hallucinogenic runes."

"Where?" said Morag, the drunkenness in her voice gone at once.

"Rockerfellers on Broad Street."

"I know the one," said Morag.

"You do?" said Nina surprised.

"The one next to the Chinese casino? Yeah, twenty quid to wrestle to music in a giant darkened sauna where drink prices start at a fiver and go up steeply."

"Yeah, although that's pretty much every club." Ricky slowed, aiming for the cluster of emergency vehicles a little way ahead. "We could use your expertise if you're in a fit state."

Morag laughed at that. "I'll be sober by the time I get there. I'm just by the Alex."

"Then you're only ten minutes behind us. See you there."

They got out, Ricky a fraction ahead of her. He was already chatting to the two cops who were blocking off the pavement. There were four police cars and two ambulances already at the scene and several dozen hysterical clubbers. Two paramedics were trying to get a woman in a pink printed T-shirt and a tutu into the ambulance but, pumped with adrenaline and wild-eyed, she was fighting them all the way. There was a violent spiral cut on her arm. Not a typical Broad Street injury.

"Do not send any officers inside," Nina told Ricky.

"Four guys have already gone in," he replied.

Nina approached a hen party – she assumed it was a hen party; it seemed an odd time to be doing a fancy-dress fun run for breast cancer which was the only other possible explanation for their clothing choices. Nina picked a woman who seemed more with it than most, a woman with a livid bruise on her neck, precise and detailed enough that Nina could see the outlines of sucker marks.

"What's in there?" said Nina.

The woman stared blankly. Nina gripped her arm.

"What did you see?"

"Nothing," said the woman. "Nothing. Something took Allana."

"But you took the drugs," said Nina and pointed at the wound on the woman's neck. "What did you see?"

"I didn't take anything. Honest. I don't even drink."

Nina looked for Ricky and spotted him in conversation with a uniformed offer.

"Chief Inspector Lee! You need to get your guys out of there."

"There are members of the public in there," he shouted back.

"And four coppers. Get them out."

She went to the call log on her phone and dialled Morag.

"I'm on my way," said Morag, puffing.

"People have been attacked," said Nina.

"If you keep the rune activated long enough then beings –"

"People who've not taken them."

"Not possible," said Morag and then, "Unless there's some sort of critical mass effect if enough people activate the runes in close proximity. I'm guessing."

"This woman says her friend was 'taken'."

"It's not a gateway," said Morag. "At least not a two-way gateway. Those particular runes are lost. Something could potentially reach through… not reach through exactly but pull someone back."

"Right."

"Nina. It can only work one way."

"Okay."

"No getting them back."

"Gotcha. One way trip to hell. See you soon. Maybe."

"What do you mean –"

Nina ended the call and went to the night club entrance. A police officer put a hand up to stop her. He was a tall chap –

everyone was taller than Nina but this guy was taller still – and looked like he lived to tell people where they could and couldn't go.

"You can't go in, miss."

"Jesus."

Nina was used to being stopped outside clubs and bars, the price she paid for her youthful good looks. This had to be the first time she had been stopped going into a club that was literally hellish.

"Ricky!" she called.

Ricky looked over.

"You're going in?"

She nodded.

"Wait there. I'm coming with you."

"Why? What good will you be?"

His wounded look made her smile.

"But…" he said. "The things in there…"

She shrugged. "YOLO," she said, gave the cop on the door a look until he stepped aside and then went in.

Knives had no effect on the monsters. Neither did bullets. Tony T had discovered this the hard way.

When the *muda* went down and the invisible *glun'u-te* started picking off the humans on the dance floor, it was like watching a fire take hold. There was an initial moment of surprise, the flaring up of something new, and then the undeniable excitement of seeing it spread outward, destruction in action, followed by the realisation that this might be *adn-bhul* dangerous and a wise *samakha* should already be heading for the nearest exit. By then, it was too late to simply run for it.

A man in a blood-soaked shirt ran towards their booth then suddenly changed course as something unseen wrapped itself around his ankle, hauled him away and slammed him against a wall.

"Ggh! This is *bhul-detar*!" Tony shouted, put his hand down the crotch of his tracksuit and pulled out the final defence pistol he kept in his pants. Death Roe tried to tip their table over to form a barricade and discovered it was bolted to the floor. His muscles straining, the big guy uprooted it and tipped it over anyway. Fluke, who had certain priorities, managed to rescue one of the fishbowl cocktails just in time.

"There!" shouted Pupfish, pointing at nothing. "There!"

Death Roe swung his knife speculatively at thin air.

"Can't see *muda*! Ggh!" said Fluke.

A bar stool rose into the air. Tony fired at an empty space just below the stool. Glass shattered somewhere, the stool remained raised.

"There!" yelled Pupfish. Death Roe swung. Tony fired. "There!" screamed the idiot Pupfish and then something took him, hooked him around the waist and hauled him back, not across the room but away and out of this world, as though the scene before them was printed on a curtain and Pupfish had been dragged into its folds.

"Pup!" yelled Fluke.

Tony was angry now. He was scared for sure but he was *adn-bhul* angry now too. These *pabbe-grru shaska* were attacking his crew and ruining the best night out they'd had in months. Nonetheless, Tony T hadn't risen to the position he held now by picking the wrong fights.

"Fire exit!" he shouted, waving his gun at a green running man sign.

"Where's Pup?" cried Fluke.

"Fire exit!" yelled Tony and shoved him.

Death Roe cleared the way, barging aside a wandering human and kicking through a cluster of chairs to get to the door. He slammed up against the door. It opened several inches and then stopped. The metal handles were chained together.

"*Bhul!*" snarled Tony, placed the nose of his little pistol against the padlock and fired. The ricochet ripped a shallow cut along Tony's thigh and smashed Fluke's fishbowl. The lock remained untouched. Not even a scratch. Tony roared in pain and frustration. Roaring didn't come easy to *samakha* – it was more like a goat bleat than a big cat roar – but he roared all the same.

Something whacked Death Roe across the head and sent him sprawling. And then Tony saw Jeffney Ray, cowering beside a pillar not ten feet away.

"*Shod-doi!*" spat Tony and grabbed Ray. "Ggh! This is your *doi* fault, *muda ben ai!*"

Ray had his hands raised to protect his ugly scarred face.

"Sold in good faith!" he protested. "All sold in good faith!"

Death Roe tried to stand up and a table came smashing down on his back.

Tony fired, hitting nothing.

"Give them to me!" said Tony and rifled through Ray's pockets. Ray didn't resist.

Tony found the bag of rune papers, ripped it open, sending them everywhere and then put one in his mouth. Suddenly he could see. A murky light that was not of this world filled the room. The pain and suffering and fear which had been hidden in the dark corners of the nightclub was now plainly visible. Around him, tree branches that weren't tree branches, weird bulbous growths and wet, dangling tendrils. It was like a cross between some David Attenborough jungle *muda* and the mould growing on his mum's kitchen wall.

Fat round creatures, with four horse feet and tentacles where their heads should be, filled the dancefloor. There was a fuckload of them, twenty at least. The thin mouths in their bellies opened and closed in unison. Tony couldn't hear them over the music that was still playing but it looked like they were singing or chanting.

One of the fat *shaska* stood over Death Roe. Death Roe was swinging his blade at it – through it – but it was like it was a hologram. It could touch him but he couldn't touch it back. And that was just unfair. Tony fired his pistol at it but it was like shooting at air. Maybe the creatures understood that he had tried to attack them. Maybe. Whatever, a pair of them began to trundle at a leisurely pace towards the *samakha* gang trapped by the fire exit.

"Ain't *adn-bhul* going out like this," said Tony.

"Like what?" said Fluke.

Tony raised the pistol. He was going to put Fluke out of his misery before these tentacled butterballs could have him.

"Tony?" said Fluke, eyeing the pistol.

There was a squeal of feedback from the club speakers and then a voice over the top of the music.

"All right! Do we have anyone from *Leng* in the house tonight?" Tony recognised the voice. He looked towards the DJ booth. It was that scrawny minx from the consular mission. Nina Seth. Tony knew her well. She was a right laugh sometimes and a stone-cold bitch at others. "*Shad ap'su byanah. Kahaiyn-de shiaufa yo-jadszoar fuabair!*" she yelled.

That got the tentacle heads' attention. Slowly, turning clumsily, they drifted towards her.

"Put your tentacles in the air like you just don't care!" hollered Nina.

"What's – ggh! – she doing?" said Fluke.

On the floor, Death Roe gasped and struggled to his feet as the monster over him lost interest.

"Hey, how many priests of *Nystar* does it take to change a lightbulb?" called Nina. "Three! One to screw the lightbulb, one to say when the stars are right and one to *pu'qalsit myek oh*. Huh? Huh? Am I right?"

In their silent other-world, the tentacled blobs shouted angrily and threw themselves against the DJ booth. Nina ducked and grabbed the microphone.

"Anyone with two legs, seriously, now's the time to run for the exit. And spit out any of that rune crap. Drugs are bad, m'kay?"

Tony T propelled Fluke towards the door, grabbed Death Roe by his jacket shoulder and pushed him forward as well. Tony T was keeping his crew close and would use them as shields if he had to.

The glass around the DJ booth shattered under a torrent of flailing pseudo-limbs. The music screeched, popped and died.

"And anyone who helps the wounded out gets free vodka jelly shots at the after-party," Nina shouted, no longer with the aid of a microphone.

Skirting wide past the mass of monsters, Tony clawed the remains of the rune paper from his mouth and threw it down. The alien light was gone. Bare electric lights shone on a dead night club, all smashed glass, broken furniture and floor that was slick with spilt drinks and blood.

Morag Junior could see the lights of police cars and ambulances ahead. She'd possibly taken a wrong turn by the Mailbox (after a month, this city was still a mystery to her) and had not yet caught up with Nina. The sheer number of emergency vehicles had drawn rubberneckers in. Traffic stood still on Broad Street. Midweek revellers stood in the road and gawped.

Morag could hear shouts and cries. There was a commotion on the pavement and the crowd swelled around the epicentre that was the Rockerfellers nightclub. Screams rose and the silhouettes of police officers struggled with containment.

The wave of people and the rapidly dissipating panic rippled down the road. Morag was jostled by a herd of drunks who were either trying to get out of the way or fighting for a better view. Then someone ran past her heading toward an Australian bar on the canalside. It took Junior's brain a long five seconds to click. The *Kal Frexo* runes. Morag Senior had mentioned a dealer or something with a scarred face and the guy running pell-mell for the canal had a face that was more scratches than actual face.

"Hey!" she yelled.

The man glanced back and then ran on. That was an admission of guilt by Junior's reckoning. She gave chase.

"Make a soup of his juices!" sang Steve from her pocket.

"Give me a chance," she replied. "I haven't caught him yet."

The towpath was in darkness. Light came from streetlamps reflected off the still water and from the balconies of a French bistro up above. The man, either out of energy or ready to take his chances against her, stopped and turned. Junior didn't even slow; she ran past him, arm held wide, and clothes-lined him across the throat.

He wasn't a big guy and he went down but he grabbed her to stop his fall. They spun around one another, she grabbed him back and they slammed against painted brickwork. He grunted like a stuck thing as he tried to get out of her grip but she refused to let go.

226

"Steal his juices! Steal his juices!" cried Steve.

"Not helping," she panted.

The man broke away by slipping out of his suit jacket. Something slapped on the towpath.

"Stupid mad bitch," he muttered and pulled a piece of paper from his pocket. Junior recognised the vague shape of a mind-sapping *zahir* and thrust her hand over her eyes before the deadly pattern could hypnotise her. She blindly lashed out and swiped the paper from his hand but he took advantage of her blindness and barged her against the wall again. She smacked her head and was suddenly lying on the ground.

Junior's hand came upon something square and leathery and she realised it was a wallet, his wallet. It was thick in her hand, like it was stuffed full of cash. More importantly, she thought, it would have ID, an address. She could let him run now and catch him at her leisure.

The man snatched his jacket off the floor and then hesitated. He'd realised it was too light. He squeezed at it.

"Where's my wallet?" he said, keening with increasing panic.

Junior got to her hands and knees and was rewarded with a kick in the ribs. She rolled.

"Where's my fucking wallet!" He was frantic now and weeping the word, "No, no, no," over and over again.

Junior curled her hands and her body about the wallet but he had spotted the action. He clawed at her.

"That's mine!"

She rolled away and came up against the edge of the towpath. Any further and she was in the water. He booted her in the side again and tried to prise her arms open. She wasn't winning.

"Harvest his vitals!" shouted Steve. The little sack doll tumbled over her torso and ran at the man's feet.

"... the fuck?" he said.

In the break in the assault, Junior tossed the wallet over the edge of the canal. It wasn't a plan as such. It was an instinctive act. If she didn't have it, he wouldn't try to get it from her.

227

"What was…? You didn't!" He was sobbing now. "That had everything in it. The Black Barge... I'm a dead man. Why did you…?"

He sniffled, took a step back and then booted her in the face. Junior's cheek exploded in a pain so sharp it blinded her for a second, maybe more.

Thursday

Morag woke. The pain in her face hauled her up into consciousness when all she wanted to do was sleep. It was only in the final moment of waking that she remembered she was one of two Morags. She was the copy, the interloper, Morag Junior.

There was a hint of industrial strength cleaner in the air and she instantly knew she was in hospital. She remembered the police and then the ambulance. After that, things had become sketchy. She opened her eyes. The light at the window was TV-static grey and the lights above her were on. It was very early morning, possibly still technically night.

Nina sat at her bedside in the private room, munching on a chocolate bar as she sorted little squares of blue paper on the C-shaped bed table and taking pictures of them with her phone. Junior rolled over to look at her properly. The side of Junior's face felt unpleasant and taut, like it had been coated in glue and sprinkled with a glitter called pain. She groaned involuntarily.

"You took a proper whack there," said Nina. It would be nice to think there was a tone of sympathy in Nina's face but, like most millennials, she seemed to struggle with expressing human warmth.

"I did," mumbled Junior, finding her tongue to be a momentarily useless lump of meat in her mouth.

"When Scotch people bruise, does it come up tartan?"

"Did you just call me Scotch?"

"Is that wrong?"

"Tell you what, go to Scotland and find out." She pushed herself upright. Her body ached but that was probably due to last night's alcohol consumption. "Where am I?"

"The restricted ward," said Nina.

Junior reached for the open can of Red Bull by Nina's hand and took a swig.

"Why the restricted ward?"

"As soon as they saw your ID, they transferred you here. Enjoy it. It's like having private health care but, you know, with a greater likelihood of something with more teeth than One Direction in the next bed."

Junior took another swig and prodded her tender cheek. It felt like the pain was inside her upper jawbone and cheekbone. She didn't think bones had any nerves in them but they hurt all the same.

"You didn't break anything," commented Nina. "The doctors mentioned a possible concussion and said that your bruises are going to make a colourful display. I assume it was that scar-faced perv that did it and not some random bloke."

"No, it was Scarface."

"Because I've had boys want to take me up the canal before and although it sounds like a good idea, it –"

"It was Scarface. I did get some good shots in but..."

Nina brought up a large cylindrical tub and set it on the table. Steve the Destroyer lay still inside it.

"And the *pabash kaj* doll?" she said. "The paramedics found it on you."

"It's mine," said Junior. She prodded the tub but Steve remained still and inert. That could be a bad sign.

"Really?" said Nina. "Okay. Thought that might be an angle we could investigate." She sighed and abruptly looked very tired. Junior looked at Nina's clothes and realised that the younger woman probably hadn't slept since the previous night.

"What happened?" said Junior.

"Huh? Oh. People off their tits on a mysterious drug. Then some ugly mofos turned up. Carnage on the dance floor. Everyone came staggering out covered in blood and their own vomit. Police. Ambulances. Some drunk girl sat on the kerb crying."

"So, a typical night on Broad Street."

"A typical night on Broad Street." Nina gathered the rune papers into a pile and bagged them up. "Two people went missing."

"Damn."

"A girl – Allana something – and a *samakha* gangsta. One of the Waters Crew."

"I'm sorry."

Nina stood. "I need a shower. Rod's coming over in a bit, he says." She stretched until something went click. "Stay frosty," she said.

When she had gone, Junior picked up the tub and rapped on the side.

"Steve? Steve? Are you still in there?"

The doll sprang into life and struck a pose.

"I am *Qulsteyvan* the Destroyer, outrider of the entourage of *Prein*, emissary of the shattered realms and loyal servant to the blind gods of *Suler'au Sukram*. I lay claim to your worthless spirit and all your *adn-bhul* kind!" it squeaked.

"Shut up, you daft bugger. I just wanted to check you were okay. Now find me my phone."

"Your phone?"

"I need to contact the other Morag," she said as she unscrewed the lid. "Everyone knows I'm in hospital. Can't have her turning up to work in a few hours' time, can we? Then we'd be well and truly rumbled."

"So what if you are rumbled?" said Steve. "We will crush them."

"If you say so."

"Bring on the rumbling, snotlings!"

"Enough of that."

"Let's get ready to rumble!"

"Phone! Now!"

Jeffney Ray got up at dawn, an unspecified dread weighing on him.

He slipped out from under his Aston Villa duvet and looked at his hands. He had forgotten to put on his sleep mittens. His nails, always kept as short as possible, were ragged. Flecks of red and dried brown clung to the underside of his nails. He went to the mirror above the bedroom hand basin. In his sleep, he had clawed at his face and mouth. His lower lip was bleeding. A shallow but

231

vicious row of scratches on his forehead was already starting to scab over. It looked like he had tried to headbutt an industrial sander.

Wondering how he could have possibly forgotten his mittens, he began to curse himself. Then he remembered the night before – the bitch on the towpath who had attacked him, who had stolen his wallet, who had tossed it in the canal. There had been over four hundred pounds in that wallet, all of Ray's money. He had until noon today to repay the Black Barge the three hundred he had borrowed or pay the penalty: ten years of indentured servitude.

No, he reminded himself, closing his eyes at his own idiocy, a hundred years. "A hundred years", he had joked.

He looked at the time. He had hours yet. There were ways and means. This early bird was as cunning as a fox.

Ray washed and then began applying bio-oil to his freshly ravaged face.

"It rubs the lotion on its skin. It rubs the lotion on its skin…"

Oh, to be hungvover, still marginally drunk even, and to find oneself at five in the morning riding the lift to the eighth floor of the Queen Elizabeth to visit oneself in hospital. Morag Senior had only herself to blame. She wanted to blame Junior but, via a circuitous route, that just meant the same thing.

The guard at the security door inspected her pass and let her through. That he didn't simply say, "Oi. Aren't you already inside?" and taser her on the spot was a small stroke of luck. She entered, found the nearest disabled toilet and texted her clone using the phone she had borrowed from Richard.

She waited for several minutes until there was a knock at the door. She opened it a crack and saw Junior's face.

"Oh, my God," said Senior and dragged her inside.

Junior's face wasn't exactly a mess but bruises seriously weren't a good look. There was a dark mark with a cut at its centre on her right cheek and a black eye on the same side.

"It was the soul cash trader you were looking for," said Junior.

"How do you know?"

"He was scarred. He mentioned the Black Barge. He panicked when I grabbed his wallet."

"You still have it?"

Junior shook her head.

"Bugger."

"Well, yes. The question is what we do about this." She flicked her hands between them.

"You go home," said Senior. "You rest up. You stay hidden. You can have a day off from the chores."

"You are too generous, mother. And that's not going to work."

"Less of the sass from you," snapped Senior. "I'm not feeling too great and I don't appreciate being called out at oh-God-hundred in the morning."

"I'm not sure I wanted to be called out of my sick bed to get abused in a public toilet," said Junior. "And it's not my fault you're hung over."

Junior looked at the bags Senior knew to be under her eyes. One of the Morags bloodied and bruised, the other tired as hell and looking like a schemie grandma. It was the most unflattering mirror for both of them and perhaps some sort of message about their life choices.

"You go home," said Senior, "and then I –"

"It won't work," said Junior. "Nina has seen this face. She knows I'm injured."

"Ah."

"You go home. This is the face of Morag for the time being."

"No," said Senior. "I've got stuff I need to do. Catch that bastard drug dealer."

"What do you think I want to do? That *muda khi umlaq* assaulted me."

"He's done far worse. There are people – innocent humans – taken by the Mammonites because of him. We could use makeup!"

Junior frowned and then winced at the pain it caused.

"You're going to recreate these injuries with makeup?"

"Or... use a lot of foundation and pretend I'm covering them up."

"That's not going to work!"

"Well, we've got to find a way of making our faces match up!"

Junior punched her in the eye. Senior gasped and clutched at her face.

"What the fuck!"

Junior punched her again. Senior staggered and sat down hard on the toilet.

"Stop!"

"Hang on, just one more," said Junior.

Senior waved her hand to ward off her copy. If the woman came any closer, Senior already had plans to rip the lid off the toilet cistern and brain her with it.

"Just stop!"

"It's working." Junior pointed at her face. "We've already got some discoloration. A couple more."

"No!"

"But…"

"No! For three very good reasons!"

Junior took a step back, fists still raised.

"One," said Senior, "you're never going to get them to match exactly. We're just going to look like two people with different bruises in the same places. Two, you're probably going to cause me brain damage before I'm bruised enough. Three, and I can't emphasise this one enough." She pointed at where Junior had punched her. "This is my left cheek!"

Junior hesitated and then understood. "Oh. I was thinking of it like a mirror. This matching that."

"Were you?" said Senior, hearing the mania rise within herself. "Were you? Were you expecting me to only talk to people while standing in front of a mirror? Huh?"

"Yeah, okay. I'm sorry."

"We match even less than before."

"Yeah…"

"So, if we want to even up…" Senior stood quickly and thumped Junior on her uninjured cheek. "That would be a start."

Junior backed up against the door and rubbed her cheek. "Bitch!"

"Me? I owe you at least one more before we're even."

"You'd hit an injured woman?"

"A woman who tried to steal my date!"

He's my ex-boyfriend too!"

Steve the Destroyer, perched on top of the toilet roll dispenser, jumped up and down and chanted, "Fight! Fight! Fight! Fight!"

The Morags looked at the ridiculous Venislarn monster, trapped in a cute and cuddly body.

"This is stupid, isn't it?" said Junior, suddenly deflated.

"Yes," said Senior, calmer now. "I'm sorry."

"Me too."

Senior reached out and brushed a thumb under Junior's cheek. "That looks really sore."

"My eyeball feels like it's three sizes too big."

"Fight, my pretty bitches!" squealed Steve.

"Shut it or we'll flush you," Junior told him.

"He did call us pretty," said Senior.

"So, how did the evening end?" said Junior. "You and Cameron...?"

Senior scoffed.

"Hardly. He's changed, hasn't he?"

"Picked up a tan."

"And a sort of new age vibe."

"And that wicked scar."

Senior laughed. "Said it was a love bite from a sea-dwelling *yon-bun*. Anyway, Cameron and Kathy..."

"Get on well, don't they?"

"They do. They've both got an interview today so they didn't stay out late. Left Rod and me to drown our sorrows."

"You don't think Cameron and Kathy went off and...?"

Senior shook her head. "No. I don't think it was like that. Although she was closer to charming him out of his pants that I was. She definitely won on points."

"I don't know what guys see in her."

"Yeah, you do," said Senior. "Big eyes, big tits and enough underwired lingerie to set the metal detectors off at the airport."

"Harsh," said Junior.

Senior nodded in admission. "Okay. Big eyes, big tits plus she's smarter than the pair of us combined. And she's funny too."

"And she's quite lovely."

"She is."

Junior considered this.

"Bitch," she said, finally.

"Fucking bitch," Senior agreed.

"So, what's the plan?"

Senior thought for a second. "We pretend we like her to her face but slag her off behind her back."

"I meant about this situation. The one we're in now."

"Oh. We – or one of us – goes back to your room and collects your clothes. We then discreetly discharge ourselves and go back to the flat to plan properly."

"How are two of us going to get past the one security guard? He's going to notice."

"We could do that thing where we wrap up one of us in bandages. Cover our face."

"Cos that won't look suspicious."

"Then we just blag it. Tell him he's mistaken. He knows there can't be two of us. The important thing is that no one at the office finds out. I do not want to get fired over this and you don't want to get deleted or whatever."

"Agreed." Junior scooped up Steve. "Let's do this. Stealth mode."

Senior unlocked and opened the door. Rod, walking along the corridor at that moment, saw her. The timing was impeccably awful.

"Morag."

"I can explain," said Senior.

"Explain what?" he said and then looked past her at Junior.

"This," said Junior.

There really wasn't room for three people in the hospital toilet cubicle, particularly, Rod thought, since one of them was only wearing a surgical gown and Rod wasn't necessarily okay with being close up to a female work colleague wearing quite so little clothing. A female work colleague's temporary copy. Whatever. It was Morag Murray. Being in a confined space with two Morag Murrays, one of them entirely underdressed, was not half as appealing as Rod might have previously imagined. Also, the obscene squeaks from the animated ragdoll on the toilet roll thingy weren't helping.

"You okay there, Rod?" said the uninjured Morag. "You look a bit uncomfortable."

"Um," he said. "It's a lot to take in."

"I know."

He took a couple of deep, reflective breaths. "I mean, it is classic Morag."

"Is it?"

"Oh, aye. If anyone asked me which of my workmates would accidentally create a dozen mirror universes containing copies of herself, use a demonic puzzle box and a voodoo doll to break out of a magical prison and then wind up playing tag team dinner date before getting beaten up by a rogue occultist, I can't think there'd be anyone else on that list apart from you."

"Thanks," said the Morags sourly.

"You're a bleeding menace," he told them. "The pair of you."

"Kill him!" shrieked the ragdoll. "He will betray you all!"

"But you've got to keep this secret," said the injured Morag. "If they find out, I could be killed."

"Hardly."

"Magicked away, which is the same thing."

"And I could be fired," said the other.

"Slightly different priority levels," said Rod.

"First up, we've got to bluff our way out of this place."

"Security will spot two Morag Murrays trying to leave," said Rod. "They're not stupid."

"I said that," said the uninjured Morag.

"No, you didn't," said the other.

"I was thinking it. That's why I said we need a disguise."

"Bandages are not a disguise."

"Well, we're not going to be able to whip you up a whole new face, are we? You all right, Rod?"

"A thought's just occurred to me," he said.

"Good," said the uninjured Morag. "Care to share?"

"I can get you a new face."

"A disguise?"

"A face."

"Give me a scalpel and chloroform and I can get you a face!" shouted the ragdoll.

"Not like that. Not quite," said Rod. "Stay here. I'll be back."

He retreated from the toilet, made sure they locked the door behind him and set off along the corridor in search. He had a fair memory for names but a better memory for faces. He was looking for any of the three women or one man who had spent Tuesday locked in with the demented Venislarn, Barbara. Rod remembered one of them was Paula, another was Angie and there was…

"Marco!"

The orderly looked up from the station he was clearing.

"Ah, it's Mr…"

"Rod. Rod Campbell. You remember me from the other day? I need to ask you a favour."

Marco's general demeanour was a relaxed and unhurried one so the suspicious look he gave Rod was a long time in coming together.

"I need you to pop into Barbara Gudge's room," said Rod.

"And?" said Marco.

"Do you know how to use the 3D food printer thing?"

Marco was in Barbara's room for what seemed a very long time. When he emerged from the makeshift airlock (the plywood exterior now plastered with office-printed signs saying "Do not Enter. Danger of Death") he had a small package for Rod wrapped up in paper hand towels.

"I printed one," said Marco, "and then Barbara woke up and said she wanted to eat it so I had to print another."

"You did a grand job," said Rod.

"No worries. What do you want it for?"

Rod looked at the package and then at Marco.

"I could tell you an almost believable lie," he offered.

Marco shrugged happily and went back to his work.

"I'm not wearing this," said Junior.

"Come on," said Senior. "Be a sport."

Junior held it in her hands, unwrapped but still laying on the paper towels.

"It's a man's face."

"As promised," said Rod.

Junior looked at it. Looking didn't make it any better. It was face down in her hands, the bulge of the nose poking between her fingers. The reverse side was raw but dry flesh like glazed turkey leftovers or something seen in a burns unit.

"It's made..." She struggled. "It's made of meat."

"Faces usually are," said Senior.

"And you want me to put it over my own face?"

"Yes."

"It's not rotten or anything," said Rod as if that helped. "It's fresh."

"I don't care," said Junior. "It's not like it's a slice of ham or some Billy Bear, is it?"

"You're making a fuss," said Senior.

"Then you wear it," said Junior, offering.

"We agreed," said Senior. "They're more likely to stop you with your obvious injuries."

"We agreed? You agreed."

"Just put it on."

"Wear the face!" cried Steve the Destroyer. "Feel the meat!"

Junior raised it a little, hesitated.

"Look, it's not the meat thing. It's just..."

"What?" said Rod.

"It's black," said Junior. "It is a black man's face."

239

"Is this a racist thing?" said Rod.

Junior shook the face. "*This* is a racist thing! You're telling me to put on a black man's face."

"Yes?"

"It is literally blackface."

"It's not like you're getting blacked-up for *The Black and White Minstrel Show*," said Senior.

"I had a limited number of faces to choose from," argued Rod. "I went for the biggest one since you've got to wear it over your own face. Marco himself printed it off."

"You see," said Senior. "Marco says it's okay."

Junior could feel the situation sliding out of her control.

"Getting permission from a black man does not make this okay."

"It's not like you're pretending to be a black man," said Rod.

"I think it is," said Junior.

"But when someone wears blackface, they're doing an impression of a black person, a parody. That is a black man's face and you want me to wear it."

"And shall I point out that I have ginger hair?" said Junior. "Even if – God help us – even if I get away with the face, I've got a ton of red hair sticking out of the top."

"A hat," said Senior simply, with a shrug.

"A big hat," agreed Rod.

"Oh, I know," said Junior. "Maybe I could wear a big Rastafarian hat, red, yellow and green and saunter out swaying to some reggae beats."

"I think that would be racially insensitive," said Rod.

"I was being sarcastic!"

Dressed in his second suit (he'd scuffed the knees of his first in the tussle with that cow on the canal), Ray went downstairs.

His mom was at the kitchen sink, smoking a fag. Ray got his probiotic yoghurt from the fridge and gave her a peck on the cheek.

"You were late last night," she said.

"I was working," he said.

She tore her eyes away from whatever it was that had her attention in the back garden and looked at him. Her eyes lingered painfully on the fresh wounds on his face.

"They've got you working nights?"

"It's a twenty-four/seven business," he said.

"They are paying you, aren't they, Jeffney?" she asked.

"Yeah, about that," said Ray.

Her expression stiffened. She went to stub out her cigarette, looked at it, took one more big drag and then extinguished it.

"I told you they'd take advantage of you," she said. "I told you."

"It's just a cashflow problem."

She put her hand on his lapels and smoothed them down.

"I need some money, mom."

"What do you mean, you need some money?"

"I need some money."

She picked up her purse from the side and opened it.

"I need three hundred pounds," he said.

She stopped and looked at him. "I've got twenty in here."

"What about your post office account?"

She shook her head.

"An overdraft?" he said.

"They don't give people like me an overdraft."

Ray felt his anger rise towards this stupid little woman. "What do you spend it all on?"

"Spend all of what?" she said.

"Throwing your money away on your cigarettes and... and..."

"And what, Jeffney Ray?" she said, biting the words. "On food for you? On bills for this house? On your clothes and your creams and your silly little health yoghurts?"

Ray slammed his probiotic yoghurt down on the side.

"God, you're like all the rest of them," he snapped. "Stupid. Stupid. Trying to take our power, our essence. Draining us. Bitches."

"Jeffney Ray!"

241

He knew he'd overstepped a line and would regret it later. If he got through the day, he'd have to make it up to her. A box of Terry's All Gold or maybe some of those little Baileys miniatures she liked. But, now, right now, he was furious with her.

He took the purse from her hands, took the twenty pounds out and thrust the purse back at her before storming out.

Morag Junior pulled the beanie hat over her hair and down low to cover her ears. Her hands were the wrong colour so she tucked them into the pockets of her jeans. She realised in dismay that this made her walk with a swagger. She'd especially wanted to avoid a swagger or any other kind of over-the-top display of cartoonishly black body language. She tried to walk in whatever way the opposite of that was, but then found herself not having the slightest idea of how to do that. She'd heard the saying about it being impossible to walk normally if someone watches how you walk, and decided that this was a hundred times worse. How did models manage on the catwalk? The ones that didn't fall over in their ludicrous heels anyway. She tried to walk like a runway model, carefully placing one foot in front of the other and loosely swaying her hips. No! NO! This was even worse. She briefly considered going back to find a walking frame or wheelchair, but then she was within sight of the security guard. She just needed to keep going. The meaty mask meant that she couldn't see his face as she passed him, and it was all that she could do not to break into a run when she finally saw the bank of lifts ahead of her.

Rod and Senior appeared as the lift doors opened and they all entered the lift together

"He didn't even bloody look at me!" she hissed at them.

"We got away with it, didn't we?"

"But he didn't even look!"

"What are you complaining for?"

"I don't know! Maybe because I've got racially insensitive meat stuck to my face!"

The lift doors closed.

"We're clear," said Rod.

The Morag copy ripped off the Marco mask and the beanie cap. She rubbed her face in disgust and then winced loudly as she encountered her bruised cheek.

"No bones broken," said Rod. "You were lucky."

"Lucky, right." The Morag copy looked at her phone. "A message from the office. Vaughn wants a meeting with us all at nine."

Rod checked his phone. "Must be serious. How often does that man call meetings? It's like an incurably shy introvert throwing a party."

Rod saw a look pass between the two Morags. He couldn't say what it was; he wasn't one for reading the looks that women gave each other.

"Rock, paper, scissors," said the copy Morag.

"It's not up for discussion," said the real Morag. "This is my world. You're the visitor from a parallel dimension. Go home. Rest."

"Yes!" agreed the ragdoll Steve from a pocket somewhere. "We shall watch the *Pointless* and the *Eggheads* and I would like to see the one where the man says 'Pact or No Pact'."

"*Deal or No Deal*," said the copy Morag.

"Yes!" said Steve. "It has mysterious boxes. I like mysterious boxes. They should put a poisonous *ranndhu* in one of them. It could bite the bearded man in the face. I would like that."

There was a moment of quiet reflection and general nodding as all three humans considered the entertainment value of Noel Edmonds getting bitten in the face.

And then the arguing started again.

Ray fumbled with the shed padlock with one hand while trying to make a phone call with the other. The padlock sprung open just as Mrs Lee-Mammonson answered the phone.

"*San-shu*, Mrs Lee-Mammonson. It's Jeffney Ray."

"Are you aware of what time it is, Mr Ray?" said the Mammonite sternly. "Our regular hours do not begin until nine o'clock."

"My deepest apologies, Mrs Lee-Mammonson," said Ray. "I wouldn't normally call so early but I did say I would be able to deliver your *lu'crik oyh* today."

"And I said I would be in after one."

Ray looked in his tanks. The one he had added eggs and seeds to the day before was now home to more than a dozen creatures, little more than blobs with tails and a chitinous outer shell – like armour-plated tadpoles. They were weeks away from maturity. It was the two closed tubs at the far right of the shelves that were to be the saving of his skin today.

"Indeed, Mrs Lee-Mammonson. I remember it clearly," he said. "Unfortunately, I can now only make deliveries to your area this morning."

"But that simply isn't convenient. I have a *helle'p kren* ceremony to attend and cakes to prepare for the school fayre."

"Ah, no. Sorry. Very well." He paused deliberately. "I suppose I could deliver to the next customer on the list. The – let's see – the Andrews-Mammonsons."

He counted silently and got as far as three before the Mammonite caved in.

"Very well," she said, "but you must get here as soon as possible."

"And it will be cash on delivery," said Ray smoothly.

"We already paid you a substantial deposit."

Ray swore in his head. He'd forgotten that.

"Then it will be just the balance left to pay. Four hundred pounds."

"Two hundred, Mr Ray," she said instantly.

"Are you sure?"

"Are you accusing me of financial irregularities, Mr Ray?" she asked and he was instantly reminded that the Mammonites might be greedy but they were precise and, whilst not exactly litigious, they would exact retribution from anyone who tried to con them.

"Not at all, Mrs Lee-Mammonson," he said. "I will be at your door shortly."

He ended the conversation and searched for the number of a taxi cab company that would transport him and a couple of tubs of energetic *lu'crik oyh* to Dickens Heath.

Rod pulled up outside 27 Franklin Road and, diplomatically, said nothing.

The real Morag had taken the train into the city from the QE Hospital and asked Rod to drive her copy home before coming into work. The argument between the two women hadn't reached any sort of conclusion but copy Morag had at least got in the car with Rod and had sat there sullenly while he drove the short distance to Bournville.

Copy Morag sat beside Rod. She didn't get out, just sat there, arms crossed, fuming.

Rod wondered whether he should wait it out or whether this was a signal from her that she wanted him to say something. He decided on the former but he cracked after less than a minute.

"We're here," he said, gesturing to the house.

"It's not fair!" said Morag.

Rod crumpled within. He was trapped in a car with an angry woman who expected him to engage in conversation which would no doubt require him to second-guess what she wanted him to say. That wasn't fair. It wasn't like she was even his girlfriend or anything. Rod felt quite certain that if Morag was his girlfriend, he would be able to accept the situation with far more stoicism. A small part of him thought that perhaps he could make things better by kissing her but he instantly recognised it as the very stupid part of him and mentally told it to shut up.

"But it's not fair!" said Morag.

Ah. She definitely expected some form of contribution from him.

"Not fair," said Rod, making it neither a statement nor a question.

"Why should she be allowed to do this to me, huh?"

Rod nodded carefully.

"I wouldn't do this to her," said Morag.

Rod bit down on the powerful temptation to point out that recent history suggested this was exactly what she would do to a copy of herself.

"No," he said.

"So, you agree with me?" she said.

Bugger, thought Rod. He'd been caught expressing an opinion. He could lamely agree with her and then get caught out in some moral trap (either now or even weeks down the line) or he could risk a gambit and deflect it.

"What do you think she should do?" he said.

That made Morag think for a while.

"She could at least share a bit more," she said finally. "We alternate days at work."

"Since when did you love work so much?"

"It's about responsibility. About not treating me like a child." She pointed an angry finger at her angry bruise. "I did this in the line of duty. I chased that *pabbe* drug dealer. I had his wallet and ID for a moment before I was forced to chuck it in the canal. I'm doing good work. But did she thank me?"

"Maybe she feels you're treading on her toes."

"So… what? Should I just fade away? Go off and become a shadow? A nobody?"

He gave a cautious shrug.

"Maybe one Morag Murray is enough."

Unexpectedly, she laughed at that. "That's what my Uncle Ramsay used to say."

"And you know," said Rod, "there are plenty of people who would love an excuse to leave their old life behind."

"Like my Uncle Ramsay: run away to the rigs and live a life of near solitude doing crane work and deep-sea welding."

Morag bowed her head and suddenly looked small and lost. The small bit of Rod's brain that wanted him to reach out and kiss her reared its idiotic head again. He slapped it down hard.

"I've done stupid things," said Morag.

"Like shooting a god in the face."

"It was one of the August Handmaidens of *Prein*."

"One of those enormous crab monsters with screaming baby faces on it? I didn't think they could be killed."

"I caught it by surprise. They swore to kill me. The last man I..." She looked at Rod and laughed. "Why am I telling you this?"

"Because I care?" he suggested and then regretted it because, for a dangerous moment or two, it looked like she might be about to cry.

"You remember the week I started? The last guy I had sex with... he..."

"The Handmaidens murdered him in the cathedral. I know. Well, I worked it out. Just now. And if you'd had the weaponry you'd have taken them all down and kickstarted the apocalypse."

"I would have," she said honestly. "The Handmaidens still want me dead."

"They will have their vengeance!" squeaked Steve from somewhere but they both ignored him.

"If I could just walk away from all that," said Morag thoughtfully.

"Turn a challenge into an opportunity," offered Rod.

The final look Morag gave him before she got out of the car was one of resignation.

"Maybe so," she said. "Come on, Steve. Let's go watch Pact or No Pact."

When Nina came in, drinking her fourth energy drink of the morning, Lois the receptionist directed her to meeting room three. Vivian, Morag and Vaughn Sitterson were already there. Vaughn had placed himself at the head of the table and laid a protective semicircle of documents, folders and wallets around himself to keep everyone at a safe distance. He held his tablet up to read from and hide behind, just in case anyone broke through his outer shield.

"You're late, Miss Seth," said Vaughn without looking up.

Nina looked at the clock.

"Have you already started?" she said.

"Not yet."

"But I'm late?" she said, rubbing the last vestiges of sleep from her eyes. "Huh."

"Poor punctuality is inexcusable," commented Vivian, giving Nina a clear and unwavering look.

"It's as bad as chemical warfare and punching kittens," agreed Nina facetiously. "Anyway, Rod's not here."

Rod almost stumbled through the door.

"Sorry I'm late," he said, moving swiftly to a seat. "I had to drop… a package off in Bournville."

"We haven't started," said Nina, looking to Vaughn and then to Vivian when it was clear Vaughn wasn't going to meet her eye. "Aren't you going to give Rod hell about his lateness?"

"He apologised," said Vivian.

Nina noticed Morag's face. Morag was wearing an ugly pendant necklace, a sort of Viennese swirl of frosted glass. Nina would have assumed Morag was wearing it to distract people from her bruises but she didn't seem to have any.

"You're looking a lot better."

"Concealer," said Morag.

"Also, she heals quick," said Rod. "Like that superhero with claws."

"The correct adverb is 'quickly'," said Vivian. "Poor grammar –"

"Up there with bad timekeeping and genocide," said Nina. "Gotcha."

"If I could start this meeting," said Vaughn tetchily, "now that we're all here." He opened a folder on the table and slid out a letter printed on thick paper. "I tend to allow the response team to operate without much managerial involvement. I believe that teams of expertise should lead the way rather than be guided by a top-down management structure." It was the kind of statement that was clearly going to be followed by a 'but'. Vaughn left it hanging. He unfolded the letter and addressed himself to it rather than the people in the room. "I have received a formal complaint."

"Who from?" said Rod.

"Mammon-Mammonson Investments," said Vivian.

"Indeed, Mrs Grey," said Vaughn. "You were aware they had grounds for complaint?"

248

"I know how the Mammonites think and behave, Mr Sitterson. I should imagine that letter contains a lot of bluster and empty business-speak but that their complaint amounts to our arguably unjustifiable intrusion into their legitimate business affairs, to wit: trading in human bodies and souls."

"It does," said Vaughn. "The complaints, which are listed, numbered and cross-referenced, include wasting of company time, disruption of the workings of their central office, obstruction of a retrievals officer in the execution of his duty, refusal to take action when the same retrievals officer was hurt by a human –"

"He was hurt while trying to stuff a woman in a cage," said Rod fiercely.

"And the making of baseless accusations that Mammon-Mammonson Investments was either circumventing or ignoring the treaties that govern Venislarn action within the city."

"They are slimy scumbags," said Rod.

"Slime, I would have thought, Mr Campbell, was an aspect of the job you were well used to," said Vaughn, allowing himself an indulgent smile.

"They are evil," said Nina. "The kids too. They tied me to a tree and were going to livestream my murder."

"Yes," said Vaughn, "there is a reference here to you trespassing on Mammonite school property."

Vaughn put the letter down and then gazed out of the window. Beyond the interlocking metal circles that covered the exterior of the Library of Birmingham, this room looked out over the Jewellery Quarter and Handsworth. It was hardly an inspiring view.

"I've never met the Mammonites," said Morag.

"Whether you have or haven't," said Vaughn. "Whether there is a basis to the Mammonites' complaints or not, this letter raises questions about what you have been doing with your time."

"Do you think we've been skiving off, sir?" asked Rod.

Vaughn looked at a notepad. "There are reports of attacks on cyclists that haven't been followed up and I've had numerous communications from British Telecom asking when they will be allowed to access the Anchor Exchange hardened facility again."

249

"They won't," said Rod.

"Mr Sitterson," said Vivian, placing her hands together on the table, fingers interlocked. "I tend to deal in precise matters. Facts. I don't like vagaries, uncertainties or hunches."

"No, you don't," said Vaughn.

"However," she said in that clear glacial tone that Nina hoped to master one day and use on pretty much everybody, "I feel, with some conviction, that Xerxes Mammon-Mammonson is up to something."

"Up to something?" said Vaughn, surprised at the words.

"Yes," said Vivian.

"Up to what?"

"I don't know."

"He's buying up people," said Rod.

"Legally," said Vaughn.

"But not just holding soul cash certificates. He's stockpiling live human beings."

"Again, legally."

"He's working with one or more human occultists, probably unregistered."

"Then you must pursue them, not him."

"Which is what I'm trying to do," said Nina. "He was selling activated *Kal Frexo* runes at the Rockerfellers night club last night. He attacked Morag."

"He did," said Morag with oddly emphatic insistence.

"Runes?" said Vaughn.

"Used as a psychotropic drug," explained Vivian.

Nina tossed the bag of seized rune papers onto the table. Vaughn picked up the plastic bag and turned them over.

"Seventeen different runes," said Nina, "each of them bringing about a trippy mindfuck."

"Twelve," said Vivian.

Nina shook her head. "Seventeen. I counted and I took pictures."

"You must be mistaken," said Vivian. "Of the original twenty summoning runes of *Kal Frexo*, eight are lost. The eight lost runes of *Kal Frexo*. Papers have been written about them by educated people who, one assumes, can count."

"I'm educated," said Nina. "I got a GCSE in Maths which means I can count too."

"No, you didn't," said Vivian.

"I got a D."

"That isn't a pass, Miss Seth. It's a little ribbon given out to the child who comes last to stop them crying." Vivian gestured to Vaughn for the bag of runes. He passed them over automatically. "I will check these myself today. I'm sure there will be time during the selection process."

"You do not need to be present during the interviews today, Mrs Grey," said Vaughn.

"No," she insisted. "I know you appreciate my input on these matters."

Vaughn didn't look particularly appreciative but said nothing more.

"We'll find this occultist drug-dealer whatever," said Nina. "Me and Wolverine here saw him at the Black Barge."

"Wolverine!" said Morag with a sudden smile.

"With the claws!" said Rod.

"We couldn't remember," Morag explained to Nina. "It had been bugging us." She looked at Rod. "Who did we think it was?"

"Asbestos?" said Rod.

"No one thought his name was Asbestos."

"I think you did."

"Enough," said Vaughn. "Follow up this... *rune* avenue of investigation, yes, but remember the role is more than just firefighting each emergency as it arises. I require follow-up on the alleged attacks on cyclists, an account of any dealings with the Mammonite community in the past few days plus I regard it as vital that we bring all of these matters to the Venislarn court, as I am sure the Mammonites have done."

"Mammon-Mammonson has lodged a complaint with *Yo-Morgantus*?" said Rod.

"If he hasn't, I'm sure he will," said Vivian.

251

"As our registrar and court liaison, Mrs Grey..." Vaughn began.

"I think I am busy enough for today," said Vivian. "I am given to understand that *Yo-Morgantus* looks upon Miss Murray favourably..."

"Got a crap job? Give it to the ginger," muttered Morag.

"I don't wish to micro-manage this team," said Vaughn. "Organise yourselves as you will. But I want to see a return to the thoroughness and unquestionable professionalism that this mission embodies."

"In short, leave the Mammonites alone?" said Vivian.

Vaughn inclined his head a fraction, gathered his papers and left. Rod leapt up to follow him.

"Could you help me requisition a new firearm?" Rod asked. "Admin won't authorise a new one unless I return the previous one."

"And you haven't returned the previous one because?" said Vaughn, halfway down the corridor already.

"First up, it's inside a giant spider," said Rod. "Secondly, the spider is..." The door swung closed on the meeting room and Nina didn't hear the rest.

Nina looked at Vivian across the table.

"Did you just get all sarky with Vaughn then?"

"When?"

"'Leave the Mammonites alone.'"

"Sarcasm is poor wit indeed," said Vivian. "I was merely seeking clarification."

"Ah, there might have been a smidge of sass in there," said Morag, holding thumb and forefinger an inch apart.

"Not at all," said Vivian, standing and straightening her jacket. "I don't believe in any obfuscation in communication. I say what I think, openly, honestly and clearly. And I wish other people would do the same."

"Careful what you wish for," said Nina.

Vivian gave her a look as if she was an idiot child. Vivian gave Nina that look a lot.

"So, we going to catch ourselves a scumbag occultist?" said Morag.

"Sure," said Nina and took out the vial of *rehpat viarr* truth potion she had confiscated from Mystic Trevor. "In a minute. I'm just going to offer the interview candidates refreshments."

"In tea, truth. Eh?" said Morag.

Rod did not have a replacement firearm. He did now, however, have three multi-part forms provided by Lois: a 3BGG to request a new firearm from the quartermaster, a SWAT7D to report the loss of his original firearm, and a GAT3B to report an incident that might lead to the removal of his right to carry a firearm. It wasn't what Rod had hoped for. Lois said it was almost as good as getting his gun back. Rod thought it was a poor substitute. You couldn't take down a threat with paperwork, not unless you first fashioned it into a very sharp paper dart. (Some months ago, Rod had spent a full week watching YouTube videos on making offensive weapons out of paper. He had perfected the technique of embedding a thrown playing card into a watermelon but he doubted he'd have much cause or opportunity to use that skill.)

"There's a woman in reception," Lois said. "Do you have time to talk to her?"

"Who is it?"

"Kirsten Jones. She's come about her son, Michael."

Rod frowned. The name meant nothing.

"Pupfish," said Lois.

"Oh."

Rod couldn't imagine that any conversation with Pupfish's mum would be easy but that was part of the job, wasn't it?

Rod went through to the reception area. The sallow-faced young woman in a stained tracksuit stood with a big *samakha* lad by her side. The *samakha,* wearing a Tupac T-shirt, had a hand on the woman's shoulder: comforting, not possessive. Rod was sure he recognised the *samakha* but he didn't think it racist that he struggled to tell one fish-man from another. Security Bob, who had brought them up to the seventh floor, inclined his chin at Rod.

"Can I leave these two with you?" he said.

"Aye. Thanks, Bob." Rod reached out a hand to the woman. "Ms Jones. I'm Rod Campbell."

Kirsten Jones stared at his hand as though human decency and social etiquette was a mystery to her. "It's, er, Fluke, isn't it?" Rod said to the *samakha*.

"Ggh! You know it," said the fish boy in cautious greeting.

"I'm very sorry about what happened with Pupfish, that is, Michael," said Rod.

The woman wrung her hands ceaselessly: hand over hand over hand, like she was either desperate for a cigarette or wanted to claw at something. Her face was tired, prematurely aged. Rod guessed that losing your child – even if he was a fish – would do that to a person but he reckoned that life in Fish Town had robbed plenty from her already.

"Where is he?" she said.

"Michael?" said Rod. "My colleague, Nina Seth, is probably the best one to answer that. She was in the club last night."

"Bitch saved everyone," said Fluke.

"I gather," said Rod. "As best as I understand it, Michael – your son – was taken by creatures from something called *leng*-space."

"And you're gonna get him back," said Kirsten.

"I don't think it's as easy as that," said Rod.

Her composure began to break. This was going to go one of two ways, anger or tears, and Rod wasn't sure which he liked least. He'd already had to deal with one upset woman today. He didn't deserve another. He had definitely met his daily quota, possibly weekly.

"What fucking use are you?" she trembled, not angry yet but teetering towards it.

"*Leng*-space," Rod began. "It's not like it's a regular place we can just…"

"They took him."

"I know."

"It's all right, Kirsten," said Fluke and gave her shoulder a squeeze. Rod realised that this wasn't just Pupfish's mum and one of his mates; something else was going on between these two. "G-man," said Fluke. "We know that Pupfish is – ggh! – gone. He was a soldier and he's fallen. What we want to know is what you're doing 'bout it."

"We are following all lines of enquiry," said Rod.

"Bullshit!" said Kirsten.

"What you doing?" demanded Fluke.

"We are trying to find the man who sold Pupfish the drugs he took that –"

"Drugs?" said Kirsten and then, shrugging off his hand, turned on Fluke. "You were supposed to be looking after him!"

"I was, doll," said Fluke.

"He was doing drugs?"

"It wasn't anything. It – ggh! – was just some magic rune *muda*."

"You watched him take them?"

There was a panic in Fluke's huge eyes now. This was much better, thought Rod. Women getting upset with someone else. He was fine with that.

"He's a grown man," argued Fluke. "He knew what he was doing."

"He was eighteen years old! He had his whole life ahead of him!"

"Ggh! Tupac was twenty-five when they gunned him down. Death, babe, it just –"

Rod didn't get to hear what death just was because Kirsten slapped Fluke hard in the gills at that moment. The fish boy staggered away.

"I don't fucking care about Tupac, you stupid boy!" she screamed.

"I know you're – ggh! – angry," Fluke coughed, "but there's no reason to disrespect –"

Kirsten followed up the slap with a kick to the groin. The *samakha* gangster went down, clutching himself.

"Enough," said Rod and stepped between them. He quickly but firmly steered the weeping woman to the row of seats by the wall. "Lois," he called to the glass-fronted reception hatch. "A cup of tea for Ms Jones, please."

"That bastard," sobbed Kirsten. "Why do I fall for the ones who live at the bottom of a canal."

"That's a good question," said Rod charitably and then had a thought.

He looked round at Fluke, sitting on the hard floor and cradling his codpiece.

"Fluke."

"What, man?" hissed the wounded *samakha*.

"You can swim, right?"

Lois went into the office kitchenette to find Nina there stacking cups in the sink.

"Don't mind me," said Nina. "I was just sorting out drinks for the interview people."

"Didn't know that was on your job description, bab." Lois found a mug to make tea in. "Anyway, isn't that Professor Thingy in for interview?"

"He is."

"I thought you hated him."

"I do."

Lois pulled a face, confused, and then nodded. "You spat in his drink."

Nina put her hands on her hips. "Come on, Lois. I'm better than that."

Lois swirled the metal teapot that was resting on the counter and felt the side to see how warm it was.

"I wouldn't if I was you," said Nina.

"You did spit in it," grinned Lois, though not entirely approvingly.

"Nope. I just thought that the interviews would go a lot better if there was bit of honesty from the candidates," said Nina. "Let them see what that *bhul-gen* Omar is really like."

The three interview candidates had been placed in meeting room two. As Vivian entered, they sat at their individual tables like well-behaved school children. Cameron Barnes put down his pen and looked up from the notebook in which he had been sketching

Venislarn decals. Dr Kathy Kaur placed her phone face down to give Vivian her full attention. Professor Sheikh Omar, waiting patiently, gave Vivian a toothy smile.

"You have the schedule for today," she told them. "We will start with an in-tray exercise and psychological evaluations before finally taking one or more of you to interview panel with the consular mission chief, Ms Clement from Personnel and myself. At the end of the day, one of you will have succeeded and become the new tech support officer for this facility. The other two will have failed. Any questions?"

"No."

"No."

"One," said Omar, "I would very much like to know what happened to the bull sculpture that adorned the old Bullring shopping centre before it was demolished in the nineties."

"Is that really pertinent to this interview situation, Professor Omar?"

"Pertinent?" he said. "No. Sorry, you just asked if we had any questions."

"About today."

"No."

"Quite."

Vivian could not ascertain whether the man was being facetious, perhaps even flirtatious, although for a moment Omar had seemed as surprised by his own question as she had been. Regardless, it was a mark against him, literally. Vivian made a note on her clipboard.

"Slay him!"

Morag Junior squeezed the tea bag against the side of the cup and then plonked it in the bin.

"Slay him!"

There was only an inch of milk in the fridge. She sniffed it to see if it was off, decided it was on the turn but poured it into her tea anyway.

"Slay him!"

She looked in the biscuit tin but there was nothing there. She slouched into the living room.

Steve the Destroyer capered on the arm of the sofa, incandescent with rage.

"What is it?" said Junior.

"The Kyle has presented the ugly oaf with proof that the child is his but does not kill him!"

She looked at the TV screen. "Yeah. That's not how it works. Jeremy Kyle comes on, accuses him of cheating on her or accuses her of being a gold digger or something and then they shout at each other and maybe start a fight. The audience all start whooping or hurling abuse. And then Jeremy looks all smug."

The stuffed toy demon turned to give her a full-body *"what the hell"* gesture. "Then why do they do it?"

"I think they do it because they're chavs and they think being on TV gives their pointless lives meaning. The audience watch it because they like to see the personal lives of others torn apart. And the presenter and the TV company put it on because they can dress it up as a human interest piece even though it's just cruel voyeurism. I don't know. Daytime TV isn't a speciality area for me."

Steve turned back to the TV for a second and then returned to Junior.

"So, all existence is futile and meaningless and the only truth to be gained is through creating artificial confrontation and then sharing our pain with others?"

"That's pretty much every reality TV show."

"Even the baking off one?"

"God, yeah," she said as her phone began to ring. "This is just *Great British Bake Off* with no cakes and more swearing. Hello?"

"Do you remember exactly where he attacked you?" said Rod.

"I do," said Junior. "It was just under the balcony of the French bistro place. Pierre something. Why?"

"We're going to find that wallet. I've got us a search diver. Up for it?"

Junior considered the prospect of watching daytime TV until Morag Senior got home. "Totally."

Vivian sternly put her finger to her lips as Vaughn entered the assessment room. Vaughn pretended not to notice, which came quite naturally to him.

The three candidates were busily writing answers to the in-tray exercise. Vaughn stood next to Vivian and attempted to look over at the question paper. She slid it across so that he could see it more clearly without having to invade her personal space.

PRIORITISE THESE (1-10) AND GIVE A BRIEF DESCRIPTION OF HOW YOU WOULD RESPOND TO EACH.

A) EIGHTEEN TONS OF *YOBHANI XO* HAVE BEEN DELIVERED TO THE VENISLARN MATERIALS RECLAMATION CENTRE. YOU HAVE NO ROOM TO TAKE THEM.

B) A NEW EXHIBIT HAS JUST OPENED AT A LOCAL GALLERY. THE SUBJECT OF THE PAINTINGS APPEARS TO BE A *GUPREE*, ACCURATELY RENDERED. SEVERAL GUESTS AT THE OPENING HAVE FALLEN ILL, THE ARTIST NOT AMONG THEM.

C) YOU HAVE COMPELLING EVIDENCE THAT THE WORLD WILL END ON THURSDAY. YOUR BUDGET ANALYSIS REPORT IS DUE ON FRIDAY.

D) PRINCE *HOLUNH ADHULAS* IS VISITING THE CITY AND DEMANDS A FRESH HUMAN BRAIN FOR HIS DINNER.

E) THE *FAHAIB'SOREE* ARE RISING AGAIN. YOU HAVE NO BONE MARROW IN STOCK.

F) IN TWO HOURS, YOUR COLLEAGUE WILL GIVE BIRTH TO THE *KAATBARI* WHICH WILL SIGNAL THE END OF THE WORLD.

G) FOR A BET, TWO STUDENTS HAVE BROKEN INTO THE VENISLARN "MENAGERIE" IN DUDLEY.

H) YOUR GRANDMOTHER HAS COME TO VISIT. YOUR GRANDMOTHER DIED SOME YEARS AGO. IT IS TUESDAY.

I) A CHILD HAS FOUND A *YETSID* SHELL AND IS CURRENTLY IN HOSPITAL SPEAKING IN THE LANGUAGE OF *AKLO*.

J) A MAMMONITE BUSINESSMAN HAS STARTED THE WIDESPREAD PURCHASING AND STOCKPILING OF HUMANS.

Vaughn pointed a finger at the last item.

"Really?" he said witheringly.

Vivian shushed him.

His finger roved over to the blue rune squares she was sorting through on the desk. She had made two piles.

"Why the two piles?" he whispered.

"Mr Sitterson, I will have to ask you to be quiet or leave," she said. "There is a test taking place."

She could have told him that the largest pile was of papers marked with the twelve known runes of *Kal Frexo*. The others, in the much smaller pile, were marked with runes unknown to her (although a couple looked vexingly familiar). The natural assumption was that these were examples of the lost runes, now found, but she wasn't going to be making any hasty judgements on the matter. Even in the Venislarn world, there were such things as hoaxes.

"7 Mermaid Drive. 15th April."

Morag Senior wrote the address and the date on a Post-it note and stuck it on the map, close to Mermaid Drive. Nina shuffled through to the next photocopy and read out the address and the date.

Senior knew she could have done it electronically but it was sometimes just better to plot things out physically. Nina had disagreed on that point, more than once, but Senior was in a determined mood and was using her non-existent injuries to garner sympathy.

She had pinned a large city-wide map to the office wall and they were working their way through the copies of soul cash certificates Vivian had taken from Mammon-Mammonson Investments. An indistinct pattern – but a pattern nonetheless – had emerged very quickly. The soul cash certificates had been sold throughout the centre of the city but, beyond that, only in a fairly narrow corridor that led away from the city at a four o'clock angle.

260

Senior placed the next Post-it, representing one of the first certificates the dealer had sold.

"I reckon he lives near here," she said.

"Where? Shirley?" said Nina.

"Here. And don't call me Shirley."

"The place is called Shirley."

"Um. I know. I was being funny. It's like that joke off *Airplane*."

"*Airplane*?"

"It's a film." Senior sighed. "Before your time."

Nina nodded slowly. She had a low opinion of things that were "before her time".

"I know what this is," she said, indicating the line of Post-its coming out of the city. "It's the number six bus route. Except here." She drew a finger along the relatively short spur that jutted away from the Shirley high street.

"No," said Senior. "That's the route he walks to get to the bus stop."

Vivian placed a box in front of each of the candidates. The boxes were white, unmarked and the approximate size of a shoe box. She returned to her own table.

"You have fifteen minutes."

"What is this?" asked Cameron Barnes.

"The next activity," said Vivian. She had already glanced at his answers to the in-tray exercise. Cameron's answers had demonstrated a level of technical expertise but his handwriting suggested a lack of organisation and a libertarian mindset. She had noted as much on her clipboard.

"Vivian tends towards the enigmatic," said Sheikh Omar.

Kathy put her ear to the box, sat back and then carefully lifted off the lid. Her apprehensive expression softened at once.

"Awww." She pulled out the *Dendooshi* pup and hugged its hairy body to her chest.

"Oh, okay," said Cameron and opened his box.

On spring legs, a red and black *ranndhu* leapt out and attached itself to his face. He kicked, pivoted backwards and fell off his chair. Vivian raised her pen to make a final, damning mark on her clipboard… But then the man did redeem himself some small amount by binding the creature with a *shadz* line and immediately asking Vivian if it was carrying eggs.

"No, Mr Barnes. It was a sterile female."

As Cameron returned the struggling *ranndhu* to its box and himself to his seat, rubbing the red puncture marks on his face, Vivian turned to Professor Sheikh Omar. He sat with his hands on the table either side of the box, perfectly still.

"Aren't you going to open it, professor?" she asked.

"Is there a reason why I should?" he replied.

"Is there a reason why you shouldn't?"

"Plenty," he said. "Shall I list them?"

"If you would."

Morag Junior paced along the canal. In daylight, the stretch of water from Broad Street to the Cube looked entirely different. Gone were the shadowy doorways and cold lights on water, replaced now by non-descript brickwork and a squadron of ducks that had swum over in optimistic expectation of bread. She looked up at the balcony seating area of the French restaurant above their heads. She looked down at the small mooring posts set into the edge of the canal.

"This one," she said, more to herself than anyone.

"What's that?" said Rod.

She pointed at the water. "I threw the wallet in here."

Rod turned to Fluke. "You heard the lady."

The *samakha* gangster-boy looked at the murky brown. "That's some manky *muda*, man."

"The name and address of the man who did for your friend is down there. It might have drifted a bit but there's no current."

"Ggh!" spat Fluke distastefully and began to undress.

"I'm sure Pupfish's mum will be very grateful," Rod added.

Fluke laughed at that. He stripped to his trousers and passed his T-shirt and baseball cap to Junior as though they were the holy relics.

"None of this shit touches the ground, y'hear?" he said and then dove in, slicing into the water like a knife through flesh.

The ripples spread out and died.

"We could have got a police diver, you know," said Junior.

"This is a low-profile operation," said Rod. "Vaughn gave us all a bit of a bollocking this morning. We've been warned to stay away from the Mammonites."

"This has got nothing to do with the Mammonites," said Junior, waving at the canal.

"Not yet," said Rod. "But when we follow the trail..."

Fluke emerged from the water with a splash, a Brummie-style Creature from the Black Lagoon. He slapped something flat and soggy on the towpath. Rod nudged it with his toe.

"That's a kebab, lad."

Fluke sneezed out a mouthful of brown silt. "And..."

A webbed hand dumped a load of loose change next to the kebab.

"Where there's muck there's brass," said Rod.

"You what?" said Fluke.

"You're meant to be looking for a wallet," said Junior.

"All right, girl. Ggh! It's blacker than Darth Vader's helmet down there."

"I thought you might be able to..." Junior made vague sensory gestures.

"You wanted echolocation, you should've got yourself a dolphin," snorted the *samakha* and dived again.

"Echolocation," said Rod. "That's a big word for a fish boy."

"Doesn't mean he can spell it," said Junior.

Vivian looked across the interview panel table, Vaughn Sitterson to her left, the ineffectual Cheryl Clement to her right. In the interview chair, Kathy Kaur sat primly alert, hands on knees, knees pressed tightly together.

"This is quite a departure from your current job, isn't it?" said Cheryl.

"In some ways," said Kathy and then reconsidered. "It's very different. A much more technical role that will challenge me in a new way."

"Are you sick of dealing with sick people?" said Vivian.

"Yes." Kathy looked shocked at her own response. "I like helping people. I like having helped people. It makes me feel good about myself." She stared as though she couldn't believe she had said that. "Christ, that makes me sound I have a God complex."

"Do you have a God complex?" said Vivian.

Kathy responded carefully. "I think I have no more of a God complex than the next person."

"Do you think Mr Sitterson here has a God complex?"

"I don't know. I don't know him."

"Do you think I have a God complex?"

"Yes. Definitely."

"Interesting," said Vivian, watching the candidate's hands scrunch into tense balls in her lap.

"I seem to be unaccountably honest at the moment," said Kathy. "I do apologise."

Vaughn shuffled his papers uncomfortably.

"On your responses to the in-tray exercise, Dr Kaur… Would you care to explain your response to scenario A and how you would deal with the unexpected delivery of eighteen tons of *Yobhani Xo*?"

"Yes?" said Kathy.

"You said that you would have room but the scenario said that there was none."

"Yes. I would operate the Dumping Ground so that it would always register as full. It's like departmental budgets. You have to spend them or someone will take them away. It's the same thing. We would make sure that there was no obvious visible space in the Dumping Ground or else someone would fill it."

"You would lie?"

"No," said Kathy. "Not directly. It would be a matter of organisation. Creating an element of flexibility." She paused and then spoke, almost as an aside, as though she was host to two competing personalities. "I believe that's how the previous post-holder operated. Please understand, I know this is not an okay answer to give at interview. I really do. For some reason, I can't help myself."

Cheryl Clement leaned forward. "Do you feel unnaturally compelled to tell the truth?"

"I do."

"Why do you think that is?" asked Vivian.

Kathy thought. "Have you cast a spell on me?"

Over the next ten minutes, Fluke came up with three phones, a skateboard, a very soggy copy of *Fifty Shades of Grey* and a child's bike.

"It's not just a bike," said Rod defensively as he marvelled over the rusted and muck-smeared thing. "This is a Raleigh Grifter, king of bikes. They haven't made these in decades."

"This must be what it was like when they found the Staffordshire Hoard," said Junior, failing to share his excitement.

"You may mock," said Rod.

"I believe I will."

Fluke surfaced, waving something that was at least the right shape and size to be a wallet. He tossed it ashore.

"Let's take a look," said Rod and pulled the wet thing open. "A lot of cash." He passed the notes to Junior. "Bank card, travel card. Ah, provisional driving licence." The card came out with some resistance. "Jeffney Wilson Ray. He lives in Shirley."

Fluke pulled himself out onto the path with powerful arms. It was rare to see a fish with a six pack. Junior could almost understand why a certain type of woman might find that attractive. Almost. Apart from the big fish head, obviously. Fluke shook himself off and pressed the worst of the silty water from his trousers.

"Give us the address, fed. We'll sort him out."

"Ha," Rod smiled. "We'll take it from here."

Junior tossed Fluke's T-shirt back to him.

"Hey," he said, "we – ggh! – got some vengeance to deal out."

"Which is why we will handle it," said Rod.

"Besides," said Junior, tapping her bruised cheek, "we've got some vengeance to deal out ourselves." She peeled away approximately half of the banknotes and offered them to him. "Here," she said.

"Ggh! A payoff from the *adn-bhul* five-oh?" spat Fluke, although that might have just been him spitting out canal water.

"A reward," said Junior and pressed the cash into his hand. "There's several hundred there."

"Treat your girlfriend – Kirsten, isn't it – to something nice," said Rod. "Something to cheer her up."

"Like a Nando's?" said Fluke, his eyes ashine.

"Aye. Sure," said Rod despairingly. "A Nando's."

Fluke smoothed out his T-shirt, touched Tupac's face for good luck and headed off.

"Shirley, then," said Rod.

"Yeah. Let's get back to your car. I'm worried about Steve."

"He's a possessed doll in a jam jar," said Rod. "He's not a Labrador we left behind in a hot car."

"I'm just… you know."

"Soft," said Rod. "Aye. Come on."

"I'm just saying, this is a waste of time."

"We're going to find him," said Morag Senior.

"Yeah, maybe," said Nina. "But we could have just tweeted, 'Have you seen this man? Hashtag Shirley. Hashtag douchebag drug dealer' and waited for responses."

"Is Twitter the future of criminal investigation?"

"It'd save all this legwork."

The two of them had been doing house enquiries for a little over an hour, taking the oldest of the soul cash contracts as a starting point. So far, they had elicited a lot of blank faces and a few vague maybes. More than a couple of individuals had wanted to share their very specific opinions on door-to-door salesmen or the state of the neighbourhood or whatever cuckoo nonsense was on their mind at that moment. In many respects, just like Twitter.

Away from its long, drawn out high street, Shirley was mostly a mass of post-war housing estates: crescent after avenue after cul-de-sac of Englishmen and their semi-detached castles. If it weren't for the map on her phone, Senior wouldn't know whether they were re-treading old ground or not.

"Shall we just play chappie-knockie at the next one?" she said.

"What?" said Nina.

"Chappie-knockie."

"What the hell?"

"You know, when you knock on someone's door and run away."

"Oh," said Nina, uninterested. "One, it's called knock down ginger –"

"Bit gingerist."

"– and two, no one plays that anymore. Is that what people did before the television was invented?"

"How old do you think I am?" said Senior as she rang the doorbell of the next house.

A balding bloke opened the door sharply as though expecting to catch chappie knockers or knock down gingerists in the act.

"Can you read?" he said.

"Yes, thank you," said Nina cheerily.

He pointed at a home-printed sign stuck in the porch window which read: NO JUNK MAIL, NO FREE PAPERS, NO LEAFLETS, NO COLD CALLERS, NO SALESMEN, NO JEHOVAH'S WITNESSES.

"Nope, we're none of them," said Nina.

"Or Mormons," he said.

"We just wanted to ask some questions," said Senior, flashing her ID card.

"I'm not letting you in until I've checked your credentials."

"We don't want to come in."

The man clicked his fingers for her ID. Senior passed it over.

"We're actually trying to track down a fraudulent door-to-door salesman who's been targeting this area."

"Is that so?" said the man, his interest suddenly piqued. "Cos they're everywhere, aren't they?" There was something in the way he said "they" which made Senior think the conversation might take a sudden turn into nationalistic/xenophobic/UKIP/Enoch Powell and Rivers of Blood territory.

"We're looking for a young white male," said Senior, "with a number of scars on his face. He's been selling what he says are broadband contracts to people up and –"

"You mean Linda Ray's lad. He's got one of them conditions."

Senior frowned.

"His face," the man said. "He does it to himself. Can't help himself."

"Linda Ray?" said Nina.

"The lad's called Jeffney. Not Jeffrey but Jeffney. He's harmless really. They live round the corner on Shakespeare Drive. Number four."

"That's brilliant," said Senior. As she reached to take her ID, the man pulled back a little and tapped the card.

"This picture. It ain't you," he said. "It's that Black Widow woman from the superhero film."

"Thank you!" said Senior with bitter gratitude. "Three weeks I've been on this job and you're the first to notice." She snatched it from him. "Let's go, Nina."

Cameron Barnes looked very relaxed in the interview chair. Vivian did not approve. With that casual tan, that untamed haircut and the bead bracelet he thought she couldn't see under his cuff (or worse, didn't care) the man looked like a surfer who had been stuffed into a suit, a hippy come in from the cold.

"The in-tray exercise," said Cheryl Clement. "Your answers were superb."

"*Tendhu*," he said, gratefully.

"Apart from scenario H."

"Is that the ghost of your dead granny one?"

"Yes. And you wrote, 'Hold a spontaneous fireworks display in a nearby park'."

"I did."

"Why?" said Cheryl, baffled.

"It struck me as obvious," said Cameron, rather smugly. "Apparitions of dead loved ones could have a number of causes. However, the scenario mentioned it was Tuesday. Why Tuesday?"

"Random detail," said Vivian.

"But is it?" said Cameron.

"Yes," said Vivian.

"But is it? Tuesday is the day when stress and depression are statistically likely to be at their highest. The psychic *lo-frax* field, the pre-Soulgate net that surrounds our *durigan* world, might have responded to those energy changes by manifesting ghostly images of those who have already gone."

"Yes?"

"So, I was suggesting some form of massive public celebration to lift spirits and remove the underlying cause."

"But the Tuesday thing is irrelevant," said Vivian.

"That might be the way you wrote it," said Cameron, "but the reader is the final arbiter."

"But I could have written Thursday."

Cameron paused for only a moment. "Then I would look at an almost opposite cause. Woman are significantly more likely to give birth on a Thursday. An increase in *randhu gefit ta-ta* – that's background soul-pressure to you and me – might draw a response from the *lo-frax* field."

"Friday then!"

"Oh, that would be different," said Cameron. "I would probably be looking for a specific human agent, unregistered occultist prodding the cosmic horrors with a stick. The criminal element are most active on Fridays."

Vivian held her tongue. The man was insistent on subverting test scenarios she had written, infuriatingly so. It was doubly annoying that his answers were intelligent and insightful.

"Very good," said Vaughn. "Tell me, Mr Barnes, what strengths do you bring to this job?"

"Direct personal experience with the Venislarn is number one," said Cameron. "The time I spent in Pohnpei and aboard the research platform over *Cary'yeh* meant I was dealing with individual Venislarn and their *em-shadt* accoutrement on a daily basis. My contributions to our understanding of the citizens of *Cary'yeh* were invaluable."

"And yet you were there for only a matter of months."

"My rotation had come to an end. There are dangerous colour fields in the area so no one can stay there for too long."

"But," said Vaughn, intently looking at his notes, "some staff rotate to nearby islands for a few weeks and then return. You weren't asked to."

Cameron smiled. It was deep and warm and, even Vivian could see, entirely artificial. "Has Dr Rolf said something?"

"What would she say?"

"She would say I became too close to the Venislarn. Personally. She might have said I developed an attachment to the *yon-bun* dweller called *Chagulameya*." Cameron stopped and shook himself as though he had just spoken from within a trance. "But I don't want to go into that."

"I think we should," said Vivian.

"I would want to tell you that Dr Rolf was jealous that she was unable to build up a similar personal and cultural bond with the Venislarn."

"You'd want to?"

"Yes," said Cameron, "but I think she was showing an understandable professional concern about a sexual relationship between a man and a twenty-foot sea cucumber." He shook himself again. "Why am I telling you this?"

"You feel inexplicably compelled to tell the truth?" suggested Vivian.

"I do."

"Why do you think that is?"

Cameron looked blank.

"If it's any help," said Vivian, "today's Thursday."

Rod pulled up outside the house on Shakespeare Road.

"I'm unarmed," he said.

"This guy, Jeffney, isn't exactly the physical type," said Morag.

Rod raised a hand meaningfully towards Morag's bruised face.

"You'd squash him like a fly," she assured him.

Besides, Rod reasoned, even though he hadn't yet acquired a new sidearm, he wasn't unarmed. The pen in his breast pocket contained a one-shot taser, he had a paracord bracelet threaded with monofilament which could be used as a garrotte, his belt could be reassembled as a hunting bow and he had a survival penknife which opened out into, well, a knife. He was also, by chance, wearing his Kevlar-lined waistcoat today.

Morag put the jam jar containing the freaky doll, Steve, in her bag.

"Does he have to come with us?" said Rod.

"Yes," said Morag.

"I want to see the man squashed like a fly, fleshling!" cried Steve.

"Fine."

They walked up the cracked driveway to the front door. Morag knocked on the frosted glass. Rod casually took out his taser pen and put his thumb over the trigger stud. The door opened.

"Hey," said Nina in the hallway and then looked at Morag in deep puzzlement. "What are you doing there? And your face…"

"I got hit, remember?" said Morag.

Nina turned round. The other Morag, the original, stood in the hallway.

"This might require explaining," said Rod.

Nina had no trouble in accepting the existence of multiple Morags and was, if anything, only put out that they hadn't confided in her earlier. Linda Ray, Jeffney's mother, stood silently in the kitchen while they all (one Rod, one Nina, two Morags plus a member of the entourage of *Prein* trapped in a *pabash kaj* doll), caught up with each other.

"Jeffney's not here," said Morag Senior. "He left an hour or so ago. Where did he say he was heading, Linda?"

"He didn't," said the mother in a dead monotone, staring out of the window.

Morag indicated a cardboard box on the counter.

"We searched his room and collected these. No major clues."

"We were going to have a look in the shed next."

"He said he was going to take it down for me," said Linda.

Morag Junior flicked through the box. Amulets, fetishes and symbols. Mass-produced rubbish or cheap imitations.

"We had to wade through a sea of happy tissues to find those," said Nina. "We deserve a fricking medal."

"Happy tissues?" said Rod.

"That boy spends a lot of time alone in his room," explained Nina.

"Oh. Eww."

"*Venislarn: A Language Primer*," said Junior, pulling out a slim but well-thumbed book. "What's this?"

"An unauthorised and illegally-distributed book," said Senior.

"And I think I recognise the writing style," said Nina. "That's one of Sheik Omar's."

"Interesting," said Rod. "You think he's behind this?"

"Could be. And if we want to question him, we know exactly where he is."

Professor Sheikh Omar sat patiently in the interview chair while the interviewers considered the test results before them. He gave his fingernails a cursory inspection while he waited (they were perfectly manicured, Vivian had noticed) and gave his glasses a brief polish with a paisley handkerchief.

"Some of your answers to the in-tray exercise were... interesting," said Cheryl Clement and Vaughn nodded in agreement.

"I aim to be interesting," said Omar genially.

"Most interesting is your answer to scenario I, regarding the child in hospital. Can you clarify what you wrote?"

"I believe I wrote that we should kill the child," said Omar simply.

"Kill the child?"

"Kill the child."

"Many would say that's a morally repugnant answer," put in Vaughn.

"Yes. And it is."

"The child could be saved."

Omar smoothly uncrossed and recrossed his legs. "Could. But shouldn't be. Its quality of life would be very poor. Besides, Prince *Holunh Adhulas* needs the child's brain and we can use the child's bone marrow to placate the *Fahaib'soree*."

"You've made a decision about the individual's life based on its basic usefulness to your needs," said Cheryl, displeased.

"We do that all the time," said Sheikh Omar. "This interview situation being a case in point."

"But this is a person's life – their death. Can you put a value on it?"

"The life insurance industry is built around that very idea."

Cheryl made a disagreeable noise.

"Our other candidates," said Vivian, "claimed that they felt compelled – against their will – to tell nothing but the truth in this interview."

Omar nodded but said nothing.

"Are you perhaps under a similar compulsion?" she asked.

Omar considered this, opened his mouth, croaked a little and then closed it.

"Yes. Although I still stand by the answers I've just given."

"As you should," said Vivian, who approved of his pragmatism. "Care to speculate on the cause of this sudden honesty?"

"Tea," he said.

Vivian was not going to rise to enigmatically monosyllabic responses. "Go on, professor."

"Nina Seth went out of her way to provide us all with refreshments this morning. I know from certain sources that she confiscated a vial of *rehpat viarr* from a visitor to the Black Barge yesterday. Nina's animosity towards me is well known. It all seems probable."

Vaughn threw down the paper he held. For a man who was usually about as extroverted as a corpse, this was a dramatic gesture.

"One of our own staff attempting to sabotage the recruitment process!" he said to the air above them.

"Quite!" said Cheryl, attempting to be equally incensed.

"I think it's been enlightening," said Vivian. "We should even consider making it policy. But while we have you in this condition, professor..."

"Yes, Vivian?"

"Why do you want this job?"

"I'm seeking new opportunities," said Omar.

"That's an empty statement. Are you not happy with your current job?"

"It's a means to an end."

"Then to what end is the tech support role with the consular mission a means?"

"Morag Murray," said Omar and then pursed his lips and looked savagely aside.

"Morag Murray?" said Cheryl.

He stood, furious with himself and half-turned away. "I can't speak about this. Please ignore what I just said."

"I think it's fair to say that the professor has an ulterior motive in coming here today," said Vivian.

Omar said nothing, perhaps knowing any further comment would be incriminating.

"Smash it down, freakishly large man!" yelled Steve the Destroyer from within Junior's bag.

"Nearly there," said Rod, probing his tie clip lock picks in the padlock on the shed door.

"You should have left Steve at home," said Senior. "You were meant to be at home too."

"I was working this case," said Junior. "And getting results."

"We got here before you," said Senior.

"It's not a race, girls," said Nina. "Come on, Rod. Haven't you done that yet?"

Rod growled, grabbed the padlock and, with a savage twist, ripped it – lock, latch, hasp, screws and all – off the rotten shed wall.

"It's done," he said and pulled the door open. The interior was dark and musty with an unwholesome stink that crept up on Junior and then leapt at her like a repellent ninja.

"Smells like an open drain," she said, wafting a hand in front of her nose.

"Smells like fish," said Senior, doing likewise.

"Be prepared for more happy tissues," said Nina.

Rod stepped carefully inside. The damp floorboards creaked under his weight. "I think it might actually be fish."

The three women followed him into the cramped space and regarded the tanks, tubs and other paraphernalia: fifty-percent occultism and fifty-percent aquarium supplies, the laboratory of an alchemist trying to turn base metals into goldfish.

"Aren't these *Dinh'r* eggs?" said Rod.

"They are," said Nina, "and this stuff is *khei-ba drel*."

"What's that?"

"Dried fish jizz."

Rod grimaced. "This Jeffney kid needs to get out more, get a hobby."

"Oh, he has hobbies," said Senior, crouching beside Junior to inspect a tank. "I think that's the problem."

Junior tracked one of the little swimming creatures with her finger. Limbs and fins, mandibles and claws. The agility of a fish and the armour of a lobster.

"You know what," she said, "I don't think these are the mummy and daddy ones."

"Me neither," said Senior.

There were damp and empty spaces on the shelves nearest the door. Senior tugged at a sodden label that had fallen off. "*Lu'crik oyh* – Handle with Care. Isn't that just badly-phrased Venislarn for 'big fish'?"

"*Lu'crik oyh*," said Nina. "Wait. I've heard that recently." She blinked several times. "Yes! The Mammonite woman. She was going to give me a muffin but Vivian said no."

"You've slipped into gibberish mode," said Rod.

"No," said Nina. "It was on Monday. Yes. The Smith-Mammonson woman, the Mammonite in Dickens Heath. She said they had one in their garden."

"Coincidence?"

"Or the latest designer pet, cooked up right here by this amateur," said Nina.

"A little knowledge is a dangerous thing," said Rod. "I think I'm starting to dislike this guy."

"Get in line. There's a queue."

Vivian spoke with Vaughn outside meeting room three while the two remaining candidates waited inside to hear their fate.

"Cheryl made her feelings clear," said Vaughn. "Illegally administering a truth drug to the candidates invalidates the whole process. And yet we have successfully discounted Professor Omar as a viable candidate."

"We have him held in room two so we can question him about his apparent interest in Morag. He might still be the best man for the job," said Vivian.

"You would trust him with our most exotic and dangerous treasures?"

"Trust has nothing to do with it. Trust can be engineered and extorted. I would argue that, right now, we cannot afford any delays in appointing someone to this post. The Vault and the Dumping Ground desperately need an organising hand and we have a significant number of OOPArts and relics that even I cannot identify."

A thought occurred to Vivian.

"I have a further assessment activity for Mr Barnes and Ms Kaur," she said. "This afternoon, we will decide if Professor Omar is disqualified or not, conduct another round of interviews and make our selection."

Vaughn shifted uneasily. "You are aware that I am the senior member of staff here?"

"I am, Mr Sitterson."

"And that any decision on this matter is mine to make?"

"Of course."

There was a moment of silence. Vivian looked at Vaughn. Vaughn looked at his shoes.

"Very good," he said. "I'll be in my office."

Vivian went into room three. Cameron and Kathy looked up at her with the half-expectant, half-fearful "dog at the pound" look of interview candidates everywhere. Vivian produced a photocopy she'd made of the *Kal Frexo* runes and put it in front of the two of them. They looked at it and then at her.

"Tell me what you can," she said.

"These are *Kal Frexo* summoning runes," said Cameron.

"All of them?"

"There are only twelve known runes," said Kathy.

"So, five of them don't belong or are fakes or are lost no longer," said Cameron.

"And yet I think I've seen some of the supposedly lost ones elsewhere," said Vivian. "I'm wondering where? Any ideas?"

Kathy gave Vivian an arch look which Vivian did not approve of.

"Is this part of the interview or are you just getting us to do the tech support role?" asked the woman with a twitch of her improperly expressive eyebrows.

"Yes," said Vivian. "For one of you, this is just an interview exercise. For the other, this is your first task in your new role."

"Because I know one place where the lost runes can be found," she said with slow thoughtfulness.

"Where?" said Vivian.

"The Bloody Big Book. You have it in your storage vault, don't you?"

"We do."

"Have you ever read it? Any parts of it, I mean."

"Several thousand pages," said Vivian. Kathy had a point. "Perhaps we should all go down and inspect it."

Mrs Lee-Mammonson may have been desperate enough to take delivery of her *lu'crik oyh* at Ray's convenience but, now that she had him, she was going to get her money's worth from him.

She had him inspect the pond at the bottom of the long rear garden that backed onto the canal. She had him check the lining and the filter pump and then demanded a detailed description of the creature's dietary requirements, which Ray really had no expertise in. Ray had no choice. He had very little time in which to raise a further one hundred pounds and get it to the Black Barge but he couldn't risk infuriating a Mammonite.

These creatures might look human (he suspected Mrs Lee-Mammonson had too many teeth or was it that the corners of her mouth were too elastic?) but humanity was just a face they wore, a fashion they had chosen. The warning signs were everywhere in the house as he came through: a cellar door with a padlock, the sculpture of their unholy mother *Yoth Mammon* in the hallway, the oven bigger than anyone would need to cook the largest of Christmas turkeys, the sigil-surrounded mirror in the lounge that Ray avoided looking in. Ray trod carefully.

"I couldn't say if Kobe beef or wagyu beef would be best," he said. "They will eat anything."

"Yes, yes," said Mrs Lee-Mammonson, "but I have asked the man at Waitrose to put aside the best cuts for...? Oh my. I don't even know what his name is."

"He hasn't got a name yet," said Ray. "Why don't we get him in the pond and then you can think of a name for him."

"All by myself?" said Mrs Lee-Mammonson, eyes wide. "Such responsibility."

Ray hoiked the tub to the edge of the pool. The *lu'crik oyh* inside thrashed and nearly toppled the tub straight in. But Ray held it steady. If this one was like any of the others, it would come out hungry and angry. The trick was to open and tip the tub at the same time. Ray was very mindful of his fingers at the edge of the lid as he tipped and opened. The *lu'crik oyh* had sharp pincers and powerful jaws, even at this size.

The *lu'crik oyh* flopped into the pond with a meaty splash. Mrs Lee-Mammonson jumped up and down doing excited little handclaps like an over-emotional Japanese schoolgirl.

"He's so big!" she exclaimed passionately.

"He'll get bigger if you let him," said Ray.

"We've already got plans for a bigger pond. Maybe one day we'll just cut a channel into the canal so he can stretch his fins when he likes."

"I don't think that's a good idea," said Ray.

The *lu'crik oyh* circled the edge of the pool with casually powerful flicks of its segmented and armoured tail. Its legs clicked on the hard plastic lining of the pond, testing it.

"The Lodge-Mammonsons have already had to rescue theirs from the canal several times. It just keeps climbing out."

"It's done what?"

"Anyway," smiled Mrs Lee-Mammonson (yes, too many teeth), "the hard work is done. You must come in for a drink. A lie down perhaps?"

Slag, he thought.

"Um, no thank you, Mrs Lee-Mammonson."

The Mammonite woman laid a hand on his chest, fingernails tensing slightly against him.

"But you look tired," she said in a voice that was probably meant to be sultry but was as creepy as hell. "I could do something about that." She smiled.

Yes, thought Ray. The creepy slag would do something about his tiredness all right, something permanent. She'd paid him. All he needed to do was get out of there.

"I really must be going…"

"Is that the fish man?" called a voice. A head peered over the fence to next door.

"Audrey Bell-Mammonson!" snapped Mrs Lee-Mammonson. "Can't you see we're in conversation here?"

"I need the services of Mr Ray."

"Hello, Mrs Bell-Mammonson," said Ray. "Nice to see you."

"You had better not be touching that fence, Audrey," Mrs Lee-Mammonson snarled. "That is our property."

The other Mammonite held up her hands to show that no contact was being made. "Mr Ray, I demand that you come here at once and take a look at my *lu'crik oyh*."

"I'm kind of busy at the moment. I've got another *lu'crik oyh* to –"

"At once."

Ray grimaced and stepped back from Mrs Lee-Mammonson's touch. "I'd best see what she wants," he said and backed away as quickly as possible.

Vivian led Kathy and Cameron towards the Vault. Its accumulation of new pieces plus Morag Murray's demolition of local time-space with her mishandling of the Berry Mound vase of multiplication had made it a place of chaos: no longer an austere museum but a junk shop of artefacts.

"There is a lot of work to be done here," Vivian said. "We've not really had the time or expertise to properly catalogue or store some of the new acquisitions. And there have been a lot of late."

"Any reason for that?" said Kathy.

"There has certainly been a sharp increase in items being found in places they couldn't possibly have been placed. Inside trees. Within entirely inappropriate strata of soil. It's all very whimsical and I can't say I like it."

"I wrote my dissertation on OOPArts," said Cameron. "Non-Venislarn ones. I recall there are burnt mounds alongside one of the rivers in Birmingham that are, archaeologically, quite anachronistic."

Vivian made a disapproving noise. Objects and people should stick to their proper place and time. The world was messy enough without things wandering off to places they didn't belong.

She stopped at the edge of the magical barrier Omar had set up earlier in the week to contain the universes Morag had unleashed from the multiplication vase. Omar had been right. The separate realities had found their balance and settled, many had righted themselves and shrunk to accommodate their neighbours. The appearance of the whole thing had shifted from Escheresque nightmare to a simple maze of mirrors.

"As you can see," said Vivian, "we've had a little accident. Resolving this will be another job for the successful candidate. The Wittgenstein Volume is this way. Do not wander off. Your safety cannot be guaranteed."

"Oh good," said Kathy.

Morag Senior let Nina take the lead with the Smith-Mammonson woman; Nina had experience with these people. There had been no Mammonites in Edinburgh but Morag could smell crazy on this woman like cheap cider on a doorway alcoholic.

"Good morning. How are you doing today? It's Miss Nina Seth, isn't it? And you and I have not met before. My name is Melanie."

"This is Morag Murray," said Nina. "She's a colleague."

"Have you come back for a muffin?" said the Mammonite. "I haven't got any in at the moment but I could bake some if you'd care to come in and wait."

Senior could see that Nina was resisting temptation. "We've come to talk about your *lu'crik oyh*."

Mrs Smith-Mammonson's slightly skew-whiff face lit up.

"It's the absolute envy of the whole neighbourhood."

"So we hear," said Nina. "We'd love to take a look and talk about where you got it from."

"Do come through, Nina. Morag. Can I call you Morag?"

The entryway of the house was tiled white. The walls were the wipe-down white of clinic walls. The scent of lemony disinfectant hung in the air. Just across the threshold, Morag could see a tiny, perfect circle of blood on the porcelain floor. Every fibre of her body screamed out that if they went inside that house they'd never come out.

"You know what," she said, "we'll just go round the side."

"You can come through, Morag."

"Muddy feet," said Senior. "This way, Nina."

Vivian navigated a course through the Vault, never stepping across from the one true universe (or, at least, her universe) into any of the others. The tiles on ceiling and floor were her principal guide. The lines between universes were visible as breaks in the tiling pattern: ordered squares becoming diverging triangles of tiles. As they walked, they saw fallen shelves, smashed artefacts and even smears of blood: remnants of Morag's time with the

Whitehall visitor. Twice, Vivian thought she saw movement down the distant corridors of other dimensions. She looked but did not stop to investigate. Any dangers lay on the other side of the barrier.

Ten minutes of careful walking brought them to the room that housed the Wittgenstein Volume. The walls were lined with confiscated paintings by artists who had glimpsed more of the Venislarn than they should and committed what they had seen to canvas. The Wittgenstein Volume was housed in a modified pressure chamber which currently had an axe embedded in the porthole on its front.

"Naturally, this will need tidying up," said Vivian, brushing crumbs of broken glass aside with her foot.

"Naturally," said Kathy.

Vivian tapped a seven-digit code into the keypad beside the chamber door, struggled briefly with the locking wheel and pulled the door open. Inside, on a cubical pedestal, sat the Bloody Big Book.

"Tell me what you already know," said Vivian.

"It has an infinite number of pages," said Kathy, "each page has a thickness of just under fifty micrometres but the whole book is only twenty-one centimetres thick."

"Twenty-one point three seven three centimetres," cut in Cameron, "and it weighs –"

"One point oh six one kilograms," cut in Kathy, "or two hehgn'u."

"All of which is mathematically impossible but nonetheless true," said Cameron. He moved forward to get a better view of the open pages. "The binding is thought to have been made by Roedelius in the eighteenth century and although the book can be closed and opened, it's impossible to definitively turn to either the first or last page. Can I touch it?"

"I think, under the circumstances, we should take it out so that we might all have a closer look," said Vivian.

He reverently slipped his hands under the solid covers and lifted it.

"It's not heavy," he said. "It really isn't."

He stepped back from the chamber and laid it gently on a display table. The pages were yellow with age but undamaged. The Venislarn text on the open page was handwritten in a neat, uniform script in ink that was now a dark lustrous brown but might have once been either black or red. The style was quite beautiful and Vivian had modelled her own Venislarn handwriting on it, however the content of these pages was less exciting: a detailed and monotonous description of the foundations of a building. There was no mention of the building's name or purpose on either of the visible pages but there was a drawing of an engraving, vaguely anchor-like in appearance, that could be seen on one of the foundation stones.

"No one knows who or what produced the actual pages," said Cameron.

"But there are a variety of competing theories," said Kathy. "Several of them refer to the creator as *Yoth-Kreylah ap Shallas*, the 'living black and white'."

"Although that could just be another name for the book itself," said Cameron. "The black ink on the white page. *Yoth-Kreylah* is often thought of as being a god-machine, a sentient device from an alien realm."

"Very good," said Vivian primly. "You've both read things and are able to regurgitate them. Well done. Now, the question is, how do we use the book to learn more about these *Kal Frexo* runes and how they came to be rediscovered?"

The two interview candidates stood in thought, glancing at each other from time to time. Either neither had anything to say or neither wished to speak first in case they appeared foolish.

"Come now," said Vivian. "Any ideas? How do we find the page I had previously seen?"

"We drop it on the floor," said Cameron. "Statistically, the book is likely to fall open at one of the most recently opened pages."

"We are not dropping an infinitely large book," said Vivian.

"We look in the index," said Kathy.

"It has no index," said Vivian.

"That you've seen. A book that allegedly details everything that is, was or could be in our universe, would also contain information about itself. That index is not necessarily at the back."

"So, it is as lost as the page we are looking for."

"Not equally. We're trying to find one page. The size of an index is usually in proportion to the book. A one-hundred-page book might have a one page index, a two-hundred-page book a two page index. Whatever the size of the book, the chances of randomly stumbling upon the index are roughly the same."

"You might be making assumptions about book production methods and writing conventions," said Cameron.

"Then heat," said Kathy.

"Yes?" said Vivian.

"If you touched the page of the book when you read it, you will have added some heat energy to the book, however little. It might have been some time ago but if you closed the book afterward, surrounding the page you had touched with an infinite number of insulating pages, finely tuned heat detection equipment might still be able to pinpoint which section of the book you were reading."

"Interesting," said Cameron.

"Then let's also think about human residues," said Kathy. She caught Vivian's dubious look and explained. "You touched the book. Oils and cells from your skin will have been left there. You will have, infinitesimally, added mass to a book the weight of which is precisely and clearly known. We could weigh sections of the book to find the heaviest."

"That's preposterous," said Cameron.

"And you have a better suggestion?" Kathy challenged him.

"If you have seen one of these runes," Cameron said to Vivian, "a brief search through your memories with a *byhaxx* invocation would bring the memory forth."

"Yes," said Vivian who could think of nothing worse than having this new age Venislarn-lover rummage through her mind. "I think we can treat that as a last resort, don't you?"

In Dickens Heath, Rod's satnav developed a system error and crashed after he took five left turns in a row and didn't cross his own path.

"This place doesn't obey the laws of geography," he said.

"I laugh in the face of geography!" cackled Steve the Destroyer perched on the dashboard.

"Not helpful," said Rod.

"Just keep driving," said Morag Junior. "If we see Jeffney Ray here, it'll be a pure fluke. But unless the other two find a lead, this is as good a plan as any."

At a crossroads where there couldn't logically be a crossroads, Rod paused at the GIVE WAY for a pair of Mammonite women, each holding the hand of a Mammonite toddler. All four turned to look at the car.

"It's like *The Stepford Wives*, this place," said Junior.

"Village of the bleeding Damned more like," said Rod and drove on.

Morag Senior had visited Venislarn temples before, both those built by humans and those erected by the more comprehensible of the earthly Venislarn. The general principle, as far as she could grasp it, was to create something as stomach-turningly mad as possible. Irregular building materials, insane angles, smashed perspectives: all suffused with imagery of gods or symbols or secret knowledge that would turn the unsuspecting mind to mush. Senior had seen so much of it now, it had got boring and she rarely noticed it.

Nonetheless, it was nice to see an attempt at an *al fresco* version.

The Smith-Mammonson back garden was like a Renaissance artist's idea of what a classical Greek garden might have looked like, with shapely gods and goddesses caught in marble poses among neatly tended borders and babbling rills and fountains. Except, in this instance, the gods and goddesses were only moderately shapely (some could hardly be said to have a shape, some had too much shape, and at least one seemed unwilling to maintain a single shape despite being hewn from solid rock), the rills babbled with the voices of the mad and the fountains' drips were the sighs of the damned.

"Nice," said Nina.

"Artful," said Senior.

"Thank you," said the Smith-Mammonson woman. "Built to glorify our mother, in expectation of her triumphant return."

"Oh, she'd be dead pleased with this," said Nina.

"What mother wouldn't?" agreed Senior, following the Mammonite down to the furthest section of the long garden.

The pond was almost too big to be called a pond. It was a stone-lined pool that could have swallowed a car (and the truck towing it too probably). Something rolled and turned in its depths and the size of it gave Senior pause for thought.

"This is your *lu'crik oyh*?" she said.

"Titus," said Smith-Mammonson.

"And you've had him how long?"

"Two weeks."

"Right."

Senior considered the ramifications. A pet that was essentially an angry shrimp with extensive facial weaponry had grown to the size of a prize bull. From box to bull in two weeks.

"How long would you say that thing is?" said Senior. "Twelve feet? Fifteen?"

"I don't know," said Nina.

"More?"

"I mean I don't know how long a foot is, grandma."

Senior edged nearer. Silver compound eyes flashed as the thing swam beneath.

"Four metres then?"

"I don't do metric either," said Nina.

"But it's big though," said Senior and realised she was whispering so as not to disturb it.

"So," said Nina, "Mrs Smith-Mammonson, the man who sold it to you..."

"Yes?"

"Have you seen him recently?"

Mrs Smith-Mammonson stiffened. "Are you asking me to divulge details about business contacts?"

"I just wondered where we could buy one."

The Mammonite eyed her suspiciously.

"Do you think there's something wrong with him?" Mrs Bell-Mammonson asked Ray.

In the aggressively neat garden, Ray considered her pet *lu'crik oyh*. It was bigger than Ray himself but small in comparison to others he had sold at the same time. Also, there was series of pinky-yellow nodules growing along its spine, giving extra shape and prominence to its dorsal fin. It wasn't like any of the others that Ray had seen.

"What have you been feeding it?" Ray asked.

"Mostly lamb cutlets. We had veal at the weekend. Pate for occasional treats. Foie gras."

The answer meant nothing to Ray. He had bred these things. He didn't understand them beyond the moment they became sellable.

He crouched down at the poolside and tried to get a closer look. He couldn't decide if those things on its spine were a sign of disease or if they were a form of colouration in the species that he'd just not seen before.

"If you've sold me a deficient creature – and I've no idea what the neighbours will say – then I will demand a full refund," said Mrs Bell-Mammonson.

"Let's not be hasty," said Ray.

"My husband will certainly want words when he returns from work."

Ray could see the Mammonite's shadow cast over him. He was aware of how close she stood behind him.

"I'm sure it won't come to that," he said.

Without warning, the *lu'crik oyh* gave a sudden turn and flick of its tail and propelled itself upward at Ray. He pushed himself back with a tiny yelp and fell onto the grass. He felt its chisel-like legs claw at his body as it heaved itself out of the pool and landed on top of him.

287

"Shit! It's trying to eat me!"

"Oh, yes," said the Mammonite with mild interest rather than any concern.

Ray wriggled in frenzied horror. The *lu'crik oyh* continued to clamber over him. He had a view of its face, its mandibles working hungrily in a mouth that was like a diseased wound with teeth. It stank like a fishmonger's on a hot day. Its eyes flashed.

"No!" he squealed and, frantically scrambling for leverage, he brought his knees up beneath it and pushed.

"Don't you hurt it!" said Mrs Bell-Mammonson.

That just made Ray angry as well as terrified. With a huge mental *fuck you* for Mrs Bell-Mammonson, he pushed up at its belly and rolled, spilling the *lu'crik oyh* onto its back on the pool's concrete apron.

Soaking and wild with fear, Ray scrambled to his feet and away. The *lu'crik oyh*, stuck on its back for the time being, thrashed its tail from side to side and lashed at the air with its many legs.

"What have you done, Mr Ray?"

The beast on the ground cried out. From a mouth with no lungs, it produced a weak but piercing howl, a friction-filled honk, a satanic kazoo of a noise.

"You've upset him!" said Mrs Bell-Mammonson. "I will have to call my husband now."

The creature howled piteously and flailed about. Ray did not want to be around when it found its feet again.

Nina did not hear the faint honking at first.

The *lu'crik oyh* in Mrs Smith-Mammonson's pond had responded before she even recognised there was a sound coming from her neighbour's garden. It sank to the bottom of the pool, arched its back and leapt for the surface. Morag pulled back, startled, when it breached and flung itself, head and body, onto the bank. It was fat and ungainly on land but it was not immobile. With a hurried shifting of its spider legs, it rotated its carapace left then right, sensing the air.

"What the hell?"

"He's never done that before," commented Mrs Smith-Mammonson with interest.

It turned rapidly on the spot, sweeping a circle with its armour-plated tail and nearly slicing Nina's legs from beneath her. Then, with a lurch that was half scuttle and half fishy flop, it launched itself toward the fence. The *lu'crik oyh* moved without grace and, as it ran, brought down three statues. It clawed down the fence and flolloped over into the next garden.

"This is an unhelpful turn of events," said Morag.

And then Nina heard the sound: like parts rubbing in an ungreased engine, high-pitched and grating.

Rod took a turn at random and looked at a street that might have been familiar, might have been utterly new. Uniformly charming semis, box hedges, gleaming prestige saloons on driveways, carefully spaced deciduous trees on the verges. The same things he'd seen for the past fifteen minutes just shuffled into a new order.

"Okay, I'm lost," he said.

"It feels like we've driven miles," said Morag. "Surely, we'd be out of Dickens Heath by now."

"We could be in Narnia now for all I know," said Rod.

"Narnia's changed," said Morag.

A shape barrelled out of the privet next to them, slammed into the front corner of the car and slithered heavily over the bonnet and then the roof, leaving claw puncture marks and a crack in the windscreen. Its tail slapped on the tarmac on the other side and then it was gone, charging down the side between two houses.

"Demon fish!" yelled Steve the Destroyer.

"There weren't any demon fish in Narnia," said Morag faintly.

Slime smeared down the windscreen. Rod unclipped his seatbelt to jump out but then, further ahead, another creature, as large as the first, slithered and skidded into the road.

"You reckon these things are fair game?" he said.

"God, yes," said Morag, reaching to phone her older self.

"Good," said Rod. He put his foot to the floor and chased the thing as it flopped away down the road.

The Vault guards helped carry their equipment through the maze of worlds to the location of the Bloody Big Book. Vivian watched Kathy take command and direct the men to place the instruments on various surfaces. Most of the equipment they never got to use because the first thing Kathy did was weigh the book.

She calibrated the precision scales and carefully transferred the book from its pedestal.

"Huh," she said, intrigued.

"What is it?" said Cameron and looked at the readout.

"Nine hundred and fifty-four point nine grams," said Kathy.

The book was a hundred grams lighter than it should be. A fool would immediately declare it to be impossible but Vivian wasn't a fool.

"Check the scales," said Cameron.

Kathy removed the book, recalibrated the scales, checked the foot mountings and reweighed the book.

"It's shrunk," said Kathy.

"The book has been weighed dozens of times, with increasing levels of accuracy," said Cameron. "It has never shrunk."

"Conclusions?" said Vivian, who had come to her own chilling conclusions but wanted the candidates to find their own.

"Part of the book is missing," said Cameron eventually.

"Yes," said Vivian.

Morag Senior took the call from her junior self while running on a trail of broken fences that led from garden to garden.

"What?" she yelled. "Yes! We know! We're following it now!"

She frowned furiously at Junior's indistinct reply.

"There are more?"

She looked at Nina.

"What the hell's happening?"

They hurdled over the smashed remnants of a trellis and found themselves in a garden with three of the creatures. Two of the *lu'crik oyh* were equally massive, whereas the third was smaller and more brightly coloured than the others, a ridge of bobbly growths running down its back. The two huge beasts circled and snarled at each other, with the smaller one turning nervously between them.

"Fighting over dinner?" said Senior.

"It's not dinner," said Nina and Senior immediately saw she was right. It was two big males competing for a smaller and more colourful female.

"This is bad," said Senior, speaking into the phone.

"Bad how?"

"It's a female, drawing them in."

"Stop this at once!" commanded a strident voice.

There were two people in the garden. Senior's brain had not registered them until now. No, not people. The one who was about to try and scold the *lu'crik oyh* like naughty puppies was a Mammonite woman. The one cowering by the low wall that backed onto the canal was a scar-faced idiot who had already indirectly killed several innocent individuals.

"Jeffney Ray."

The Mammonite woman wagged her finger at the circling *lu'crik oyh*.

"You get out of here this instant!" she shouted at the larger creatures. "Look at what you've done!"

"Get back, lady!" Nina shouted at her.

"I'll not be bullied in my own garden," snorted the Mammonite and turned her attention back to the fishy interlopers. "Get away and leave young Caligula alone!"

One of the males swiped its tail at her, possibly instinctively, possibly accidentally. The tail was a flat blade of heavy chitin. The Mammonite woman fell apart in two neatly severed chunks, spilling what passed for Mammonite blood all over her trimmed lawn.

"*Azbhul!*" said Senior. "Nasty."

Jeffney Ray recognised Nina and Morag, stared at them goggle-eyed and then seemed to be considering whether to leap over the wall.

"You stay there!" shouted Senior and made to reach him, past the deadly tails of the *lu'crik oyh*.

The female squealed louder and this drove the males into further excitement. Senior could hear the smashing of wooden fences from somewhere in the distance.

"She's bringing all the boys to the yard, isn't she?" said Nina.

Nina picked up a garden fork as she followed Senior. Senior was about to ask her what she expected to do with it when one of the *lu'crik oyh* whirled on them and Nina jabbed it in the face. The *lu'crik oyh* spat and thrashed and, as it did, Jeffney Ray decided to take his chances and leapt over the wall into the canal.

"Is this a set-up?" asked Cameron.

Vivian directed her gaze at the man. "What do you mean?"

"The interview. This activity. The convenient mystery of the missing pages."

Vivian gestured at the Big Bloody Book on the surface between them.

"You think we dismembered an artefact whose infinite size has the potential to create singularly cataclysmic problems in order to make this selection process more *immersive*?"

"I don't like coincidences," said Cameron. "I don't buy them. It's *manan'shei*. It's just God being lazy."

"Or the gods playing with us," said Vivian.

Kathy, who had been toying with her collar thoughtfully, said, "Whether stolen or missing, an infinite number of pages have gone. A finite proportion of an infinite object is itself infinite."

"Yes?" said Vivian.

"And although key information would be missing from those pages, one might extrapolate any missing information for the infinite data already present. It would mean…"

"Yes?"

"It would mean that whoever has those pages possesses a form of omniscience."

"A little knowledge is a *graz* dangerous thing," said Cameron. "Infinite knowledge is…"

"Apocalyptic," said Kathy.

"Yes," said Vivian. "A tad over-dramatic, Dr Kaur, but essentially true. So, what questions do we need to ask ourselves?"

Cameron touched the edges of the book with his fingertips. "Where are the pages now?"

"And who took them?" said Kathy. "This is meant to be a secure facility and it has been breached."

Behind her, Andy the security guard rolled his shoulders in disagreement and cleared his throat.

"You may posture all you wish," Vivian said to him. "She is right. We have been victims of theft."

"It could be that the missing pages have been used to uncover or extrapolate the no-longer-missing *Kal Frexo* runes," said Cameron. He suddenly clicked his fingers. "*Heyun'toth!*" he exclaimed. "You've had a recent surge in OOPArts in the city."

"We have," said Vivian, who did not see the connection.

"Ontological necessity," said Cameron.

"No," said Kathy. "Really?"

"Explain," said Vivian, who did not enjoy being the only Venislarn expert in the room who did not understand.

"It could be said that truth demands physical expression," said Cameron. "Logical truth becomes *em-shadt* reality: new knowledge created the items."

"Is there any scientific basis to this?" asked Vivian, who suspected that Cameron was talking hippy mumbo-jumbo.

"The Mathematical Universe hypothesis is not universally accepted," admitted Kathy. "And this is an unsubstantiated variant."

"But," said Cameron with an abrupt passion, "if someone is using the stolen pages to generate new 'truths' then the OOPArts could be simply bubbling into existence in response."

Vivian found it all very doubtful.

293

"Or it's magic," said Cameron. "Describe it however you like."

"I would prefer to describe things as they are, Mr Barnes. But, to the questions: who took them and where are they now?"

Kathy looked up at the ceiling and the walls. "Assuming it wasn't a cat burglar or Tom Cruise crawling through the air vents, the pages were taken by someone who was allowed in here. There's CCTV and security records. Apart from permanent staff who has been down here?"

Andy the guard coughed meaningfully. Vivian looked at him sharply. He gave her an innocent look.

"Professor Omar was in my view the entire time we were down here," she said.

"Just saying," Andy replied.

"What's this?" said Kathy.

Vivian gave a rueful shake of the head. "It proved necessary to bring Professor Omar down here. On Tuesday."

"And his little assistant friend," said Andy.

"Yes," said Vivian slowly.

Morag Junior and Rod were almost on top of the creature when it crested a humpbacked bridge at the edge of the village, flung itself up onto the wall and cartwheeled down into the canal.

"Bugger," said Rod with quiet feeling and slammed to a halt on the bridge.

He was already out of the door by the time Junior could speak.

"Are we chasing after that thing? On foot?"

"What else?" said Rod.

"And if we catch it?"

"Restrain it. Kill it," he said and then actually gave it some thought. "With my bare hands if need be."

"You have city hands, gobbet!" yelled Steve but the big guy was already running toward the steps to the canalside below.

Junior, with Steve the Destroyer clinging to her sleeve, thumbed the number for the office. They were going to need police to set up a cordon at the very least. And maybe, she thought giddily, the RAF to bring in an airstrike.

The *lu'crik oyh* lunged at Nina again and she stabbed it cleanly with the garden fork, driving one tine into its eye and the other three into the fleshy corner of its mouth. It reared back, pulling the fork from her hand.

Morag saw this as the opportunity to run past but the other male, who had been trying to monopolise the female's attention, saw this as some sort of threat and lunged at her. Morag stumbled into the borders and got briefly entangled in a thorny rose bush.

Nina's fork was currently embedded in the other *lu'crik oyh*'s face – it was doing a spectacularly bad job of trying to dislodge it by headbutting the back wall of the house – and she looked about for another weapon. She picked up a plastic can of weed killer and hurled it at the *lu'crik oyh* threatening Morag. The can bounced and splashed across the creature's face. It reared as though burned.

Morag pushed herself out of her thorny bush, ran to the wall and stepped over onto whatever narrow bank was on the other side in pursuit of Jeffney Ray.

The forked *lu'crik oyh* (which clearly subscribed to the 'try, try again' school of thought) charged at the house one last time and, in a single, swift and noisy act, skewered itself and fell dead. There was a loud *ploosh* and Nina turned away from the self-kebabbed spiderfish to see that the other male had disappeared into the canal. There was no sign of Morag.

The female, who had gone from two suitors to none in the flap of a fin, turned this way and that, hollering her weird squeaky cry. From not far away – not far enough at all – came answering sounds of destruction as prized pond pets were drawn to the flirty female.

"Bitch, you need to shut up," said Nina and considered what gardening implement would be her next weapon of choice.

A narrow strip of land ran along the backs of the canalside houses, a balance beam of muddy turf between garden borders and the Stratford-upon-Avon canal. Morag Senior worked her way along it, foot by tricky foot, following Jeffney Ray. The desperate fool was in the water, splashing his way across the canal. He was some distance ahead of her but Senior's eyes kept returning to the waters at her feet. She had seen the *lu'crik oyh* go under and could picture it all too clearly in her mind's eye, cruising through its element. It might have been clumsily dangerous on land, but underwater it was an agile and hidden terror. She studied Jeffney's inefficient breaststroke and wondered whether *lu'crik oyh* preyed on frogs.

Jeffney clutched at the grass verge of the opposite bank.

"You can't get away!" she shouted.

Probably spurred on by the prospect of death from below rather than a desire to prove Senior wrong, Jeffney Ray hauled himself up and rolled exhausted onto the towpath. Senior looked up and down the waterway. There was a bridge a couple of hundred yards ahead. She hurried towards it because there was no way she would be swimming with a *lu'crik oyh* in the water.

Nina was rapidly working on her hoe-wielding skills.

The female *lu'crik oyh* might have been a fraction of the size of the males but it was still as big as Nina and, to the extent that insect-fish hybrids' faces could convey intentions, it looked like it was eyeing her up for lunch.

Nina just wanted the damned bitch to shut up with the whining and go quietly. It wasn't much to ask, but every time Nina whacked at it with the long-handled hoe to drive it back to its pond, the *adn-bhul* creature would blart out another horrid honk.

Trying to drive it away wasn't working. Nina wondered whether trying to lure it might be more effective, so she gave it a tempting waggle of leg, a cry of "come and try my tasty thighs" and hopped and skipped enticingly into the open rear door of the house. The *lu'crik oyh* needed no further encouragement and slithered in behind her. All she needed to do now was circle around and shut the door from the outside to trap it in the house.

Nina ran to the front of the house and pulled at the front door handle. It was locked. There was no key.

"What kind of person locks their front door and hides the key?" she demanded of the world.

The *lu'crik oyh* was in the kitchen, turning towards the hallway and Nina. Nina went back partway towards it and opened the downstairs toilet door, pulling it open as a barrier between herself and the *lu'crik oyh* a second before the creature ran into it.

The door swung back on its hinges. Nina leaned her weight against it and dug in her heels. The *lu'crik oyh* was stronger but Nina felt the pressure on the door ease. The damned thing had gone into the toilet. She slammed the door shut after it and pulled the fat and hideous carving of *Yoth Mammon* off the hallway table to brace the door closed.

She heard angry thrashing noises from within and then the sound of breaking ceramic. A pool of water spread under the doorway.

"Drown yourself if you like," said Nina but then the noise took on a curiously subterranean tone, a drain-ey noise. "No, you're too big," she whispered.

She ran out to the back garden and round to the side of the house but the sounds from underground were already moving on.

"Come on, bitch. Play fair."

The sounds moved under the partition fence and onward toward the house next door. Nina stepped through the smashed fence, over the tangled remains of a rotary clothes line. She had no idea where the drains might lead next but she had no time to wonder. There was a scream from the upstairs of the house. Someone had probably just developed a lifelong phobia of toilets. How long that life would be remained to be seen.

Vivian entered the meeting room bearing a tea pot and two cups on a tray. Professor Sheikh Omar sat with his chair angled towards the window. The metal rings that shrouded the Library of Birmingham building barely impeded the view of Centenary Square and the demolition site over Chamberlain Square next door. A crane, higher than any building around, swung its arm round with titanic slowness.

"It never stops, does it?" said Omar. "It's quite beautiful."

Vivian set the tray down.

"'One could tear out any number of pages from the Wittgenstein Volume and it would not change its contents a single jot,'" said Vivian. "Your words, professor."

"Near enough," said Omar. He regarded the pot. "Are you going to be mother?"

Vivian had not intended it to be any other way. She poured.

"Either you are being dashed civil, my dear," said Omar, "or you intend to ply me with more truth potion."

"I can do both," she said and passed cup and saucer across.

He looked at the colour of the tea before adding a splash of milk. "Tea-making is an art," he said, not indicating at all whether he thought Vivian had mastered it or not.

"The cornerstone of civilisation."

"I'm always amazed," he said, "that the staff in cafeteria these days seem utterly unable to perform the task. They give you a pot of hot water and a tea bag as though they can't be bothered to introduce one to the other themselves. I'm sure if they took the same approach with sandwiches – here's your bread, here's your cheese, chop-chop – they'd soon be out of business."

"I don't tolerate it," said Vivian. "I tell them to get their finger out and make the tea for me."

"Hear, hear."

"I've had one young incompetent point out that the reason they don't do teas properly is that they're all coffee shops these days. I don't know where all the tea shops went."

"Died or fled to Yorkshire," said Omar and sipped gently.

"Your assistant, Maurice," said Vivian.

"Ah, if it wasn't for his tea-making skills, I'm sure I would have got bored with him years ago."

"He's on his way."

"You're letting me go."

"No. We're having him arrested."

Omar put the cup down on the saucer with a soft chink. There was a tremor of emotion in his hands though his voice didn't betray it. "He's of a delicate disposition. He doesn't take kindly to big burly types manhandling him."

298

"Either you or he stole a section from the Wittgenstein Volume."

Omar downed his cup of tea, swallowed noisily and put the cup down heavily. He gave Vivian a pointedly emphatic look and said, "Neither Maurice or I stole your book on Tuesday. That's the truth."

Vivian opened her mouth to speak. Omar raised his hand to stop her.

"Neither of us stole it on Tuesday. Neither of us has stolen it, part or all, at any point in time. We have not engaged or asked anyone to steal it for us. I have not offered advice or assistance to anyone who has. I know of no one who has stolen part or all of the book or who has expressed any intention of doing so. If you were to ask me who has taken, had taken it or has plans to take it I would have to say, in all honesty, that I do not know." He heaved a heavy breath. "Have you genuinely sent officers to arrest Maurice?"

Vivian nodded. "They won't be there yet."

"Please," said Omar. "Don't."

Vivian gave it some thought.

Omar tilted his cup to regard the dregs. "Was there any *rehpat viarr* in there?"

"There was barely anything in the pot left over from this morning," said Vivian.

Omar nodded in understanding.

"Do you trust me, Mrs Grey?"

"Not an inch, Professor Omar," she replied.

"So, if I were to tell you that despite any scurrilous rumours and despicable truths told about me, I regard the Venislarn threat just as you do, you wouldn't believe me?"

"I would be surprised that you presume to know my opinions."

"It is said that the Big Bloody Book was written by a machine or a god or some other horror," said Omar. "Clearly something not confined by the notions of time and space inherent in our universe. It is said that the author, *Yoth-Kreylah ap Shallas*, was a being with a thousand limbs, each holding a pen, fed by the ink of its own blood. I can't help but picture some sort of literary squid."

"Yes," said Vivian. "All very vague and unhelpful nonsense."

"If one had one of the pens, some simple sympathetic magic would have it direct you to any missing pages."

"If."

Omar dabbed at his shirt with a handkerchief where a stray drop of hastily drunk tea had splashed him. "Call off the boys in blue and do not harass my Maurice and I will tell you where you can find such a pen."

"Oh, please, professor," said Vivian. "If you are going to waste my time…"

"Cross my honest little heart," he said and did so.

Vivian had already made her decision but let Omar squirm for several seconds. "Very well," she said. "Where is the pen?"

"In Birmingham," he said.

"Yes. I require a little more information than that."

"No, you don't, my dear," said Omar. "Just apply a little thought. Where is the best place to hide a leaf?"

Morag Junior ran after Rod along the towpath in pursuit of the *lu'crik oyh*. He might have been ex-SAS and a specimen of peak physical fitness but Rod Campbell was built for strength and endurance, not speed. As Junior overtook him, Steve offered words of encouragement.

"Come on, meatsack. This isn't no boy scout picnic!"

Rod growled wordlessly.

Ahead, the *lu'crik oyh* was visible as a shallow bow wave, a dark V-shape in the water. Further on, there was potential trouble: two cyclists on the towpath, humans (only humans would think yellow Lycra tops, skin-tight trunks and cycling helmets were acceptable clothing to wear in public). The bow wave was definitely edging towards them.

"The noise!" shouted Rod.

"What?" shouted Junior.

"The noise! The wheels!"

It took Junior a good few seconds to work out what he meant. The wheels of the bikes, the brakes... they sounded remarkably like the honking of the female that had driven the *lu'crik oyh* wild in the village.

"Stop!" she yelled at the cyclists and waved her arms urgently. "Get off! Get off!"

"But it's our right of way," she heard one of them say to the other and then the bow wave was at the bank.

In perhaps a life-saving accident, the water splashing over the edge of the bank startled the lead cyclist, who came to a wobbly stop and stumbled off his bike as it fell over. The other could not help but do the same. By the time the *lu'crik oyh* had lugged itself up onto the path, the noise of squeaking brakes had ended and the cyclists were a few feet away from their bikes.

Both cyclists screamed and swore and shot up the wooded bank next to the canal with the kind of speed one would expect of Lycra-clad athletes. The *lu'crik oyh* clawed experimentally at one of the bikes.

Now that they were upon the beast, Junior had no idea what they were going to do about it. She slowed but Rod rushed forward, apparently intent on attacking it with a pen.

"Go, giant man!" cried Steve.

Rod raised the pen to stab at it. The *lu'crik oyh* swung his way and slammed him to the ground with its head. Morag looked for a weapon. She had nothing. There weren't even any handy sticks or stones on the towpath. With a flicker of mental apology, she plucked Steve off her shoulder and hurled him at the creature. It was a distraction at least.

The creature's insect eyes shimmered silver as it turned.

"From hell's heart, I –" yelled Steve and then was gone into its maw.

The creature shook itself and Steve briefly resurfaced between its jaws, apparently trying to pick a fight with the *lu'crik oyh*'s tongue.

"– for hate's sake, I –"

The *lu'crik oyh* jerked its head and swallowed. On the ground, Rod jabbed up with the pen. There was an electric fizz and a hiss of pain from the *lu'crik oyh* as it spasmed backwards into the canal and disappeared.

Junior realised she was panting.

"So, that crackpot who said canal monsters were eating cyclists?" she said.

"Aye. Might have been correct," he conceded, "sound of a breeding female."

He looked at the bicycles.

"At least we now know how to lure them in. Fancy a ride?"

"Ah, a classic Rod pick-up line. Unfortunately..." She nodded toward one of the bikes. A chunk of wheel had been clawed out, tyre, rim and spokes. "Bicycle for one," she said.

Kathy Kaur drove a small red Italian car. Vivian approved of the size; economy and modesty were admirable traits. She did not approve of the colour or the leather interior; it was flashy and suggested lax morals and deep personal insecurity.

"Is this still part of the interview process?" asked Kathy.

"Why do you ask?" said Vivian.

"I'm suddenly having flashbacks to my test. Mirror, signal, manoeuvre."

"You're right about Birmingham," said Cameron from the confines of the back seat. "I'm lost already."

Kathy took a right at the traffic lights by the Sikh gurdwara and pulled up beside an archway into a tall red brick building.

"The Pen Museum," she said, peering up at the sign on the wall. "I can honestly say I had no idea such a place even existed."

Vivian unclipped her seatbelt and stepped out.

"It seems they'll give you a grant for anything these days," she said. "Pen museum here. A coffin works museum down towards St Paul's Square."

"A coffin museum?" said Cameron, squeezing out of the back seat.

"Too kooky for my tastes," said Vivian.

"Coffins? Kooky?"

"Oh, I'm all for celebrating our industrial history but, just because something's old, doesn't mean it deserves a museum." She straightened her jacket. The leather seats had put quite a crease in it. "Next challenge. We have a pen to find."

Nina was about to investigate the noises inside the house when the investigation came to her. A Mammonite man wearing fewer clothes than was normally considered modest burst out of the patio doors, closely followed by a hungry female *lu'crik oyh*. Wounded and terrified he might have been but he still had the presence of mind to say to Nina as he ran past, "Who are you? This is private property, you know!"

Fixated on the tasty semi-naked man, the *lu'crik oyh* scuttled past Nina and over the mangled rotary washing line. Nina grabbed a loose length of trailing flex and pulled hard, drawing the lines taught and entangling the creature. It struggled and turned. Nina pulled again and the thing got itself tied up further, but it still struggled powerfully on – now dragging the entire contraption behind it.

Nina picked up the central pole and pulled against the aquatic demon. It was stronger than her but not smarter and almost immediately it was running in a circle with Nina as the pivoting centre. She leaned back and let the *lu'crik oyh* do all the work. Two swift rotations and then she let go: the thing, carried by its own momentum, ran straight into a trellis-covered brick wall. It collapsed in a heap of clothes line and smashed trellis, with perfect specimen roses scattered on top.

Nina caught her breath and thought that there must surely be an excellent kiss-off line for such an occasion. She had a thing that was half spider, half fish, a clothes line and a garden trellis. Witty puns should just be lining up in her mind.

"Just taking out the laundry? No. That's one web you won't get out of? No? Net?" She shook her head. "When I tell this in the pub later, I'll have said something so cool."

Senior, running for the bridge, found her path along the narrow spit of land blocked by a *lu'crik oyh* half in and half out of the water. She scissor-leaped over into a back garden and dashed through the broken fence.

The *lu'crik oyh* that had blocked her path was leaning into the garden and harassing a Mammonite couple who had taken cover in a brightly painted and entirely ostentatious gazebo. The Mammonite man, in whom fear had made his off-human countenance look even worse, waggled an ineffectual hand at the beast.

"Ivana! It's ruined the clematis!"

"There will be words at the next Neighbourhood Watch meeting!" shrilled the female Mammonite. "There will be words!"

The *lu'crik oyh*, apparently confounded by the gazebo, heaved itself into the garden and slither-scurried towards Senior.

"Hell, no," she muttered and took brief cover behind a gas barbecue on wheels.

"It's going for the Broil King Super Gem, Ivana!" cried the man.

The *lu'crik oyh* mounted the barbecue to get at Senior. She reached aside, pulled a mass of green netting from a soft fruit bed and threw it over the creature. It could only be a diversion. Plastic netting might as well be tissue paper to this thing. It shook at the netting and worked its jaw with breathless grunts.

And then it froze, twitched, and gazed upward for a long second before its left eyeball exploded and a fat lump of wetness tumbled out onto the ground. The *lu'crik oyh* reared in agony and bucked like a fish on a hook. Then it turned, with no consideration for its surroundings, and rushed down the garden, dragging netting and barbecue behind it, over the wall and into the canal.

"It's taken the Broil King Super Gem!" shouted the man. "We've not even had chance to use it yet!"

Senior simply stared. The loss seemed acceptable in the circumstances.

The wet blob of cloth at her feet shook itself like a dog, dislodging barely any of the slime that coated it.

"And I thought they smelled bad on the outside," said Steve.

Rod had cycled off, up to the bridge and towards the village, with a half-formed plan to draw the *lu'crik oyh* to a central location. Junior had called the authorities and, above the fading squeak of Rod's intermittent and fish-baiting braking, she thought she heard the distant approach of the first police helicopter.

In the opposite direction from which she'd come, Junior saw a slouched figure walking along the towpath. It was Jeffney Ray, totally drenched but unmistakeably Jeffney Ray. He was picking through a wad of wet banknotes and hadn't seen her but the moment she stepped towards him, he looked up and ran.

Junior was struck by the déjà vu of the situation: a canal, him running, her chasing. It had not ended well last time but it looked like the fight had gone out of Jeffney now. He ran towards the distant bridge. There was someone on it. Nina. Junior waved and pointed but Jeffney had seen her too and cut off to the side through the woods.

Junior ran on. Nina came the other way, converging.

Leaving the incandescently miffed gazebo-dwellers to rant about what the *lu'crik oyh* had done to their garden, Senior stepped back onto the narrow canal edge and continued towards the bridge. She was momentarily distracted by the sight of her other self, running at full pelt in the other direction on the opposite path, but she was too slow to call out to her before she had gone.

"I prefer the other one to you," said Steve the Destroyer conversationally.

Senior paid the slime-sodden doll in her pocket no mind.

"She's not grumpy like you," he said.

"She doesn't have you making her jacket wetter than an otter's pocket."

Eventually, she reached the bridge to find Rod's car parked at the brow, empty and doors open.

"Okay," she said, nonplussed. "Where is everyone?"

"They've abandoned you, morsel!" sneered Steve. "None of them like you!"

"That's very hurtful," said Senior.

Steve the Destroyer cackled happily.

Nina was thirty seconds into the woods before it struck her that the undergrowth of lush ferns and sprawling brambles were particularly familiar. Some distance ahead between the trees, she could make out a regular silhouette pattern that might have been a security fence.

"The school's over there," she said.

"What school?"

"The Mammonite one."

Morag cast about. "Where's Jeffney Ray?"

"He's a slippery *vangru* all right," said Nina.

She led the way towards the path and then to the gap in the fence she had climbed through on Monday.

"What trees are these?" she said.

"Birch trees," said Morag. "Why?"

"How do you old people know useless *muda* like that?"

"They're trees. They're everywhere. They're kind of important."

Nina snorted.

The Pen Museum was not overly busy and Vivian was, in that assessment, being very charitable. The arrival of Kathy Kaur, Cameron Barnes and herself had increased the occupancy of the tiny museum by three hundred percent. And the other person present was the current curator.

"Thursday afternoons are not our busiest time," said the short moustachioed curator, "but that gives you all the more opportunity to explore the world of pens and pen production."

"Yippee," said Kathy.

The museum consisted of two rooms. The first reminded Vivian of the classrooms where boys were taught woodworking before the war. It was dominated by benches and vices and other pieces of mounted and well-greased equipment apparently essential for the production of pens. They hurried through to the second, much larger, room. Its windows were wide (to admit as much natural light as possible), high (to prevent anyone inside being distracted by the world beyond) and sealed shut. The place smelled of grease and wood. Dust angels hung motionless in the air. Apart from a TV screen playing a rolling presentation on pen manufacture, the room might not have changed for fifty or even a hundred and fifty years.

And then there were the pens.

"That's a lot of pens," said Kathy.

Vivian tutted. She despised statements of the obvious. But there were a lot of pens.

"A lot of nibs," said Cameron. "Don't you have any of the pen – 'bodies', is it?"

"That's a common misconception," said the curator in tones that suggested he was tired of people's ignorance but delighted to correct it. "These are the pens. The word 'pen' refers to the metal piece used to write."

"Oh."

The walls were covered in pens. Thousands of pens were mounted on green felt, like butterflies. Thousands more crowded the shelves of glass display cases. Huge boards, pocket-sized sample boxes and folding cases for travelling salesmen held thousands more. There was an elaborate display of silver pens, and a cabinet of outsized pens for calligraphy or demonstration purposes. And not a drop of ink in sight.

"So many," said Kathy.

"In the 1840s, Birmingham provided three quarters of the world's pens," said the curator. "This is but a small sample, I can assure you, and not all of it yet catalogued."

"And they're all fountain pens," said Cameron. "You don't have any biros or –"

The curator's considerable moustache fluttered as he blew out with annoyance. "The ballpoint is not a pen."

"It's an abomination?" suggested Cameron.

"It killed off the local pen industry nearly a hundred years ago, supplanting the divinely elegant dip pens and fountain pens."

"Right," said Cameron. "Pens good, biros bad. Got it."

There was the ring of the front door of the museum opening.

"Oh, it's bedlam here," said the curator and with a very old-fashioned bob of his head, departed to see who it was.

"Which one's the one we want?" said Kathy, scanning the exhibits.

"That's the challenge," said Vivian.

Cameron spread out his hands, palms up and intoned, *"As vanir'gi finarl beraayh-kreeh!"*

Nothing happened. Kathy gave him a look.

"Did you just try to cast *'accio* pen'?" said Kathy.

"Worth a shot," said Cameron.

Vivian watched the two explore the room. Kathy appeared to be inspecting each pen nib in turn, one by one, second by second.

"Choose wisely," she muttered. "For while the true pen brings everlasting life…"

Ray hunkered down at the base of the largest tree he could find to hide behind. He had two hundred in wet notes on him. It wasn't enough. When he took his phone out of his pocket to check the time, water streamed out of the corner of the case. But it was too late. He knew it was too late.

He sniffed. He was cold and he was miserable. Those two slag bitches were somewhere nearby. He didn't know who they were but they clearly had it in for him.

Bet they were bloody lesbians, he thought sourly.

His plans now? He could try to grab some cash somehow – rob a corner shop or something – and then throw himself on the mercy of the Black Barge. He could just stay away from canals from now on and Gas Street Basin in particular. They could hardly get him if he wasn't around. Maybe he should just leave town, he thought, leave the country. He could go to Amsterdam. He'd heard the place was full of hot chicks just gagging for it. A stud like him could clean up in a town like that. Did they have canals in Amsterdam? He wasn't sure.

Whatever. He needed to be away from here. Let these people clean their own shit up.

There was a rustle of undergrowth and the snap of dry wood. Ray looked round. A *lu'crik oyh* stood next to him, its huge head an arm's length from his own. Its slick mouth was a quivering tube of sausagey pinks and greys. Down that throat he could see gill slits, daylight in the windows of its cold maw. The dripping mandibles twitched, ready to pull Ray in, work him through. His eyes flicked up. Ray saw no emotion in those silver eyes, no intelligence, no life to speak of.

Ray couldn't run. He couldn't speak. He had nothing. He was too scared to even pee himself.

The mandibles widened, curved fangs flexing to grip the sides of his head. The *lu'crik oyh* leaned in slowly, delicately.

A distant squeal went up. The *lu'crik oyh* pulled away at once, raised itself up on its front legs and looked away. There was another squeal and another. The sound of children playing, high-pitched and discordant. Did the *lu'crik oyh* think it was another female calling?

It was hooked. Ignoring Ray completely, the *lu'crik oyh* bounded over him and away.

Ray burst into tears.

Nina saw the big shape flash by through nearby trees.
"There!"
"Is it him?" said Morag.
"I really don't think so…"

The shape flung itself over the fence and across the school playing fields. Nina dashed through the gap in the fence. The *lu'crik oyh* – its hybrid movement looked ridiculous in such an open space – wriggle-crawled towards the Mammonite students on the rear playground of Thatcher Academy.

There were children. Mammonite children, evil monster children from the suburbs of hell, but they were children nonetheless and that meant something.

Nina sprinted after the *lu'crik oyh*, screaming for anyone to listen.

The Mammonites were evil monsters from the suburbs of hell but most of them weren't idiots. As soon as they saw the *lu'crik oyh* coming, they screamed and scattered. Unfortunately, the increase in noise drove the creature to run faster. The children fleeing in all directions drove it wild with indecision and it ran here and there, back and forth, not chasing any one individual and therefore catching none. It leapt over a stack of industrial rubbish bins, sending a handful of kids running from their hiding position, and then climbed up the side of a teaching building to explore an open window.

Nina stumbled to a stop in the playground. The schoolchildren had fled and the creature was about to find its own way inside. A school army cadet came around the corner, took up position with his rifle and fired at the *lu'crik oyh*, striking it several times before it slithered through the window and out of sight.

"Bloody hell, kid," said Nina. "Nice going."

The boy sneered like she had just vomited on his shoes. "Don't talk to me, human *shaska*."

He ran off into the building in pursuit.

Morag finally caught up with Nina.

"What the hell?" she panted, pointed at the departing boy.

"Army cadets. They have a fully stocked armoury in the sports hall." She gave it half a second's thought. "They have a fully stocked armoury in the sports hall."

Vivian had decided to let the candidates suffer for five minutes before she put them out of their misery. Kathy was still working her way through the first pen display case; Vivian had no idea what she expected to see. Cameron stood in the centre of the room, eyes closed and arms spread as though waiting for the answers to descend on him from above. None of it was particularly inspiring.

But, partway through the fourth minute, Cameron opened his eyes and said, "You know what we need."

"Yes, Mr Barnes?" said Vivian.

"A Venislarn resonator. An *apudam-rha* piece."

"Detection equipment?" said Kathy.

Vivian opened her purse and removed an arrow-shaped charm on a chain.

"Always useful," she said, dangled it by the chain and watched it spin. As though misbalanced, the downward pointing tip of the arrow rose as it drifted round, pulling minutely in one direction. Vivian followed it across the room, toward the corner by Kathy.

"I was near," said Kathy.

Vivian slowed, let the arrow pull at her, raised it up along the rows and then across. And then back. And then stopped.

Cameron and Kathy crowded in to look. The pen nib in the case was black, not a spooky and ominous black but the black of silver that had tarnish for centuries until only the tarnish remained. It was fat and sharply pointed. It had no other noteworthy features, no aura of importance.

"Is that it?" said Kathy.

"Let's see," said Cameron.

The display case had a latch and a lock but second's brutish waggling with a thin key in the gap forced the latch up.

Nina ran through the teaching block. She'd not yet found the *lu'crik oyh* or the sports hall. It was a confusing place, possibly because of the dimension-bending qualities of Venislarn design or possibly because it was a school. At every classroom door she yelled at the students to shut it and keep hidden. She could hear Morag doing the same on some other level.

Mrs Cook-Mammonson appeared at the top of the stairs ahead and held out a hand.

"There will be no running in the corridors, Miss Seth," the headteacher said curtly.

"You *adn-bhul* kidding me?"

"Or swearing."

The Mammonite woman didn't look like a woman whose school had just been invaded by killer pondlife.

"There's a *lu'crik oyh* loose in y–"

"I'm perfectly aware," said Cook-Mammonson. "I should be insulted by the insinuation that I wouldn't be but the opinion of a woman of your low education is hardly –"

"It's dangerous!"

"It's someone's pet," said the headteacher.

"An *adn-bhul* dangerous pet."

"I shall not warn you about your swearing again. You do not have authorisation to be here. This is a gross breach of protocol. You are interfering with the scheduled lessons of the school."

"It will eat the students!"

Cook-Mammonson gave her a tiredly superior look. "And if it does?"

Nina was speechless.

"What is school?" said the headteacher smoothly, "It is a testing ground. It exists to winnow the chaff from the grain, to separate the weak from the strong. And if a student is eaten, then what?"

"You're *adn-bhul* mad."

"Third time, Miss Seth." Something bony moved under the skin beneath the Mammonite's cheek. "You will leave now and allow us to return to our timetabled lessons."

Nina shook her head, furious, and made to go past the headteacher. The Mammonite grabbed her elbow to stop her and Nina decided the time to be a professional was over. She punched the headteacher in the face, hard. Nina had boys for cousins and she had learned how to punch. The Mammonite didn't go down immediately so Nina punched her again.

Cook-Mammonson fell to her knees. Behind the mask of her skin, something truly hideous occurred and any illusions that this thing was human were gone. Nina punched her again.

"You dare touch us!" spat the Mammonite, struggling with a tongue and jaw that were no longer shaped for human speech. "You are too stupid to know fear?"

The creature still had hold of Nina so she punched it a fourth time. The thing let go and slumped the floor.

"This girl isn't afraid of nothing," said Nina.

Cook-Mammonson made a noise that might have been a laugh.

"That was a double negative, idiot!"

"I was using it for deliberate emphasis, bitch," said Nina and stalked off.

"Just you wait," hollered Cook-Mammonson through bloodied lips. "When our mother rises in all her glory and takes this city again, you will plead for death."

"Yeah?" Nina shouted back. "Well, I'm calling Ofsted. So, who's in trouble now, eh?"

She hurried down the stairs.

"Through here," Morag called to her, standing at a pair of double doors.

Nina followed her through a canteen area.

"The thing's behind those screen doors," said Morag. "The sports hall..." She pointed to another set of double doors.

The huge high space of the sports hall, benches along the sides, tape marking out the courts and areas for various games on the floor, brought memories flooding back to Nina, few of them particularly happy ones. Getting thrashed at volleyball by taller girls, getting told off for having too much fun while playing badminton with Anita and Saba... Sports halls had been, in her experience, places of belittlement, oppression and soul-crushing boredom. That said, the sports halls Nina recalled did not have rows of rifles in racks, stacks of munitions to one side and concrete-backed targets at one end. PE at school might have been more fun if they had.

Morag ran her hand along the rifle rack. "These aren't even locked away."

"Mammonites," said Nina. "If one of them wants to go postal, that's their lookout." She considered the empty slots on the rack. "It looks like some already have."

In the large hall, the sound of a rifle bolt echoed loudly. A school boy stood, taking aim at them over the top of one of the concrete targets. Another came up at the target beside him.

"We're here to help," said Morag.

"Leave now or we shoot," said the first boy.

"We're not leaving," said Nina, walking slowly towards them.

The boy aimed deliberately low and shot a groove in the floor just off to Nina's right.

"The *lu'crik oyh* is in the room next door. Together we can take it down."

"It's her," said another voice and a girl stepped out. Nina recognised the blonde pigtails, the constantly spiteful expression and the plush toy clutched in her arms.

"It's Yang, isn't it?" said Nina.

"We should have killed you," said Yang.

313

"Maybe," said Nina. "That can wait. We do need your help."

"We don't help," the girl spat. "And only the weak ask for it."

"Right," said Nina, "because everyone gets one chance, yeah?"

"And this is it," said Yang.

Nina walked up to her and held up her fist. Her knuckles had split from the pounding she'd given the headteacher and some of the Mammonite's blood smeared the back of her fingers.

"Then I'm giving you a chance," said Nina.

Yang began to sneer at the threat and then sniffed. Her gaze narrowed. "Cook-Mammonson?"

"You better believe it," said Nina.

"Or we could pay you to help us," offered Morag and held out a thick wodge of filthy notes.

"It's dirty," said Yang.

"It's still money," said Morag. "I mean, we did get it out of a drug dealer's wallet so it is sort of dirty but…"

"Drug dealer?" said one of the boys. "That's pretty hardcore."

Yang looked at the money. She was at least thinking about it.

Using the bicycle as a lure had worked. It had *really* worked. Two or three circuits of Dickens Heath village (it was hard to tell what was new and what wasn't) and Rod had eight of the beasts following him, including a massive one-eyed freak apparently trailing a net and ton of gardening equipment behind it.

The problem now, Rod realised, was what the hell to do next. He was riding the metaphorical tiger. He had what he wanted but the moment he stopped he was dead. Ahead was the bridge on which he'd initially abandoned his car. One of the Morags was there. She had a phone to her ear and was shouting at him. He accelerated towards her. She pointed vigorously.

"The school! To the school!"

That didn't make a whole lot of sense, taking a herd of predators into a kiddies' school, not unless they wanted to solve the spider-fish problem at the same time as classroom overcrowding.

"Go!" shouted Morag and slid into the car as the first *lu'crik oyh* came barrelling by.

Morag Junior pocketed her phone.

"Okay," she declared to the sports hall. "We have a plan. And I use that term in the loosest possible sense."

She threw open the external double doors of the sports hall and then hurried back to the shelter of the concrete targets they had piled up as a barricade.

Cameron Barnes had an impressive repertoire of Venislarn incantations. Vivian had mixed feelings in that regard. Of the two candidates, he was clearly the greater Venislarn scholar but, seeing him touch the pen to the scar on his neck and to his tongue and then balance it on his fingertip – speaking in the tongues of *aklo* all the while – made her uneasy. He might not be the first human to have "gone Venislarn" but she was disinclined to be the first to appoint such a person to a role within the Birmingham consular mission.

Nonetheless, his knowledge was proving useful. He stood on the pavement outside the Pen Museum and weighed the black nib on his fingertip.

"That way," he said, nodding down the hill towards the city centre.

"Very good, Mr Barnes," said Vivian. "Dr Kaur, you're driving."

Morag Senior fought the car through a fishtail turn onto the school driveway, snapped the flimsy car park barrier off against the windscreen and accelerated on towards the sports hall. A distance away to her left, Rod had cycled in through the student pedestrian entrance – his cheeks puffing and his rhythm faltering but still a bike-length ahead of the snarling, love-crazed *lu'crik oyh*.

"He's gonna need a bigger bike," commented Steve the Destroyer.

"He's fine," said Senior.

She steered tightly through a car park crowded with Audis and Jags – either human teachers vastly underexaggerated their salaries or Mammonites commanded higher fees – and then slammed her foot on the brake when she saw the sports hall entrance. Steve slapped against the windscreen and fell onto the dashboard. She grabbed him, leapt out and ran into the sports hall.

"They're coming!" she yelled before she even saw the figures crouched behind the targets. She ran towards them. "Do not shoot at Rod!"

She gave a start as a *lu'crik oyh* crawled in from a side room. Rifles cracked and she flung her hands up to shield her face and veered away.

"And don't shoot me!"

She had barely made it to the barricade when Rod rode in, cycling hard across the floor. Senior scuttled behind the targets and peered round. Just outside the double doors, two *lu'crik oyh* fought over which would be first with the squealing female that was Rod on his bike. He was going to be such a sexual disappointment, she thought.

Ten metres from the barricade, he awkwardly threw himself from the bike, rolled and ran low for cover. The *lu'crik oyh* charged forward into a volley of shots from the Mammonite kids. Senior grabbed a rifle, raised it over the top of a target and tried to remember what little she knew about the workings of a gun.

"Shoot them! Shoot them now!" cried Steve.

Morag Junior looked across from the other end of the line. "Steve? How the hell...?"

Rod had picked up a rifle and started shooting before Senior even had remembered how on earth she was supposed to manually chamber the first round.

Out in the centre of the sports hall, some very optimistic *lu'crik oyh* shoved and barged one another away from the prized bicycle while the school defence forces shot divots of armoured flesh out of their hides. Others spun in confusion and rage at the attack. It was only a matter of time before they realised where the pain was coming from.

Senior spotted the one-eyed net-covered monstrosity among the pile of rolling creatures.

"The Broil King Super Gem!" she shouted. "Shoot the Broil King Super Gem!"

Rod gave her a quizzical look.

"The barbecue!" she shouted over the gunshots.

Rod nodded and resumed firing.

"Twenty quid to the first one to shoot the barbecue!" yelled Nina.

Two or three shots sparked off the black metal lid of a wheeled barbecue that hung, snagged, in the *lu'crik oyh*'s net. A second later a bullet – it would be impossible to tell whose – punctured the gas cylinder underneath.

"Kids! Down!" barked Rod but no one had time.

The flash was momentarily blinding. The bang left Senior's ears ringing for much longer. Something heavy smashed into the basketball board above their heads and dropped wetly to the ground before the targets. By the time Senior had come to herself once more the exploding gas had burned itself out.

Everything was suddenly still.

Rod stepped round the barricade and approached the *lu'crik oyh*. Chunks of *lu'crik oyh* decorated most of the floor, much of the walls and, here and there, bits of the ceiling. Steve the Destroyer leapt from Senior's shoulder and ran out into the hall, giving a good post-mortem slapping to any lumps of *lu'crik oyh* he passed. The air stank of smoke and something that was almost like cooked fish but not quite.

Rod walked among the *lu'crik oyh*, putting three bullets in each one that remained remotely whole. The Mammonite children cautiously followed him, weapons ready.

"Fleshling!" shouted Steve. "Take a picture of me, victorious!"

The doll man stood beside the severed upper body and head of the one-eyed *lu'crik oyh*. Morag Junior went forward, taking her phone out.

A soft toy on the floor, incongruous in this place, caught Senior's eye. She picked it up and turned it over in her hands. She had held one just like it in a marketing meeting at the office some weeks before. She remembered the googly eyes and the entirely inappropriate tartan spines. It was meant to be *Yoth Mammon*. If only the gods really were this cuddly...

"This is one of the My Little Venislarn dolls," she said.

"It belongs to Yang there," said Nina, beside her.

"I didn't think these toys ever went into production. Just one of Chad and Leandra's stupid ideas that went nowhere."

Nina shrugged and sniffed deeply.

"Is it wrong to say that smell makes me hungry for fish and chips?"

Senior laughed weakly.

"I think if you want fish and chips you deserve them."

There was the sound of approaching sirens.

"I'll get one of Ricky's boys to pick some up for me."

Rod shouldered his rifle, spoke to the Mammonite children – Senior couldn't hear what he said but the body language was of a captain congratulating his troops – and walked stiffly back to the barricades.

"I've never cycled so hard," he said with a faint groan. "My thighs are burning."

"You did good, old man," said Nina.

"Gonna need some Deep Heat rubbed on them and no mistake. Any volunteers?"

"I said you did good," said Nina. "I didn't say you cured cancer. Do your own rubbing."

Morag Junior was taking several snaps of tiny Steve the Destroyer leaning up against the head of his trophy. The *pabash kaj* doll gave the lolling jaw of the dead beast a merry kick.

"Smile, you son of a bitch!"

Senior considered the doll in her hands.

Ray trudged along the canal path. He was wet and now he was cold too. The only direction he had chosen was away. He wasn't going back into Birmingham. He wasn't going back to his selfish mum – no Terry's All Gold or miniature Baileys for her! He'd had enough. His geography beyond the city wasn't great but he'd walk until he got to a main road, catch a lift to somewhere he could beg or steal some clothes and then he'd start again. No more Jeffney Ray. This lone wolf would take on a new name, find fresh flocks to prey on.

Distracted by his own misery, he only slowly became aware of the faint splashing and the slow bow wave drawing close behind him. He turned and saw, with the calm horror of a nightmare, the Black Barge. It followed him at little more than a walking pace. There was no one at the tiller, no faces visible at the dark membranous windows.

Ray stopped. His heart pounded in his cold chest.

"I was going to find you!" he called out to the boat. "I was going to bring you the money."

The Black Barge slowed.

"I just ran into some difficulties, that's all," he said.

The Black Barge drifted.

"It was just three hundred quid, right?" he said. "I can get that tomorrow. Double even."

No movement on deck. It was a ghost of a barge, a desiccated shell, a discarded insect casing.

"Ten years we said," said Ray. "That thing about a hundred was just a joke. I will get you the money. Whatever you want."

Still no life on board. Ray's fear gave way to irritation, anger and bravado. It wasn't like an empty canal barge was even remotely threatening. Yeah, it looked like something force-grown from bone or constructed by nest-building insects but it was still a bloody canal barge. It was about as spooky as a pedalo.

"You know what, fuck you!" he shouted. "That money? You can whistle for it. What are you going to do?" He took a step back from the path, onto the grassy verge. "Go back to your bosses and tell them you failed!"

The Black Barge jigged closer to the shore, bobbing in a sideways motion that seemed quite wrong for a barge.

"I'm not scared of you!" he shouted.

The Black Barge suddenly lifted upwards from the canal. Water streamed down a hull that was not a hull. The bony lines of the window frames of the barge ran down over the shell – or was it

319

the head crest? – of the giant creature beneath. Barnacles clustered around her black shark eyes. Pond weed, frayed strands of rope and the dredged detritus of a hundred canals dangled like a beard beneath her whale jaw. Rising from a depth far greater than the canal, the goddess stretched her bleached white limbs, her uneven water-smoothed fingers. The barge, her skull crest, was now gone from sight above Ray.

"*Yoth-Qahake-Pysh*," Ray whispered, hoarsely.

She reached out dreamily for Ray. Ray's mind, drowning, reached for whatever it could.

"*Skeidl hraim yeg courxean. Oyo-map-ehu merishimsha meren'froi,*" he breathed. Do not kill me, honoured friend. I was only admiring your beauty. "*Skeidl hraim yeg courxean. Oyo-map-ehu merishimsha meren'froi.*"

Her fingers, each as fat as a ship's mast, curled around him. She was gentle. She didn't want to damage him. As she lifted him, Ray instinctively grabbed her topmost finger for support. He had moved beyond fear into a blank insanity. His lips moved but his mind no longer knew what the words meant. He had never really got to grips with spoken Venislarn but she took what little he had from him. He had never known as much magic as he would have liked and she took that from him too. *Yoth-Qahake-Pysh*, Goddess of the Deep, sank beneath the surface and Ray went with her.

Vivian had Kathy drive round the Mammon-Mammonson Investment building twice, which was hard because the roadwork diversions associated with the redevelopment of Chamberlain Square meant that circling the building involved circling the Town Hall, the Council House and the crane-filled demolition site of the old Central Library. After they'd parked up, Cameron led them, black pen nib in hand, back along the road and round the building on foot to confirm.

"It's in there," said Cameron, having to raise his voice over the noise of traffic from the dual carriageway next to them as they looked up at the former stock exchange building. "All the missing pages as far as this *samoha* dowsing method can detect."

Vivian looked at her two candidates. "Mammonites have the missing pages from the Big Bloody Book. Speculate."

"It's very valuable," said Kathy. "They could have stolen it simply for its value."

"No," said Cameron. "The Mammonites are not law-breakers. They operate entirely within the laws and treaties that govern the local Venislarn."

"Then they bought it from the thieves."

"The recovery of lost *Kal Frexo* runes might suggest the book has been used in that research."

Kathy's eyebrows shot up in alarm. The woman really ought to do something to get them under control, thought Vivian.

"A thought, Dr Kaur?" said Vivian.

"*Yoth Mammon* is currently residing in *Kal Frexo* leng-space."

And there it was, thought Vivian. The candidates were now on the same page as her. It had taken them long enough.

"The lost runes of *Kal Frexo* are summoning runes," said Cameron.

"But we've only seen seventeen out of the twenty," said Kathy.

"Doesn't mean the Mammonites haven't seen the others," Cameron replied. "And those OOPArts in the Vault that might have been brought into existence by someone uncovering truths in the missing pages…"

"What of them?" said Vivian.

"A vase of creation. The cube of *Prein*. The keys of *Trek-lehn*. They all have association with summonings, creations, openings. It may be no coincidence."

"They are going to bring Yoth Mammon back," said Kathy.

"*Yoth Mammon* the corruptor, the defiler of souls, the dredger in the lake of desires," said Cameron.

"You're smiling," said Kathy.

"What? No."

She was right. Vivian could see the man's eyes positively glittering.

"It's just… exhilarating," said Cameron. "A goddess no one alive today has ever glimpsed."

"A shapeless space-worm that's all teeth and spikes. As big as… as big as…. well, she's just bloody huge."

"Exactly," said Cameron, failing to keep the excitement from his face. "I mean it's terrible, really terrible and we should do everything we can to stop it. But – *jebor vas ur!* – it's still very thrilling."

Vivian gestured to the building behind them. "So, what do we do now?"

"We go in," said Cameron. "We have probable cause. We talk to whoever's in charge and we ask them their intentions."

Kathy had a deeply perturbed look on her face. "Can't we just call for backup? I don't think this is our job."

Vivian brought up the contacts on her phone and selected Morag Murray.

"Indeed, Dr Kaur. It's not your job, is it?"

The clean-up job on the blasted body parts of nearly a dozen *lu'crik oyh* was passed down the line from the response team to the police, back to the response team and then down to the school caretakers. The band of indentured human workers took a look at the mass of spider-fish bits in the sports hall and set about digging a pit on the back field.

Morag Senior, Morag Junior, Nina and Rod stood at the police cordon at the end of the school drive where Rod had now relocated his car. The show was over here. There would have to be a thorough inspection of Mammonite back gardens for any overlooked beasts but, apart from that, matters were back in Mammonite hands. The rogue occultist Jeffney Ray had given them the slip in the chaos and their search for him would have to begin afresh.

As Morag Senior's phone started to ring, Rod gestured questioningly at the soft toy she carried in her hand.

"It's odd, isn't it?" she said, passing it over. "This is one of ours."

"Ours?" said Rod.

Senior answered the call. "Hello?"

"Ms Murray," said Vivian, "I would like an update on your meeting with *Yo-Morgantus*."

"Um, yes."

"You were going to brief the Venislarn court on our concerns with Mammon-Mammonson Investments and their tiresome complaints against us."

"That's exactly right. That was the plan."

"I think it's important to go back and inform him that we have compelling evidence they have, in their possession, a stolen section of the Wittgenstein Volume."

"What?"

There was a sigh. "Please don't feign deafness as a stand-in for surprise, Ms Murray. You heard me well enough. I am going to speak to Rod Campbell next and advise him to come down to the Mammon-Mammonson building to join me while I speak to the managing director."

"I'm sure I can tell Rod that for you," said Senior. Rod frowned at her. "I'm sure he'd be delighted to come down to Mammon-Mammonson and help you question the boss."

Rod looked to the heavens in tedium and nodded.

"Oh, I don't need his help," said Vivian. "The man's conversational skills are functional at best. I just need an armed escort in case – in case – the Mammonites decide to attempt anything unwise."

"I'll make sure he comes armed."

"With what?" mouthed Rod, pulling the trio of claims forms from his pocket.

"Speak later," said Senior and ended the call. "Looks like my meeting with *Yo-Morgantus* is a bit overdue."

Nina put her fingers between her lips and produced a wonderfully unladylike whistle. Chief Inspector Ricky Lee, talking to a uniformed colleague, looked round and waved.

"Ricky and I will give you a lift to the Cube," Nina said to Senior.

"Thanks."

"On the understanding that we're stopping for fish and chips on the way."

Morag Junior paused in the seemingly impossible task of trying to clean the *lu'crik oyh* slime from Steve the Destroyer. "Where the hell are you going to find a chippy open in the middle of Thursday afternoon?"

"Ask and you shall find answers," said Nina, getting out her phone.

On the corner of Margaret Street and Great Charles Street, Vivian stood with the two remaining candidates for the tech support role. The day had not gone as she had anticipated but it had given her a superb idea for future recruitment. She made several short notes in her pad and was already mentally drafting a proposal document to present to Personnel.

"When will the successful applicant be informed?" asked Kathy Kaur.

"I should think it will be today," said Vivian.

"And the final decision will be made by…?"

"The most qualified person to do so."

"Er, ladies," said Cameron and nodded behind them.

Three Mammonite suits approached. The middle one smiled. His teeth were brighter than his shirt.

"Mrs Vivian Grey," he said. "A pleasure to find you here. A happy accident, you being in the vicinity?"

"Yes, Mr Lodge-Mammonson." She nodded politely. "Let's say that."

"And I don't believe we've met your colleagues before," said the Mammonite.

"Only one colleague."

"Oh. Which…" He looked from one to the other.

"That remains to be seen," said Vivian.

"Mr Mammon-Mammonson has asked me to escort you in for your meeting."

"We had no meeting scheduled."

"Really?" said Lodge-Mammonson. The surprise on his face was entirely false. "But you had intended to speak to him today, surely."

The Mammonites that flanked Lodge-Mammonson were silent and impassive. One looked like his skin was several sizes too large. The other had tombstone looks and might have been more at home on a slab somewhere.

"Yes," said Vivian. It did no good to lie to Mammonites. "But I am waiting for my other colleagues to arrive first."

"And yet, it shames one to say, Mr Mammon-Mammonson was quite insistent the meeting be brought forward."

"I am sure we will be with him soon enough."

"As I say," said Lodge-Mammonson with what appeared to be genuine regret, "he was quite insistent."

The two other Mammonites had knives in their hands. There was no menace in their body language; they held their blades as carpenters would hold their saws, painters their brushes.

"Are you threatening us in public?" said Vivian, voice raised in pique.

Lodge-Mammonson leaned a little closer.

"We can do it in private if you wish, Mrs Grey. Business is all about putting the customer at ease."

Morag Senior unbuckled her seatbelt as Ricky Lee pulled the police car in on Wharfside Street in the shadow of the Cube.

"Are you coming in, Nina?" she said.

"Nah," said Nina from the front passenger seat.

"Why? Scared?"

"I don't want any of them stealing my chips. Want one?" Nina offered the mass of chip papers through the gap to Senior.

In the ten minutes since she'd bought them, Nina had eaten most of the chips and all the batter off the fish, leaving a scraggly piece of cod.

Senior shook her head.

"You know, you shouldn't encourage her," Senior said to Ricky.

The chief inspector gave her a hopelessly happy look. "Does she need encouragement?"

"I will be as quick as I can," said Senior and got out.

The cube was twenty-five storeys of apartments, businesses and retail spaces and most of it was occupied by humans who had no idea that they were living in the basement of the gods. The concierge, a human servant of the Venislarn whose body had taken a relaxed attitude to which bits should be sporting hair and which should not, directed Senior with a hairy finger to the lift.

Yo-Morgantus would be expecting her and, she was sure, one day he would kill her. It was odd, she thought as she went up, to be ascending into hell, not descending.

The lift door opened. There was no one there to greet her. The only sound was the constant moan of a heating vent.

Senior checked herself. There was a drying grey stain where the slime-soaked *pabash kaj* doll had struck her jacket. Senior debated for a second what to do and then simply took the jacket off and bundled it up beside a waste bin. There was no putting things off.

She pushed open the only set of doors leading off from the lobby and entered the court of the Venislarn.

There were gods. Small g. The Venislarn. Vastly intelligent or dribblingly insane; it was hard to tell. Hideous and angelic. Strange and formless. As familiar as childhood terrors. Hungry. It was impossible to say where or when they had come from but the place they had come to was here.

The hall was higher than it architecturally had any right to be. It was dressed in black and steel and mirrors and monsters. *Draybbea* hung from rafters and observed Senior coolly. *Presz'lings* clustered at their dark tables and barely looked up to acknowledge her. A stone *Skrendul* loomed large and still in the corner, waiting out the days, months or years until the Venislarn Soulgate closed around the earth and it could romp through the playground of the eternal hell that would follow. Off to her right, a trio of August Handmaidens of *Prein*, raised themselves up on their jointed legs, massive shells rotating across their bodies to present the frozen faces of screaming babies to Senior. There were allegedly twelve Handmaidens of *Prein*. Were. That number was down to ten now and Senior admitted she was at least partly responsible. She wasn't sure why they hadn't already exacted their bloody revenge.

There were courts like this across the world. Senior imagined that they all looked pretty much like this one except in perhaps two small regards. Firstly, long vine-like fronds hung down from the hot vents in the high ceiling: those were *Yo-Morgantus*'s tendrils, his presence in the room. The other key difference was the sheer number of naked ginger men and women in the room.

Yo-Morgantus liked redheads. And he liked them naked because being a redhead was not degrading enough. They mingled with the gods and goddesses and the things that aspired to godhood, playing in secluded mud pools, chatting amiably like friends at dinner; but they were definitely *Yo-Morgantus*'s playthings. Occasionally, one of the tendrils would descend a few feet to touch a ginger head and the human would immediately move off on a new course of action.

A middle-aged man with heavy moobs and an apron of stomach fat that nearly covered his genitals waddled up to Senior.

"Our lord is waiting," he said. "This way."

He turned, absently scratching his bum, and led her through a door, along a corridor and through to another hall, more realistic in dimensions and (although as dark as the first hall) not decorated by someone who thought shiny was the hallmark of superior design. This hall was empty, but for the usual tendrils hanging from the ceiling and a naked young woman at its centre. Senior recognised her as the woman who had been watching the Black Barge in Gas Street Basin.

Senior looked up at the ceiling, toward the mass of amorphous flesh that resided in the spaces beyond. "Greetings, my Lord *Morgantus*," she called.

She approached the woman but kept a respectful distance. Senior liked to keep her distance from casually naked people; it was a little rule of hers.

"Good afternoon. We've not been formally introduced."

327

"I am Brigit," said the young woman coldly. Senior reckoned that someone with a body like that could afford a few manners, but such was life.

So, this was Brigit, *Yo-Morgantus*'s favourite mouthpiece. The one time Morag had previously been brought to court, *Morgantus* had spoken through a man, Drew, a man Morag had unwisely taken to her bed and then seen murdered by the August Handmaiden of *Prein* she had obviously slighted.

"You have come to explain yourself," said Brigit.

"Does Lord *Morgantus* need me to explain myself?"

"We have had... troubling reports about the consular mission. Getting ideas above our station, are we?"

A streamer-tendril lolled across the woman's shoulder. *Yo-Morgantus* could make her thoughts his, put an idea into anyone he touched. Where this emissary ended and the most powerful god in the city began was a debatable point. All Senior could be certain of was that one of them was talking like a complete douche.

"I don't know what you've heard but we have – as always – acted in accordance with your wishes."

"Oh," said Brigit haughtily, "you presume to know our wishes."

Senior stepped forward, naked lady or no naked lady.

"Do you want to tell me what we've supposedly done? I can then put you straight on what you –"

"What," said Brigit loudly, cutting across Senior and pointing at Senior's throat, "is that?"

Senior put her hand to the pendant necklace, the swirl of translucent impossibleness that Cameron had given to her – had given to Junior first before it was passed onto her.

"It's just a necklace. It's glass. *Cquluman'i* I think."

"That's a claim marker, from a *shodu-bon*."

"Is it?" said Senior. "Lovely." *Shodu-bon*. The name was vaguely familiar. One of the deep sea Venislarn? A vassal species?

"You cannot give yourself to them."

"It was just a gift."

"No."

Senior saw the tendril descend and tried to step out of its reach but wasn't fast enough. It brushed her scalp –

Green. The ocean was green but the surface was thousands of feet overhead and there was no light. The ocean was the green of alien night. The life-extinguishing pressure of these depths weighed down on all things. Motes of dirt, crumbs of stone and slivers of rotten flesh all hung in the water, unable to rise, unable to sink. This was a place of the unliving. Below, dark arches, fallen columns and abandoned temples appeared as only silhouettes: the city of Cary'yeh, a necropolis of sunken gods.

Cameron Barnes hung in the water, in the bulky shell of his Newtsuit atmospheric diving suit.

– Morag Senior had not known what a Newtsuit was but the information arrived in her consciousness, like a lost memory regained –

An umbilical line and a faint stream of super-compressed bubbles ran up toward the distant surface. There was an electronic commlink in the helmet but Cameron had turned it off. He enjoyed the silence. The weightlessness, the silence and the enshrouding dark; it was a fragment of oblivion.

Chagulameya *swam up from the black silent city, fading into existence. Cameron watched the* yon-bun *dweller approach, her papillae undulating, her tube feet paddling. She made straight for him at speed, her feeding tentacles already distending hungrily from her calcarate mouth.*

Four times more massive than the human diver, Chagulameya *wrapped herself around Cameron and prised the plates of his Newtsuit apart, shelling him like a nut. The pressure of the deep ocean should have squished him like a tomato under a tyre but she kept him whole, wrapped in her lucid frills. And now she could hold back no longer. He reached out his arms toward her cylindrical body.* Chagulameya *disgorged her upper intestine over his chest and head to consume him.*

No, not consume him. She placed her mucosal tentacles upon his thighs and worked the claim marker into his chest while he worked his tongue against her milky tentacles.

Morag Senior fought her way back to her own consciousness and her own body and batted *Yo-Morgantus*'s tendril away. She shuddered and ripped the necklace from around her neck.

She spat. She physically spat.

"He was... was canoodling with that thing."

"Canoodling," said Brigit, tasting the word. "Yes."

Cameron Barnes. The one that got away. Yep, she was definitely over him now. She threw the pendant aside where it bounced across the floor.

"Now," said Brigit, "to the matter in hand: your interfering with the legal business of our subjects in this city..."

Rod parked up on Margaret Street, got out of the car and looked around.

"They're not here," he said.

"Liars and swindlers!" yelled Steve the Destroyer in Morag's hand, causing a passing office suit to look round in alarm.

"She's a ventriloquist," said Rod.

The office suit gave Morag's bruised face a sceptical look.

"Not a very popular one," said Morag.

"Everyone's a critic," said Rod.

The suit, vaguely mollified, walked away munching on his lunchtime baguette.

"You need to keep quiet, puppet," Morag told Steve, "or you will get my hand up your rear end."

"Do that and you will enter a realm of horrors!" he squeaked warningly.

"I'll be sure to wash my hand afterwards."

"Maybe Vivian got tired of waiting," said Rod and took out his phone to call her, only to find a text from Kathy waiting.

"Captured by manicure at Malkin monsoon," he read.

"What?" said Morag.

"A text from Kathy. Followed by 'Going to summon youth maroon'."

"Predictive text. Probably pocket texting."

"Either that or there's a new beauty place opened up and they've all gone to get their nails done."

He crossed the road to the Mammon-Mammonson Investment building. The steel shutters were down on the car park entrance at the rear. They followed the pavement round to the front. Even before they climbed the short flight of stone steps, Rod could see that the lights weren't on inside. There was only the gloom of a business shut for the day. Rod tried the ornate Edwardian door handles anyway.

"Locked." He peered in, gave it a second's thought and raised his elbow to smash the window.

"I wouldn't," said Morag and dragged her toe along the brass bar inlaid across the tiled entrance. Rod wasn't even going to pretend to know what the engraved squiggles in the brass meant.

"No?" he said.

"I don't think you'd get two steps inside. We'll have to find another way in."

They stepped back onto the street and looked up.

"I could climb up to one of those windows, although none of them are open."

Morag's gaze shifted across to the side, to the nearby Chamberlain Square.

"Did I ever tell you about my Uncle Ramsay?" she said.

"Was he the deep-sea welder uncle who only ever told anecdotes about the Dutch and oral sex?"

"Wow, you do pay attention sometimes."

"Aye," said Rod. "Some things tend to stick in the mind."

"Well, he wasn't just a diver," she said.

Rod followed Morag's gaze.

Nina was picking at the flecks of batter in the bottom of her chip papers when Rod rang.

"Yo," she said.

"Vivian's been taken prisoner by the Mammonites," said Rod.

"They tied me to a tree on Monday."

"That was schoolkids," said Rod. "They're planning to summon *Yoth Mammon* back to this world."

331

Nina tried to imagine a goddess that was all insatiable appetite and mounds of fleshy horror wrapped in spiky, armour-plated death devouring the city piece by piece. But her imagination didn't have a huge special effects budget and in her mind's eye she saw something like a body bopper in a sleeping bag rolling across a miniature city made of cardboard boxes.

"When?" she said.

"Today."

"But I've got plans for the weekend."

"If the city survives until Friday, let's call that a win. Is Morag still with *Yo-Morgantus*?"

"Yep," she said. "Should we tell him?"

"Tough call. He's not going to be pleased and we don't want him trying to fix this himself."

"No." In her mind's eye, the sleeping bag monster was met in battle by a giant mattress made of ham. The cardboard city didn't fare well. "We need to tell her though."

"Aye. But I need you over here in Chamberlain Square. Morag's got a plan to get us inside."

The first floor of Mammon-Mammonson Investments had undergone some changes since Vivian's visit the day before. Desks and computers still crowded the periphery of the open-plan office, dwarfed by a wall-size display of live financial data. But additional space had been cleared around the giant floor mosaic of *Yoth Mammon*, and the ritual circle that bounded it was now encompassed by a new ring of tall network router cabinets. Eleven racks of flickering lights (that looked like they belonged in a data centre) were spaced evenly around the magic circle, each with a gagged and bound human strapped to the front of it, as though an entire IT department had decided to play Cowboys and Indians and were preparing for a historically inaccurate and culturally insensitive scalping. Yellow networking cables ran from the cabinets in a swirl about the circle and away to the computers. Vivian observed a few red cables among the yellow ones, then realised they were not cables but intravenous tubing, feeding blood from the eleven wild-eyed sacrifices to the circle. Blood trickled into the cracks in the mosaic, filled the hollows of the Venislarn symbols around the outside with color and transfused life itself into the rendering of the unholy mother of the Mammonites at its centre.

"Mrs Grey," said Xerxes Mammon-Mammonson, striding across the mosaic, open-armed to greet her. He left smears of bloody footprints under his designer shoes as he came. "Do you know how much you've cost us?" he said, smiling broadly as he did so.

Arranged around the circle, collars sharp, cufflinks gleaming, nearly twenty other Mammonites regarded her with hungry, hateful eyes. Vivian recognised some of them as members of the board of directors from the portrait she'd seen hanging in reception. This was, she concluded, an executive meeting; the underlings had been sent home for the day.

"You are an expensive indulgence," said Xerxes. "I hope you're worth it. We've had to bring our timetable forward because of you."

"This," said Vivian, refusing to be cowed by his sinister charm. "*All of this* is your doing. Everything that happens today will be on you."

Xerxes pulled a "yeah, so what?" face, distending the rubbery mask of his almost handsome, almost human face.

"You know the difference between winners and losers, Mrs Grey?"

Vivian said nothing. She was happy to let this egotist monologue as much as he liked.

"Timing," said Xerxes.

"I think that's comedy," said Kathy next to Vivian.

Xerxes gave a nod to Lodge-Mammonson. Kathy didn't even have time to turn. A knife tip jabbed into the back of her shoulder and levered her down to the ground. Cameron turned to object but one of the Mammonites already had his wrist and he was forced down too, grunting in pain as he went.

"People who see someone make it big, make a fortune, say 'I could have thought of that idea' or 'if I'd bought my stock at the same time then I'd be rich too'." Xerxes gave a knowing shake of the head. "Fools. It's all timing. And, yes, some are lucky but some are smart – like me – and that's why they're a success. If you're planning to short sell, to bet against the market, then timing is everything. How much has Mrs Grey cost us, Truman?"

"Three hundred and seventeen million," said Lodge-Mammonson.

Xerxes's eyes widened. If eyes could laugh, they would be giggling.

"You are an expensive indulgence indeed," he said to Vivian.

On the floor, Kathy was whimpering softly and putting pressure on the wound in her shoulder. Vivian ignored her for now.

"You are going to engineer a market crash and make a fortune from it?" she said. "I thought this was about summoning *Yoth Mammon* back to this world."

"Oh, it is!" said Xerxes. "But we'd be idiots not to take advantage of the impact it will have on global finances. Our mother would expect nothing less."

"*Yo-Morgantus* won't accept her return lightly. There will be consequences."

"There will be blood. And rubble. We're counting on it. We own a number of construction companies already lined up for the rebuild."

There were murmurs of approval from the Mammonite directors, the lip-smacking of diners before a feast.

"But now that everyone's here, the investors" – he gestured to the bound humans – "the witnesses" – he nodded to Vivian – "and, of course, our keynote speaker..."

He gestured across the large room and Vivian realised that the Mammonites and their human captives were not the only individuals at the edge of the circle; there was one more. Standing at a low lectern was a Carcosan word mage. Vivian had never met one before but there was hardly mistaking it for anything else. It was an unpleasantly tall and slender humanoid, albino-pale, an autumn leaf bleached of colour and substance and ready to fly apart at the slightest breeze. It must have travelled from beyond worlds, step by frail step to be here.

Xerxes saw Vivian looking.

"Of course, the other secret to success is knowledge. The *be'ae tyez* here has been very helpful."

On the lectern, the word mage's hands hovered above the pages of a book. The book, little more than a sheaf of loosely bound pages, was less than a centimetre thick but had a substance to it, a gravity of importance. Vivian recognised the stolen pages of the Big Bloody Book.

"Our friend is being paid in mutually-shared knowledge. His stock in trade is a little different to ours."

The word mage either had no interest in conversation or did not even recognise that Xerxes was speaking. It scratched thoughtfully at the brand mark in its forehead and raised its pen. A blood-filled tube ran from the nib up and away to, presumably, one of the humans.

"I believe we'll be ready to begin soon," said Xerxes. "Bind them." Xerxes reached out and stroked Vivian's cheek as she was led past. "Gently, but bind them. There can be no deal without witnesses."

Rod walked towards the police car as it stopped in the sliver of Chamberlain Square that was not fenced off by the demolition and construction crews around the site of the old library. Nina got out, balled up her chip papers and lobbed them at a nearby bin. She wasn't even close to getting it in.

"I've updated Vaughn," said Rod. "That didn't go down well."

"Did he have a right moan at you about pestering the Mammonites?" said Nina.

"Something like that, aye."

Ricky Lee stood in the open door of the car. "What's going on?"

"Well, either nothing at all or a goddess of unspeakable power and hunger is going to manifest in the immediate vicinity."

"They're quite... different options there," said Ricky.

"It's sort of end of the city as we know it. Or not," agreed Rod. He looked round at the pedestrians filing through the squeezed space, filing between the museums and the council houses and Victoria Square and the shops beyond. "We need to clear the area."

"You have authorisation?" said Ricky.

"No," said Rod.

The three of them looked from one to another.

"Where's Morag?" said Nina. "Your Morag. The one with the face."

"Up there," said Rod.

He pointed at the static crane more than a hundred metres overhead. Nearing the top now were two figures, climbing the internal ladder. In their gestures and positions, one could almost imagine an argument going on between them, the man demanding that the woman come down, the woman refusing and climbing onwards to the cabin.

Rod's finger drew a line along the crane jib arm to the heavy bucket at the furthest end.

"That is so cool," said Nina.

"Within the context of a potentially city-ending event," Rod reminded her.

"YOLO," she said and then, after a moment's thought, "We could phone in a bomb threat. You know, to clear the area."

"That would be grossly unprofessional," said Rod.

"Effective," countered Nina.

"And your Jihadi John accent is borderline racist."

"It's authentic."

"Authentically racist."

"What is it you think is happening here?" said Brigit, spokesperson and literal mouthpiece of *Yo-Morgantus*.

"Here?" said Morag Senior.

"The world is headed for Armageddon, an eternity of exquisite horrors. And here we are, the *em-shadt* Venislarn, here already. Do you think we are merely slumming it, hanging out until some unspecified moment?"

"I wouldn't presume to think anything," said Senior.

"No, you wouldn't. You are like the Aztecs witnessing the arrival of Cortez and his conquistadors in their incomprehensibly advanced wooden ships. No, you are like the children of those Aztecs, the infants. You cannot look beyond the sea, grasp the distances covered. You cannot know the plans of kings and popes."

"We're Aztec babies. Got it," said Senior, trying to keep the flippant edge out of her voice. "I'm just asking you for a little clemency. There are humans, kept prisoner through no real fault of their own, in an office –"

"And yet you persist," said Brigit. "If you were not well favoured by Lord *Morgantus* I would have you killed where you stand."

"You promised us justice," said a voice in the darkness.

"There will be justice, Watts-Mammonson," said Brigit.

Senior peered into the dark distances of the hall. The figure approached slowly, tossing an impractically jagged blade from one hand to the other. His suit was painfully sharp. There was something wrong with his jaws and eyes, as if a trace of crocodilian ancestry couldn't help but shine through.

"The consular mission must pay," said the Mammonite.

He passed close to Brigit and ran his fingers over her naked behind, the curve of her hips.

"Remember your place!" the woman snapped.

Watts-Mammonson stepped aside, spread his hands innocently and lifted his head to the ceiling.

"Just admiring the goods, my Lord. It's a compliment."

A tendril brushed Brigit's head and the sneer of affronted disgust was wiped away and replaced with an appreciative smile.

"Do not touch what you can't afford," she said with a roguish pout.

Watts-Mammonson gave her a little comic bow and turned to face Morag Senior again.

"We were discussing compensation for the offence we have suffered," he said, "for the impugning of our fine reputation."

Vivian tested the networking cables that tied her to the phone box-sized router cabinet. There was a rubbery flexibility to the individual cables but the mass of them was tight about her body.

Now that Xerxes Mammon-Mammonson had her tied and pinned in place, he ignored her utterly.

The Mammonites were about the business of their ritual now. Vivian had seen a lot of rituals in her time: weddings, banishments, christenings, summonings, graduations, funerals, initiations, blood libations and Christmas dinners. They all had the same four elements, starting with the set dressing – the flowers in the aisle, the holly wreath, the black robes of Baphomet. Next came the words of preamble that, no matter how you rearranged them, amounted to "we are gathered here today to *whatever-it-is-we're-here-to-do.*" Then came the words of the ceremony itself, which could be spoken perfectly well without any of the other nonsense but without which there was no ritual at all – the "I now pronounce you man and wife", the "the power of Christ compels you", the "I have no mouth but I must scream." And finally came the symbolic act that sealed the ritual, made of it a sacrament or covenant – the rings, the plunging dagger, the soil on a coffin lid.

Vivian had no time for pointless frivolities. Nothing as self-congratulatory as the pulling of a cracker was allowed in her home, no mortarboards had been flung at her graduation. If she had her way, all weddings would be "Do you? Yes. Do you? Yes. Then you're married." And, because she did have her way, her own wedding had been barely more than that. Mr Grey's funeral had been a bit more extravagant than practicality required but she forgave herself that moment's decadence; it had been a trying week after all.

The Mammonites' tediously self-important ritual to summon their goddess mother from *Kal Frexo leng*-space contained more superfluous extras than a top of the range sports car. Yes, the circle probably did need to be charged with a slow but constant libation of human blood. Yes, there was probably some key phrase in the word mage's litany that unlocked the barriers between worlds. But, the router cabinets were impractical decoration, a cheap analogy of a stone circle. The nightmare storm of data on the giant display – in a spiky red font, for goodness sake! – was hackneyed mumbo-jumbo. And the chanting... Why were the Mammonite businessmen chanting? What could they possibly add?

338

A literally captive audience member, Vivian could do nothing but silently tut and bemoan each theatrical excess. What next? Black candles? Incense? She found small solace in the fact that the more time they wasted on this twaddle, the better chance that someone else might intervene and put a stop to it.

The site manager had stayed in the crane operator's cab just long enough to a) see that Morag Junior had zero intentions of leaving and b) get freaked out by the capering sack cloth doll she had brought with her. Junior looked at the controls. It wasn't rocket science: a green button and a red one, and then a nice comfy seat with a joystick on each armrest. She'd need to figure out which one was for the trolley and which one was for the hoist, but there was a little diagram at the side of each, so she was confident that she could master it quickly. Conversations with Uncle Ramsay about his time operating lifting cranes on the rigs covered many of the basics but Junior was aware she still knew no more about crane operation than a person who had never driven a car but knew what the pedals did. Fortunately, this did look as though it had been deliberately idiot-proofed. Having Steve the Destroyer jump up and down on her chair yelling, "Pull that one! Pull that one!" was less helpful.

"Steve…" she said.

"No, that one! That one!"

"Um, I think I'm going to need you to be my eyes and ears out there."

"Out where?"

"Out there," she said and pointed along the seventy-metre jib. "To tell me when I'm in position."

"I am not your lookout, meatsack!"

Junior slid the window open a crack.

"Here," she said and thrust a spare communication headset at the creature. The headset encircled the doll like a hula hoop. "Get out there and tell me when we're over the Mammonite's building."

She lifted him over to the gap in the window and gave him a little prod as he struggled to squeeze his pudgy stuffed body through.

339

"You do not give me orders, creature!" he protested but went anyway, trotting along the upper bars of the jib, leaning this way and then that against the wind.

"Good," said Junior to the now silent cab. "Let's see."

She reached for the controls. The two main joysticks were helpfully labelled and the readouts of trolley height and jib direction were very clear. She remembered the one key lesson Uncle Ramsay had taught her about crane operation when she was younger (she liked hearing him talk about cranes far more than about the sexual proclivities of Dutchmen). He told her to hold out her arm and gave her an unwound yo-yo to hold and demonstrated what happened if you moved your arm too quickly. He'd set up an obstacle course of empty beer cans and watched her try to navigate the yo-yo through. Slow and steady was the key.

The jib began to rotate, slewing clockwise over the roofs of the nearby council house and museum.

"Slow and steady," she told herself.

The whole city was below her gaze and beneath her reach. Millennium Point, Town Hall, the Bullring, New Street, the Rotunda and, further out, one of the football stadiums (she couldn't say which), the tower blocks of distant estates, the streets of Digbeth, Aston, Moseley and beyond. Junior had seen prettier cities but she was damned sure this one wouldn't be made any better by the addition of an enormous interdimensional demon-goddess.

Black candles!

Vivian stared in furious amazement at the thick candles each of the Mammonite executives now held in their hands as they stared intently at the circle, chanting with the word mage.

"Where the hell did they come from?" she hissed in furious surprise.

"I think it's just... magic," said Kathy from the router cabinet next to her. The young doctor seemed to be in considerable discomfort, all the life and energy had gone from her usually oh-so-expressive eyebrows. Blood had soaked through her clothes all down her shoulder and arm although the bleeding might finally have stopped.

"I mean, it's not even a natural colour for wax!" said Vivian and, twisting against her bonds, looked in the other direction at Cameron, seeking confirmation of her righteous indignation. "What do you..." She stopped. "Are you chanting along, Mr Barnes?"

"What?" he said, guiltily. "No, I was just... Okay, maybe. It's fairly meaningless *feskir* stuff and I'm not actually contributing to the ritual incantation."

Vivian stared at him.

"It's catchy," he said, unrepentant. "It clears the mind. We're all going to die in the next few minutes and I think I would like to spend that time sharing in a Carcosan cultural activity, thank you."

Vivian turned back to Kathy.

"Welcome to the team, Dr Kaur. We'd like to offer you a position."

"Oh, yay," said Kathy, deadpan.

The funnel-shaped bucket touched down hard in Chamberlain Square, cracking several paving bricks as it landed.

"In," said Rod.

"Just texting Morag. The other Morag," she said and then grabbed the high lip and swung her legs up. Rod followed. He might have been taller but he had more bulk to get over the six-foot-high edge. He rolled in and narrowly avoided squashing Nina. They stood. Rod waved his arms for Morag to take them up.

"You need to clear the area," Nina said to Ricky Lee.

"I'm not phoning in a terrorist threat," he said.

"Think of something else then."

The slack crane line tightened and slowly began to pull them up.

"Say they found an old World War Two bomb while they were clearing rubble," shouted Rod.

"Yeah," added Nina enthusiastically. "We used that one when the *Krysill* was uncovered in Aston. We closed the expressway for three days and no one complained."

341

Ricky reluctantly began to make the call.

Rod watched their progress carefully as they rose. There were plenty of buildings immediately around them and the rooftop of Mammon-Mammonson Investments was one street over. There was a lot they could bump into on their way. He realised that he had automatically braced his arms for any unexpected impact.

"Nina," he said.

"Yep."

"This is definitely one of them 'keep your hands and legs inside the carriage at all times' situations, okay?"

"Sure," she said, mildly put out that he felt it needed saying.

"We don't want a repeat of the big wheel incident, do we?"

"No. No, we don't."

Watts-Mammonson approached Morag Senior, knife at the ready.

"There will be no killing without my say so," said Brigit.

"The life of one member of the consular mission will be the least of our demands," said the Mammonite.

"Demands?" said Brigit, intrigued.

"Which I am sure you will be granting." Watts-Mammonson gave Brigit a smile which sat at the wrong end of the charming-creepy spectrum. "In your infinite wisdom."

Senior's phone buzzed again. She took it out.

"I'm sorry," said Watts-Mammonson. "Am I distracting you from something?"

"Ooh," said Senior. "This is actually quite interesting." She held the phone out. "Just heard that Mammon-Mammonson are planning to open a doorway to *Kal-Frexo leng*-space and bring *Yoth Mammon* back to Birmingham. How would Lord *Morgantus* feel about that?"

"Is this true?" said Brigit.

Watts-Mammonson re-attempted the smile but rather than sliding over into charming it took a tangential swing into desperate.

"Planning," he said. "My lord, you have always known that we would ultimately – *ultimately* – desire the return of our mother. This would be within the strategic framework of –"

Watts-Mammonson froze mid-speech as a strand of *Yo-Morgantus* reached down and tapped into his consciousness. He was still for several seconds and then he gave a little strangled squeak and pushed himself away.

"It's not like that!" he said to Brigit. "We have broken no commands! We have acted entirely within the letter of the law!"

Brigit was shaking her head.

"You think I will allow this?" she said.

"It's a big city," said Watts-Mammonson. "We can share."

Seeing no leniency in Brigit, Watts-Mammonson changed his grip on the knife and ran at Morag Senior. He got barely a dozen feet before a tendril found him again and he stopped. Blank-eyed, he took the knife in both hands and calmly and slowly turned it to point at his own throat.

"Share?" said Brigit.

A crack had appeared in the large mosaic in the centre of the floor, a ragged line along the nuggets of stone in the image of *Yoth Mammon*. A couple of pieces fell away – fell through – admitting a powerful pink light from the space beneath.

"It's opening!" declared Cameron, sounding far more excited that Vivian thought appropriate.

He was, nonetheless, right.

Accompanied by the muffled screams of the human blood donors, a pit yawned open in the middle of the room. Initially, chunks of mosaic and masonry fell into the void, but as the opening expanded, the floor began to pull away in large, connected sections: wide circular strips, the unpeeling of one world by another.

The hole before Vivian's feet did not open into the ground floor of the building or the bedrock beneath but into a whole other space. At the fringes of the circle, the floor fell away in a rough helix and the pit became a spiral bore shaft.

The word mage intoned a final syllable and, trick of the eldritch light or not, the blood-soaked circle of sigils flashed fixedly in response.

"Behold!" declared Xerxes Mammon-Mammonson.

343

Vivian beheld. A doorway, flung wide to *Kal Frexo leng-*space.

"Hell," said Kathy softly, not as an expletive but as an acknowledgement.

"Down a bit, you useless snackling! Down!"

"What do you think I'm doing?" said Morag Junior.

The Mammon-Mammonson Investments building was behind a section of what Junior took to be the museum. Getting the bucket over the top without taking out a gallery was a minor achievement. Now, with her eyes on the trolley position and the height of the bucket, she lowered away.

As the bucket settled onto the flat, tarmacked roof of the MMI building, Rod remembered footage of the Lunar Excursion Module touching down on the Sea of Tranquillity. He might have shared the thought with Nina but, given her ignorance of everything that had happened before the millennium, such sharing would require a detailed preamble about the Apollo programme, the space race and, inevitably, the Cold War, Operation Paperclip and the Second World War. Nina would then ask Rod if he had fought in the Second World War and he would get snippy – partly because he wouldn't be able to tell if she was joking.

"The Eagle has landed," he murmured as the bucket made solid contact with the roof.

Nina gave him a funny look. "Really?"

"What?" he said.

"My dad always used to say that after his morning dump."

"I haven't crapped myself, Nina. I was…" He growled and gave up.

The link chain on the bucket slackened and the crane cable began to spool down the side of the bucket and onto the rooftop.

Rod heaved himself over the side and onto the roof. The cable was still coming down in rough loops on the tarmac. Rod turned towards the distant crane and waved with both hands.

"Get her on the phone, will you?" he said to Nina.

344

The roof shook: a brief but sharp vibration, as though a truck had run into the side of the building. They put out their arms to steady themselves.

"Earthquake?" said Rod optimistically.

"Nah," said Nina. "Shit just got real."

Rod straightened up.

"We've had words about that, Nina. You are not to use that line every time something really bad is about the happen. I'm not right happy with the prospect of dying with a line from *Bad Boys* as one of the last things I ever hear."

"*Bad Boys 2.*"

"I don't care! Come on." He made for the roof access door.

"Sure," he could hear her muttering. "I can't say 'shit got real' but you can use my dad's dump-line. That's fine, apparently."

Yellow lightning flashed in the pit. Questing fingers of wild electricity crept up the sides of the shaft and earthed themselves against the walls of the trading office. Vivian felt an unpleasant sensation in her ears and her sinuses as though the air pressure was rapidly changing. Below the howls of distant, interdimensional winds, she heard the stone building about her creak. That didn't bode well, for the city in general and her in particular.

A flat section of plaster fell from the ceiling above and into the pit, tumbling apart in the hot rising wind.

"Floor four, floor three... wait."

Rod stopped on the landing. Nina smacked into his back with a tiny *oof.*

"Why are we stopping?"

He ignored her, got his bearings and ran through a door.

"Aren't we looking for the evil business dudes?" said Nina.

"Not until we rescue these chaps."

They were in the Mammonites' storage area: the recess-lined corridor where human acquisitions were held in trances behind glass. Rod put his hand on the nearest pane.

"Tell me we can just smash these open."

Nina looked it up and down.

"It's just glass." She peered at the bloke in the hi-vis tabard behind the glass. "But they're under some charm."

"But you can break it?" said Rod hopefully.

"Me?"

Rod looked down at his diminutive colleague. "Nina. I'm good at a number of things. I can hit things very hard. I can shoot better than ninety-nine percent of the population" – he slapped his side where a gun should have hung but where he now had only a pocketful of claims forms – "Drop me in a desert, a warzone or a burning building and I can probably get myself and everyone with me out alive. What I can't do is this alien magic stuff."

"Yes," she said patiently, "but I'm going to need to know what 'alien magic stuff' was cast over them."

Rod grimaced. He knew it. The oily one, Lodge-Mammonson, had told them. It was...

"Wisteria Farm," he hazarded.

"That's not a thing."

"Interior bar?"

"Still not a thing."

"Malaria tar? No, it's definitely 'bar'."

"Malaria bar?"

"No, no." He closed his eyes. "It's... mmm... cap, cup, car... cartoon. Cartoo-oo-oo bar."

"*Ka'teriah Ba*?" she suggested.

"Yes!" he shouted. "That's it!"

"Oh, fine. Not a problem. You smash these in. I'll warm up my mad hot skills," she said and cracked her knuckles.

Rod went to fetch the fire extinguisher he'd seen on the landing.

Vivian stood less than a metre from the edge but she could not see to the bottom of the long shaft into *leng*-space. Shadows moved in the deep. Voices clamoured. On the lowest visible level of the helical ramp, creatures marched. Through hot mist Vivian glimpsed waving tentacles, fat bodies and misshapen, hoofed feet. Climbing.

"Priests of *Nystar*!" said Cameron, fascinated.

"Too late to impress us with your knowledge, Mr Barnes," said Vivian. "My decision is final. What you could both put your minds to is how we close this opening."

"While we're tied up?"

"Let us be optimistic and assume that we also manage to free ourselves."

Xerxes stood at the very lip of the pit and gazed down. Rising air toyed with his sculpted coiffure.

Yoth Mammon, meh skirr'ish," he called down to his mother goddess. *"Shan-shan prui. Sogho fer juriska, te made. Vashan! Vashan!"*

There was a cry in reply from below: a vocal assault of foghorn roars, throaty bellows and electric screams. It was a cry that could have brought down the walls of Jericho. Perhaps it had. The world shook and a supersonic nimbus of energy blasted upward from the pit, smashing through the ceiling above.

Nina smacked the last captive human on his forehead with the palm of her hand.

"And you're back," she said.

"Who are you?" said the pyjama-wearing young man suspiciously.

"Questions later," said Nina. "Follow my mate, Rod. Watch out for broken glass on the floor."

The man did as he was told, stepping cautiously along the corridor.

The background hum of distant chanting abruptly rose in pitch and volume. There was a scream, like God had dropped a brick on his toe, and the floor beneath Nina's feet buckled upwards. She fell – she ran – down a corridor that was now a rapidly breaking wave of shattered marble. She shoved pyjama boy hard in the back and he slammed into lollipop man, who stood frozen at the door to the stairs. Momentum carried them through to the landing, where they would have slid to a stop had Rod not caught all three in a bear hug and jumped.

Morag Junior saw the ripple of energy from *leng*-space as a momentary glow on the roof of Mammon-Mammonson, an equally momentary flash of Barbie-pink light and then a plume of dust and fire that tossed the crane bucket into the sky and buffeted the jib arm of the crane itself. The crane shook like a car racing down a potholed road. She grabbed for something secure but there was nothing; either she was safe or she was dead.

In her earpiece, she heard a squeaky voice swearing for all it was worth.

As quickly as it had come, the geyser of energy collapsed and, for a second, the cab was still.

And then she saw the crane bucket: a hundred feet or more above where it had just been, tumbling end over end, falling like a carelessly tossed yo-yo. But those weren't beer cans down there.

Every time one of the recently-woken humans slowed or stopped on the stairs, Rod urged them on with quiet words and the occasional flat of his hand.

"Just keeping going down," he said.

"How far, mate?" said one bloke.

"To the bottom. The basement. The garage, whatever. Find a door. Get far away."

"Why? What's happening?"

Rod's reply didn't get beyond the first syllable.

From on high, something crashed noisily through the floors above.

Amid the dazzle of unearthly lights, transdimensional pressures and the accompanying cataclysmic rumbles, Vivian almost missed the sudden entrance of a giant steel bucket through the ceiling. When she did see it, she was unsurprised; the human brain had a fixed capacity for astonishment, beyond which everything took on a dream-like normality, no matter how insane.

The bucket plummeted down, snagged on the end of its cable tether and swung erratically to the side, a wild pendulum. A Mammonite executive screamed briefly as he was mashed into the

348

wall plaster. Then the bucket swung back and his flattened remains fell wordlessly through the gateway to *leng*.

The crane jib shuddered and, for a sickening second, Morag Junior could feel the cab pull forward – maybe only a degree or two off vertical, but forward nonetheless – towards the glowing ruin of Mammon-Mammonson's roof.

Steve was still shrieking on the line although she was not certain whether it was a shriek of fear or the exhilarated shriek of a demon enjoying a skydive into hell.

Several lights were flashing on the control panel. Junior had no idea what they meant but doubted that any of them had been designed to warn of apocalyptic Venislarn crap.

"Yes, yes," she said, slapping the console in an attempt to calm them. "The world's gone crazy. I know."

The bucket's swing became an elliptical twirl. It bounced off the wall, smashed one of the router cabinets onto its side and then, with a balletically slow inevitability, slammed the word mage, lectern and Big Bloody Book fragment across the edge of the circle and down into the shaft. The word mage fell like a shot bird, his robes flapping about him like useless wings. The infinite book section fluttered down with him.

Xerxes Mammon-Mammonson either had not seen the word mage fall or no longer cared now that his work was done but several of the company directors gave immediate chase, running down the ragged spiral slope that circled into the pit.

"We have to get that book," said Vivian.

"And close the gate," said Kathy.

"Once we're freed," Cameron reminded them.

Vivian felt a slackening of the cables across her chest.

"One thing at a time," said Nina from behind them.

Vivian craned her head round as best she could. Nina was pulling at the mass of cables behind Cameron's router. Directly behind her, Vivian could hear the regular snip-snip of cables coming loose, one at a time. That would be Rod, a man with a tool for every occasion.

349

"Are we too late?" he said.

"Let's pretend we're not," said Vivian. "We must go after the book otherwise there's nothing to stop this happening all over again."

Nina had her phone out. It was like the thing was glued to the girl's hand.

"Morag," she said, raising her voice about the din. "Are you still up there?"

Watts-Mammonson lay dead on the floor of *Yo-Morgantus*'s audience chamber, blood pooling slowly around his body. Morag Senior was sure someone or something would be along soon to clean up, or just eat.

"With your permission," said Senior, "we'll put a stop to Mammon-Mammonson's ritual, free the human prisoners and everything can go back to business as normal."

"Stop the ritual?" said Brigit. "Why would we want to do that?"

The reasons were obvious. To stop the arrival of a rival god. To maintain the current status quo.

"To... um." She frowned at Brigit. "Why wouldn't you want to stop *Yoth Mammon?*"

"You think Lord *Morgantus* is afraid of challengers? Let her come."

In the space beyond the vents and panels above, something shifted and groaned: a sea of tissue and muscle and fat and gnarly folds of skin, a sucking tar pit of flesh. Senior couldn't picture *Yo-Morgantus* in motion, had always thought of him as a bed-bound emperor, covered with bed sores and cankers, imprisoned in his own palace by his corpulence. She could not imagine how he would meet *Yoth Mammon* in battle. She didn't want to.

"My lord," she said, "I implore you, don't do this."

"Well then, implore," said Brigit. "Plead. Beg."

"I do," said Senior. "I am. If you would only let us handle this, we would be beyond grateful."

The beautiful woman stroked her jaw and shifted her hips thoughtfully.

"What is beyond grateful? Here is grateful." She put a hand out, slicing the air. "What's on the other side?"

The spreading pool of blood touched Brigit's feet. She scrunched her toes in it.

"What have you got to offer?" she said.

Nina backed up against a wall and then, with a silent YOLO, she sprinted toward the bucket. She leapt the eight-foot gap, slammed her chest against the rim of the bucket and grabbed on with all the might her body could muster. Moments later she had tipped herself in, whacked her head against the metal bottom and was on the phone again.

"Take me down," she said.

The line fizzed and crackled but there was definitely some form of affirmation in there.

Morag Junior pushed the stick forward.

The Distance to Ground readout on the control panel flickered between a few metres and a whole row of nines.

"Going down," she said.

As Cameron shoved the last remaining cables from his feet, Vivian made a snap assessment of the situation. The Mammonites were distracted by the imminent arrival of their mother, the loss of the word mage, Nina's rash antics on the descending crane bucket and, now, a brewing argument (or possibly fight to the death) with the bloated priests of *Nystar* coming up the path from below.

"We need to fathom out how to close this gate," she said to Kathy. "We need to retrieve or destroy that book," she said Rod.

Cameron looked expectantly at her.

"Freeing the other humans would be a bonus," she said.

Rod tossed Cameron the pocket wire cutters.

"Don't lose them," he said.

Nina looked down over the edge of the bucket. Below her was a world that refused to play by the rules of common sense or physics. Down walls of bubbling rock that bled and swayed, the

351

path descended round and round. Jungle vines and deep-sea plant monsters sprang from the walls and, here and there where *leng*-space thought Nina wasn't paying attention, the vertical became the horizontal and plains stretched away into starlit darkness. The scorched air shimmered in front of her and Nina couldn't discern whether she was looking at weird rock outcrops and campfires or demonic cities and vast sacrificial pyres. Monsters crawled like insects or, possibly, insects strutted like monsters. Her eyes watered simply looking at it.

Directly below, both just out of reach and infinitely far away, was *Yoth Mammon*. The goddess filled the shaft, a mouth big enough to swallow aircraft carriers stretched wide to greet the world.

"Yeah, you stay down there, bitch," Nina muttered, though she doubted that was going to happen.

Rod and Vivian ran down the spiral slope.

"Keep close to the wall," he said, redundantly. The path was a good ten feet wide and Vivian felt no compulsion to get closer to the edge than she absolutely needed to.

She clutched the black pen nib as she ran. It might prove essential in locating the book pages. Its sharpness against her palm was a comforting touchstone of reality.

They stepped over fissures and fallen masonry, maintaining a good pace. Vivian followed in Rod's footsteps as closely as possible. He was her guide and her shield and she made a mental note to thank him if they survived the day.

Nina's crane bucket was a considerable distance below them although, as charitable as she tried to be about the young woman, Vivian doubted Nina would be of any use in locating the pages. Of more immediate concern was the crowd of Mammonites and priests of *Nystar* half a turn ahead. A shoving match between the off-human city traders and the tentacle-headed priests took up the full width of the path.

The priests of *Nystar* sung with one voice, *"Ey un nue ken-daa! Ey un nue ken-daa!"*

"What are they saying?" yelled Rod.

"Go back. You're too early."

"It's half-day closing in hell or what?"

"Maybe…" Vivian puffed as the exertion of running began to wind her. "Maybe Xerxes hadn't considered whether his mother actually wanted to be summoned."

"Stay close to me!" Rod shouted.

Easier said than done, thought Vivian, who lacked the breath to say it.

Rod ploughed into the rear of the crowding Mammonites and barged on through. He lowered his rugby player shoulder and with a roar, slid between two of the mostly spherical priests, pitching one aside into the abyss. Vivian hurried through behind him before the ranks could close.

A fallen Mammonite lashed out at Rod's leg and he stumbled. Vivian was past him when he tried to get up, only to fall again as the Mammonite clutched his trouser turn-ups.

"Go!" he shouted at her. She had no intention of doing otherwise.

A dozen turns of the path, several storeys in height below her, there was a wide level area and a white shape that might have possibly been the word mage or indeed his book.

The phone line between Nina and Morag in the crane was deteriorating rapidly. Clearly hell didn't get good phone coverage.

"I'd better not have to pay data roaming charges." She looked at her phone. "*Muda*! There's a wi-fi hotspot here. Hell has wi-fi."

"*kxxx–* what?" said Morag.

"Nothing. Swing me left."

"*kxxxk*."

The bucket swung right.

"Left!" Nina said.

"That is left!"

Nina looked up at the small disc of light high above that was the sky of Birmingham and wondered if she'd got turned around in the descent.

"I mean my left!" she said.

"What's your left?"

"Right!"

"*kxxxk*'s sake!" said Morag.

The bucket swung left. It was looking good. She was descending in a smooth arc toward the broad ledge where she thought she'd seen the book.

"Slowly now," she said.

"I'm almost out of line anyway," said Morag.

Rod rolled onto his back and kicked Truman Lodge-Mammonson in the face. He felt teeth and something more besides crunch under his heel. Lodge-Mammonson spat and elbowed Rod's stomach, crawling forward to get from under a priest of *Nystar*'s hoofs.

"Our staff," he grunted, "have the right to work without" – he jabbed his elbow down again, this time into Rod's ribs – "abuse or threats of violence."

Rod caught him cleanly with a left hook but Mammonites were made of strong stuff. Lodge-Mammonson pulled a spiked zombie knife from within his tailored jacket and swung down to impale Rod with it.

Rod grabbed the Mammonite's wrist to hold him off.

"Strong manly grip you've got there, Rod," Lodge-Mammonson snorted and put his weight on the hilt to force the knife down.

Kathy skirted round the edge of the circle, identifying and translating as she went.

"Outer circle is the summoning, enhanced by the *Kal Frexo* runes," she said to herself. "The inner circle…"

She ran her hands over the engraved symbols. They were tacky with congealing blood.

A distance away, Cameron nipped at another captive's cable bonds with Rod's wire cutters. Xerxes Mammon-Mammonson loomed over the far edge of the pit, arms raised in an almost Nixonian salute. He didn't care about the humans now. He only had eyes for the world below.

354

"She rises!" he cried, not for the first time. The first time it had been in exultation. Now there was a hint of desperate exhortation.

There was another unholy roar from the pit and a newer more profound rumbling echoed up.

"Christ," muttered Kathy. "Maybe she is rising. The inner circle…"

Vivian ran down the slope. She held out her left hand to the wall for support until something with teeth that looked like claws (or maybe claws that looked like teeth) tried to take an opportunistic bite of her fingers from its crevice home. She watched her feet and the path ahead. Vivian did not hold with casual footwear in the workplace. However, she had a deep sense of the practical and had bought for herself several pairs of stout women's shoes that also had solid rubber grip soles. People who said you couldn't have formality and function were just too lazy to find it.

From time to time, her erratic path brought her closer to the edge and she saw down into the pit. It was impossible to gauge how far below *Yoth Mammon* truly was or indeed how fast she was rising. The sheer scale of the goddess made it impossible to tell. Vivian was sure that the dinosaurs of the Cretaceous, if they had the wherewithal to look up and ponder, would have had no idea how far off that meteor was until it struck them.

The tip of Lodge-Mammonson's wicked knife cut into Rod's waistcoat and found the Kevlar lining. It was a temporary reprieve at best. They were called anti-stab vests rather than stab-proof vests for a reason.

Lodge-Mammonson's weight was entirely bearing down on him, preventing him from reaching his own knife in his trouser pocket. He could, with his marginally freer right hand, reach inside his jacket where it would have been really handy to have a gun right now.

Over them, priests of *Nystar* jostled. Hoofs stamped heavily on the path around them. Rod's view from the floor was mostly composed of huge green *Nystar* butts. Dying here would be a bloody poor way to go.

Rod tried kicking but he couldn't get the angle with his legs. Lodge-Mammonson smiled at his struggles. Rod saw a glint of gold in Lodge-Mammonson's breast pocket and reached for it. Made by an artisanal printer in Milan, he remembered.

Rod snagged one of the gold-edged business cards between fore and index fingers and sliced sideways across Lodge-Mammonson's cheek. They were sharp. Lodge-Mammonson gasped. Rod sliced the other way, taking one of the Mammonite's eyes. Lodge-Mammonson roared this time and clutched his face.

"Lawsuit!" he yelled as Rod shoved him off and scrambled up the slope and away from the melee.

Rod freed the knife that was embedded in his armoured waistcoat and sought the sanctuary of the nearest wall. Lodge-Mammonson was still rolling on the floor. "I need witnesses! Someone take photos! You all saw it! You all saw what he did! I'm suing!"

A priest of *Nystar* trod on Lodge-Mammonson and thoughts of litigation (and probably a lot else as well) went from the Mammonite's head.

In the deeps, a goddess, clearly on the move now, roared.

Leng shook as the bucket was about to touch down. The gentle landing became a graceless thump and the bucket tipped over, dumping Nina. She rolled out like a tiny acrobat and sprang to her feet. "Stuck it!"

She was standing on a table of broken stone, as unbeautiful and as lifeless as factory concrete. Steam and smoke and Venislarn indifference made everything beyond her immediate vicinity an indecipherable nonsense. If this was hell, it was bloody irritating. Overall, she was unimpressed, although the existence of wi-fi was a chink of hope for the place.

She looked at her phone. A Bluetooth device was trying to connect with it.

"What the *bhul*..."

"Hey!"

From a cavern entrance, two figures shuffled towards her, filthy ripped clothes on their backs, a pained weariness in their stride. Nina prepared to take on these demons with the best she had (a combat method she called "pub car park bitch gone apeshit") and then stopped. She didn't reckon many demons wore New York Yankees baseball caps or carried mobile phones.

"I – ggh! – know her!" said the taller one, picking up speed.

Nina peered at them. "Pupfish?"

"It's Nina!" said the *samakha* gangsta. "We're saved."

Arm in arm, the fish boy and the human woman (who looked as if she'd had the worst possible night on the town) hurried towards her.

"It's a brace," said Kathy.

"What?" said Cameron.

She hadn't even realised he was there with her. She looked up. All the human captives were freed and fled. It was probably too late for them anyway. If *Yoth Mammon* made it to the surface this would be ground zero and the metaphysical blast radius was going to be huge.

"The inner circle is a brace," Kathy said, making a ring of her hands. "It's holding the gateway open."

"Makes sense," said Cameron. "So, if we destroy even one of the symbols…"

"Foom! It's gone. Closed."

"Right."

Both of them looked around.

"A sledgehammer?" said Cameron.

"In an office?" said Kathy.

"Or something like one."

Vivian found the word mage and the remains of the Big Bloody Book beside him. The word mage was dead. He was bent in half, a snapped twig. The Big Bloody Book, pages held together with a spine binder of wood and twine, rested under the elongated fingers of his outstretched hand. She lifted it gently. The binding weighed more than the book. It was odd that something so light could be so dangerous.

Vivian mentally shook herself. There was no time for such cod-philosophical musings. She'd leave that to the millennials. Clearly the fumes in this place were getting to her.

She looked up at the distance she had run. She looked down to the place where Nina had landed. Going down would be quicker than going up.

One half of Pupfish's face was solid bruise. The woman with him had a series of lacerations running down her ruined dress and her leg.

"I thought you were dead," said Nina, "after what happened in the nightclub."

"After the first week here, we wished we were," said Pupfish.

"Week? No. It was last night."

"Time is different here, dog."

The woman took hold of Nina's arm like she was the pope come visiting.

"I'm not ever doing E again. It's nothing like the stuff we took in Magaluf."

"Allana, babe," said Pupfish. "It wasn't no E. Ggh! I told you."

Allana's face was a mask of dirt grey, mascara streaks and skin-pink tear tracks. She looked like someone ready for their Goth weekender or possibly someone with an upcoming walk-on role in a Mad Max movie.

"Michael's been keeping me straight," she said.

"Michael, huh?"

Nina gave Pupfish a wry look. She didn't know fish boys could blush.

Allana rooted around in her purse and pulled out a pack of cigarettes and a lighter.

"And they say you never meet good guys in nightclubs," she said.

"They do, don't they?"

Allana attempted to light the measliest of dogends.

"You've no idea what we've been through," said Pupfish.

"You can tell me when we're out of here," said Nina.

"We ain't had nothing to eat – ggh! – except some nasty-ass paste stuff we found. I need me some Burger King or some KFC."

"I've got a family-sized bucket for you," said Nina, pointing back at the crane bucket. "First we've got to find a book and Vivian."

"Mrs G?" said the *samakha*. "That her there?"

It damn well was.

Vivian was running at them, spritely for such an old biddy, a bunch of papers clutched in her hand.

"We are leaving, Miss Seth!" she shouted. "Now!"

Morag Junior had sat with only silence for company for several minutes. Weird light still played around the roof of Mammon-Mammonson Investments. Steve's voice was gone from the headset. The line to Nina was still open but there had been only interference and muffled voices. Suddenly, there was a sharp burst of static.

"–s up," said Nina.

"Come again?" said Junior.

"*Kxxxk* – take us up."

"Now?"

"Now!" said Nina.

Junior pulled the joystick to retract the line.

"Scream if you want to go faster," she said.

"*Kxxx* –" said Nina.

Rod wished he understood Venislarn a little better – no, a heck of a lot better – because something had changed between the arguing Mammonites and priests of *Nystar*. As he climbed the shaking slope to the surface he noted a definite shift in tone in the blobby monsters' chanting. Had it stopped being too early? Was it now okay for the Mammonites to greet their dear old mama?

He looked down over the edge.

The crane bucket was swinging as it came up, three or possibly four figures squeezed into it. *Yoth Mammon*, that great wall-to-wall orifice, was powering up the shaft only just below them.

Vivian saw her error as they drew level with where the word mage had fallen. Paper fluttered under the edge of his robes and at least one piece was stuck to the wall by the constant updraft.

"Take this," she said to Nina and passed her the book pages.

She gripped the supporting chains above her and pulled herself up to the rim of the bucket.

"What are you doing?" said Nina.

"I've left some pages behind."

Nina shook her head. "Vivian. You'll never jump that."

Nina was wrong, as she often was. The bucket was swinging in a shifting ellipse.

"It'll bring me close enough in a minute. It's like a Spirograph. It will eventually bring me round to..."

Vivian levered herself up, crouched unsupported on the lip for a second and leapt. It was a good leap. She landed solidly on the path – stumbled, yes, and cut herself on the rocks, yes, but landed solidly.

She ran back down the half turn to the word mage.

Nina was shouting. Vivian ignored her.

Nina turned to the *samakha* and the woman.

"What the hell's a Spirograph?"

Kathy discovered that offices were generally lacking in sledgehammers and sledgehammer-like objects. Given the situation, she considered this a gross oversight on the part of office furnishers everywhere.

Thirty seconds into the search, she had found a long-armed stapler and Cameron had located a printer. Neither seemed wholly suitable for the job.

A jeer went up from the Mammonites at the pit's edge. She looked back.

A pair of Mammonites had hauled Rod from the path and held him pinned, in a double armlock.

Vivian grabbed at the wind-tossed pages. Theoretically, any selection of multiple pages from the Big Bloody Book had the capacity to contain infinite knowledge, to allow those with ability to unlock forbidden doors and loose fresh terrors. She cast about for stray pages and prepared to run.

Fingers closed around her ankle. It was the Carcosan word mage, bent horribly in two but not yet dead. Amber eyes beneath paper-white lids blinked at her. He mouthed something.

Vivian had no time for this but a whisper of his words reached her ears.

"Tei gharri cor ap Shallas."

She shook her head at such nonsense.

"Kash ka..." he said and attempted a nod.

Nonsense, she told herself. The nonsense product of a dying mind.

The crane bucket was a distance above her now. *Yoth Mammon* was below her, much closer now, and ascending at speed. Vivian shook herself free of the word mage's weak grip and ran.

Nina saw Vivian running. She saw the goddess rising.

"She's not going to make it," she said.

She looked up at the distance they still had to go.

"We're not going to make it."

"I thought you were rescuing us, blood," said Pupfish.

She gave him a blast of her stone-cold bitch look.

"Lighter," she said to Allana.

The woman was slow in retrieving it from her purse. Nina snatched it from her and lit it beneath the bound pages of the Big Bloody Book.

"Do you know what happens when you set fire to a book with an infinite number of pages?" she said as it began to catch alight.

"What?" said Allana.

361

Nina shrugged. "Let's find out."

She held on as long as she dared – the flames turning from orange to yellow to blue-white – and then dropped it over the side. By the time it entered Yoth Mammon's gaping piehole, the book, no bigger than a glossy magazine, had become a fireball of searing intensity.

Pupfish was awestruck. "You – ggh! – would try to kill a god? *Kos-kho bhul!*"

"Just give her a little heartburn," said Nina. She put her phone to her ear. "Morag, we need to swing over and pick up Vivian."

Kathy shouted to the Mammonites who held Rod.

"Let him go!"

They didn't comply. They didn't argue back. It was worse than that; they simply ignored her.

"Hey!" she yelled. "Let him go or *Yoth Mammon* gets trapped in *leng*-space forever."

They looked at her then but with no great urgency.

"What are you going to do?" called Xerxes Mammon-Mammonson. "Threaten us with a stapler and a printer?"

"Yeah!" said Cameron. "You'd better *adn-bhul* believe it."

Xerxes shook his head, bored. "Kill them," he said simply.

Three Mammonite executives began circling the pit to come at them.

"Do it!" yelled Rod. "Close it!"

Kathy's eyes flicked to the crane bucket. It was coming up now. Not far to the surface.

Morag Junior watched the crane readouts.

The bucket was nearly back up to the height at which Nina had first climbed aboard. Only a few seconds until it was clear.

The phone line was a squall of noise and static that might once have been speech.

Yoth Mammon screamed as she climbed. Maybe it was excitement. Maybe it was anger. Maybe it had something to do with the sun-bright fireball she appeared to be gargling. Anger, excitement or pain, it was being translated into earth-shaking spasms that sent those in the world above stumbling.

Kathy stepped back. The Mammonite running at her tripped and fell aside. Cameron swung his printer and clouted another one on the side of the head.

"Now, Kathy!" yelled Rod.

The bucket wasn't up yet. It wasn't quite through.

Yoth Mammon ripped apart the spiral path as she wriggled past. Priests of *Nystar* and Mammonites fell together, crying out to their goddess.

Rod wrestled one arm free and punched his other captor.

"Now!"

The fallen Mammonite had found its feet. Kathy raised the long-armed stapler over her head and hammered it into the nearest symbol of the inner ring. The symbol cracked apart.

Nina fell onto broken ground. Oofing and eeking, Pupfish and Allana landed with her. The world had fallen silent. No roaring deities. No chanting blob-priests. No earthquake rumbles. She stood in the centre of a circle of ruined mosaic on a floor that was otherwise complete and whole. The gateway to *leng*-space was gone.

Above her, the crane bucket rose onwards, its bottom an open circle, sliced away by the closing gate. She immediately inspected her shoes and saw that a few millimetres had been shaved off the soles.

"Too close," she said.

Any closer and she'd have lost precious centimetres of her own foot. And she was short enough as it was.

But it was done. The ritual had failed. Against all odds, the city was saved. Kathy Kaur, her arm wet with blood, stood with Cameron Barnes at the edge of the circle. They were inexplicably armed with a stapler and a printer. Rod had backed off some distance from the nine remaining Mammonites. Xerxes Mammon-Mammonson, the boss, stared in disbelief at the ruin of his plan.

Pupfish, Allana, Kathy, Cameron, Rod, Mammonites. She whirled on the spot.

"Where's Vivian?"

No one piped up. There was no "here I am."

"Where's Vivian?" she demanded, angrily.

"She was running," said Cameron which was no answer at all.

"I had to..." said Kathy which was even less.

Nina dropped to her knees and brushed broken mosaic aside and, when pieces didn't come, she pulled at the floor. But it was just stone and concrete. *Leng* was somewhere else entirely now.

Rod put a hand under her arm and lifted her.

"I told Kathy to do it," he said.

A great and terrible emotion bubbled up inside Nina. She abruptly wanted to hurt and hold Rod at the same time and was instead caught in a numb nowhere in between.

Xerxes Mammon-Mammonson swung a finger at all of them.

"You have transgressed," he said. "The laws you have broken, the treaties you have violated. Never, in all history, has a legitimate business enterprise been treated so unfairly, so unjustly."

Nina felt Rod slowly guiding her back to where Kathy and Cameron stood. Pupfish and Allana had already hurried for cover. Nine Mammonites, all of them either already armed or now drawing their impractical but deadly blades, were ranged before them.

"Stock theft," said Xerxes, furious. "Capital destruction. Material damage. Misuse of office equipment."

"We submit to the judgement of the Venislarn court," said Rod. "There will be restitution."

Xerxes shook his head, advancing.

"The accounts have been tallied. We know what we're owed."

Five humans and a *samakha* and barely a weapon between them. The Mammonites drew in.

"This will not be over quickly," said Xerxes. There was a hungry set to his mouth and a manic glitter in his inhuman eyes.

"When I attack," Rod whispered to Nina, "you run for that fire exit."

"Attack with what?" she whispered back.

"I've got a penknife somewhere."

"A penknife? Don't be a cretin," she said, knowing that it was the best of all the bloody stupid things they could do right now.

Morag Senior slammed through a door and into a huge office space that looked as if it had just been visited by a small but persistent tornado.

"Stop!" she shouted.

The Mammonites, in their dirt-smeared suits, with their knives out, turned to look at her. Before any of them could speak, she held up the sheet of paper she had just run across town with.

"This is an order from *Yo-Morgantus*, prince of Venislarn, ruler absolute of this city and all of its residents, human and non-human."

They didn't run over and stab her at once so that was a good start.

"It commands Mammon-Mammonson Investments and all its senior officers to cease and desist in any current attempts to summon *Yoth Mammon*, the corruptor, the defiler of souls, the dredger in the lake of desires, back to this world, *schluri'o bento frei*. It also commands Mammon-Mammonson Investments to surrender into the authority of the consular mission to the Venislarn any human beings it is holding, living or dead, as well as any material goods that they require for current or future criminal investigations into the senior officers or the company entire."

"She's going to get murdered," Rod whispered to Nina.

"No, wait," said Nina. "This actually might work."

Xerxes walked towards Morag. Rod could see the nervousness in Morag's stance.

"Are you sure?" he said.

"Furthermore," said Morag, "the consular mission staff are not to be hindered, delayed or harmed in the execution of their duty. The penalty for non-compliance will be the total and immediate eradication of the Mammonite species from their enclave in Dickens Heath and anywhere else they might be found in Lord *Morgantus*'s domain."

"Let me see that," said Xerxes and held out his hand.

Morag edged forward and presented the sheet to him.

He read it slowly, nodding occasionally. He then folded it carefully and tucked it inside his jacket.

"Everything appears to be in order," he said.

Rod waited. Xerxes looked round at first his board of directors and then at the humans.

"You are free to go."

Friday

There was no body to bury and there was no family to inform. There would be a stone on a crematorium wall at some point and certainly there would be reminiscences and drinks in the pub even though Vivian did not approve of drinking. There would be a lot of things that Vivian did not approve of that she wouldn't be around to disapprove of anymore and they would have to do a lot of disapproving on her behalf. But, for now, there was a quiet moment in the response team office and cheap wine in plastic cups.

The response team operated a hot-desking policy. This tended to mean that every person's crap didn't just occupy one desk but any desk they had ever sat at. However, Vivian's desk was Vivian's desk and no one dared hot-desk it and that was the way it was going to stay for a long time yet.

Rod raised a cup to the labelled filing trays and the savagely ordered desk tidy, to the neatly aligned computer and keyboard, to the drinks coaster, and to the tub of gloopy keyboard cleaner. There was no indication that a real and fallible human being had ever worked there and that was how Vivian would have wanted it.

"I have no mouth," he said.

"And I must scream," the others replied and drank and then went about the business of the day.

Kathy looked across the desk at Vaughn Sitterson.

He seemed intent on the computer screen before him. No matter how she smiled or waggled her eyebrows at him, he didn't seem capable of acknowledging her presence. Did he do this to everyone? Had he forgotten she was there?

"Excuse me," she said.

"Yes?"

"Is there some doubt about my appointment?"

"Oh, no. Not at all, Dr Kaur," said Vaughn, still utterly avoiding looking at her. "Mr Barnes was very clear on the matter

367

and I both respect and agree with Mrs Grey's decision. Her final decision."

"Good, so…"

Vaughn swivelled his chair and gazed out of the window.

"The tech support job is yours if you want it."

"Thank you, sir," she said and made to stand.

"But," said Vaughn, "with the very unfortunate death of Mrs Grey, we do have two vacancies to fill…"

Morag Senior met Cameron at New Street station to see him off.

He had spent his final night in the city in his hotel. After the events of the day before, she didn't have the energy or emotional capacity to spend time catching up in the evening and he hadn't asked, but she came to the station to see him off.

"You'll have to put up with the Edinburgh job for a while yet," she said as they waited for his train to come up on the departures board.

"Do you miss the old town?" he asked.

"Yes," she said. "I do."

"Bannerman will no doubt be asking after you."

"And how is chief Bannerman?"

Cameron shrugged. "He always had a soft spot for you. Never had one for me."

He tossed his fringe out of his eyes. There was a dark red mark near his temple but he'd otherwise survived his visit to Birmingham unscathed.

"Ah, before I forget," said Senior. She took the *shodu-bon* claim marker pendant from her pocket and put it in his hand.

"It was a present for you," he said.

"Ah, well. Some girls like diamonds. Some like gold. Very few like dried Venislarn mucous. Besides, it was a present to you first."

He pulled an uncomfortable expression. "I really hadn't planned to see her again," he said.

"So, this thing with you and – *Chagulameya*, was it? – it was a serious thing?"

"It perhaps was," he said, "but that kind of relationship is hard to maintain. I'm in Britain, she's in the South Pacific. I work for the consular mission, she's..."

"A fucking huge sea slug from another world, yeah," said Junior with unfiltered sarcasm. "It's Romeo and Juliet all over again, isn't it?"

His expression stiffened a degree.

"We're not all the same, are we?" he said. "The heart wants what the heart wants. And, you know, as they say, *yofehngeta muesulma-dia bheros chinn-ha*." He gave her a raffish grin.

"No, Cameron," she replied. "No one says that. Ever."

She turned and walked to the exit.

Mrs Cook-Mammonson, headteacher at the Thatcher Academy, was partway through her assembly address to the year sevens when she saw that a student in one of the middle rows had stood up.

After the unwanted intrusion on school grounds and the assault on her person by that genetically deficient runt, Nina Seth, Mrs Cook-Mammonson had come into school this morning with a bloody nose and the script for a powerful assembly about perseverance in the face of adversity under her strong and stable leadership.

She had barely warmed to her theme and this child had stood up. It was Yang Mammon-Mammonson.

"Sit down," said Cook-Mammonson but the girl was walking up the aisle to the front, a tablet in her hand. "Return to your seat at once."

Yang did not slow, did not deviate. She came to front and presented her tablet to the headteacher. Yang's score on the screen was nine point eight.

"Yes, very good. Now, for the final time. Return to your seat."

"Not my score," said the girl and scrolled helpfully. "Yours."

Cook-Mammonson saw her own name at the top of the screen now and next to it a pathetic zero point two. Students in the hall had their tablets out too and, as Cook-Mammonson watched, it dropped one notch and then two.

"You let her beat you, miss," said Yang coldly. "You let her."

Behind Yang, other students were standing. Oh, look, thought Cook-Mammonson, they've even brought their own knives. And, despite herself, her heart swelled with pride at a job well done.

Morag Junior turned at the sound of footsteps.

"She's coming," she said.

"Then we can proceed," said Professor Sheikh Omar.

Morag Senior walked through the Vault security doors with a helpless gesture of apology.

"You're late," said Junior. "You're letting Team Morag down."

"Security Bob wouldn't let me in on account of me 'already being inside'."

"Ladies," said Omar. "Or is that just lady? Shall we begin?"

The professor stood beside the line of symbols he had drawn in marker pen on the Vault floor two days earlier, a line that held back the mish-mash of alternative universes Cattress had created by breaking the Berry Mound vase.

"Are you both happy that you wish to do this?" he asked. "I have a client friend in Santiago who would furnish one of you with a new identity if you'd care to act as his private advisor on the Venislarn and all things outré. An absolute gentleman."

Maurice, who had dressed for the day in a bold lemon sweater and a pair of deck shoes, as though he couldn't decide if he was going golfing or sailing, gave a tiny snort of derision.

"Paulo is a gentleman," said Omar and turned to the women. "Ignore, my lovely assistant. He's bitter after he and Paulo had a disagreement regarding the novels of Jilly Cooper."

"We're doing this," said Junior, butterflies in her stomach.

"*Yo-Morgantus* says we must."

"And Vaughn won't pay two salaries."

"Very good," said Omar. "The gin please, Maurice."

Maurice extracted a bottle from his Gladstone bag and passed it to Omar, along with a white cloth. Omar wrapped the cloth around his fingers and upended the bottle to dampen the cloth.

"Finest cleaning substance known to man," said Omar. "And, given where Maurice does our drinks shopping, not good for much else."

He bent to rub out one of the symbols.

"Wait," said Junior. "Just wait."

"Yes?"

"This isn't going to kill me, is it? And it's not going to kill her?"

"No," said Omar. "I promise."

Senior took hold of Junior's hand. "But which of us will remain?"

"When the weekend comes, which Morag are you?" said Omar. "The Morag who lived through Thursday? Or the one who lived through Wednesday?"

"But they're the same person," said Junior.

Omar smiled and bent with his cloth. "I like to pretend that the trick to a good disenchantment is like – oh, Maurice what's that game we spent the evening playing on that wet weekend in Barry?"

"Jenga," said the lithe little man.

"Yes, like Jenga. It's all a matter of the order in which it's done. But, you know, truthfully, all the bricks come tumbling down in the end."

One of Pupfish's eyes was clouded with blood but the other widened as he spoke.

"Then, to cap it all off, we all – ggh! – went out for Nando's," he told Rod. "And Fluke paid for all of it out of his own pocket."

"Did he now?" said Rod.

"And my mum was really grateful. Ggh!"

"Is that so?"

"She gave him a big kiss cos, I guess we don't go out for Nando's much mum and me. But Fluke's – ggh! – like a second son to you, isn't it?"

Next to Pupfish in the office reception, his mum, Kirsten, squirmed uncomfortably and put on a smile that could only possibly fool a half-blind fish.

"Yeah," she said, unconvincingly.

"But we just wanted to say thanks to you and Nina and Mrs G and that," said Pupfish.

"We do," said Kirsten, finally able to say something genuine.

"All part of the service." said Rod. "Anyroads, look, I've got to…"

"Sho thing. Sho thing," said Pupfish. "Go do."

Rod directed them to the lift.

"Got things to do myself," said Pupfish. "Me and Allana are meeting up later."

"A date?"

"Takin' it slow, dog," said Pupfish like he was coolest cat on earth.

"Aye. Slow is good," said Rod and waited for the door to close before swearing softly to himself.

The *samakha* thank you party had been a momentary diversion. He went down the corridor a way and into the marketing office.

Leandra was alone in the office, sorting through headshots of pretty young men on the central meeting table.

"Rod!" she smiled. "You can help me find the stars of the future. We're auditioning for *Tentacular*. We're going to have a number one album next year. Unless you're looking for Chad. He's out at a *chakra* realignment seminar. His vibrational energies have been off all –"

Rod set the plush *Yoth Mammon* toy on the table.

Leandra looked at it.

"What was it you mentioned?" said Rod. "Mutual fact-pooling outreach programme with the local Venislarn community or some other horse muck?"

"They were never going to be taken up for mass production," said Leandra sadly, touching a floppy tartan spike.

"By any chance was there anything else you shared with the local Venislarn community?" he asked. Rod was rarely angry and it was a novel and exhilarating experience as he now tried to contain his rage. "A book perhaps?"

Leandra frowned.

"It's just a book, isn't it? Just words."

Xerxes Mammon-Mammonson stalked the floors and corridors of his company office. Colleagues and underlings were keeping their heads down, buried in their ledgers and screens. An unsettled mood had come over the place from the very start of the day. Saul Smith-Mammonson had declared in an open meeting that a change of management was clearly needed. His skinned body now hung in the lobby as a reminder to all that the board still had confidence in their managing director and if they didn't then they'd better come armed.

Xerxes polished his knife with a silk handkerchief as he walked. His chief accountant, Scott-Mammonson, had to scuttle to keep pace with him.

"The surveyors will be in tomorrow to assess the structural damage, sir. It may be that this whole building has to be condemned."

"We must be able to sue someone for that at least," said Xerxes.

"Our lawyers are analysing the wording of Lord *Morgantus*'s edict. If there's any loophole or wiggle room, they will find it."

"Good."

Xerxes stomped down the broad stairs to the lobby.

"And confiscation of our property by the consular mission?"

The accountant flicked through his pad. "All the humans in our storage facility plus all soul cash certificates, redeemed and unredeemed. They made it clear that those won't be returned and we won't be receiving any compensation either."

Xerxes huffed and then spotted a blank space on the lobby wall where there shouldn't have been one.

"And where's the picture gone?" he demanded.

"Er, yes," said the accountant. "They took that too. The little woman was quite insistent. She didn't say why."

"I caught the big spider-fish in the washing line, swung it round and smashed it into the fence and I said, 'Dry yourself off, pal.' Boom."

"Yes?" said Barbara politely.

"Never mind," said Nina. She'd tell it better next time.

Barbara Gudge, the demented *Koloba*, went back to her lunch of human face. It was Nina's own face. It was intriguing to see someone tucking into a cold plate meal of your own face. Nina wasn't sure if she felt flattered, disgusted or even slightly aroused.

The screen on the hospital room wall was showing *Marco the Orderly Reads Purple Ronny Poems*. So far, Barbara's diet (televisual and actual) of the same faces, again and again, had kept them all fresh in her memory and thus in the world.

"You want some?" said Barbara, offering Nina the plate.

"I'm fine, thanks," said Nina. "I brought something for you."

"Did you, dear?"

Nina unwrapped the picture. It was wider than she was tall and she'd had a hell of a time fitting it in the lift and then in through the airlock around Barbara's door. She propped the picture on one of the free chairs.

"Now, this man here. This is Xerxes Mammon-Mammonson. Get a good look at him, Barbara. He's the managing director of Mammon-Mammonson Investments. Xerxes Mammon-Mammonson. And these are all the blokes on the board."

"Not one single woman," noted Barbara. "For shame."

"For shame indeed," said Nina. "Now this one…"

Nina went along the two rows, naming everyone and making sure that Barbara got a good look at each of the executives in the corporate portrait. Then she made tea.

"I had a friend," said Nina. "She told me there were five steps to making a perfect cup of tea."

"And what are they?" asked Barbara, taking her first sip.

"I don't know," said Nina softly. "I never asked her."

374

Barbara gestured at the picture of the Mammonites with her cup. "It's very... kind of you to bring it, dear," said the wrinkly baggage. "But what's it for?"

"Don't worry," said Nina. "Just forget about it."

Morag stood and thought. The Vault was back to its original, horrifically disorganised former self. There was probably a lot of tidying up to do somewhere. The merging of dozens of universes must have resulted in at least some breakages.

"Do you have any of that gin left?" she said.

"I'm afraid we're lacking glasses and a decent tonic water," said Professor Omar.

Maurice, a man of silent insights, simply passed Morag the bottle and she took a swig.

"Ah, you can take the bonnie lass out of Scotland..." said Omar.

Morag could feel the tight tenderness around her right cheek where Jeffney Ray had struck Morag Junior and, additionally, the lesser but nonetheless real soreness on her left cheek where Junior had punched Senior.

"So, which Morag are you?" said Omar.

Morag didn't have an answer to that yet so took another swig. Omar put his hand on the bottle.

"Easy now. We need to take care of ourselves."

"Vaughn told me a funny thing," she said.

"Mr Sitterson has many fine qualities," said Omar. "I was unaware that humour was one of them."

"He told me why you had applied for the tech support job. Sorry you didn't get it, by the way."

"And yet" – Omar performed a slow and merry pirouette – "I am down here and the week is not yet over."

"What did you mean when you told him I was the reason you applied? That's pure creepy uncle territory. Fancy me or something?"

"Miss Murray, I have absolutely no designs on you or, to be perfectly specific, your body."

"Uh-huh," she said and raised the bottle again. Omar took hold of it before it could reach her lips.

"However," he said heavily, "I am sure you've had your fair share of gentleman callers."

"None of your *adn-bhul* business, prof."

"I believe there was a young man, one of *Morgantus*'s human puppets…"

"Again," she said hotly, "business, as in none of your, as in *bhul-zhu*."

"Sorry," said the professor. "I meant no offence. Feminine ways are a mystery to me."

Maurice tittered.

"And my understanding of the internal plumbing is wholly theoretical," Omar added.

"Right," she said. "Thanks for sorting out the old two-Morag problem but you can fuck right off now, gents."

"But despite all this, Maurice and I might be of some small use in a few months' time, fetching towels and hot water and such."

The words cut through her annoyance and the edge of the neat gin. She felt a tremble in her legs and reached out for something to hold. Maurice nipped forward and took her arm.

"Oh, God," she whispered.

"Well, quite," said Omar gently.

"Or gods," suggested Maurice. "It might be twins."

Leng-time, leng-space

Vivian pushed away the rock directly above her and wriggled and hauled her way towards the light. The light was pink, the pink of inflamed wounds and cheap costume jewellery, but it was the only light there was.

Scraping herself savagely but choosing not to care, she emerged, pushed herself over the edge of the hole in the rubble and allowed herself to roll down the pile to the ground.

She hurt and she suspected that wasn't going to change. She would do an inventory of her injuries eventually. Death was a stranger in this place and so she could wait until she had the time to check herself over.

Time, she thought.

She still had the screwed-up remnants of the Big Bloody Book in her hand. She straightened the pages out, folded them neatly and placed them in her jacket pocket next to the pen nib and her arrow pendant.

She stood. She had lost a shoe.

She distracted herself from that annoyance by inspecting the horizon. The geography of hell did not remain constant but there were definable moods to the landscape. There, a crawling forest of fire. There, jagged peaks and the suggestion of a city. There, a ripple across the world, a sea perhaps, pink on pink. She saw the movement of creatures in the distance, some humanoid, most not. From far, far away there came a desperate volcanic roar: *Yoth Mammon*, she supposed, a fire of infinite size stuck in her craw. Death was a stranger here even if one wished it otherwise.

Something scrambled across the rocks towards her. It was a handspan high and appeared to be made from poorly stitched sack cloth.

"Ha ha!" it crowed. "You are now mine, fleshing!"

"Your stuffing is coming loose," she said and pointed.

The ragdoll looked in alarm at the brown wool spilling from its side.

"I am wounded!"

"I can fix it if we can find a needle," said Vivian. "What is your name?"

The creature immediately forgot its wound. "I am Steve the Destroyer, gobbet! Fear me!"

"No," said Vivian.

"Yes!"

"Steve the Destroyer is a ridiculous, twee and juvenile name. Whoever gave you it should be ashamed."

"I don't know," said Steve. "I think it sounds dangerous. Steve!" It struck a dynamic pose. "Mysterious even. *Steeeeve.*"

"No," she told it. "Not at all."

Steve kicked at a pebble contemptuously.

"Which way are you heading?" it said.

"I thought I'd try down there," she said, pointing towards the sea. Things that might or might not have been *draybbea* oozed along the beach. Something very much like a *Croyi-Takk* wheeled in the nightmare sky above.

"This your first time in hell?" asked Steve.

"This hell," Vivian nodded.

"Come!" it boomed as ominously as a doll could boom. "We have such sights to show you."

"I believe I shall be the judge of that," said Vivian haughtily.

She debated whether to keep her one shoe on or abandon it. In the end, she took it off and carried it as she and the doll walked down the hill to the shores of hell.

Authors' Notes

YES – Birmingham's brutalist Central Library was demolished following the construction of the new, shiny Library of Birmingham, despite requests for it to be made a listed building and it being put on the World Monuments Fund's watch list.

NO – There are no mysterious artefacts to be found embedded in its foundations.

YES – There is a hardened telephone exchange and nuclear bunker underneath the city of Birmingham, built to preserve the city's telecommunications (and a few precious lives) in the event of a nuclear strike. The Anchor Exchange is one of three such bunkers in the UK, although there is alleged to be a fourth in Glasgow that remains classified. The Anchor tunnels run from the Jewellery Quarter to Southside, a distance of around one and a half miles. Their exact dimensions and function remain a secret and members of the public are not permitted entry.

YES – Astonishingly, the decline of heavy industry in the city has so reduced the demand for water that the local water table has risen to the extent that the Anchor Telephone Exchange must be continually pumped out to prevent it flooding.

NO – There is not an illegal nest of alien spiders in the Anchor Exchange.

YES – Dickens Heath is a village on the outskirts of the Birmingham conurbation developed as a considerable housing estate in the 1990s.

NO – Despite the confusing road layout and uniformity of the housing, Dickens Heath was not deliberately constructed to bewilder and deter the casual visitor.

NO – Thatcher Academy (formerly Tythe Barn Lane secondary school) is not a real school. Any similarity to nearby schools, in layout or management practices, is entirely accidental.

YES – In 2016, the Defence Secretary launched an army cadets scheme in targeted Birmingham schools with the stated intention of using them to combat religious extremism and instil "British Values".

NO – Army cadets in Birmingham schools do not engage in live fire exercises.

NO – The giant rings on the outside of the Library of Birmingham are not forged from a tungsten-magnesium alloy with a selenium core.

YES – There are the remains of an Iron Age fort at Berry Mound on the edge of Shirley.

NO – There are no magical vases to be found in those remains.

YES – There are the remains of a Roman fort at Metchley Park next to the Queen Elizabeth Hospital.

NO – There is no secret "restricted ward" on the top floor of the hospital.

YES – A wire-mesh statue called "Manangel" by David Begbie, installed ten feet off the ground on the wall of the Jam House in St Paul's Square, disappeared overnight in 2016. Its current location is unknown.

NO – There isn't a secret fishman town on the Warwick and Birmingham Junction canal.

NO – Although there are floating cafes, restaurants, tour boats, shops and taxis at Gas Street Basin, the Black Barge has never paid a visit.

YES – The building on the corner of Great Charles Street and Margaret Street housed the Birmingham stock exchange until its closure in 1987.

NO – The building is not currently occupied by Mammon-Mammonson Investments.

YES – There is a mine underneath Birmingham University, excavated by mining students in the 1930s. The entrance is near the South Gate, not far from the Bristol Road.

NO – The mine is not used anymore and certainly not by Professor Sheikh Omar.

NO – There is no menagerie of alien creatures in Dudley.

NO – There is no Rockerfellers night club on Broad Street.

YES – Birmingham does have more miles of canal than Venice and more acres of parkland that Paris. It is also the birthplace of the balti. Its claims to be the birthplace of the

Industrial Revolution, the British Enlightenment and Heavy Metal are good ones but are reasonably disputed by other cities.

YES – There are many examples of burnt mounds by the rivers of Birmingham. These are the piled remains of stones, heated to high temperature and then shattered by plunging into cold water. These remains are mostly between 3000 and 4000 years old and, since there is no evidence that the heated stones were used for cooking, their purpose is a mystery. The hypothesis that these were some form of stone age sauna has led to speculation that the stones are anachronistic Out Of Place Artefacts.

YES – There is a coffin works museum on Fleet St in Birmingham. It's really good.

YES – The Pen Museum is a real thing. It's on Frederick St in the Jewellery Quarter. It's also really good.

NO – The Pen Museum is not the hiding place for any mystical or magical pens, as far as we know.

YES – In the 1840s, Birmingham provided 75% of the world's pens. This market share slowly declined until the rollerball pen effectively killed off the industry in the early 20th Century.

YES – In May 2017, a 500-pound unexploded wartime bomb was found by construction workers in Aston. The A38 expressway and many other routes into the north and centre of the city were closed for two days while it was dealt with.

NO – The unexploded bomb wasn't a cover story for the discovery of a buried Venislarn. Not unless the army then decided to blow it up. The controlled on-site detonation destroyed windows and door shutters on nearby business premises.

The authors would like to extend their thanks to Paul Hepburn for his invaluable advice in the operation of tower cranes. Any error in the text is ours not his.

Printed in Great Britain
by Amazon